Richard F Burton

Supplemental Nights

To the Book of the Thousand and One Nights with Notes Anthropological and Explanatory,

Volume Two

Richard F Burton

Supplemental Nights
To the Book of the Thousand and One Nights with Notes Anthropological and Explanatory,
Volume Two

ISBN/EAN: 9783743417632

Manufactured in Europe, USA, Canada, Australia, Japa

Cover: Foto ©Andreas Hilbeck / pixelio.de

Manufactured and distributed by brebook publishing software (www.brebook.com)

Richard F Burton

Supplemental Nights

SUPPLEMENTAL NIGHTS

TO·THE·BOOK·OF·THE·THOUSAND
AND·ONE·NIGHTS·WITH·NOTES
ANTHROPOLOGICAL·AND
EXPLANATORY

BY

RICHARD·F·BURTON

VOLUME
TWO

PRIVATELY·PRINTED
BY·THE·BURTON·CLUB

TO HENRY IRVING, Esq.

My Dear Irving,

   To a consummate artist like yourself I need hardly suggest that The Nights still offers many a virgin mine to the Playwright; and I inscribe this volume to you, not only in admiration of your genius but in the hope that you will find means of exploiting the hidden wealth which awaits only your "Open, Sesame!"

Ever yours sincerely,

RICHARD F. BURTON.

London, *August* 1, 1886.

CONTENTS OF THE TWELFTH VOLUME.

VOL. XII.

CONTENTS.

APPENDIX: VARIANTS AND ANALOGUES
OF SOME OF THE TALES IN VOLS. XI. AND XII.

By W. A. CLOUSTON.

CONTENTS.

SUPPLEMENTAL NIGHTS

TO THE BOOK OF THE

THOUSAND NIGHTS AND A NIGHT

———◆———

AL-MALIK AL-ZAHIR RUKN AL-DIN BIBARS AL-BUNDUKDARI AND THE SIXTEEN CAPTAINS OF POLICE.[1]

THERE was once in the climes[2] of Egypt and the city of Cairo, under the Turks, a king of the valiant kings and the exceeding mighty Soldans, hight Al-Malik al-Záhir Rukn al-Din Bibars al-Bundukdári,[3] who was used to storm the Islamite sconces and the strongholds of "The Shore"[4] and the Nazarene citadels. His Chief of Police in the capital of his kingdom, was just to the folk, all of them; and Al-Malik al-Zahir delighted in stories of the common sort and of that which men purposed in thought; and he loved to see this with his own eyes and to hear their sayings with his own ears. Now it fortuned that he heard one night

---

[1] Bresl. Edit., vol. xi. pp. 321-99, Nights dccccxxx-xl.

[2] Arab. "Iklím" from the Gr. κλίμα, often used as amongst us (*e.g.* "other climes") for land.

[3] Bibars whose name is still famous and mostly pronounced "Baybars," the fourth of the Baharite Mamelukes whom I would call the "Soldans." Originally a slave of Al-Sálih, seventh of the Ayyubites, he rose to power by the normal process, murdering his predecessor, in A. D. 1260; and he pushed his conquests from Syria to Armenia. In his day "Saint" Louis died before Tunis (A. D. 1270).

[4] There are sundry Sáhils or shore-lands. "Sahil Misr" is the River-side of Cairo often extended to the whole of Lower Egypt (vol. i. 290): here it means the lowlands of Palestine once the abode of the noble Philistines; and lastly the term extends to the sea-board of Zanzibar, where, however, it is mostly used in the plur. "Sawáhil" — the Shores.

from a certain of his nocturnal reciters[1] that among women are
those who are doughtier than the doughtiest men and prower of
prowess, and that among them are some who will engage in fight
singular with the sword and others who beguile the quickest-
witted of Walis and baffle them and bring down on them all
manner of miseries; wherefore said the Soldan, "I would lief hear
this of their legerdemain from one of those who have had to do
with it, so I may hearken unto him and cause him discourse."
And one of the story-tellers said, "O king, send for the Chief of
Police of this thy city." Now 'Alam al-Dín[2] Sanjar was at that
time Wali and he was a man of experience, in affairs well versed;
so the king sent for him and when he came before him, he discovered to him that which was in his mind. Quoth Sanjar, "I
will do my endeavour for that which our lord seeketh." Then he
arose and returning to his house, summoned the Captains of the
watch and the Lieutenants of the ward and said to them,
"Know that I purpose to marry my son and make him a bridal
banquet, and I desire that ye assemble, all of you, in one place.
I also will be present, I and my company, and do ye relate that
which you have heard of rare occurrences and that which hath
betided you of experiences." And the Captains and Runners
and Agents of Police answered him, " 'Tis well: Bismillah—in
the name of Allah! We will make thee see all this with thine own
eyes and hear it with thine own ears." Then the Chief of Police
arose and going up to Al-Malik al-Zahir, informed him that the
assembly would meet on such a day at his house; and the Soldan
said, " 'Tis well," and gave him somewhat of coin for his spend-
ing-money. When the appointed day came the Chief of Police
set apart for his officers and constables a saloon, which had
latticed casements ranged in order and giving upon the flower-
garden, and Al-Malik al-Zahir came to him, and he seated himself
and the Soldan, in the alcove. Then the tables were spread for
them with food and they ate: and when the bowl went round
amongst them and their souls were gladdened by meat and
drink, they mutually related that which was with them and,
revealed their secrets from concealment. The first to discourse
was a man, a Captain of the Watch, hight Mu'ín al-Dín,[3] whose

---

[1] Arab. "Sammár" (from Samar, = conversatio nocturna), = the story-teller who in
camp or house whiles away the evening hours.
[2] "Flag of the Faith:" Sanjar in old Persian = a Prince, a King.
[3] "Aider of the Faith."

heart was wholly occupied with the love of fair women; and he said, "Harkye, all ye people of high degree, I will acquaint you with an extraordinary affair which fortuned me aforetime." Then he began to tell

The First Constable's History.[1]

KNOW ye that when I entered the service of this Emir,[2] I had a great repute and every low fellow and lewd feared me most of all mankind, and when I rode through the city, each and every of the folk would point at me with their fingers and sign at me with their eyes. It happened one day, as I sat in the palace of the Prefecture, back-propped against a wall, considering in myself, suddenly there fell somewhat in my lap, and behold, it was a purse sealed and tied. So I hent it in hand and lo! it had in it an hundred dirhams,[3] but I found not who threw it and I said, "Lauded be the Lord, the King of the Kingdoms!"[4] Another day, as I sat in the same way, somewhat fell on me and startled me, and lookye, 'twas a purse like the first: I took it and hiding the matter, made as though I slept, albeit sleep was not with me. One day as I thus shammed sleep, I suddenly sensed in my lap a hand, and in it a purse of the finest; so I seized the hand and behold, 'twas that of a fair woman. Quoth I to her, "O my lady, who art thou?" and quoth she, "Rise and come away from here, that I may make myself known to thee." Presently I rose up and following her, walked on, without tarrying, till we stopped at the door of a high-builded house, whereupon I asked her, "O my lady, who art thou? Indeed, thou hast done me kindness, and what is the reason of this?" She answered, "By Allah, O Captain[5]

---

[1] These policemen's tales present a curious contrast with the detective stories of M. Gaboriau and his host of imitators. In the East the police, like the old Bow Street runners, were and are still recruited principally amongst the criminal classes on the principle of "Set a thief," &c. We have seen that the Barmecide Wazirs of Baghdad "anticipated Fourier's doctrine of the *passionel* treatment of lawless inclinations," and employed as subordinate officers, under the Wali or Prefect of Police, accomplished villains like Ahmad al-Danaf (vol. iv. 75), Hasan Shuuman and Mercury Ali (ibid.) and even women (Dalilah the Crafty) to coerce and checkmate their former comrades. Moreover a gird at the police is always acceptable, not only to a coffee-house audience, but even to a more educated crowd; witness the treatment of the "Charley" and the "Bobby" in our truly English pantomimes.

[2] *i.e.* the Chief of Police, as the sequel shows.

[3] About £4.

[4] *i.e.* of the worlds visible and invisible.

[5] Arab. "Mukaddam:" see vol. iv. 42.

Mu'in, I am a woman on whom love and longing are sore for
desire of the daughter of the Kazi Amín al-Hukm.[1] Now there
was between me and her what was and fondness for her fell
upon my heart and I agreed upon an assignation with her,
according to possibility and convenience; but her father Amin
al-Hukm took her and went away, and my heart cleaveth to her
and yearning and distraction waxed sore upon me for her sake."
I said to her, marvelling the while at her words, "What wouldst
thou have me do?" and said she, "O Captain Mu'in, I would have
thee lend me a helping hand." Quoth I, "Where am I and where
is the daughter of the Kazi Amin al-Hukm?"[2] and quoth she
"Be assured that I would not have thee intrude upon the Kazi's
daughter, but I would fain work for the winning of my wishes.
This is my will and my want which may not be wroughten
save by thine aid." Then she added, "I mean this night to go
with heart enheartened and hire me bracelets and armlets and
anklets of price; then will I hie me and sit in the street wherein
is the house of Amin al-Hukm; and when 'tis the season of the
round and folk are asleep, do thou pass, thou and those who are
with thee of the men, and thou wilt see me sitting and on me
fine raiment and ornaments and wilt smell on me the odour of
Ottars; whereupon do thou question me of my case and I will
say, 'I hail from the Citadel and am of the daughters of the
deputies[3] and I came down into the town for a purpose; but
night overtook me all unawares and the Zuwaylah Gate[4] was
shut against me and all the other portals and I knew not whither
I should wend this night. Presently I saw this street and noting

---

[1] "Faithful of Command;" it may be a title as well as a P. N. For "Al-Amín," see vol.
iv. 261.

[2] i. e. "What have I to do with, etc.?" or "How great is the difference between me and
her." The phrase is still popular in Egypt and Syria; and the interrogative form only
intensifies it. The student of Egyptian should always try to answer a question by a
question. His labours have been greatly facilitated by the conscientious work of my late
friend Spitta Bey. I tried hard to persuade the late Rogers Bey, whose knowledge of
Egyptian and Syrian (as opposed to Arabic) was considerable, that a simple grammar of
Egyptian was much wanted; he promised to undertake it, but death cut short the design.

[3] Arab. "Nawwáb," plur. of Náib (lit. deputies, lieutenants) = a Nabob. Till the
unhappy English occupation of Egypt, the grand old Kil'ah (Citadel) contained the palace
of the Pasha and the lodgings and offices of the various officials. Foreign rulers, if they are
wise, should convert it into a fort with batteries commanding the town, like that of Hydera-
bad, in Sind.

[4] For this famous and time-honoured building, see vol. i. 269.

the goodly fashion of its ordinance and its cleanliness, I sheltered me therein against break of day.' When I speak these words to thee with complete self-possession,[1] the Chief of the watch will have no ill suspicion of me, but will say, 'There's no help but that we leave her with one who will take care of her till morning.' Thereto do thou rejoin, ' 'Twere best that she night with Amin al-Hukm and lie with his wives[2] and children until dawn of day.' Then straightway knock at the Kazi's door, and thus shall I have secured admission into his house, without inconvenience, and won my wish; and—the Peace!" I said to her, "By Allah, this is an easy matter." So, when the night was blackest, we rose to make our round, followed by men with girded swords, and went about the ways and compassed the city, till we came to the street[3] where was the woman, and it was the middle of the night. Here we smelt mighty rich scents and heard the clink of rings: so I said to my comrades, "Methinks I espy a spectre;" and the Captain of the watch cried, "See what it is." Accordingly, I undertook the work and entering the thoroughfare presently came out again and said, "I have found a fair woman and she telleth me that she is from the Citadel and that dark night surprised her and she saw this street and noting its cleanness and goodly fashion of ordinance, knew that it belonged to a great man[4] and that needs must there be in it a guardian to keep watch over it, so she sheltered her therein." Quoth the Captain of the watch to me, "Take her and carry her to thy house;" but quoth I, "I seek refuge with Allah![5] My house is no strong box[6] and on this woman are trinkets and fine clothing. By Allah, we will not deposit the lady save with Amin al-Hukm, in whose street she hath been since the first starkening of the darkness; therefore do thou leave her with him till the break of day." He rejoined, "Do whatso thou willest." So I rapped at the

---

[1] Arab. "Tamkín," gravity, assurance.

[2] Arab. " 'Iyál-hu" lit. his family, a decorous circumlocution for his wives and concubines.

[3] Arab. "Darb," lit. a road; here a large thoroughfare.

[4] When Mohammed Ali Pasha (the "Great") began to rule, he found Cairo "stifled" with filth, and gave orders that each householder, under pain of confiscation, should keep the street before his house perfectly clean. This was done after some examples had been made and the result was that since that time Cairo never knew the plague. I am writing at Tangier where a Mohammed Ali is much wanted.

[5] i.e. Allah forfend!

[6] Arab. "Mustauda' " = a strong place where goods are deposited and left in charge.

Kazi's gate and out came a black slave of his slaves, to whom said I, "O my lord, take this woman and let her be with you till day shall dawn, for that the lieutenant of the Emir Alam al-Din hath found her with trinkets and fine apparel on her, sitting at the door of your house, and we feared lest her responsibility be upon you;[1] wherefore I suggested 'twere meetest she night with you." So the chattel opened and took her in with him. Now when the morning morrowed, the first who presented himself before the Emir was the Kazi Amin al-Hukm, leaning on two of his negro slaves; and he was crying out and calling for aid and saying, "O Emir, crafty and perfidious, yesternight thou depositedst with me a woman and broughtest her into my house and home, and she arose in the dark and took from me the monies of the little orphans my wards,[2] six great bags, each containing a thousand dinars,[3] and made off; but as for me, I will say no syllable to thee except in the Soldan's presence."[4] When the Wali heard these words, he was troubled and rose and sat down in his agitation; then he took the Judge and placing him by his side, soothed him and exhorted him to patience, till he had made an end of talk, when he turned to the officers and questioned them of that. They fixed the affair on me and said, "We know nothing of this matter but from Captain Mu'in al-Din." So the Kazi turned to me and said, "Thou wast of accord to practice upon me with this woman, for she said she came from the Citadel." As for me, I stood, with my head bowed groundwards, forgetting both Sunnah and Farz,[5] and remained sunk in thought, saying, "How came I to be the dupe of that randy wench?" Then cried the Emir to me, "What aileth thee that thou

---

[1] Because, if she came to grief, the people of the street, and especially those of the adjoining houses would get into trouble. Hence in Moslem cities, like Damascus and Fez, the Hárát or quarters are closed at night with strong wooden doors, and the guards will not open them except by means of a silver key. Mohammed Ali abolished this inconvenience, but fined and imprisoned all night-walkers who carried no lanterns. See Pilgrimage, vol. i. 173.

[2] As Kazi of the quarter he was ex-officio guardian of the orphans and their property, and liable to severe punishment (unless he could pay for the luxury) in case of fraud or neglect.

[3] Altogether six thousand dinars = £3000. This sentence is borrowed from the sequel and necessary to make the sense clear.

[4] i.e. "I am going at once to complain of thee before the king unless thou give me due satisfaction by restoring the money and finding the thief."

[5] The Practice (of the Prophet) and the Holy Law (Koranic): see vols. v. 36, 167 and i. 169.

answerest not?" Thereupon I replied, "O my lord, 'tis a custom among the folk that he who hath a payment to make at a certain date is allowed three days' grace: do thou have patience with me so long, and if, at the end of that time, the culprit be not found, I will be responsible for that which is lost." When the folk heard my speech they all approved it as reasonable and the Wali turned to the Kazi and sware to him that he would do his utmost to recover the stolen monies adding, "And they shall be restored to thee." Then he went away, whilst I mounted without stay or delay and began to-ing and fro-ing about the world without purpose, and indeed I was become the underling of a woman without honesty or honour; and I went my rounds in this way all that my day and that my night, but happened not upon tidings of her; and thus I did on the morrow. On the third day I said to myself, "Thou art mad or silly;" for I was wandering in quest of a woman who knew me[1] and I knew her not, she being veiled when I met her. Then I went round about the third day till the hour of mid-afternoon prayer, and sore waxed my cark and my care for I kenned that there remained to me of my life but the morrow, when the Chief of Police would send for me. However, as sundown-time came, I passed through one of the main streets, and saw a woman at a window; her door was ajar and she was clapping her hands and casting sidelong glances at me, as who should say, "Come up by the door." So I went up, without fear or suspicion, and when I entered, she rose and clasped me to her breast. I marvelled at the matter and quoth she to me, "I am she whom thou depositedst with Amin al-Hukm." Quoth I to her, "O my sister, I have been going round and round in request of thee, for indeed thou hast done a deed which will be chronicled and hast cast me into red death[2] on thine account." She asked me, "Dost thou speak thus to me and thou a captain of men?" and I answered, "How should I not be troubled, seeing that I be in concern for an affair I turn over and over in mind, more by token that I continue my day long going about searching for thee and in the night I watch its stars and planets?"[3] Cried she, "Naught shall betide save weal, and thou

---

[1] In the corrupt text "Who knew me not;" thus spoiling the point.

[2] Arab. "Maut Ahmar" = violent or bloody death. For the various coloured deaths, see vol. vi. 250.

[3] i.e. for lack of sleep.

shalt get the better of him."[1] So saying, she rose and going to a
chest, drew out therefrom six bags full of gold and said to me,
"This is what I took from Amin al-Hukm's house. So an thou
wilt, restore it; else the whole is lawfully[2] thine; and if thou
desire other than this, thou shalt obtain it; for I have monies in
plenty and I had no design herein save to marry thee." Then she
arose and opening other chests, brought out therefrom wealth
galore and I said to her, "O my sister, I have no wish for all this,
nor do I want aught except to be quit of that wherein I am."
Quoth she, "I came not forth of the Kazi's house without pre-
paring for thine acquittance." Then said she to me, "When the
morrow shall morn and Amin al-Hukm shall come to thee bear
with him till he have made an end of his speech, and when he is
silent, return him no reply; and if the Wali ask, 'What aileth
thee that thou answerest me not?' do thou rejoin, 'O lord and
master[3] know that the two words are not alike, but there is no
helper for the conquered one[4] save Allah Almighty.' The Kazi
will cry, 'What is the meaning of thy saying, The two words
are not alike?' And do thou retort, 'I deposited with thee a
damsel from the palace of the Sultan, and most likely some enemy
of hers in thy household hath transgressed against her or she hath
been secretly murdered. Verily, there were on her raiment and
ornaments worth a thousand ducats, and hadst thou put to the
question those who are with thee of slaves and slave-girls, needs
must thou have litten on some traces of the crime.' When he
heareth this from thee, his trouble will redouble and he will be
amated and will make oath that thou hast no help for it but to go
with him to his house: however, do thou say, 'That will I not do,
for I'am the party aggrieved, more especially because I am under
suspicion with thee.' If he redouble in calling on Allah's aid
and conjure thee by the oath of divorce saying, 'Thou must
assuredly come,' do thou reply, 'By Allah, I will not go, unless
the Chief also go with me.' Then, as soon as thou comest to the
house, begin by searching the terrace-roofs; then rummage the

---

[1] *i.e.* of the Kazi.

[2] Arab. "Mubáh," in the theologic sense, an action which is not sinful (*harám*) or quasi-
sinful (*makruh*); vulgarly "permitted, allowed"; so Shahrazad "ceased to say her say
permitted" (by Shahryar).

[3] Arab. "Yá Khawand"; see vol. vii. 315.

[4] *i.e.* we both make different statements equally credible, but without proof, and the case
will go against me, because thou art the greater man.

closets and cabinets; and if thou find naught, humble thyself
before the Kazi and be abject and feign thyself subjected, and
after stand at the door and look as if thou soughtest a place
wherein to make water,[1] because there is a dark corner there.
Then come forward, with heart harder than syenite-stone, and
lay hold upon a jar of the jars and raise it from its place. Thou
wilt find there under it a mantilla-skirt; bring it out publicly and
call the Wali in a loud voice, before those who are present.
Then open it and thou wilt find it full of blood, exceeding for
freshness, and therein a woman's walking-boots and a pair of
petticoat-trousers and somewhat of linen." When I heard from
her these words, I rose to go out and she said to me, "Take these
hundred sequins, so they may succour thee; and such is my
guest-gift to thee." Accordingly I took them and leaving her
door ajar returned to my lodging. Next morning, up came the
Judge, with his face like the ox-eye,[2] and asked, "In the name of
Allah, where is my debtor and where is my property?" Then he
wept and cried out and said to the Wali, "Where is that ill-
omened fellow, who aboundeth in robbery and villainy?"
Thereupon the Chief turned to me and said, "Why dost thou
not answer the Kazi?" and I replied, "O Emir, the two heads[3]
are not equal, and I, I have no helper;[4] but, an the right be on my
side 'twill appear." At this the Judge grew hotter of temper and
cried out, "Woe to thee, O ill-omened wight! How wilt thou
make manifest that the right is on thy side?" I replied "O our
lord the Kazi, I deposited with thee and in thy charge a woman
whom we found at thy door, and on her raiment and ornaments
of price. Now she is gone, even as yesterday is gone;[5] and after
this thou turnest upon us and suest me for six thousand gold
pieces. By Allah, this is none other than a mighty great wrong,
and assuredly some foe[6] of hers in thy household hath transgressed against her!" With this the Judge's wrath redoubled
and he swore by the most solemn of oaths that I should go with

---

[1] Arab. "Irtiyád" = seeking a place where to stale, soft and sloping, so that the urine
spray may not defile the dress. All this in one word!

[2] Arab. "Bahár," the red *buphthalmus sylvester* often used for such comparisons. In
Algeria it is called 'Aráwah: see the Jardin Parfumé, p. 245, note 144.

[3] *i.e.* parties.

[4] *i.e.* amongst men.

[5] Almost as neat as "oú sont les neiges d'autan?"

[6] Arab. "Ádí," one transgressing, an enemy, a scoundrel.

him and search his house. I replied, "By Allah I will not go, unless the Wali go with us; for, an he be present, he and the officers, thou wilt not dare to work thy wicked will upon me." So the Kazi rose and swore an oath, saying, "By the truth of Him who created mankind, we will not go but with the Emir!" Accordingly we repaired to the Judge's house, accompanied by the Chief, and going up, searched it through, but found naught; whereat fear fell upon me and the Wali turned to me and said, "Fie upon thee, O ill-omened fellow! thou hast put us to shame before the men." All this, and I wept and went round about right and left, with the tears running down my face, till we were about to go forth and drew near the door of the house. I looked at the place which the woman had mentioned and asked, "What is yonder dark place I see?" Then said I to the men, "Pull up[1] this jar with me." They did my bidding and I saw somewhat appearing under the jar and said, "Rummage and look at what is under it." So they searched, and behold, they came upon a woman's mantilla and petticoat-trousers full of blood, which when I espied, I fell down in a fainting-fit. Now when the Wali saw this, he said, "By Allah, the Captain is excused!" Then my comrades came round about me and sprinkled water on my face till I recovered, when I arose and accosting the Kazi (who was covered with confusion), said to him, "Thou seest that suspicion is fallen on thee, and indeed this affair is no light matter, because this woman's family will assuredly not sit down quietly under her loss." Therewith the Kazi's heart quaked and fluttered for that he knew the suspicion had reverted upon him, wherefore his colour yellowed and his limbs smote together; and he paid of his own money, after the measure of that he had lost, so we would quench that fire for him.[2] Then we departed from him in peace, whilst I said within myself, "Indeed, the woman falsed me not." After that I tarried till three days had passed, when I went to the Hammam and changing my clothes, betook myself to her home, but found the door shut and covered with dust. So I asked the neighbours of her and they answered, "This house hath been empty of habitants these many days; but three days agone there came a woman with an ass, and at supper-time last night she took her gear and went away." Hereat I turned back,

---

[1] It was probably stuck in the ground like an amphora.
[2] i.e. hush up the matter.

bewildered in my wit, and for many a day after I inquired of the dwellers in that street concerning her, but could happen on no tidings of her. And indeed I wondered at the eloquence of her tongue and the readiness of her talk; and this is the most admirable of all I have seen and of whatso hath betided me. When Al-Malik al-Zahir heard the tale of Mu'in al-Din, he marvelled thereat. Then rose another constable and said, "O lord, hear what befel me in bygone days."

The Second Constable's History.

I WAS once an overseer in the household of the Emir Jamál al-Din al-Atwash al-Mujhidi, who was made governor of the two provinces, Sharkíyah and Gharbíyah,[1] and I was dear to his heart and he hid from me naught of whatso he desired to do; and he was eke master of his reason.[2] It came to pass one day of the days that it was reported to him how the daughter of Such-an-one had a mint of monies and raiment and ornaments and at that present she loved a Jewish man, whom every day she invited to be private with her, and they passed the light hours eating and drinking in company and he lay the night with her. The Wali feigned not to believe a word of this story, but he summoned the watchmen of the quarter one night and questioned them of this tittle-tattle. Quoth one of them, "As for me, O my lord, I saw none save a Jew[3] enter the street in question one night; but I have not made certain to whom he went in;" and quoth the Chief, "Keep thine eye on him from this time forward and note what place he entereth." So the watchman went out and kept his eye on the Judæan. One day as the Prefect sat in his house, the watchman came in to him and said, "O my lord, in very sooth the Jew goeth to the house of Such-an-one." Whereupon Al-Atwash sprang to his feet and went forth alone, taking with him none save myself."[4] As he went along, he said to me,

---

[1] In Egypt; the former being the Eastern of the Seven Provinces extending to the Pelusium branch, and the latter to the Canobic. The "Barári" or deserts, i.e. grounds not watered by the Nile, lie scattered between the two and both are bounded South by the Kalúbíyah Province and Middle Egypt.

[2] i.e. a man ready of wit and immediate of action, as opposed to his name Al-Atwash = one notable for levity of mind.

[3] The negative is emphatic, "I certainly saw a Jew," etc.

[4] The "Irish bull" is in the text; justified by—
> They hand-in-hand, with wand'ring steps and slow
> Through Eden took their solitary way.

"Indeed, this girl is a fat piece of meat."[1] And we gave not over going till we came to the door of the house and stood there until a hand-maid came out, as if to buy them something wanted. We waited till she opened the door, whereupon, without question or answer, we forced our way into the house and rushed in upon the girl, whom we found seated with the Jew in a saloon with four daïses, and cooking-pots and candles therein. When her eyes fell on the Wali, she knew him and rising to her feet, said, "Well come and welcome and fair cheer! By Allah, great honour hath betided me by my lord's visit and indeed thou dignifiest my dwelling." Hereat she carried him up to the daïs and seating him on the couch, brought him meat and wine and gave him to drink; after which she put off all that was upon her of raiment and ornaments and tying them up in a kerchief, said to him, "O my lord, this is thy portion, all of it." Then she turned to the Jew and said to him, "Rise, thou also, and do even as I:" so he arose in haste and went out very hardly crediting his deliverance.[2] When the girl was assured of his escape, she put out her hand to her clothes and jewels and taking them, said to the Chief, "O Emir, is the requital of kindness other than kindness? Thou hast deigned to visit me and eat of my bread and salt; so now arise and depart from us without ill-doing; or I will give a single outcry and all who are in the street will come forth." So the Emir went out from her, without having gotten a single dirham; and on this wise she delivered the Jew by the seemliness of her stratagem. The company admired this tale, and as for the Wali and Al-Malik al-Zahir, they said, "Ever devised any the like of this device?" and they marvelled with the utterest of marvel. Then arose a third constable and said, "Hear what betided me, for it is yet stranger and rarer."

The Third Constable's History.

I was one day abroad on business with certain of my comrades; and, as we walked along behold, we fell in with a company of

---

[1] As we should say, "There are good pickings to be had out of this job." Even in the last generation a Jew or a Christian intriguing with an Egyptian or Syrian Moslemah would be offered the choice of death or Al-Islam. The Wali dared not break open the door because he was not sure of his game.

[2] The Jew rose seemingly to fetch his valuables and ran away, thus leaving the Wali no proof that he had been there in Moslem law which demands ocular testimony, rejects

women, as they were moons, and among them one, the tallest of
them and the handsomest. When I saw her and she saw me, she
lagged behind her companions and waited for me till I came up to
her and bespake her. Quoth she, "O my lord (Allah favour thee!)
I saw thee prolong thy looking on me and I fancied that thou
knewest me. An it be thus, let me learn more of thee." Quoth
I, "By Allah, I know thee not, save that the Most High Lord
hath cast the love of thee into my heart and the goodliness of thy
qualities hath confounded me; and that wherewith the Almighty hath gifted thee of those eyes that shoot with shafts
hath captivated me." And she rejoined, "By Allah, indeed I
feel the like of that which thou feelest; ay, and even more; so
that meseemeth I have known thee from childhood." Then said
I, "A man cannot well effect all whereof he hath need in the
market-places." She asked me, "Hast thou a house?" and I
answered, "No, by Allah, nor is this city my dwelling-place."
Rejoined she, "By Allah, nor have I a place; but I will contrive
for thee." Then she went on before me and I followed her till
she came to a lodging-house[1] and said to the Housekeeper,
"Hast thou an empty room?" The other replied, "Yes:"[2] and
my mistress said, "Give us the key." So we took the key and
going up to see the room, entered to inspect it; after which she
went out to the Housekeeper and giving her a dirham, said to her
"Take the *douceur* of the key[3] for the chamber pleaseth us, and
here is another dirham for thy trouble. Go, fetch us a gugglet of
water, so we may refresh ourselves and rest till siesta-time pass
and the heat decline, when the man will depart and bring our bag
and baggage." Therewith the Housekeeper rejoiced and brought
us a mat, two gugglets of water on a tray, a fan and a leather
rug. We abode thus till the setting-in of mid-afternoon, when
she said, "Needs must I make the Ghusl-ablution ere I fare."[4]

---

circumstantial evidence and ignores such partial witnesses as the policeman who accompanied his Chief. This I have before explained.

[1] Arab. "Raba'," lit. = spring-quarters. See Marba', iii. 79.

[2] Arab. "Ni'am," an exception to the Abbé Sicard's rule. "La consonne N est l'expression naturelle du doute chez toutes les nations, par ce que le son que rend la touche nasale,
quand l'homme incertain examine s'il fera ce qu'on lui demande; ainsi NE ON, NE OT, NE
EC, NE IL, d'où l'on a fait *non*, *not*, *nec*, *nil*.

[3] For this "Haláwat al-Miftáh," or sweetmeat of the key-money, the French *denier à
Dieu*, Old English "God's penny," see vol. vii. 212, and Pilgrimage i. 62.

[4] Showing that car. cop. had taken place. Here we find the irregular use of the inn,
perpetuated in not a few of the monster hotels throughout Europe.

Said I, "Get water wherewith we may both wash," and drew forth from my pocket a score or so of dirhams, thinking to give them to her; but she cried, "Refuge with Allah!" and brought out of her pocket a handful of silver, saying, "But for destiny and that the Almighty hath caused the love of thee fall into my heart, there had not happened that which hath happened." Quoth I, "Accept this in requital of that which thou hast spent;" and quoth she, "O my lord, by and by, whenas mating is prolonged between us, thou wilt see if the like of me looketh unto money and means or no." Then the lady took a jar of water and going into the lavatory, made the Ghusl-ablution[1] and presently coming forth, prayed the mid-afternoon prayer and craved pardon of Allah Almighty for the sin into which she had fallen. Now I had asked her name and she answered, "Rayhánah,"[2] and described to me her dwelling-place. When I saw her make the ablution, I said within myself, "This woman doth on this wise, and shall I not do the like of her doing?" Then quoth I to her, "Peradventure[3] thou wilt seek us another jar of water?" Accordingly she went out to the Housekeeper and said to her, "O my sister, take this Nusf and fetch us for it water wherewith we may wash the flags."[4] So the Housekeeper brought two jars of water and I took one of them and giving her my clothes, entered the lavatory and bathed. When I had made an end of bathing, I cried out, saying, "Harkye, my lady Rayhanah!" However none answered me. So I went out and found her not; but I did find that she had taken my clothes and all that was in them of silver, to wit, four hundred dirhams. She had also carried off my turband and my kerchief and I lacked the wherewithal to veil my shame; so I suffered somewhat than which death is less grievous and abode looking about the place, hoping that haply I might espy a rag wherewith to hide my nakedness. Then I sat a little and presently going up to the door, smote upon it; whereat up came the Housekeeper and I said to her, "O my sister, what hath Allah done with the woman who was here?"

---

[1] For its rules and right performance see vol. vi. 199.

[2] *i.e.* the "Basil(issa)," mostly a servile name, see vol. i. 19.

[3] Arab. "La'alla," used to express the hope or expectation of some event of possible occurrence; thus distinguished from "Layta"—Would heaven! utinam! O si! etc.—expressing desire or volition.

[4] Arab. "Balát," in Cairo the flat slabs of limestone and sandstone brought from the Turah quarries, which supplied stone for the Jízah Pyramids.

She replied, "The lady came down just now and said, 'I'm going to cover the boys with the clothes,' adding, 'and I have left him sleeping; an he awake, tell him not to stir till the clothes come to him.'" Then cried I, "O my sister, secrets are safe with the fair-dealing and the freeborn. By Allah, this woman is not my wife, nor ever in my life have I seen her before this day!" And I recounted to her the whole affair and begged of her to cover me, informing her that my private parts were clean unconcealed. She laughed and cried out to the women of the lodging-house, saying, "Ho, Fátimah! Ho, Khadíjah! Ho, Harífah! Ho, Sanínah!" Whereupon all those who were in the place of women and neighbours flocked to me and fell a-mocking me and saying, "O pimp,[1] what hadst thou to do with gallantry?" Then one of them came and looked in my face and laughed, and another said, "By Allah, thou mightest have known that she lied, from the time she said she liked thee and was in love with thee! What is there in thee to love?" A third said, "This is an old man without wisdom;" and all vied one with other in exercising their wits upon me, I suffering mighty sore chagrin. However, one of the women took compassion on me after a while, and brought me a rag of thin stuff and cast it on me. With this I covered my shame, and no more, and abode awhile thus: then said I in myself, "The husbands of these women will presently gather together upon me and I shall be disgraced." So I went out by another door of the lodging-house, and young and old crowded about me, running after me and crying, "A madman! A madman!"[2] till I came to my house and knocked at the door; whereupon out came my wife and seeing me naked, tall, bare of head, cried out and ran in again, saying, "This is a maniac, a Satan!" But, when my family and spouse knew me, they rejoiced and said to me, "What aileth thee?" I told them that thieves had taken my clothes and stripped me and had been like to slay me; and when I assured them that the rogues would have slaughtered me, they praised Allah Almighty and gave me joy of my safety. So consider the craft this woman practised upon me, and I pretending to cleverness and wiliness. Those present marvelled at this story and at the

---

[1] Arab. "Yá Mu'arras!" here = O fool and disreputable; see vol. i. 338.

[2] These unfortunates in hot climates enjoy nothing so much as throwing off the clothes which burn their feverish skins: see Pilgrimage iii. 385. Hence the boys of Eastern cities, who are perfect imps and flibbertigibbets, always raise the cry "Majnún" when they see a man naked whose sanctity does not account for his nudity.

doings of women; then came forward a fourth constable and said, "Now that which hath betided me of strange adventures is yet stranger than this, and 'twas after the following fashion."

The Fourth Constable's History.

WE were sleeping one night on the terrace-roof, when a woman made her way through the darkness into the house and, gathering into a bundle all that was therein, took it up that she might go away with it. Now she was big with child and nigh upon her time of delivery; so, when she packed up the bundle and prepared to shoulder it and make off with it, she hastened the coming of the labour-pangs and bare a child in the dark. Then she sought for the fire-sticks and when they burned, kindled the lamp and went round about the house with the little one, and it was weeping. The wail awoke us, as we lay on the roof, and we marvelled. So we rose to see what was to do, and looking down through the opening of the saloon,[1] saw a woman, who had lit the lamp, and heard the little one crying. As we were peering, she heard our words and raising her head to us, said, "Are ye not ashamed to deal thus with us and bare our shame? Wist ye not that the day belongeth to you and the night to us? Begone from us! By Allah, were it not that ye have been my neighbours these many years, I would assuredly[2] bring down the house upon you!" We doubted not but that she was of the Jinn and drew back our heads; but, when we rose on the morrow, we found that she had taken all that was with us and made off with it;[3] wherefore we knew that she was a thief and had practised on us a device,

---

[1] Arab. "Daur al-Ká'ah" = the round opening made in the ceiling for light and ventilation.

[2] Arab. "La-nakhsifanna" with the emphatic termination called by grammarians "Nún al-taakid"—the N of injunction. Here it is the reduplicated form, the Nun al-Sakílah or heavy N. The addition of Lá (not) e.g. "Lá yazrabanna" = let him certainly not strike, answers to the intensive or corroborative negative of the Greek effected by two negations or even more. In Arabic as in Latin and English two negatives make an affirmative.

[3] Parturition and death in warm climates, especially the damp-hot like Egypt are easy compared with both processes in the temperates of Europe. This is noticed by every traveller. Hence probably Easterns have never studied the artificial Euthanasia which is now appearing in literature. See p. 143 "My Path to Atheism," by Annie Besant, London: Freethought Publishing Company, 28, Stonecutter Street, E. C., 1877; based upon the Utopia of the highly religious Thomas Moore. Also "Essay on Euthanasia," by P. D. Williams, Jun., and Mr. Tollemache in the "Nineteenth Century."

such as was never before practised; and we repented, whenas
repentance availed us naught. The company, hearing this tale,
marvelled thereat with the utmost marvelling. Then the fifth
constable, who was the lieutenant of the bench,[1] came forward
and said, "This is no wonder and there befel me a story which
is rarer and stranger than this."

The Fifth Constable's History.

As I sat one day at the door of the Prefecture, behold, a woman
suddenly entered and said as though consulting me. "O my lord,
I am the wife of Such-an-one the Leach, and with him is a company of the notables[2] of the city, drinking fermented drinks in
such a place." When I heard this, I misliked to make a scandal;
so I bluffed her off and sent her away unsatisfied. Then I rose
and walked alone to the place in question and sat without till the
door opened, when I rushed in and entering, found the company
even as the woman aforesaid had set out, and she herself with
them. I saluted them and they returned my salam and rising,
treated me with honour and seated me and served me with meat.
Then I informed them how one had denounced them to me, but I
had driven him away and had come to them by myself; so they
thanked me and praising me for my kindness, brought out to me
from among them two thousand dirhams[3] and I took them and
went away. Now two months after this adventure, there came to
me one of the Kazi's officers, with a paper, wherein was the
judge's writ, summoning me to him. So I accompanied the
officer and went in to the Kazi, whereupon the plaintiff, he who
had taken out the summons, sued me for two thousand dirhams,
declaring I had borrowed them of him as the agent or guardian of
the woman. I denied the debt, but he produced against me a
bond for that sum, attested by four of those who were in company on the occasion; and they were present and bore witness to
the loan. I reminded them of my kindness and paid the amount,
swearing that I would never again follow a woman's counsel. Is
not this marvellous? The company admired the goodliness of his

---

[1] *i.e.* he whose turn it is to sit on the bench outside the police-office in readiness for
emergencies.

[2] Arab. " 'Udúl" (plur. of 'Ádil), gen. men of good repute, qualified as witnesses in the
law-court, see vol. iv. 271. It is also used (as below) for the Kazi's Assessors.

[3] About £80.

tale and it pleased Al-Malik al-Zahir; and the Wali said, "By
Allah, this is a strange story!" Then came forward the sixth
constable and said to those present, "Hear my adventure and that
which befel me, to wit, that which befel Such-an-one the Assessor, for 'tis rarer than this and finer."

The Sixth Constable's History.

A CERTAIN Assessor one day of the days was taken with a woman
and much people assembled before his house and the Lieutenant
of police and his posse came to him and rapped at the door. The
Assessor peered from house-top and seeing the folk, said, "What
do ye want?" Replied they, "Speak with the Lieutenant of
police Such-an-one." So he came down and as he opened the
door they cried to him, "Bring forth the woman who is with
thee." "Are ye not ashamed? How shall I bring forth my wife?"
"Is she thy wife by book[1] or without marriage-lines?" "She is my
wife according to the Book of Allah and the Institutes of His
Apostle." "Where is the contract?" "Her lines are in her
mother's house." "Arise thou and come down and show us the
writ." "Go from her way, so she may come forth." Now, as
soon as he got wind of the matter, he had written the bond and
fashioned it after the fashion of his wife,[2] to suit with the case,
and he had written therein the names of certain of his friends to
serve as witnesses and forged the signatures of the drawer and the
wife's next friend and made it a contract of marriage with his
wife and a legal deed.[3] Accordingly, when the woman was about
to go out from him, he gave her the contract he had forged, and
the Emir sent with her a servant of his, to carry her home to her
father. So the servant went with her and when she was inside
she said to him, "I will not return to the citation of the Emir;
but let the Assessors present themselves and take my contract."

---

[1] Arab. "Kitáb" = book, written bond. This officiousness of the neighbours is thoroughly justified by Moslem custom; and the same scene would take place in this our
day. Like the Hindú's, but in a minor degree, the Moslem's neighbours form a volunteer
police which oversees his every action. In the case of the Hindú this is required by the
exigencies of caste, an admirable institution much bedevilled by ignorant Mlenchhas, and
if "dynamiting" become the fashion in England, as it threatens to become, we shall be
obliged to establish "Vigilance Committees" which will be as inquisitorial as caste.

[2] e.g. writing The contract of A. with B., daughter of Such-an-one, etc.

[3] Arab. "Hujjat," which may also mean an excuse.

Hereupon the servant carried this message to the Lieutenant of police, who was standing at the Assessor's door, and he said, "This is permissible." Then said the Assessor to the servant, "Fare, O eunuch, and fetch us Such-an-one the Notary;" for that he was his friend and 'twas he whose name he had forged as the drawer-up of the contract.[1] So the Lieutenant sent after him and fetched him to the Assessor, who, when he saw him, said to him, "Get thee to Such-an-one, her with whom thou marriedst me, and cry out upon her, and when she cometh to thee,[2] demand of her the contract and take it from her and bring it to us." And he signed to him, as much as to say, "Bear me out in the lie and screen me, for that she is a strange woman and I[3] am in fear of the Lieutenant who standeth at the door; and we beseech Allah Almighty to screen us and you from the woes of this world. Amen." So the Notary went up to the Lieutenant, who was among the witnesses, and said, " 'Tis well. Is she not Such-an-one whose marriage-contract we drew up in such a place?" Then he betook himself to the woman's house and cried out upon her; whereat she brought him the forged contract and he took it and returned with it to the Lieutenant of police.[4] When the officer had taken cognizance of the document and professed himself satisfied, the Assessor said to the Notary, "Go to our lord and master, the Kazi of the Kazis, and acquaint him with that which befalleth his Assessors." The Notary rose to go, but the Lieutenant feared for himself and was urgent in beseeching the Assessor and in kissing his hands till he forgave him; whereupon the Lieutenant went away in the utmost concern and affright. On such wise the Assessor ordered the case and carried out the forgery and feigned marriage with the woman; and thus escaped calumny and calamity by the seemliness of his stratagem.[5] The folk marvelled at this with the uttermost marvel and the seventh constable said, "There befel me in Alexandria the God-guarded a wondrous thing, and 'twas this."[6]

---

[1] The last clause is supplied by Mr. Payne to stop a gap in the broken text.

[2] The text idiotically says "To the King."

[3] In the text "Nahnu" = we, for I; a common vulgarism in Egypt and Syria.

[4] This clause has required extensive trimming; the text making the Notary write out the contract (which was already written) in the woman's house.

[5] Arab. "Husn tadbír" = lit. "beauty of his contrivance." Husn, like pulcher, beau and bello, is applied to moral intellectual qualities as well as to physical and material. Hence the καλὸ γέρων, or old gentleman which in Romaic becomes Calogero, a monk.

[6] i.e. that some one told me the following tale.

The Seventh Constable's History.

THERE came one day an old woman to the stuff-bazar, with a casket of mighty fine workmanship, containing trinkets, and she was accompanied by a young baggage big with child. The crone sat down at the shop of a draper and giving him to know that the girl was pregnant by the Prefect[1] of Police of the city, took of him, on credit, stuffs to the value of a thousand dinars and deposited with him the casket as security. She opened the casket and showed him that which was therein and he found it full of trinkets of price; so he trusted her with the goods and she farewelled him and carrying the stuffs to the girl who was with her, went her way. Then the old woman was absent from him a great while, and when her absence was prolonged, the draper despaired of her; so he went up to the Prefect's house and asked anent the woman of his household who had taken his stuffs on credit; but could obtain no tidings of her nor happen on any trace of her. Then he brought out the casket of jewellery and showed it to experts, who told him that the trinkets were gilt and that their worth was but an hundred dirhams. When he heard this, he was sore concerned thereat and presenting himself before the Deputy of the Sultan made his complaint to him; whereupon the official knew that a sleight had been served upon him and that the sons of Adam[2] had cozened him and conquered him and cribbed his stuffs. Now the magistrate in question was a man of experience and judgment, well versed in affairs; so he said to the draper, "Remove somewhat from thy shop, including the casket, and to-morrow morning break the lock and cry out and come to me and complain that they have plundered all thy shop.[3] Also mind thou call upon Allah for aid and wail aloud and acquaint the people, so that a world of folk may flock to thee and sight the breach of the lock and that which is missing from thy shop: and on this wise display it to every one who presenteth himself that the news may be noised abroad, and tell them that thy chief concern is for a casket of great value, deposited with thee by a great man of the town and that thou standest in fear of him.

---

[1] Arab. "Mutawallí": see vol. i. 259.
[2] i.e. his Moslem neighbours.
[3] In the text is a fearful confusion of genders.

But be thou not afraid and still say ever and anon in thy saying, 'My casket was the casket of Such-an-one, and I fear him and dare not bespeak him; but you, O company and all ye who are present, I call you to witness of this for me.' And if there be with thee more than this saying, say it; and the old woman will assuredly come to thee." The draper answered with "To hear is to obey" and going forth from the Deputy's presence, betook himself to his shop and brought out thence the casket and a somewhat making a great display, which he removed to his house. At break of day he arose and going to his shop, broke the lock and shouted and shrieked and called on Allah for aid, till each and every of the folk assembled about him and all who were in the city were present, whereupon he cried out to them, saying even as the Prefect had bidden him; and this was bruited abroad. Then he made for the Prefecture and presenting himself before the Chief of Police, cried out and complained and made a show of distraction. After three days, the old woman came to him and bringing him the thousand dinars, the price of the stuffs, de-manded the casket.[1] When he saw her, he seized her and carried her to the Prefect of the city; and when she came before the Kazi, he said to her, "Woe to thee O Sataness; did not thy first deed suffice thee, but thou must come a second time?" She replied, "I am of those who seek their salvation[2] in the cities, and we foregather every month: and, yesterday we foregathered." He asked her, "Canst thou cause me to catch them?" and she answered, "Yes; but, an thou wait till to-morrow, they will have dispersed; so I will deliver them to thee to-night." The Emir said to her, "Go;" and said she, "Send with me one who shall go with me to them and obey me in whatso I shall say to him, and all that I bid him he shall not gainsay and therein con-form to my way." Accordingly, he gave her a company of men and she took them and bringing them to a certain door, said to them, "Stand ye here, at this door, and whoso cometh out to you, seize him; and I will come out to you last of all." "Hearing and obeying," answered they and stood at the door, whilst the crone went in. They waited a whole hour, even as the Sultan's deputy had bidden them, but none came out to them and their standing waxed longsome, and when they were weary of waiting,

---

[1] Her object was to sue him for the loss of the pledge and to demand fabulous damages.

[2] Arab. "Ya'tamidúna hudà-hum" = purpose the right direction, a skit at the devotees of her age and sex; and an impudent comment upon the Prefect's address "O she-devil!"

they went up to the door and smote upon it a heavy blow and a violent, so that they came nigh to break the wooden bolt. Then one of them entered and was absent a long while, but found naught; so he returned to his comrades and said to them, "This is the door of a dark passage, leading to such a thoroughfare; and indeed she laughed at you and left you and went away."[1] When they heard his words, they returned to the Emir and acquainted him with the case, whereby he knew that the old woman was a cunning craft-mistress and that she had mocked at them and cozened them and put a cheat on them, to save herself. Witness, then, the wiles of this woman and that which she contrived of guile, for all her lack of foresight in presenting herself a second time to the draper and not suspecting that his conduct was but a sleight; yet, when she found herself hard upon calamity, she straightway devised a device for her deliverance. When the company heard the seventh constable's story, they were moved to mirth galore, than which naught could be more; and Al-Malik al-Zahir Bíbars rejoiced in that which he heard and said, "Verily, there betide things in this world wherefrom kings are shut out, by reason of their exalted degree!" Then came forward another person from amongst the company and said, "There hath reached me through one of my friends a similar story bearing on the malice of women and their wiles, and it is more wondrous and marvellous, more diverting and more delectable than all that hath been told to you." Quoth the company there present, "Tell us thy tale and expound it unto us, so we may see that which it hath of extraordinary." And he began to relate

The Eighth Constable's History.

YE must know that a company, amongst whom was a friend of mine, once invited me to an entertainment; so I went with him, and when we came into his house and sat down on his couch, he said to me, "This is a blessed day and a day of gladness, and who is he that liveth to see the like of this day? I desire that thou practise with us and disapprove not our proceedings, for that thou hast been accustomed to fall in with those who offer this."[2]

---

[1] The trick has often been played in modern times at fairs, shows, etc. Witness the old Joe Miller of the "Moving Multitude."

[2] Apparently meaning the forbidden pleasures of wine and wassail, loose talk and tales of women's wiles, a favourite subject with the lewder sort of Moslem.

I consented thereto and their talk happened upon the like of this subject.[1] Presently, my friend, who had invited me, arose from among them and said to them, Listen to me and I will acquaint you with an adventure which happened to me. There was a certain person who used to visit me in my shop, and I knew him not nor he knew me, nor ever in his life had he seen me; but he was wont, whenever he wanted a dirham or two, by way of loan, to come to me and ask me, without acquaintance or introduction between me and him, and I would give him what he required. I told none of him, and matters abode thus between us a long while till he began a-borrowing at a time ten or twenty dirhams, more or less. One day, as I stood in my shop, behold, a woman suddenly came up to me and stopped before me; and she was a presence as she were the full moon rising from among the constellations, and the place was a-light by her light. When I saw her, I fixed my eyes on her and stared in her face; and she fell to bespeaking me with soft voice. When I heard her words and the sweetness of her speech, I lusted after her; and as soon as she saw that I longed for her, she did her errand and promising me an assignation, went away, leaving my thoughts occupied with her and fire a-flame in my heart. Accordingly I abode, perplexed and pondering my affair, the fire still burning in my heart, till the third day, when she came again and I could hardly credit her coming. When I saw her, I talked with her and cajoled her and courted her and craved her favour with speech and invited her to my house; but, hearing all this, she only answered, "I will not go up into any one's house." Quoth I, "I will go with thee" and quoth she, "Arise and come with me." So I rose and putting into my sleeve a kerchief, wherein was a fair sum of silver and a considerable, followed the woman, who forwent me and ceased not walking till she brought me to a lane and to a door, which she bade me unlock. I refused and she opened it and led me into the vestibule. As soon as I had entered, she bolted the entrance door from within and said to me, "Sit here till I go in to the slave-girls and cause them enter a place whence they shall not see me." " 'Tis well," answered I and sat down: whereupon she entered and was absent from me an eye-twinkling, after which she returned to me, without a veil, and straightway said, "Arise and enter in the name of Allah." So I arose and went in after her

---

[1] *i.e.* women's tricks.

and we gave not over going till we reached a saloon. When I
examined the place, I found it neither handsome nor pleasant,
but desolate and dreadful without symmetry or cleanliness;
indeed, it was loathsome to look upon and there was in it a foul
smell. After this inspection I seated myself amiddlemost the
saloon, misdoubting; and lo and behold! as I sat, there came
down on me from the daïs a body of seven naked men, without
other clothing than leather belts about their waists. One of
them walked up to me and took my turband, whilst another
seized my kerchief that was in my sleeve, with my money, and a
third stripped me of my clothes; after which a forth came and
bound my hands behind my back with his belt. Then they all
took me up, pinioned as I was, and casting me down, fell a-haling
me towards a sink-hole that was there and were about to cut my
throat, when suddenly there came a violent knocking at the door.
As they heard the raps, they were afraid and their minds were
diverted from me by affright; so the woman went out and presently returning, said to them, "Fear not; no harm shall betide
you this day. 'Tis only your comrade who hath brought you
your dinner." With this the new-comer entered, bringing with
him a roasted lamb; and when he came in to them, he asked,
"What is to do with you, that ye have tucked up sleeves and
bag-trousers?" Replied they, "This is a head of game we've
caught." As he heard these words, he came up to me and peering
in my face, cried out and said, "By Allah, this is my brother, the
son of my mother and father! Allah! Allah!" Then he loosed me
from my pinion-bonds and bussed my head, and behold it was my
friend who used to borrow silver of me. When I kissed his head,
he kissed mine and said, "O my brother, be not affrighted;" and
he called for my clothes and coin and restored all to me nor was
aught missing. Also, he brought me a porcelain bowl full of
sherbet of sugar, with lemons therein, and gave me to drink; and
the company came and seated me at a table. So I ate with them
and he said to me, "O my lord and my brother, now have bread
and salt passed between us and thou hast discovered our secret
and our case; but secrets with the noble are safe." I replied,
"As I am a lawfully-begotten child and a well-born, I will not
name aught of this nor denounce you!" They assured themselves
of me by an oath; then they brought me out and I went my way,
very hardly crediting but that I was of the dead. I lay ill in my
house a whole month; after which I went to the Hammam and

coming out, opened my shop and sat selling and buying as was
my wont, but saw no more of that man or that woman till, one
day, there stopped before my shop a young Turkoman,[1] as he
were the full moon; and he was a sheep-merchant and had with
him a leathern bag, wherein was money, the price of sheep he
had sold. He was followed by the woman, and when he stopped
over against my shop, she stood by his side and cajoled him, and
indeed he inclined to her with great inclination. As for me, I
was dying of solicitude for him and began casting furtive glances
at him and winked at him, till he chanced to look round and saw
me signing to him; whereupon the woman gazed at me and made
a signal with her hand and went away. The Turkoman followed
her and I deemed him dead without a doubt; wherefore I feared
with exceeding fear and shut my shop. Then I journeyed for a
year's space and returning, opened my shop; whereupon, behold, the woman as she walked by came up to me and said,
"This is none other than a great absence." I replied, "I have
been on a journey;" and she asked, "Why didst thou wink at the
Turkoman?" I answered, "Allah forfend! I did not wink at him."
Quoth she, "Beware lest thou thwart me;" and went away.
Awhile after this a familiar of mine invited me to his house and
when I came to him, we ate and drank and chatted. Then he
asked me, "O my friend, hath there befallen thee aught of sore
trouble in the length of thy life?" Answered I, "Tell me first,
hath there befallen thee aught?" He rejoined, "Know that one
day I espied a fair woman; so I followed her and sued her to
come home with me. Quoth she, 'I will not enter any one's
house but my own; so come thou to my home, an thou wilt,
and be it on such a day.' Accordingly, on the appointed day,
her messenger[2] came to me, proposing to carry me to her; and
when he announced his purpose I arose and went with him, till
we arrived at a goodly house and a great door. He opened the
door and I entered, whereupon he bolted it behind me and
would have gone in; but I feared with exceeding fear and foregoing him to the second door, whereby he would have had me
enter, bolted it and cried out at him, saying, 'By Allah, an thou
open not to me, I will slay thee;[3] for I am none of those whom

---

[1] The "Turkoman" in the text first comes in afterwards.
[2] Arab. "Kásid," the old Anglo-Indian "Cossid"; see vol. vii. 340.
[3] Being a merchant he wore dagger and sword, a safe practice as it deters attack and far

thou canst readily cozen!' 'What deemest thou of cozening?' 'Verily, I am startled by the loneliness of the house and the lack of any keeper at its door; for I see none appear.' 'O my lord, this is a private door.' 'Private or public, open to me.' So he opened to me and I went out and had gone but a little way from the door when I met a woman, who said to me, 'A long life was fore-ordained to thee; else hadst thou never come forth of yonder house.' I asked, 'How so?' and she answered, 'Enquire of thy friend Such-an-one,' (naming thee), 'and he will acquaint thee with strange things.' So, Allah upon thee, O my friend, tell me what befel thee of wondrous and marvellous, for I have told thee what befel me." "O my brother, I am bound by a solemn oath." "O my friend, false thine oath and tell me."[1] "Indeed, I dread the issue of this." But he urged me till I told him all, whereat he marvelled. Then I went away from him and abode a long while, without further news. One day, I met another of my friends who said to me, "A neighbour of mine hath invited me to hear singers" but I said:—"I will not fore-gather with any one." However, he prevailed upon me; so we repaired to the place and found there a person, who came to meet us and said, "Bismillah!"[2] Then he pulled out a key and opened the door, whereupon we entered and he locked the door after us. Quoth I, "We are the first of the folk; but where be the singers' voices?" He replied, "They're within the house: this is but a private door; so be not amazed at the absence of the folk." My friend said to me, "Behold, we are two, and what can they dare to do with us?" Then he brought us into the house, and when we entered the saloon, we found it desolate exceedingly and dreadful of aspect. Quoth my friend, "We are fallen into a trap; but there is no Majesty and there is no Might save in Allah, the Glorious, the Great!" And quoth I, "May God never requite thee for me with good!"[3] Then we sat down on the edge of the daïs and suddenly I espied a closet beside me; so I peered into it and my friend asked me, "What seest thou?" I answered, "I see there wealth in store and corpses of murdered

---

better than carrying hidden weapons, derringers and revolvers which, originating in the United States, have now been adopted by the most civilised nations in Europe.

[1] I have noted (vol. ii. 186, iv. 175) the easy expiation of perjury amongst Moslems, an ugly blot in their moral code.

[2] *i.e.* Enter in the name of Allah.

[3] *i.e.* Damn your soul for leading me into this danger!

men galore. Look." So he looked and cried, "By Allah, we are down among the dead!" and we fell a-weeping, I and he. As we were thus, behold, four men came in upon us, by the door at which we had entered, and they were naked, wearing only leather belts about their waists, and made for my friend. He ran at them and dealing one of them a blow with his sword-pommel, knocked him down, whereupon the other three rushed upon him. I seized the opportunity to escape while they were occupied with him, and espying a door by my side, slipped into it and found myself in an underground room, without issue, even a window. So I made sure of death, and said, "There is no Majesty and there is no Might save in Allah, the Glorious, the Great!" Then I looked at the top of the vault and saw in it a range of glazed and coloured lunettes;[1] so I clambered up for dear life, till I reached the lunettes, and I out of my wits for fear. I made shift to remove the glass and scrambling out through the setting, found behind them a wall which I bestrode. Thence I saw folk walking in the street; so I cast myself down on the ground and Allah Almighty preserved me, and when I reached the face of earth, unhurt, the folk flocked round me and I acquainted them with my adventure. Now as Destiny decreed, the Chief of Police was passing through the market-street; so the people told him what was to do and he made for the door and bade raise it off its hinges. We entered with a rush and found the thieves, as they had thrown my friend down and cut his throat; for they occupied not themselves with me, but said, "Whither shall yonder fellow wend? Verily, he is in our grasp." So the Wali hent them with the hand[2] and questioned them of their case, and they confessed against the woman and against their associates in Cairo. Then he took them and went forth, after he had locked up the house and sealed it; and I accompanied him till he came without the first house. He found the door bolted from within;

---

[1] Arab. "Saff Kamaríyát min al-Zujáj." The Kamaríyah is derived by Lane (Introd. M. F.) from Kamar = moon; by Baron Von Hammer from Khumárawayh, second of the Banu-Tulún dynasty, at the end of the ixth century A. D., when stained glass was introduced into Egypt. N. B.—It must date from many centuries before. The Kamaríyah are coloured glass windows about 2 feet high by 18 inches wide, placed in a row along the upper part of the Mashrabíyah or projecting lattice-window, and are formed of small panes of brightly-stained glass set in rims of gypsum-plaster, the whole framed in wood. Here the allusion is to the "Mamrak" or dome-shaped skylight crowning the room. See vol. viii. 156.

[2] i.e. easily arrested them.

so he bade raise it and we entered and found another door. This also he caused pull up, enjoining his men to silence till the doors should be lifted, and we entered and found the band occupied with new game, whom the woman had just brought in and whose throat they were about to cut. The Chief released the man and gave him back whatso the thieves had taken from him; and he laid hands on the woman and the rest and took forth of the house a mint of money, with which they found the purse of the Turkoman sheep-merchant. They at once nailed up the thieves against the house-wall, whilst, as for the woman, they wrapped her in one of her mantillas and nailing her to a board, set her upon a camel and went round about the town with her. Thus Allah razed their dwelling-places and did away from me that which I feared from them. All this befel, whilst I looked on, and I saw not my friend who had saved me from them the first time, whereat I wondered to the utterest of wonderment. However, some days afterward, he came up to me, and indeed he had renounced the world and donned a Fakir's dress; and he saluted me and went away.[1] Then he again began to pay me frequent visits and I entered into conversation with him and questioned him of the band and how he came to escape, he alone of them all. He replied "I left them from the day on which Allah the Most High delivered thee from them, for that they would not obey my say; so I sware I would no longer consort with them." Quoth I, "By Allah, I marvel at thee, for that assuredly thou wast the cause of my preservation!" Quoth he, "The world is full of this sort; and we beseech the Almighty to send us safety, for that these wretches practise upon men with every kind of malpractice." Then I said to him, "Tell me the rarest adventure of all that befel thee in this villainy thou wast wont to work." And he answered, "O my brother, I was not present when they did such deeds, for that my part with them was to concern myself with selling and buying and feeding them; but it hath reached me that the rarest thing which befel them was on this wise."

The Thief's Tale.

THE woman who acted decoy for them and trapped their game and used to inveigle damsels from marriage-banquets, once caught

---

[1] The reader will not forget the half-penitent Captain of Bandits in Gil Blas.

them a woman from a bride-feast, under pretence that she had a
wedding in her own house, and fixed for her a day when she
should come to her. As soon as the appointed time arrived, the
woman presented herself and the other carried her into the house
by a door, declaring that it was a private wicket. When she
entered the saloon, she saw men and braves[1] and knew that she
had fallen into a snare; so she looked at them and said, "Harkye,
my fine fellows![2] I am a woman and in my slaughter there is no
glory, nor have ye against me any feud of blood-wite wherefor
ye should pursue me; and that which is upon me of raiment and
ornaments ye are free to take as lawful loot." Quoth they, "We
fear thy denunciation;" but quoth she, "I will abide with you,
neither coming in nor going out." So they said, "We grant thee
thy life." Then the Captain looked on her and she pleased him;
so he took her for himself, and she abode with him a whole year
doing her very best in their service, till they became familiar with
her and felt assured of her faith. One night of the nights she
plied them with drink and they drank till they became drunken;
whereupon she arose and took her clothes and five hundred dinars
from the Captain; after which she fetched a razor and shaved off
all their beards. Then she took soot from the cooking-pots and
blackening their faces[3] opened the doors and fared forth; and
when the thieves recovered from their drink, they abode confounded and knew that the woman had practiced upon them.
All present marvelled at this his story and the ninth constable
came forward and said, "I will tell you a right pleasant tale I
heard at a wedding."

The Ninth Constable's History.

A CERTAIN singing-girl was fair of favour and bruited of repute,
and it happened one day that she fared forth to a garden a-pleasuring. As she sat in the summer-house, behold, a man lopped of
the hand stopped to beg of her, and suddenly entered in at the
door. Then he touched her with his stump, saying, "An alms,

---

[1] Arab. "Abtál" = champions, athletes, etc., plur. of Batal, a brave: so Batalat = a
virago. As the root Batala = it was vain, the form "Battál" may mean either a hero or a
bad lot: see vol. viii. 335; x. 72, 73.

[2] Arab. "Fityán;" plur. of Fatá; see vol. i, 67.

[3] This was in popular parlance "adding insult to injury:" the blackening their faces
was a promise of Hell-fire.

for the love of Allah!"[1] but she answered, "Allah open!" and in-
sulted him. Many days after this, there came to her a messenger
and gave her the hire of her going forth.[2] So she took with her a
hand-maid and an accompanyist;[3] and when she came to the place
appointed, the messenger brought her into a long passage, at the
end whereof was a saloon. "So" (quoth she) "we entered therein
and found nobody, but we saw the room made ready for an entertainment with candles, dried fruits and wine, and in another
place we saw food and in a third beds. Thereupon we sat down
and I looked at him who had opened the door to us, and behold
he was lopped of the hand. I misliked this, and when I sat a little
longer, there entered a man, who filled the candelabra in the
saloon and lit the waxen candles; and behold, he also was hand-
lopped. Then flocked the folk and there entered none except he
were lopped of the hand, and indeed the house was full of these
companions.[4] When the session was complete, the host came in
and the company rose to him and seated him in the place of
honour. Now he was none other than the man who had fetched
me, and he was clad in sumptuous clothes, but his hands were in
his sleeves, so that I knew not how it was with them. They
brought him food and he ate, he and the company; after which
they washed hands and the host began casting at me furtive
glances. Then they drank till they were drunken, and when they
had taken leave of their wits, the host turned to me and said,
'Thou dealtest not in friendly fashion with him who sought an
alms of thee, and thou saidst to him, "How loathsome art thou!"'
I considered him and behold, he was the lophand who had accosted me in my pleasance.[5] So I asked, 'O my lord, what is this
thou sayest?' and he answered, 'Wait; thou shalt remember it.'
So saying, he shook his head and stroked his beard, whilst I sat
down for fear. Then he put out his hand to my mantilla and
walking-boots and laying them by his side, cried to me, 'Sing, O

[1] Arab. "Shayyan li 'lláh!" lit. = (Give me some) Thing for (the love of) Allah. The
answer in Egypt. is "Allah ya'tík:" = Allah will give it thee (not I), or, "Yaftah 'Allah," =
Allah open (to thee the door of subsistence): in Marocco "Sir fí hálik" (pron. Sirf hák) =
Go about thy business. In all cities there is a formula which suffices the asker; but the
Ghashím (Johny Raw) who ignores it, is pestered only the more by his protestations that
"he left his purse at home," etc.

[2] i.e. engaged her for a revel and paid her in advance.

[3] Arab. "Rasílah" = a (she) partner, to accompany her on the lute.

[4] Suggesting that they are all thieves who had undergone legal mutilation.

[5] Arab. "Nuzhat-í:" see vol. ii. 81.

accursed!' Accordingly, I sang till I was tired out, what while they occupied themselves with their case and drank themselves drunk and the heat of their drink redoubled. Presently, the doorkeeper came to me and said, 'O my lady, fear not; but when thou hast a mind to go, let me know.' Quoth I, 'Thinkest thou to delude me?' and quoth he, 'Nay, by Allah! But I have ruth on thee for that our Captain and Chief purposeth thee no good and methinketh he will kill thee this night.' Said I to him, 'An thou be minded to do me a favour, now is its time;' and said he, 'When our Chief riseth to his need and goeth to the Chapel of Ease, I will precede him with the light and leave the door open; and do thou wend whithersoever thou willest.' Then I sang and the Captain cried, ' 'Tis good.' Replied I, 'Nay, but thou'rt loath-some.' He looked at me and rejoined, 'By Allah, thou shalt never more scent the odour of the world!' But his comrades said to him, 'Do it not,' and gentled him, till he added, 'An it must be so, and there be no help for it, she shall tarry here a whole year and not fare forth.' My answer was, 'I am content to submit to whatso pleaseth thee: if I have failed in respect to thee, thou art of the clement.' He shook his head and drank, then arose and went out to do his need, whilst his comrades were occupied with what they were about of merry-making and drunkenness and sport. So I winked to my friends and we all slipped out into the corridor. We found the door open and fled forth, unveiled[1] and unknowing whither we went; nor did we halt till we had fared afar from the house and happened on a Cook cooking, of whom I asked, 'Hast thou a mind to quicken the dead?' He said, 'Come up;' so we went up into the shop, and he whispered, 'Lie down.' Accordingly, we lay down and he covered us with the Halfah grass,[2] wherewith he was used to kindle the fire under the food. Hardly had we settled ourselves in the place when we heard a noise of kicking at the door and people running right and left and questioning the Cook and asking, 'Hath any one passed by thee?' Answered he, 'None hath passed by me.' But they ceased not to go round about the shop till the day broke, when they turned back, disappointed. Then the Cook removed the reeds and said to us, 'Rise, for ye are delivered from death.' So we arose, and

---

[1] Arab. "Muhattakát;" usually "with torn veils" (fem. plur.) here "without veils," metaphor. meaning in disgrace, in dishonour.

[2] For this reedy Poa, see vol. ii. 18.

we were uncovered, sans veil or mantilla; but the Cook carried us up into his house and we sent to our homes and fetched us veils; and we repented to Allah Almighty and renounced singing, for indeed this was a mighty narrow escape after stress."[1] Those present marvelled at this, and the tenth constable came forward and said, "As for me, there befel me that which was yet rarer than all ye have yet heard." Quoth Al-Malik al-Zahir, "What was that?" And quoth he, "Deign give ear to me."

The Tenth Constable's History.

A ROBBERY of stuffs had been committed in the city and as it was a great matter I was cited,[2] I and my fellows: they[3] pressed hard upon us: but we obtained of them some days' grace and dispersed in search of the stolen goods. As for me, I sallied forth with five men and went round about the city that day; and on the morrow we fared forth into the suburbs. When we found ourselves a parasang or two parasangs away from the city, we waxed athirst; and presently we came to a garden. There I went in alone and going up to the waterwheel,[4] entered it and drank and made the Wuzu-ablution and prayed. Presently, up came the keeper of the garden and said to me, "Woe to thee! Who brought thee to this waterwheel?" and he smote me and squeezed my ribs[5] till I was like to die. Then he bound me with one of his bulls and made me work the waterwheel, flogging me as I walked round with a cattle-whip[6] he had with him, till my heart was a-fire; after which he loosed me and I went out, knowing not the way. Now when I came forth, I fainted: so I sat down till my trouble subsided; then I made for my comrades and said to them, "'I have found

---

[1] I have repeatedly noticed that singing and all music are, in religious parlance, "Makrúh," blameable though not actually damnable; and that the first step after "getting religion" is to forswear them.

[2] *i.e.* to find the thief or make good the loss.

[3] *i.e.* the claimants.

[4] Arab. "Sakiyah:" see vol. i. 123.

[5] The lower orders of Egypt and Syria are addicted to this bear-like attack; so the negroes imitate fighting-rams by butting with their stony heads. Let me remark that when Herodotus (iii. 12), after Psammenitus' battle of Pelusium in B.C. 524, made the remark that the Egyptian crania were hardened by shaving and insolation and the Persians were softened by wearing head-cloths, he tripped in his anthropology. The Iranian skull is naturally thin compared with that of the negroid Egyptian and the negro.

[6] Arab. "Farkalah," φραγέλλιον from flagellum; cattle-whip with leathern thongs. Lane, M.E.; Fleischer Glos. 83–84; Dozy *s.v.*

money and malefactor, and I affrighted him not neither troubled him, lest he should flee; but now, come, let us go to him, so we may contrive to lay hold upon him." Then I took them and we repaired to the keeper of the garden, who had tortured me with tunding, with the intent to make him taste the like of that which he had done with me and lie against him and cause him eat many a stick. So we rushed to the waterwheel and seized the keeper. Now there was with him a youth and, as we were pinioning the gardener, he said, "By Allah, I was not with him and indeed 'tis six months since I entered this city, nor did I set eyes on the stuffs until they were brought hither." Quoth we, "Show us the stuffs;" upon which he carried us to a place wherein was a pit, beside the waterwheel, and digging there, brought out the stolen goods with not a thread or a stitch of them missing. So we took them and carried the keeper to the Prefecture of Police where we stripped him and beat him with palm-rods till he confessed to thefts manifold. Now I did this by way of mockery against my comrades, and it succeeded. The company marvelled at this story with the utmost marvelling, and the eleventh constable rose and said, "I know a story yet stranger than this: but it happened not to myself."

The Eleventh Constable's History.

THERE was once in times of yore a Chief Officer of Police and there passed by him one day of the days a Jew, hending in hand a basket wherein were five thousand dinars; whereupon quoth that officer to one of his slaves, "Art able to take that money from yonder Jew's basket?" "Yes," quoth he, nor did he tarry beyond the next day ere he came to his lord, bringing the basket. "So" (said the officer) "I bade him 'Go, bury it in such a place;' whereupon he went and buried it and returned and told me. Hardly had he reported this when there arose a clamour like that of Doomsday and up came the Jew, with one of the King's officers, declaring that the gold pieces belonged to the Sultan and that he looked to none but us for it. We demanded of him three days' delay, according to custom and I said to him who had taken the money, 'Go and set in the Jew's house somewhat that shall occupy him with himself.' Accordingly he went and played a mighty fine trick, which was, he laid in a basket a dead woman's hand, painted with henna and having a gold seal-ring on one of the fingers, and buried that basket under a slab in the Jew's home. Then we came and searched and found the basket, whereupon without a moment of delay we clapped the Jew in irons for the murder of a woman. As soon as it was the appointed time, there entered to us the man of the Sultan's guards, who had accompanied the Jew, when he came to complain of the loss of the money,[1] and said, 'The Sultan sayeth to you, Nail up[2] the Jew and bring the money, for there is no way by which five thousand gold pieces can be lost.' Wherefore we knew that our device did not suffice. So I went forth and finding a young man, a Hauráni,[3] passing along the road, laid hands on him forthright and stripped him, and whipped him with palm-rods. Then I threw him in jail, ironed, and carrying him to the Prefecture, beat him again, saying to them, 'This be the robber who stole the coin.' And we strove to make him confess; but he would not. Accordingly, we beat him a third and a fourth time, till we were aweary and exhausted and he became unable to return a reply; but, when we had made an end of beating and tormenting him, he said, 'I will fetch the money this very moment.' Presently we went with him till he came to the place where my slave had buried the gold and he dug there and brought it out; whereat I marvelled with the utmost marvel and we carried it to the Prefect's house. When the Wali saw the money and made sure of it with his own eyes, he rejoiced with joy exceeding and bestowed on me a robe of honour. Then he restored the coin straightway to the Sultan and we left the youth in durance vile; whilst I said to my slave who had taken the money, 'Say me, did yonder young man see thee, what time thou buriedst the money?' and he replied, 'No, by Allah the Great!' So I went in to the young man, the prisoner, and

---

[1] This clause is supplied to make sense.

[2] *i.e.* to crucify him by nailing him to an upright board.

[3] *i.e.* a native of the Hauran, Job's country east of Damascus, now a luxuriant waste, haunted only by the plundering Badawin and the Druzes of the hills, who are no better; but its stretches of ruins and league-long swathes of stone over which the vine was trained, show what it has been and what it will be again when the incubus of Turkish mis-rule shall be removed from it. Herr Schuhmacher has lately noted in the Hauran sundry Arab traditions of Job; the village Nawá, where he lived; the Hammam 'Ayyúb, where he washed his leprous skin; the Dayr Ayyúb, a monastery said to date from the third century; and the Makan Ayyub at Al-Markáz, where the semi-mythical patriarch and his wife are buried. The "Rock of Job", covered by a mosque, is a basaltic monolith 7 feet high by 4, and is probably connected with the solar worship of the old Phœnicians.

plied him with wine[1] till he recovered, when I said to him, 'Tell me how thou stolest the money?' Answered he, 'By Allah, I stole it not, nor did I ever set eyes on it till I brought it forth of the earth!' Quoth I, 'How so?' and quoth he, 'Know that the cause of my falling into your hands was my parent's imprecation against me; because I entreated her evilly yesternight and beat her and she said to me, 'By Allah, O my son, the Lord shall assuredly gar the oppressor prevail over thee!' Now she is a pious woman. So I went out forthright and thou sawest me on my way and didst that which thou didst; and when beating was prolonged on me, my senses failed me and I heard a voice saying to me, 'Fetch it.' So I said to you what I said and the Speaker[2] guided me till I came to the place and there befel what befel of the bringing out of the money.' I admired this with the utmost admiration and knew that he was of the sons of the pious. So I bestirred myself for his release and cured him and besought him of acquittance and absolution of responsibility." All those who were present marvelled at this story with the utmost marvel, and the twelfth constable came forward and said, "I will tell you a pleasant trait that I heard from a certain person, concerning an adventure which befel him with one of the thieves.

The Twelfth Constable's History.

I was passing one day in the market, when I found that a robber had broken into the shop of a shroff, a changer of monies, and thence taken a casket, wherewith he had made off to the burial-ground. Accordingly I followed him thither and came up to him, as he opened the casket and fell a-looking into it; whereupon I accosted him, saying, "Peace be on you!"[3] And he was

---

[1] This habit "torquere mero," was a favourite with the mediæval Arabs. Its effect varies greatly with men's characters, making some open-hearted and communicative, and others more cunning and secretive than in the normal state. So far it is an excellent detection of disposition, and many a man passes off well when sober who has shown himself in liquor a rank snob. Among the lower orders it provokes what the Persians call Bad-mastí (le vin méchant) see Pilgrimage iii. 385.

[2] This mystery is not unfamiliar to the modern "spiritualist;" and all Eastern tongues have a special term for the mysterious Voice. See vol. i. 142.

[3] Arab. "Alaykum:" addressed to a single person. This is generally explained by the "Salam" reaching the ears of Invisible Controls, and even the Apostle. We find the words cruelly distorted in the Pentamerone of Giambattista Basile (partly translated by

startled at me; so I left him and went away from him. Some
months after this, I met him again under arrest, in the midst of
the guards and "men of violence,"[1] and he said to them, "Seize this
man." So they laid hands on me and carried me to the Chief of
Police, who said, "What hast thou to do with this wight?" The
robber turned to me and looking a long while in my face, asked,
"Who took this man?" and the officer answered, "Thou badest
us take him; so we took him." And he cried, "I ask refuge of
Allah! I know not this man, nor knoweth he me; and I said not
that to you but of a person other than this." So they released
me, and a while after the thief met me in the street and saluted
me with the salam, saying, "O my lord, fright for fright! Hadst
thou taken aught from me, thou hadst a part in the calamity."[2]
I replied to him, "Allah be the judge between thee and me!"[3]
And this is what I have to recount. Then came forward the
thirteenth constable and said, "'I will tell you a tale which a man
of my friends told me."

The Thirteenth Constable's History.

I WENT out one night of the nights to the house of a friend and
when it was the middle of the night, I sallied forth alone to hie
me home. When I came into the road, I espied a sort of thieves
and they espied me, whereupon my spittle dried up; but I
feigned myself drunken and staggered from side to side, crying
out and saying, "I am drunken." And I went up to the walls
right and left and made as if I saw not the thieves, who followed
me afoot till I reached my home and knocked at the door, when
they went away. Some few days after this, as I stood at the
door of my house, behold, there came up to me a young man,
with a chain about his neck and with him a trooper, and he said
to me, "O my lord, an alms for the love of Allah!" I replied,
"Allah open!" and he looked at me a long while and cried,
"That which thou shouldst give me would not come to the worth
of thy turband or thy waistcloth or what not else of thy habit, to

---

John F. Taylor, London: Bogue, 1848), "The Prince, coming up to the old woman heard
an hundred Licasalemme," p. 383.
[1] Arab. "Al-Zalamah"; the policeman; see vol. vi. 214.
[2] *i.e.* in my punishment.
[3] *i.e.* on Doomsday thou shalt get thy deserts.

say nothing of the gold and the silver which were about thy person." I asked, "And how so?" and he answered, "On such a night, when thou fellest into peril and the thieves would have stripped thee, I was with them and said to them, Yonder man is my lord and my master who reared me. So was I and only I the cause of thy deliverance and thus I saved thee from them." When I heard this, I said to him, "Stop;" and entering my house, brought him that which Allah Almighty made easy to me.[1] So he went his way; and this is all I have to say. Then came forward the fourteenth constable and said, "Know that the tale I have to tell is rarer and pleasanter than this; and 'tis as follows."

The Fourteenth Constable's History.

I HAD a draper's shop before I entered this corporation,[2] and there used to come to me a person whom I know not, save by his face, and I would give him whatso he sought and have patience with him, till he could pay me. One night, I foregathered with certain of my friends and we sat down to liquor: so we drank and were merry and played at Táb;[3] and we made one of us Wazir and another Sultan and a third Torchbearer or Headsman.[4] Presently, there came in upon us a spunger, without bidding, and we went on playing, whilst he played with us. Then quoth the Sultan to the Wazir, "Bring the Parasite who cometh in to the folk, without leave or license, that we may enquire into his case; after which I will cut off his head;" so the headsman arose and dragged the spunger before the Sultan who bade cut off his head. Now there was with them a sword, that would not cut clotted curd;[5] so the headsman smote him therewith and his head flew

---

[1] *i.e.* what I could well afford.

[2] Arab. Hirfah = a trade, a guild, a corporation: here the officers of police.

[3] Gen. "tip-cat" (vol. ii. 314.) Here it would mean a rude form of tables or backgammon, in which the players who throw certain numbers are dubbed Sultan and Wazir, and demean themselves accordingly. A favourite bit of fun with Cairene boys of a past generation was to "make a Pasha;" and for this proceeding, see Pilgrimage, vol. i. 119.

[4] In Marocco there is great difficulty about finding an executioner who becomes obnoxious to the Thár, *vendetta* or blood-revenge. For salting the criminal's head, however, the soldiers seize upon the nearest Jew and compel him to clean out the brain and to prepare it for what is often a long journey. Hence, according to some, the local name of the Ghetto, Al-Malláh, = the salting-ground.

[5] Mr. Payne suspects that "laban," milk, esp. artificially soured (see vol. vi, 201), is a clerical error for "jubn" = cheese. This may be; but I follow the text as the exaggeration is greater.

from his body. When we saw this, the wine fled from our brains and we became in the foulest of plights. Then my friends lifted up the corpse and went out with it, that they might hide it, whilst I took the head and made for the river. Now I was drunken and my clothes were drenched with the blood; and as I passed along the road, I met a robber. When he saw me, he knew me and cried to me, "Such-an-one!" "Well?" said I, and he rejoined, "What is that thou hast with thee?" So I acquainted him with the case and he took the head from me. Then we fared on till we came to the river, where he washed the head and considering it straitly, exclaimed, "By Allah, verily this be my brother, the son of my sire, and he used to spunge upon the folk;" after which he threw that head into the river. As for me, I was like a dead man for dread; but he said to me, "Fear not, neither do thou grieve, for I acquit thee of my brother's blood." Presently, he took my clothes and washed them and dried them and put them on me; after which he said to me, "Get thee gone to thy house." So I returned to my house and he accompanied me, till I came thither, when he said to me, "Allah never desolate thee! I am thy friend Such-an-one, who used to take of thee goods on credit, and I owe thee a kindness; but henceforward thou wilt never see me more." Then he went his ways. The company marvelled at the manliness of this man and his clemency[1] and courtesy, and the Sultan said, "Tell us another of thy stories, O Shahrazad."[2] She replied, " 'Tis well! They set forth[3]

A Merry Jest of a Clever Thief.

A THIEF of the thieves of the Arabs went one night to a certain man's house, to steal from a heap of wheat there, and the people of the house surprised him. Now on the heap was a great copper tasse, and the thief buried himself in the corn and covered his head with the tasse, so that the folk found him not and went their ways: but as they were going, behold, there came a mighty great fart[4] forth of the corn. So they went up to the tasse and raising

---

[1] *i.e.* in relinquishing his blood-wite for his brother.

[2] The Story-teller, probably to relieve the monotony of the Constables' histories, here returns to the original cadre. We must not forget that in the Bresl. Edit. the Nights are running on, and that the charming queen is relating the adventure of Al-Malik al-Zahir.

[3] Arab. "Za'amu" = they opine, they declare; a favourite term with the Bresl. Edit.

[4] Arab. "Zirtah" the coarsest of terms for what the French nuns prettily termed *un*

it, discovered the thief and laid hands on him. Quoth he, "I have
saved you the trouble of seeking me: for I purposed, in breaking
wind, to direct you to my hiding-place; wherefore do you be
easy with me and have ruth on me, so may Allah have ruth on
you!" Accordingly they let him go and harmed him not. "And
for another story of the same kind" (she continued), "hearken to

The Tale of the Old Sharper.

THERE was once an old man renowned for clever roguery, and
he went, he and his mates, to one of the markets and stole thence
a quantity of stuffs: then they separated and returned each to his
quarter. Awhile after this, the old man assembled a company of
his fellows and, as they sat at drink, one of them pulled out a
costly piece of cloth and said, "Is there any one of you will dare
sell this in its own market whence it was stolen, that we may confess his superior subtlety?" Quoth the old man, "I will;" and
they said, "Go, and Allah Almighty open to thee the door!"
So early on the morrow, he took the stuff and carrying it to the
market whence it had been stolen, sat down at the very shop out
of which it had been purloined and gave it to the broker, who
hent it in hand and cried it for sale. Its owner knew it and
bidding for it, bought it and sent after the Chief of Police, who
seized the Sharper and seeing him an old man of grave presence
and handsomely clad said to him, "Whence hadst thou this
piece of stuff?" Quoth he, "I had it from this market and from
yonder shop where I was sitting." Quoth the Wali, "Did its
owner sell it to thee?" and quoth the robber, "Not so; I stole
it, this and other than it." Then said the Chief, "How camest
thou to bring it for sale to the place whence thou stolest it?"
"I will not tell my tale save to the Sultan, for that I have a profitable counsel wherewith I would lief bespeak him." "Name it!"
"Art thou the Sultan?" "No!" "I'll not tell it save to himself."

---

sonnet; I find *ung sonnet* also in Nov. ii. of the Cent nouvelles Nouvelles. Captain Lockett
(p. 32) quotes Strepsiades in The Clouds βροντᾷ κομιδῇ παππάξ "because he cannot
express the bathos of the original (in the Tale of Ja'afar and the old Badawi) without
descending to the oracular language of Giacoma Rodogina, the engastrymythian pro-
phetess." But Sterne was by no means so squeamish. The literature of this subject is
extensive, beginning with "Peteriana, ou l'art de peter," which distinguishes 62 different
tones. After dining with a late friend en garcon we went into his sitting-room and found
on the table 13 books and booklets upon the Crepitus Ventris, and there was some astonishment as not a few of the party had never seen one.

Accordingly the Wali carried him up to the Sultan and he said,
"I have a counsel for thee, O my lord." Asked the Sultan,
"What is thy counsel?" And the thief said, "I repent and will
deliver into thy hand all who are evildoers; and whomsoever
I bring not, I will stand in his stead." Cried the Sultan, "Give
him a robe of honour and accept his profession of penitence."
So he went down from the presence and returning to his comrades, related to them that which had passed, when they confessed his subtlety and gave him that which they had promised
him. Then he took the rest of the booty and went up therewith
to the Sultan, who, seeing him, recognised him and he was magnified in the royal eyes and the king commanded that naught
should be taken from him. After this, when he went down, the
Sultan's attention was diverted from him, little by little, till the
case was forgotten, and so he saved the booty for himself. Those
present marvelled at this and the fifteenth constable came forward and said, "Know that among those who make a trade of
trickery are those whom Allah Almighty taketh on their own
testimony against themselves." It was asked him, "How so?"
and he began to relate

The Fifteenth Constable's History.[1]

IT is told of a thieving person, one of the braves, that he used to
rob and cut the way by himself upon caravans, and whenever the
Chief of Police and the Governors sought him, he would flee from
them and fortify himself in the mountains. Now it came to pass
that a certain man journeyed along the road wherein was that
robber, and this man was single-handed and knew not the sore
perils besetting his way. So the highwayman came out upon him
and said to him, "Bring out that which is with thee, for I mean to
kill thee and no mistake." Quoth the traveller, "Kill me not, but
annex these saddle-bags and divide that which is in them and take
to thee the fourth part." And the thief answered, "I will not

---

[1] This tale is a replica of the Cranes of Ibycus. This was a Rhegium man who when
returning to Corinth, his home, was set upon by robbers and slain. He cast his dying eyes
heavenwards and seeing a flight of cranes called upon them to avenge him and this they
did by flying over the theatre of Corinth on a day when the murderers were present and
one cried out, "Behold the avengers of Ibycus!" Whereupon they were taken and put to
death. So says Paulus Hieronymus, and the affecting old tale has newly been sung in
charming verse by Mr. Justin H. McCarthy ("Serapion." London: Chatto and Windus).

take aught but the whole."[1] Rejoined the traveller, "Take half, and let me go;" but the robber replied, "I will have naught but the whole, and eke I will kill thee." So the wayfarer said, "Take it." Accordingly the highwayman took the saddle-bags and offered to slay the traveller, who said, "What is this? Thou hast against me no blood-feud that should make my slaughter incumbent." Quoth the other, "Needs must I kill thee;" whereupon the traveller dismounted from his horse and grovelled before him, beseeching the thief and bespeaking him fair. The man hearkened not to his prayers, but cast him to the ground; whereupon the traveller raised his eyes and seeing a francolin flying over him, said, in his agony, "O Francolin,[2] bear testimony that this man slayeth me unjustly and wickedly; for indeed I have given him all that was with me and entreated him to let me go, for my children's sake; yet would he not consent. But be thou witness against him, for Allah is not unmindful of deeds which the oppressors do." The highwayman paid no heed to what he heard, but smote him and cut off his head. After this, the rulers compounded with the highwayman for his submission, and when he came before them, they enriched him and he became in such favour with the lieutenant of the Sultan that he used to eat and drink with him and there befel between them familiar converse which lasted a long while till in fine there chanced a curious chance. The lieutenant of the Sultan one day of the days made a banquet, and therein was a roasted francolin, which when the robber saw, he laughed a loud laugh. The lieutenant was angered against him and said to him, "What is the meaning of thy laughter? Seest thou any fault or dost thou mock at us, of thy lack of good manners?" Answered the highwayman, "Not so, by Allah, O my lord; but I saw yonder francolin, which brought to my mind an extraordinary thing; and 'twas on this wise. In the days of my youth, I used to cut the way, and one day I waylaid a man, who had with him a pair of saddle-bags and money therein. So I said to him, 'Leave these saddle-bags, for I mean to slay thee.' Quoth he, 'Take the fourth part of that which is in them and leave me the rest;' and quoth I, 'Needs must I take the whole and kill thee without mistake.' Then said he, 'Take the saddle-bags and let me wend my way;' but I answered,

---

[1] This scene is perfectly true to Badawi life; see my Pilgrimage iii. 68.

[2] Arab. "Durráj": so it is rendered in the French translation of Al-Masúdi, vii. 347.

'There is no help but that I slay thee.' As we were in this con‑
tention, behold, he saw a francolin and turning to it, said, 'Bear
testimony against him, O Francolin, that he slayeth me unjustly
and letteth me not go to my children, for all he hath taken my
money.' However, I had no pity on him neither hearkened to
that which he said, but smote him and slew him and concerned
not myself with the evidence of the francolin." His story
troubled the lieutenant of the Sultan and he was enraged against
him with sore rage; so he drew his sword and smiting him, cut
off his head while he sat at table; whereupon a voice recited
these couplets —

"An wouldst not be injurèd, injure not; * But do good and from Allah win
    goodly lot;

For what happeth by Allah is doomed to be * Yet thine acts are the root I
    would have thee wot."[1]

---

[1] A fair friend found the idea of Destiny in The Nights become almost a night-mare.
Yet here we suddenly alight upon the true Johnsonian idea that conduct makes fate. Both
extremes are as usual false. When one man fights a dozen battles unwounded and another
falls at the first shot we cannot but acknowledge the presence of that mysterious "luck"
whose laws, now utterly unknown to us, may become familiar with the ages. I may note
that the idea of an appointed hour beyond which life may not be prolonged, is as old as
Homer (Il. v. 487).
    The reader has been told (vol. vii. 135) that "Kazá" is Fate in a general sense, the uni-
versal and eternal Decree of Allah, while "Kadar" is its special and particular application
to man's lot, that is Allah's will in bringing forth events at a certain time and place. But
the former is popularly held to be of two categories, one Kazá al-Muham which admits of
modification and Kazá al-Muhkam, absolute and unchangeable, the doctrine of irresistible
predestination preached with so much energy by St. Paul (Romans ix. 15–24); and all the
world over men act upon the former while theoretically holding to the latter. Hence "Chinese Gordon," whose loss to England is greater than even his friends suppose, wrote "It
is a delightful thing to be a fatalist," meaning that the Divine direction and pre-ordination
of all things saved him so much trouble of forethought and afterthought. In this tenet he
was not only a Calvinist but also a Moslem whose contradictory ideas of Fate and Freewill
(with responsibility) are not only beyond Reason but are contrary to Reason; and although
we may admit the *argumentum ad verecundiam*, suggesting that there are things above (or
below) human intelligence, we are not bound so to do in the case of things which are opposed to the common sense of mankind. Practically, however, the Moslem attitude is to
be loud in confessing belief of "Fate and Fortune" before an event happens and after it
wisely to console himself with the conviction that in no way could he have escaped the
occurrence. And the belief that this destiny was in the hands of Allah gives him a certain
dignity especially in the presence of disease and death which is wanting in his rival reli-
gionist the Christian. At the same time the fanciful picture of the Turk sitting stolidly
under a shower of bullets because Fate will not find him out unless it be so written is a freak
of fancy rarely found in real life.
    There are four great points of dispute amongst the schoolmen in Al-Islam; (1) the Unity

Now this voice was the francolin which bore witness against him. The company present marvelled at this tale and all cried, "Woe to the oppressor!" Then came forward the sixteenth constable and said, "And I for another will tell you a marvellous story which is on this wise."

The Sixteenth Constable's History.

I WENT forth one day of the days, intending to travel, and suddenly fell upon a man whose wont it was to cut the way. When he came up with me he offered to slay me and I said to him, "I have naught with me whereby thou mayst profit." Quoth he, "My profit shall be the taking of thy life." I asked, "What is the cause of this? Hath there been enmity between us aforetime?" and he answered, "Nay; but needs must I slay thee." Thereupon I ran away from him to the river side; but he caught me up and casting me to the ground, sat down on my breast. So I sought help of the Shaykh of the Pilgrims[1] and cried to him, "Protect me from this oppressor!" And indeed he had drawn

---

and Attributes of Allah; (2) His promises and threats; (3) historical as the office of Imám; and (4) Predestination and the justice thereof. On the latter subject opinions range over the whole cycle of possibilities. For instance, the Mu'tazilites, whom the learned Weil makes the Protestants and Rationalists of Al-Islam, contend that the word of Allah was created *in subjecto*, *ergo*, an accident and liable to perish, and one of their school, the Kádiriyah (=having power) denies the existence of Fate and contends that Allah did not create evil but left man an absolutely free agent. On the other hand, the Jabariyah (or Mujabbar=the compelled) is an absolute Fatalist who believes in the omnipotence of Destiny and deems that all wisdom consists in conforming with its decrees. Al-Mas'udi (chapt. cxxvii.) illustrates this by the saying of a Moslem philosopher that chess was the invention of a Mu'tazil, while Nard (backgammon with dice) was that of a Mujabbar proving that play can do nothing against Destiny. Between the two are the Ashariyah; trimmers whose standpoint is hard to define; they would say, "Allah creates the power by which man acts, but man wills the action," and care not to answer the query, "Who created the will?" (See Pocock, Sale and the Dabistan ii. 352.) Thus Sa'adi says in the Gulistan (iii. 2), "The wise have pronounced that though daily bread be allotted, yet it is so conditionally upon using means to acquire it, and although calamity be predestined, yet it is right to secure oneself against the portals by which it may have access." Lastly, not a few doctors of Law and Religion hold that Kaza al-Muhkam, however absolute, regards only man's after or final state; and upon this subject they are of course as wise as other people, and—no wiser. Lane has treated the Moslem faith in Destiny very ably and fully (Arabian Nights, vol. i. pp. 58–61), and he being a man of moderate and orthodox views gives valuable testimony.

[1] Arab. "Shaykh al-Hujjáj." Some Santon like Hasan al-Marábit, then invoked by the Meccan pilgrims: see Pilgrimage, i. 321. It can hardly refer to the famous Hajjáj bin Yúsuf al-Sakafí (vol. iv. 3).

a knife to cut my throat when, lo and behold! there came a mighty
great crocodile forth of the river and snatching him up from off
my breast plunged into the water, with him still hending knife in
hand, even within the jaws of the beast: whilst I abode extolling
Almighty Allah, and rendering thanks for my preservation to
him who had delivered me from the hand of that wrong-doer.[1]

TALE OF HARUN AL-RASHID AND ABDULLAH BIN NAFI'.[2]

KNOW thou, O King of the Age, that there was in days of yore
and in ages and times long gone before, in the city of Baghdad,
the Abode of Peace, a Caliph Harun al-Rashid hight, and he
had cup-companions and tale-tellers to entertain him by night.
Among his equerries was a man named Abdullah bin Náfi', who
stood high in favour with him and dear to him, so that he did not
forget him a single hour. Now it came to pass, by the decree of
Destiny, that it became manifest to Abdullah how he was grown
of small account with the Caliph, who paid no heed unto him nor,
if he absented himself, did he ask after him, as had been his habit.
This was grievous to Abdullah and he said within himself,
"Verily, the soul of the Commander of the Faithful and his
Wazir are changed towards me and nevermore shall I see in him
that cordiality and affection wherewith he was wont to treat me."
And this was chagrin-full to him and concern grew upon him, so
that he recited these couplets:—

"Whoso's contemned in his home and land * Should, to better his case, in
　　self-exile hie:
So fly the house where contempt awaits, * Nor on fires of grief for the parting
　　fry;
Crude Ambergris[3] is but offal where * 'Tis born; but abroad on our necks shall
　　stye;
And Kohl at home is a kind of stone, * Cast on face of earth and on roads
　　to lie;
But when borne abroad it wins highest worth * And thrones between eyelid
　　and ball of eye."

---

[1] Here the Stories of the Sixteen Constables abruptly end, after the fashion of the Bresl.
Edit. They are summarily dismissed even without the normal "Bakhshísh."

[2] Bresl. Edit. vol. xi. pp. 400–473 and vol. xii. pp. 4–50, Nights dccccxli.–dcccclvii. For
Kashghar, see vol. i. 255.

[3] Mr. Payne proposes to translate "'Anbar" by amber, the semi-fossilised resin much
used in modern days, especially in Turkey and Somaliland, for bead necklaces. But, as he

(Quoth the sayer), Then he could brook this matter no longer;
so he went forth from the dominions of the Prince of True Believers, under pretence of visiting certain of his kith and kin, and
took with him nor servant nor comrade, neither acquainted any
with his intent, but betook himself to the road and fared deep into
the wold and the sandwastes, unknowing whither he went. After
awhile, he unexpectedly fell in with travellers who were making
the land of Hind and journeyed with them. When he came
thither, he lighted down in a city of that country and housed him
in one of the lodging-houses; and there he abode a while of days,
relishing not food neither solacing himself with sleep; nor was
this for lack of dirhams or dinars, but for that his mind was occupied with musing upon the shifts of Destiny and bemoaning himself for that the revolving sphere had turned against him in enmity, and the days had decreed unto him the disfavour of our lord
the Imam.[1] After such fashion he abode a space of days, and
presently he homed him in the land and took to himself friends
and got him many familiars, with whom he addressed himself to
diversion and good cheer. He used also to go a-pleasuring with his
companions and their hearts were solaced by his company and he
entertained them every evening with stories and displays of his
manifold accomplishments[2] and diverted them with delectable
verses and told them abundance of stories and histories. Presently, the report of him reached King Jamhúr, lord of Kashgar of
Hind, who sent in quest of him, and great was his desire to see
him. So Abdullah repaired to his court and going in to him,
kissed ground before him; and Jamhur welcomed him and treated
him with kindness and bade lodge him in the guest-house, where
he abode three days, at the end of which the king sent to him a
chamberlain of his chamberlains and bade bring him to the presence. When he came before him, he greeted him, and the truchman accosted him, saying, "Verily, King Jamhur hath heard of
thy report, that thou art a pleasant cup-companion and an eloquent teller of night-tales, and he would have thee company with
him o'nights and entertain him with that which thou knowest

---

says, the second line distinctly alludes to the perfume which is sewn in leather and hung
about the neck, after the fashion of our ancient pomanders (*pomme d' ambre*).

[1] *i.e.* The Caliph: see vol. i. p. 50.

[2] Arab. "Adab:" see vol. i. 132, etc. In Moslem dialects which borrow more or less
from Arabic, "Bí-adabí"=without being Adab, means rudeness, disrespect, "impertinence" (in its modern sense).

of histories and pleasant stories and verses." And he made answer, "To hear is to obey!" (Quoth Abdullah bin Nafi',) "So I became his boon-companion and entertained him by night with tales and talk; and this pleased him with the utmost pleasure and he took me into favour and bestowed on me robes of honour and set apart for me a lodging; indeed he was bountiful exceedingly to me and could not brook to be parted from me a single hour. So I sojourned with him a while of time and every night I caroused and conversed with him till the most part of the dark hours was past; and when drowsiness overcame him, he would rise and betake himself to his sleeping-place, saying to me, 'Forsake not my service and forego not my presence.' And I made answer with 'Hearing and obeying.' Now the king had a son, a nice child, called the Emir Mohammed, who was winsome of youth and sweet of speech: he had read books and had perused histories and he loved above all things in the world the telling and hearing of verses and tales and anecdotes. He was dear to his father King Jamhur, for that he owned no other son than he on life, and indeed he had reared him in the lap of love and he was gifted with exceeding beauty and loveliness, brilliancy and perfect grace: he had also learnt to play upon the lute and upon all manner instruments and he was used to converse and company with friends and brethren. Now it was his wont, when the king arose seeking his sleeping-chamber, to sit in his place and require me to entertain him with tales and verses and pleasant anecdotes; and on this wise I abode with them both a great while in all joyance and delight, and the Prince still loved me with mighty great love and treated me with the utmost tenderness. It fortuned one day that the king's son came to me, after his sire had withdrawn, and cried, 'O Ibn Nafi'!' 'At thy service, O my lord;' 'I would have thee tell me a wondrous story and a marvellous matter, which thou hast never related either to me or to my father Jamhur.' 'O my lord, what story is this that thou desirest of me and what kind shall it be of the kinds?' 'It mattereth little, so it be a goodly story, whether it befel of olden tide or in these times.' 'O my lord, I know by rote many stories of various kinds; so which of the kinds preferrest thou, and wilt thou have a story of mankind or of Jinn-kind?' ' 'Tis well! An thou have espied aught with thine eyes and heard it with thine ears, tell it me.' Then he bethought himself and said to me, 'I conjure thee by my life, tell me a tale of the tales of the Jinn and

that which thou hast heard of them and seen of them!' I replied,
'O my son, indeed thou conjurest me by a mighty conjuration;
so lend an ear to the goodliest of stories, ay, and the strangest of
them and the pleasantest and rarest.' Quoth the Prince, 'Say on,
for I am attentive to thy speech;' and quoth I, 'Hear then, O
my son,

The Tale of the Damsel Tohfat al-Kulub and the Caliph Harun al-Rashid.

THE Viceregent of the Lord of the three Worlds, Harun al-
Rashid, had a boon companion of the number of his boon-com-
panions, by name Ishak bin Ibrahim al-Nadim al-Mausili,[1] who
was the most accomplished of the folk of his time in smiting upon
the lute; and of the Commander of the Faithful's love for him,
he set apart for him a palace of the choicest of his palaces, wherein
he was wont to instruct hand-maidens in the arts of singing and
of lute-playing. If any slave-girl became, by his instruction,
clever in the craft, he carried her before the Caliph, who bade her
perform upon the lute; and if she pleased him, he would order
her to the Harim; else would he restore her to Ishak's palace.
One day, the Commander of the Faithful's breast was straitened;
so he sent after his Wazir Ja'afar the Barmecide and Ishak the
cup-companion and Masrur the eunuch, the Sworder of his vengeance; and when they came, he changed his habit and disguised himself, whilst Ja'afar and Ishak and Masrur and al-Fazl[2]
and Yúnus[3] (who were also present) did the like. Then he went
out, he and they, by the postern, to the Tigris and taking boat
fared on till they came to near Al-Táf,[4] when they landed and
walked till they came to the gate of the high street. Here there
met them an old man, handsome in his hoariness and of a vener-
able bearing and a dignified, agreeable of aspect and apparel. He
kissed the earth before Ishak al-Mausili (for that he knew only
him of the company, the Caliph being disguised, and deemed the
others certain of his friends), and said to him, "O my lord, there
is presently with me a hand-maid, a lutanist, never saw eyes the
like of her nor the like of her grace, and indeed I was on my way

---

[1] *i.e.* Isaac of Mosul, the greatest of Arab musicians: see vol. iv. 119.
[2] The elder brother of Ja'afar, by no means so genial or fitted for a royal frolic. See Terminal Essay.
[3] Ibn Habíb, a friend of Isaac, and a learned grammarian who lectured at Basrah.
[4] A suburb of Baghdad, mentioned by Al-Mas'údi.

to pay my respects to thee and give thee to know of her; but Allah, of His favour, hath spared me the trouble. So now I desire to show her to thee, and if she take thy fancy, well and good; otherwise I will sell her." Quoth Ishak, "Go before me to thy quarters,[1] till I come to thee and see her." The old man kissed his hand and went away; whereupon quoth Al-Rashid to him, "O Ishak, who is yonder man and what is his want?" The other replied, "O my lord, this is a man Sa'íd the Slave-dealer hight, and 'tis he that buyeth us maidens and Mamelukes. He declareth that with him is a fair slave, a lutanist, whom he hath withheld from sale, for that he could not fairly sell her till he had passed her before me in review." Quoth the Caliph, "Let us go to him so we may see her, by way of solace, and sight what is in the slave-dealer's quarters of slave-girls;" and quoth Ishak, "Command belongeth to Allah and to the Commander of the Faithful" Then he forewent them and they followed in his track till they came to the slave-dealer's quarters and found a building tall of wall and large of lodgment, with sleeping-cells and chambers therein, after the number of the slave-girls, and folk sitting upon the wooden benches. So Ishak entered, he and his company, and seating themselves in the place of honour, amused themselves by looking at the hand-maids and Mamelukes and watching how they were bought and sold, till the vending came to an end, when some of the folk went away and some remained seated. Then cried the slave-dealer, "Let none sit with us except whoso pur-chaseth by the thousand dinars and upwards." Accordingly those present withdrew and there remained none but Al-Rashid and his suite; whereupon the slave-dealer called the damsel, after he had caused set her a chair of Fawwák,[2] lined with Grecian brocade, and she was like the sun shining high in the shimmering sky. When she entered, she saluted and sitting down, took the lute and smote upon it, after she had touched its strings and tuned it, so that all present were amazed. Then she sang thereto these couplets:

"Breeze o' Morn, an thou breathe o'er the loved one's land, * Deliver my greeting to all the dear band!
And declare to them still I am pledged to their love * And my longing excels
  all that lover unmanned:

---

[1] Containing the rooms in which the girl or girls were sold. See Pilgrimage i. 87.
[2] Dozy quotes this passage but cannot explain the word Fawwák.

O ye who have blighted my heart, ears and eyes, * My passion and ecstasy
    grow out of hand;
And torn is my sprite every night with desire, * And nothing of sleep can my
    eyelids command."

Ishak exclaimed, "Brava, O damsel! By Allah, this is a fair
hour!" Whereupon she sprang up and kissed his hand, saying,
"O my lord, in very sooth the hands stand still before thy presence and the tongues at thy sight, and the eloquent when con-
fronting thee wax dumb; but thou art the looser of the veil."[1]
Then she clung to him and cried, "Stand;" so he stood and said
to her, "Who art thou and what is thy need?" She raised a corner of the veil, and behold she was a damsel as she were the full
moon rising or the leven glancing, with two side-locks of hair
which fell down to her anklets. She kissed his hand and said to
him, "O my lord, know that I have been in these quarters some
five months, during which I have withheld myself from sale till
thou shouldst be present and see me; and yonder slave-dealer
also made thy coming a pretext for not vending me, and forbade
me for all I sought of him night and day that he should cause thee
come hither and vouchsafe me thy company and gar me and thee
forgather." Quoth Ishak, "Tell me what thou wouldst have;"
and quoth she, "I beseech thee, by Allah Almighty, that thou
buy me, so I may be with thee by way of service." He asked,
"Is that thy desire?" and she answered, "Yes." So Ishak returned to the slave-dealer and said to him, "Ho thou, Shaykh
Sa'íd!" Said the old man, "At thy service, O my lord," and
Ishak continued, "In the corridor is a chamber and therein wones
a damsel pale and wan. What is her price in dirhams and how
much dost thou ask for her?" Quoth the slave-dealer, "She whom
thou mentionest, O my lord, is called Tohfat al-Humaká?"[2]
Ishak asked, "What is the meaning of Al-Humaka?" and the old
man answered, "Her price hath been weighed and paid an hundred times and she still saith, Show me him who would buy me;
and when I show her to him she saith, This one I mislike; he

---

[1] "A passage has apparently dropped out here. The Khalif seems to have gone away
without buying, leaving Ishak behind, whereupon the latter was accosted by another
slave-girl, who came out of a cell in the corridor." So says Mr. Payne. vol. ii. 207. The
"raiser of the veil" means a fitting purchaser.

[2] i.e. "Choice gift of the Fools," a skit upon the girl's name "Tohfat al-Kulúb" = Choice
gift of the Hearts. Her folly consisted in refusing to be sold at a high price, and this is often
seen in real life. It is a *Pundonor* amongst good Moslems not to buy a girl and not to sleep
with her, even when bought, against her will.

hath in him such and such a default. And in every one who would fain buy her she noteth some defect or other, so that none careth now to purchase her and none seeketh her, for fear lest she find some fault in him." Quoth Ishak, "She seeketh at this present to sell herself; so go thou to her and inquire of her and see her price and send her to the palace." Quoth Sa'íd, "O my lord, her price is an hundred dinars, though, were she free of this paleness that is upon her face, she would be worth a thousand gold pieces; but wanton folly and wanness have diminished her value; and behold I will go to her and consult her of this." So he betook himself to her and enquired of her, "Wilt thou be sold to Ishak bin Ibrahim al-Mausili?" She replied, "Yes," and he said, "Leave folly, for to whom doth it happen to be in the house of Ishak the cup-companion?"[1] Thereupon Ishak went forth the slave-dealer's quarters and overtook Al-Rashid who had preceded him; and they ceased not walking till they came to their landing-place, where they embarked in the boat and fared on to Thaghr al-Khánakah.[2] As for the slave-dealer, he sent the damsel to the house of Ishak al-Nadim, whose slave-girls took her and carried her to the Hammam. Then each damsel gave her somewhat of her gear and they decked her with earrings and bracelets, so that she redoubled in beauty and became as she were the moon on the night of its full. When Ishak returned home from the Caliph's palace, Tohfah rose to him and kissed his hand; and he saw that which the hand-maids had done with her and thanked them for so doing and said to them, "Let her home in the house of instruction and bring her instruments of music, and if she be apt at song teach her; and may Allah Almighty vouchsafe her health and weal!" So there passed over her three months, while she homed with him in the house of instruction, and they brought her the instruments of music. Furthermore, as time went on she was vouchsafed health and soundness and her beauty waxed many times brighter than before and her pallor was changed to white and red, so that she became a seduction to all who saw her. One day, Ishak bade summon all who were with him of slave-girls from the house of instruction and carried them up to Al-Rashid's palace, leaving none in his house save Tohfah and a cookmaid; for that he thought not of Tohfah, nor did she come to his

---

[1] "Every one cannot go to Corinth." The question makes the assertion emphatic.
[2] *i.e.* The Narrows of the (Dervishes') convent.

memory, and none of the damsels reminded him of her. When she saw that the house was empty of the slave-girls, she took the lute (now she was singular in her time for smiting upon the lute, nor had she her like in the world, no, not Ishak himself, nor any other) and sang thereto these couplets: —

"When soul desireth one that is its mate * It never winneth dear desire of Fate:
My life for him whose tortures tare my frame, * And dealt me pine he can alone abate!
He saith (that only *he* to heal mine ill, * Whose sight is medicine to my doleful state),
'O scoffer-wight, how long wilt mock my woe * As though did Allah nothing else create?' "

Now Ishak had returned to his house on an occasion that called for him; and when he entered the vestibule, he heard a sound of singing, the like whereof he had never heard in the world, for that it was soft as the breeze and more strengthening than oil[1] of almonds. So the pleasure of it gat hold of him and delight so seized him, that he fell down fainting in the vestibule. Tohfah heard the noise of footfalls and laying the lute from her hand, went out to see what was the matter. She found her lord Ishak lying aswoon in the entrance; so she took him up and strained him to her bosom, saying, "I conjure thee in Allah's name, O my lord, tell me, hath aught of ill befallen thee?" When he heard her voice, he recovered from his fainting and asked her, "Who art thou?" She answered, "I am thy slave-girl, Tohfah;" and he said to her, "Art thou indeed Tohfah?" "Yes," replied she; and he, "By Allah, I had indeed forgotten thee and remembered thee not till this moment!" Then he looked at her and said, "Verily, thy case is altered to other case and thy wanness is changed to rosiness and thou hast redoubled in beauty and loveliness. But was it thou who was singing just now?" She was troubled and affrighted and answered, "Even I, O my lord;" whereupon Ishak seized upon her hand and carrying her into the house, said to her, "Take the lute and sing; for never saw I nor heard thy like in smiting upon the lute; no, not even myself!"

---

[1] Arab. "Akwà min dahni 'l-lauz." These unguents have been used in the East from time immemorial whilst the last generation in England knew nothing of anointing with oil for incipient consumption. A late friend of mine, Dr. Stocks of the Bombay Establishment, and I proposed it as long back as 1845; but in those days it was a far cry from Sind to London.

Quoth she, "O my lord, thou mockest me. Who am I that thou shouldst say all this to me? Indeed, this is but of thy kindness." Quoth he, "Nay, by Allah, I said but the truth to thee and I am not of those on whom pretence imposeth. For these three months nature hath not moved thee to take the lute and sing thereto, and this is naught save a rare thing and a strange. But all this cometh of strength in the art and thy self-restraint." Then he bade her sing; and she said, "Hearkening and obedience." So she took the lute and tightening its strings to the sticking-point, smote thereon a number of airs, so that she confounded Ishak's wit and for delight he was like to fly. Then she returned to the first mode and sang thereto these couplets: —

"By your ruined stead aye I stand and stay, * Nor shall change or dwelling
    depart us tway!
No distance of homestead shall gar me forget * Your love, O friends, but I
    yearn alway:
Ne'er flies your phantom the babes of these eyne * You are moons in Night-
    tide's murkest array:
And with growing passion mine unrest grows * And each morn I find union
    dissolved in woes."

When she had made an end of her song and laid down the lute, Ishak looked fixedly on her, then took her hand and offered to kiss it; but she snatched it from him and said to him, "Allah, O my lord, do not that!"[1] Cried he, "Be silent. By Allah, I had said that there was not in the world the like of me; but now I have found my dinár in the art but a dánik,[2] for thou art more excellent of skill than I, beyond comparison or approximation or calculation! This very day will I carry[3] thee up to the Commander of the Faithful, Harun al-Rashid, and when his glance lighteth on thee, thou wilt become a Princess of woman-kind. So Allah, Allah upon thee, O my lady, whenas thou becomest of the household of the Prince of True Believers, do not thou forget me!" She replied, "Allah, O my lord, thou art the root of my fortunes and in thee is my heart fortified." Thereat he took her hand and made a covenant with her of this and she

---

[1] The sequel will explain why she acted in this way.

[2] i.e. Thou hast made my gold piece (10 shill.) worth only a doit by thy superiority in the art and mystery of music.

[3] Arab. "Úaddíki," Taadíyah (iid. of Adá, he assisted) means sending, forwarding. In Egypt and Syria we often find the form "Waddi" for Addi, imperative.

swore to him that she would not forget him   Then said he to her,
"By Allah, thou art the desire of the Commander of the Faithful!
Now take the lute and sing a song which thou shalt sing to the
Caliph, when thou goest in to him " So she took the lute and
tuning it, improvised these couplets:—

"His lover hath ruth on his woeful mood * And o'erwept him as still by his
couch he[1] stood:

And garred him drink of his lip-dews and wine[2] * Ere he died and this food
was his latest good."

Ishak stared at her and seizing her hand, said to her, "Know
that I am bound by an oath that, when the singing of a damsel
pleaseth me, she shall not end her song but before the Prince of
True Believers. But now tell me, how came it that thou tarriedst
with the slave-dealer five months and wast not sold to any one,
and thou of this skill, especially when the price set on thee was no
great matter?" Hereat she laughed and answered, "O my lord,
my story is a wondrous and my case a marvellous Know that I
belonged aforetime to a Maghribi merchant, who bought me when
I was three years old, and there were in his house many slave-
girls and eunuchs; but I was the dearest to him of them all So
he kept me with him and used not to address me otherwise than,
'O daughterling,' and indeed to this moment I am a clean maid.
Now there was with him a damsel, a lutanist, and she reared me
and taught me the art, even as thou seest. Then was my master
removed to the mercy of Allah Almighty[3] and his sons divided
his monies. I fell to the lot of one of them; but 'twas only a little
while ere he had wasted all his wealth and there was left him
naught of coin. So I gave up the lute, fearing lest I should fall
into the hand of a man who knew not my worth, for well I wot
that needs must my master sell me; and indeed but a few days
passed ere he carried me forth to the quarters of the slave-
merchant who buyeth damsels and displayeth them to the
Commander of the Faithful. Now I desired to learn the art and
mystery; so I refused to be sold to other than thou, until Allah
(extolled and exalted be He!) vouchsafed me my desire of thy
presence; whereupon I came out to thee, as soon as I heard of
thy coming, and besought thee to buy me. Thou heartenedst my

---

[1] Again "he" for "she".

[2] *i.e.* Honey and wine.

[3] *i.e.* he died.

heart and boughtest me; and since I entered thy house, O my
lord, I have not taken up the lute till now; but to-day, when I
was left private by the slave-girls, I took it; and my purpose in
this was that I might see if my hand were changed[1] or not. As
I was singing, I heard a footfall in the vestibule; so springing up,
I laid the lute from my hand and going forth to see what was to
do, found thee, O my lord, after this fashion." Quoth Ishak,
"Indeed, this was of thy fair fortune. By Allah, I know not
that which thou knowest in this art!" Then he arose and opening a chest, brought out therefrom striped clothes,[2] netted with
jewels and great pearls and other costly gems and said to her,
"In the name of Allah, don these, O my lady Tohfah." So she
arose and donned that dress and veiled herself and went up with
Ishak to the palace of the Caliphate, where he made her stand
without, whilst he himself went in to the Prince of True Believers (with whom was Ja'afar the Barmaki) and kissing the
ground before him, said to him, "O Commander of the Faithful,
I have brought thee a damsel, never saw eyes of seer her like for
excellence in singing and touching the lute; and her name is
Tohfah." Al-Rashid asked, "And where be this Tohfah[3] who
hath not her like in the world?" Answered Ishak, "Yonder she
standeth, O Commander of the Faithful;" and he acquainted the
Caliph with her case from first to last. Then said Al-Rashid,
" 'Tis a marvel to hear thee praise a slave-girl after this fashion.
Admit her that we may look upon her, for verily the morning
may not be hidden." Accordingly, Ishak bade admit her; so
she entered, and when her eyes fell upon the Prince of True
Believers, she kissed ground before him and said, "The Peace be
upon thee, O Commander of the faithful Fold and Asylum of all
who the true Creed hold and Quickener of justice in the Worlds
threefold! Allah make thy feet tread on safest wise and give
thee joy of what He gave thee in generous guise and make thy
harbourage Paradise and Hell-fire that of thine enemies!" Quoth
Al-Rashid, "And on thee be the Peace, O damsel! Sit." So she
sat down and he bade her sing; whereupon she took the lute and
tightening its strings, played thereon in many modes, so that the

---

[1] *i.e.* if my hand had lost its cunning.
[2] Arab. "Thiyáb 'Amúdiyah": 'Amúd=tent-prop or column, and Khatt 'Amúd = a
perpendicular line.
[3] *i.e.* a choice gift. The Caliph speaks half ironically. "Where's this wonderful present,
etc?" So further on when he compares her with the morning.

Prince of True Believers and Ja'afar were confounded in sprite
and like to fly for delight.   Then she returned to the first mode
and improvised these couplets: —

"O mine eyes! I swear by him I adore, * Whom pilgrims seek thronging
    Arafát;
An thou call my name on the grave of me, * I'll reply to thy call tho' my bones
    go rot:
I crave none for friend of my heart save thee; * So believe me, for true are the
    well-begot."

Al-Rashid considered her comeliness and the goodliness of her
singing and her eloquence and what other qualities she comprised and rejoiced with joy exceeding; and for the stress of that
which overcame him of delight, he descended from the couch and
sitting down with her upon the floor, said to her, "Thou hast
done well, O Tohfah. By Allah, thou art indeed a choice gift!"[1]
Then he turned to Ishak and said to him, "Thou dealtest not
justly, O Ishak, in the description of this damsel, nor didst thou
fairly set forth all that she comprised of charms and art; for that,
by Allah, she is inconceivably more skilful than thou; and I know
of this craft that which none knowest save I!" Exclaimed the
Wazir Ja'afar, "By Allah, thou sayst sooth, O my lord, O Commander of the Faithful.   Indeed, she hath done away my wit,
hath this damsel."   Quoth Ishak, "By Allah, O Prince of True
Believers, I had said that there was not on the face of the earth
one who knew the art of the lute like myself; but when I heard
her, my skill became nothing worth in mine eyes."   Then said the
Caliph to her, "Repeat thy playing, O Tohfah." So she repeated
it and he cried to her, "Well done!" Moreover, he said to Ishak,
"Thou hast indeed brought me a marvellous thing, one which is
worth in mine eyes the empire of the world."   Then he turned to
Masrur the eunuch and said to him, "Carry Tohfah to the chamber of honour."   Accordingly, she went away with the Castrato
and the Caliph looked at her raiment and ornaments and seeing
her clad in clothing of choice, asked Ishak, "O Ishak, whence
hath she these robes?"   Answered he, "O my lord, these are
somewhat of thy bounties and thy largesse, and they are a gift to
her from me.   By Allah, O Commander of the Faithful, the
world, all of it, were little in comparison with her!"   Then the
Caliph turned to the Wazir Ja'afar and said to him, "Give Ishak

---

[1] Again the usual pun upon the name.

fifty thousand dirhams and a robe of honour of the choicest apparel." "Hearing and obeying," replied Ja'afar and gifted him with that which the Caliph ordered him. As for Al-Rashid, he was private with Tohfah that night and found her a pure virgin and rejoiced in her; and she took high rank in his heart, so that he could not suffer her absence a single hour and committed to her the keys of the affairs of the realm, for that which he saw in her of good breeding and fine wit and leal will. He also gave her fifty slave-girls and two hundred thousand dinars and a quantity of raiment and ornaments, gems and jewels worth the kingdom of Egypt; and of the excess of his love for her, he would not entrust her to any of the hand-maids or eunuchs; but, whenever he went out from her, he locked the door upon her and took the key with him, against he should return to her, forbidding the damsels to go in to her, of his fear lest they should slay her or poison her or practise on her with the knife; and in this way he abode awhile. One day, as she sang before the Commander of the Faithful, he was delighted with exceeding delight, so that he offered to kiss her hand;[1] but she drew it away from him and smote upon her lute and broke it and wept. Al-Rashid wiped away her tears and said, "O desire of the heart, what is it maketh thee weep? May Allah not cause an eye of thine to shed tears!" Said she, "O my lord, what am I that thou shouldst kiss my hand? Wilt thou have Allah punish me for this and my term come to an end and my felicity pass away? For this is what none ever attained unto." He rejoined, "Well said, O Tohfah. Know that thy rank in my esteem is high and for that which delighted me of what I saw in thee, I offered to do this, but I will not return unto the like thereof; so be of good cheer, with eyes cool and clear, for I have no desire to other than thyself and will not die but in the love of thee, and thou to me art queen this day, to the exclusion of all humankind." Therewith she fell to kissing his feet; and this her fashion pleased him, so that his love for her redoubled and he became unable to brook severance from her a single hour. Now Al-Rashid one day went forth to the chase and left Tohfah in her pavilion. As she sat perusing a book, with a candle-branch of gold before her, wherein was a perfumed candle, behold, a musk-apple fell down before her from the top

---

[1] Throughout the East this is the action of a servant or a slave, practised by freemen only when in danger of life or extreme need and therefore humiliating.

of the saloon.[1] So she looked up and beheld the Lady Zubaydah bint al-Kasim,[2] who saluted her with a salam and acquainted her with herself, whereupon Tohfah sprang to her feet and said, "O my lady, were I not of the number of the new,[3] I had daily sought thy service; so do not thou bereave me of those noble steps."[4] The Lady Zubaydah called down blessings upon her and replied, "I knew this of thee; and, by the life of the Commander of the Faithful, but that it is not of my wont to go forth of my place, I had come out to do my service to thee." Then quoth she to her, "Know, O Tohfah, that the Commander of the Faithful hath deserted all his concubines and favourites on thine account, even myself hath he abandoned on this wise, and I am not content to be as one of the mistresses; yet hath he made me of them and forsaken me, and I have sought thee, so thou mayst beseech him to come to me, though it be but once a month, in order that I may not be the like of the hand-maids and concubines nor take rank with the slave-girls; and this is my need of thee." Answered Tohfah, "Hearkening and obedience! By Allah, O my lady, I would that he might be with thee a whole month and with me but one night, so thy heart might be heartened, for that I am one of thy hand-maids and thou in every case art my lady." The Princess Zubaydah thanked her for this and taking leave of her, returned to her palace. When the Caliph came back from the chase and course, he betook himself to Tohfah's pavilion and bringing out the key, opened the lock and went in to her. She rose to receive him and kissed his hand, and he gathered her to his breast and seated her on his knee.[5] Then food was brought to them and they ate and washed their hands; after which she took the lute and sang, till Al-Rashid was moved to sleep. When aware of this, she ceased singing and told him her adventure with the Lady Zubaydah, saying, "O Prince of True Believers, I would have thee favour me with a favour and hearten my heart and accept my intercession and reject not my supplication, but fare thee forthright to the Lady Zubaydah." Now this talk

---

[1] It had been thrown down from the Mamrak or small dome built over such pavilions for the purpose of light by day and ventilation by night. See vol. i. 257, where it is called by the Persian term "Badhánj."

[2] The Nights have more than once applied this patronymic to Zubaydah. See vol. viii. 56, 158.

[3] Arab. "Mutahaddisín" = novi homines, upstarts.

[4] *i.e.* thine auspicious visits.

[5] He being seated on the carpet at the time.

befel after he had stripped himself naked and she also had doffed her dress; and he said, "Thou shouldst have named this ere we stripped ourselves naked, I and thou!" But she answered, saying, "O Commander of the Faithful, I did this not except in accordance with the saying of the poet in these couplets,

"Of all intercessions can none succeed, * Save whatso Tohfah bint Marján
    sue'd:
No intercessor who comes enveiled;[1] * She sues the best who sues mother-
    nude."

When Al-Rashid heard this, her speech pleased him and he strained her to his bosom. Then he went forth from her and locked the door upon her, as before; whereupon she took the book and sat perusing it awhile. Presently, she set it aside and taking the lute, tightened its strings; and smote thereon, after a wondrous fashion, such as would have moved inanimate things to dance, and fell to singing marvellous melodies and chanting these couplets: —

"Cease for change to wail, * The world blames who rail;
Bear patient its shafts * That for aye prevail.
How often a joy * Grief-garbed thou shalt hail:
How oft gladding bliss * Shall appear amid bale!"

Then she turned and saw within the chamber an old man, handsome in his hoariness and stately of semblance, who was dancing in goodly and winning wise, a dance whose like none might dance. So she sought refuge with Allah Almighty from Satan the Stoned and said, "I will not give over what I am about, for whatso the Lord willeth, He fulfilleth." Accordingly, she went on singing till the Shaykh came up to her and kissed ground before her, saying, "Well done, O Highmost of the East and the West! May the world be not bereaved of thee! By Allah, indeed thou art perfect of manners and morals, O Tohfat al-Sudúr![2] Dost thou know me?" Cried she, "Nay, by Allah, but methinks thou art of the Jann." Quoth he, "Thou sayst sooth; I am Abú al-Tawáif[3] Iblis, and I come to thee every night, and with me

---

[1] A quotation from Al-Farazdat who had quarrelled with his wife Al-Howái (see the tale in Ibn Khallikan, i. 521), hence "the naked intercessor" became proverbial for one who cannot be withstood.

[2] i.e. Choice Gift of the Breasts, that is of hearts, the continens for the contentum.

[3] Pron. "Abuttawáif," the Father of the (Jinn-)tribes. It is one of the Moslem Satan's manifold names, alluding to the number of his servants and worshippers, so far agreeing with that amiable Christian doctrine, "Few shall be saved."

thy sister Kamariyah, for that she loveth thee and sweareth not
but by thy life; and her pastime is not pleasant to her, except
she come to thee and see thee whilst thou seest her not. As for
me, I approach thee upon an affair, whereby thou shalt gain and
rise to high rank with the kings of the Jann and rule them, even
as thou rulest mankind; and to that end I would have thee come
with me and be present at the festival of my daughter's wedding
and the circumcision of my son;[1] for that the Jann are agreed
upon the manifestation of thy command. And she answered,
"Bismillah; in the name of the Lord."[2] So she gave him the
lute and he forewent her, till he came to the Chapel of Ease,[3]
and behold, therein was a door and a stairway. When Tohfah
saw this, her reason fled; but Iblis cheered her with chat. Then
he descended the steps and she followed him to the bottom of the
stair, where she found a passage and they fared on therein, till
they came to a horse standing, ready saddled and bridled and
accoutred. Quoth Iblis, "Bismillah, O my lady Tohfah;" and he
held the stirrup for her. So she mounted and the horse heaved
like a wave under her and putting forth wings soared upwards
with her, while the Shaykh flew by her side; whereat she was
affrighted and clung to the pommel of the saddle;[4] nor was it but
an hour ere they came to a fair green meadow, fresh-flowered as
if the soil thereof were a fine robe, purfled with all manner
bright hues. Amiddlemost that mead was a palace towering
high in air, with crenelles of red gold, set with pearls and gems,
and a two-leaved door; and about the gateway were much
people of the chiefs of the Jann, clad in costliest clothing. When
they saw the Shaykh, they all cried out, saying, "The Lady Tohfah is come!" And as soon as she reached the palace-gate they
pressed forward in a body, and dismounting her from the horse's
back, carried her into the palace and fell to kissing her hands.
When she entered, she beheld a palace whereof seers ne'er saw

---

[1] Mr. Payne supplies this last clause from the sequence.

[2] *i.e.* "Let us go," with a euphemistic formula to defend her from evil influences. Iblis
uses the same word to prevent her being frightened.

[3] Arab. "Al-Mustaráh," a favourite haunting-place of the Jinn, like the Hammám and
other offices for human impurity. For its six names Al-Khalá, Al-Hushsh, Al-Mutawazzá,
Al-Kaníf, Al-Mustaráh, and Mirház, see Al-Mas'udi, chap. cxxvii., and Shiríshi's com-
mentary to Hariri's 47, Assembly.

[4] Which, in the East, is high and prominent whilst the cantle forms a back to the seat
and the rider sits as in a baby's chair. The object is a firm seat when fighting: "across
country" it is exceedingly dangerous.

the like; for therein were four halls, one facing other, and its walls were of gold and its ceilings of silver. It was high-builded of base, wide of space, and those who descried it would be posed to describe it. At the upper end of the hall stood a throne of red gold set with pearls and jewels, up to which led five steps of silver, and on its right and on its left were many chairs of gold and silver. Quoth Tohfah, "The Shaykh led me to the estrade and seated me on a chair of gold beside the throne, and over the dais was a curtain let down, gold and silver wrought and broidered with pearls and jewels." And she was amazed at that which she beheld in that place and magnified her Lord (extolled and exalted be He!) and hallowed Him. Then the kings of the Jann came up to that throne and seated themselves thereon; and they were in the semblance of Adam's sons, excepting two of them, who appeared in the form and aspect of the Jann, each with one eye slit endlong and jutting horns and projecting tusks.[1] After this there came up a young lady, fair of favour and seemly of stature, the light of whose face outshone that of the waxen flambeaux; and about her were other three women, than whom none fairer abode on face of earth. They saluted Tohfah with the salam and she rose to them and kissed ground before them; whereupon they embraced her after returning her greeting[2] and sat down on the chairs aforesaid. Now the four women who thus accosted Tohfah were the Princess Kamariyah, daughter of King Al-Shísbán, and her sisters; and Kamariyah loved Tohfah with exceeding love. So, when she came up to her, she fell to kissing and embracing her, and Shaykh Iblis cried, "Fair befal the accolade! Take me between you." At this Tohfah laughed and Kamariyah said, "O my sister, I love thee, and doubtless hearts have their witnesses,[3] for, since I saw thee, I have loved thee." Replied Tohfah, "By Allah, hearts have sea-like deeps, and thou, by Allah, art dear to me and I am thy hand-maid." Kamariyah thanked her for this and kissing her once more said, "These be the wives of the kings of the Jann: greet them with the salam!

---

[1] In Swedenborg's "Arcana Cœlestia" we read, "When man's inner sight is opened, which is that of his spirit; then there appear the things of another life which cannot be made visible to the bodily sight." Also "Evil spirits, when seen by eyes other than those of their infernal associates, present themselves by *correspondence* in the beast (*fera*) which represents their particular lust and life, in aspect direful and atrocious." These are the Jinns of Northern Europe.

[2] This exchange of salams was a sign of her being in safety.

[3] Arab. "Shawáhid," meaning that heart testifies to heart.

This is Queen Jamrah,[1] that is Queen Wakhímah and this other is Queen Sharárah, and they come not but for thee." So Tohfah rose to her feet and bussed their hands, and the three queens kissed her and welcomed her and honoured her with the utmost honour. Then they brought trays and tables and amongst the rest a platter of red gold, inlaid with pearls and gems; its raised rims were of or and emerald, and thereon were graven[2] these couplets:—

To bear provaunt assigned, * By hands noble designed,
For the gen'rous I'm made * Not for niggardly hind!
So eat safe all I hold * And praise God of mankind.

After reading the verses they ate and Tohfah looked at the two kings who had not changed shape and said to Kamariyah, "O my lady, what be this feral and that other like unto him? By Allah, mine eye may not suffer the sight of them." Kamariyah laughed and answered, "O my sister, that is my sire Al-Shisban and the other is hight Maymún the Sworder; and of the arrogance of their souls and their insolence, they consented not to change their created shapes. Indeed, all whom thou seest here are nature-fashioned like them; but on thine account they have changed favour, for fear lest thou be disquieted and for the comforting of thy mind, so thou mightest become familiar with them and be at thine ease." Quoth Tohfah, "O my lady, verily I cannot look at them. How frightful is this Maymun, with his monocular face! Mine eye cannot brook the sight of him, and indeed I am in affright of him." Kamariyah laughed at her speech, and Tohfah continued, "By Allah, O my lady, I cannot fill my eye with the twain!"[3] Then cried her father Al-Shisban to her, "What be this laughing?" So she bespoke him in a tongue none understood but they two and acquainted him with that which Tohfah had said; whereat he laughed a prodigious loud laugh, as it were the roaring thunder. Presently they ate and the tables were removed and they washed their hands; after which Iblis the Accursed

---

[1] *i.e.* A live coal, afterwards called Zalzalah, an earthquake; see post p. 76. "Wakhímah"=an unhealthy land, and "Sharárah"=a spark.

[2] I need hardly note the inscriptions upon the metal trays sold to Europeans. They are usually imitation words so that infidel eyes may not look upon the formulæ of prayer; and the same is the case with table-cloths, etc., showing a fancy Tohgra or Sultanic sign-manual.

[3] *i.e.* I cannot look at them long.

came up to Tohfah and said to her, "O my lady, thou gladdenest
the place and enlightenest and embellishest it with thy presence;
but now fain would these kings hear somewhat of thy singing,
for Night hath dispread her pinions for departure and there
abideth of it but a little." Quoth she, "Hearing and obeying."
So she took the lute and touching its strings with rare touch,
played thereon after wondrous wise, so that it seemed to those
who were present as if the palace surged like a wave with them
for the music. Then she began singing and chanting these
couplets,

"Folk of my faith and oath, Peace with you be! * Quoth ye not I shall meet you,
    you meet me?
I'll chide you softerwise than breeze o' morn, * Sweeter than spring of coolest
    clarity.
I' faith mine eyelids are with tears chafed sore; * My vitals plain to you some
    cure to see.
My friends! Our union to disunion changed * Was aye my fear for 'twas my
    certainty.
I'll plain to Allah of all ills I bore; * For pine and yearning misery still I dree."

The kings of the Jann were moved to delight by that sweet
singing and seemly speech and thanked Tohfah therefore; and
Queen Kamariyah rose to her and threw her arms round her neck
and kissed her between the eyes, saying, "By Allah, 'tis good, O
my sister and coolth of mine eyes and core of my heart!" Then
said she, "I conjure thee by Allah, give us more of this lovely
singing;" and Tohfah answered with "To hear is to obey." So
she took the lute and playing thereon in a mode different from the
former fashion, sang these couplets:—

"I, oft as ever grows the pine of me, * Console my soul with hope thy sight to
    see.
Haply shall Allah join our parted lives, * E'en as my fortunes far from thee
    cast He!
Then oh! who thrallest me by force of love— * Seizèd by fond affection's
    mastery,
All hardships easy wax when thou art nigh; * And all the far draws near
    when near thou be.
Ah! be the Ruthful light to lover fond, * Love-lorn, frame-wasted, ready
    Death to dree!
Were hope of seeing thee cut off, my loved; * After thine absence sleep mine
    eyes would flee!
I mourn no worldly joyance, my delight * Is but to sight thee while thou seest
    my sight."

At this the accursed Iblis was hugely pleased and thrust his
finger up his fundament,[1] whilst Maymun danced and said, "O
Tohfat al-Sudur, soften the sound;[2] for, as pleasure entereth into
my heart, it arresteth my breath and blood." So she took the
lute and altering the tune, played a third air; then she returned
to the first and sang these couplets:—

"The waves of your[3] love o'er my life have rolled; * I sink while I see you
    all aid withhold:
You have drowned my vitals in deeps of your love, * Nor can heart and sprite
    for your loss be consoled:
Deem not I forget my troth after you: * How forget what Allah decreed of old?[4]
Love clings to the lover who nights in grief, * And 'plains of unrest and of
    woes ensouled."

The kings and all those who were present rejoiced in this with
joy exceeding and the accursed Iblis came up to Tohfah and
kissing her hand, said to her, "Verily there abideth but little of the
night; so tarry with us till the morrow, when we will apply ourselves to the wedding[5] and the circumcision."[6] Then all the Jann

---

[1] Evidently a diabolical way of clapping his hands in applause. This description of the
Foul Fiend has an element of grotesqueness which is rather Christian than Moslem.

[2] Arab. "Rikkí al-Saut," which may also mean either "lower thy voice," or "change the
air to one less touching."

[3] "Your" for "thy."

[4] i.e. written on the "Guarded Tablet" from all eternity.

[5] Arab. "Al-'Urs wa'al-Tuhúr" which can only mean, "the wedding (which does not
drop out of the tale) and the circumcision."

[6] I here propose to consider at some length this curious custom which has prevailed
amongst so many widely separated races. Its object has been noted (vol. v. 209), viz. to
diminish the sensibility of the glans, no longer lubricated with prostatic lymph; thus the
part is hardened against injury and disease and its work in coition is prolonged. On the
other hand, "præputium in coitu voluptatem (of the woman) auget, unde femina præputiatis
concubitum malunt quam cum Turcis ac Judæis" says Dimerbroeck (Anatomie). I
vehemently doubt the fact. Circumcision was doubtless practised from ages immemorial
by the peoples of Central Africa, and Welcker found traces of it in a mummy of the xvith
century B.C. The Jews borrowed it from the Egyptian priesthood and made it a manner
of sacrament, "uncircumcised" being="unbaptised," that is, barbarian, heretic; it was a
seal of reconciliation, a sign of alliance between the Creator and the Chosen People, a token
of nationality imposed upon the body politic. Thus it became a cruel and odious pro-
testation against the brotherhood of man, and the cosmopolitan Romans derided the
verpæ ac verpi. The Jews also used the term figuratively as the "circumcision of fruits"
(Lev. xix. 23), and of the heart (Deut. x. 16); and the old law gives copious historical
details of its origin and continuance. Abraham first amputated his horny "calotte" at æt.
99, and did the same for his son and household (Gen. xvii. 24–27). The rite caused a separation between Moses and his wife (Exod. iv. 25). It was suspended during the Desert
Wanderings and was resumed by Joshua (v. 3–7), who cut off two tons' weight of prepuces.
The latter became, like the scalps of the Scythians and the North-American "Indians"

went away, whereupon Tohfah rose to her feet and Iblis said, "Go ye up with Tohfah to the garden for the rest of the night."

trophies of victory; Saul promised his daughter Michol to David for a dowry of one hundred, and the son-in-law brought double tale.

Amongst the early Christians opinions concerning the rite differed. Although the Founder of Christianity was circumcised, St. Paul, who aimed at a cosmopolitan faith, discouraged it in the physical phase. St. Augustine still sustained that the rite removed original sin despite the Fathers who preceded and followed him, Justus, Tertullian, Ambrose and others. But it gradually lapsed into desuetude and was preserved only in the outlying regions. Paulus Jovius and Munster found it practised in Abyssinia, but as a mark of nobility confined to the descendants of "Nicaules, queen of Sheba." The Abyssinians still follow the Jews in performing the rite within eight days after the birth and baptise boys after forty and girls after eighty days. When a circumcised man became a Jew he was bled before three witnesses at the place where the prepuce had been cut off, and this was called the "Blood of alliance." Apostate Jews effaced the sing of circumcision: so in 1 Matt. i. 16, fecerunt sibi præputia et recesserunt a Testamento Sancto. Thus making prepuces was called by the Hebrews Meshookim = recutitis, and there is an allusion to it in 1 Cor. vii. 18, 19,μὴ ἐπισπάσθαι(Farrar, Paul ii. 70). St. Jerome and others deny the possibility; but Mirabeau (Akropodie) relates how Father Conning by liniments of oil, suspending weights, and wearing the virga in a box gained in 43days 7¼ lines. The process is still practised by Armenians and other Christians who, compelled to Islamise, wish to return to Christianity. I cannot however find a similar artifice applied to a circumcised clitoris. The simplest form of circumcision is mere amputation of the prepuce and I have noted (vol. v. 209) the difference between the Moslem and the Jewish rite, the latter according to some being supposed to heal in kindlier way. But the varieties of circumcision are immense. Probably none is more terrible than that practised in the Province Al-Asír, the old Ophir, lying south of Al-Hijáz, where it is called Salkh, lit. = scarification. The patient, usually from ten to twelve years old, is placed upon raised ground holding in right hand a spear, whose heel rests upon his foot and whose point shows every tremour of the nerves. The tribe stands about him to pass judgment on his fortitude, and the barber performs the operation with the Jumbiyah-dagger, sharp as a razor. First he makes a shallow cut, severing only the skin across the belly immediately below the navel, and similar incisions down each groin; then he tears off the epidermis from the cuts downwards and flays the testicles and the penis, ending with amputation of the foreskin. Meanwhile the spear must not tremble and in some clans the lad holds a dagger over the back of the stooping barber, crying, "Cut and fear not!" When the ordeal is over, he exclaims, "Allaho Akbar!" and attempts to walk towards the tents soon falling for pain and nervous exhaustion, but the more steps he takes the more applause he gains. He is dieted with camel's milk, the wound is treated with salt and turmeric, and the chances in his favour are about ten to one. No body-pile or pecten ever grows upon the excoriated part which preserves through life a livid ashen hue. Whilst Mohammed Ali Pasha occupied the province he forbade "scarification" under pain of impalement, but it was resumed the moment he left Al-Asir. In Africa not only is circumcision indigenous, the operation varies more or less in the different tribes. In Dahome it is termed Addagwibi, and is performed between the twelfth and twentieth year. The rough operation is made peculiar by a double cut above and below; the prepuce being treated in the Moslem, not the Jewish fashion (loc. cit.). Heated sand is applied as a styptic and the patient is dieted with ginger-soup and warm drinks of ginger-water, pork being especially forbidden. The Fantis of the Gold Coast circumcise in sacred places, e.g., at Accra on a Fetish rock rising from the sea. The peoples of Sennaar, Taka, Masawwah and the adjacent regions follow the Abyssinian custom. The barbarous Bissagos and Fellups of North Western Guinea make cuts on the prepuce without amputating it; while the Baquens and Papels circumcise like Moslems. The blacks of Loango are all "verpæ," otherwise they would be rejected by the

So Kamariyah took her and went with her into the garden, which
contained all manner birds, nightingale and mocking-bird and

---

women. The Bantu or Caffre tribes are circumcised between the ages of fifteen and eigh-
teen; the "Fetish boys," as we call them, are chalked white and wear only grass belts;
they live outside the villages in special houses under an old "medicine-man," who teaches
them not only virile arts but also to rob and fight. The "man-making" may last five
months and ends in fêtes and dances: the patients are washed in the river, they burn down
their quarters, take new names, and become adults, donning a kind of straw thimble over
the prepuce. In Madagascar three several cuts are made causing much suffering to the
children; and the nearest male relative swallows the prepuce. The Polynesians circumcise
when childhood ends and thus consecrate the fecundating organ to the Deity. In Tahiti
the operation is performed by the priest, and in Tonga only the priest is exempt. The
Maories on the other hand, fasten the prepuce over the glans, and the women of the Mar-
quesas Islands have shown great cruelty to shipwrecked sailors who expose the glans.
Almost all the known Australian tribes circumcise after some fashion: Bennett supposes
the rite to have been borrowed from the Malays, while Gason enumerates the "Kurra-
wellie wonkauna" among the five mutilations of puberty. Leichhardt found circumcision
about the Gulf of Carpentaria and in the river-valleys of the Robinson and Macarthur:
others observed it on the Southern Coast and among the savages of Perth, where it is
noticed by Salvado. James Dawson tells us "Circumciduntur pueri," etc., in Western
Victoria. Brough Smyth, who supposes the object is to limit population (?), describes on
the Western Coast and in Central Australia the "Corrobery"-dance and the operation performed with a quartz-flake. Teichelmann details the rite in Southern Australia where the
assistants — all men, women, and children being driven away — form a "manner of human
altar" upon which the youth is laid for circumcision. He then receives the normal two
names, public and secret, and is initiated into the mysteries proper for men. The Australians also for Malthusian reasons produce an artificial hypospadias, while the Karens of
New Guinea only split the prepuce longitudinally (Cosmos p. 369, Oct. 1876); the indigens
of Port Lincoln on the West Coast split the virga: — Fenditur usque ad urethram a parte
infera penis between the ages of twelve and fourteen, says E. J. Eyre in 1845. Missionary
Schürmann declares that they open the urethra. Gason describes in the Dieyerie tribe
the operation "Kulpi" which is performed when the beard is long enough for tying. The
member is placed upon a slab of tree-bark, the urethra is incised with a quartz-flake
mounted in a gum handle and a splinter of bark is inserted to keep the cut open. These
men may appear naked before women who expect others to clothe themselves. Miklucho
Maclay calls it "Mika'" in Central Australia: he was told by a squatter that of three hundred men only three or four had the member intact in order to get children, and that in
one tribe the female births greatly outnumbered the male. Those mutilated also marry:
when making water they sit like women slightly raising the penis, this in coition becomes
flat and broad and the semen does not enter the matrix. The explorer believes that the
deed of kind is more quickly done (?). Circumcision was also known to the New World.
Herrera relates that certain Mexicans cut off the ears and prepuce of the newly-born child,
causing many to die. The Jews did not adopt the female circumcision of Egypt described
by Huet on Origen. — "Circumcisio feminarum fit resectione τῆς νυμφῆς (sive clitoridis)
quæ pars in Australium mulieribus ita crescit ut ferro est coërcenda." Here we have the
normal confusion between excision of the nymphæ (usually for fibulation) and circumcision of the clitoris. Bruce notices this clitoridectomy among the Aybssinians. Werne
describes the excision on the Upper White Nile and I have noted the complicated operation
among the Somali tribes. Girls in Dahome are circumcised by ancient *sages femmes*, and a
woman in the natural state would be derided by every one (See my Mission to Dahome,
ii. 159) The Australians cut out the clitoris, and as I have noted elsewhere extirpate the
ovary for Malthusian purposes (Journ. Anthrop. Inst., vol. viii. of 1884).

ringdove and curlew[1] and other than these of all the kinds. Therein were all manner of fruits: its channels[2] were of gold and silver and the water thereof, as it broke forth of its conduits, was like the bellies of fleeing serpents, and indeed it was as it were the Garden of Eden.[3] When Tohfah beheld this, she called to mind her lord and wept sore and said, "I beseech Allah the Most High to vouchsafe me speedy deliverance and return to my palace and to my high estate and queendom and glory, and re-union with my lord and master Al-Rashid." Then she walked about that garden and saw in its midst a dome of white marble, raised on columns of black teak whereto hung curtains purfled with pearls and gems. Amiddlemost this pavilion was a foun-tain, inlaid with all kinds of jacinths, and thereon a golden statue of a man and beside it a little door. She opened the door and found herself in a long corridor: so she followed it and entered a Hammam-bath walled with all kinds of costly marbles and floored with a mosaic of pearls and jewels. Therein were four cisterns of alabaster, one facing other, and the ceiling of the bath was of glass coloured with all varieties of colours, such as confounded the understanding of those who have insight and amazed the wit of every wight. Tohfah entered the bath, after she had doffed her dress, and behold the Hammam-basin was overlaid with gold set with pearls and red balasses and green emeralds and other jewels: so she extolled Allah Almighty and hallowed Him for the magnificence of that which she saw of the appointments of that bath. Then she made her Wuzu-ablution in that basin and pronouncing the Prohibition,[4] prayed the dawn-prayer and what else had escaped her of orisons;[5] after which she went out and walked in that garden among jessamine and lavender and roses and chamomile and gillyflowers and thyme and violets and

---

[1] Arab. "Kayrawán" which is still the common name for curlew; the peewit and plover being called (onomatopoetically) "Bíbat" and in Marocco Yahúdi, certain impious Jews having been turned into the Vanellus Cristatus which still wears the black skullcap of the Hebrews.

[2] Arab. "Sawáki," the leats which irrigate the ground and are opened and closed with the foot.

[3] The eighth (in altitude) of the many-storied Heavens.

[4] Arab. "Ihramat li al-Salát,"*i.e.*, she pronounced the formula of Intention (Niyat) with-out which prayer is not valid, ending with Allaho Akbar — Allah is All-great. Thus she had clothed herself, as it were, in prayer and had retired from the world pro temp.

[5] *i.e.* the prayers of the last day and night which she had neglected while in company with the Jinns. The Hammam is not a pure place to pray in; but the Farz or Koranic orisons should be recited there if the legal term be hard upon its end.

basil royal, till she came to the door of the pavilion aforesaid.
There she sat down, pondering that which would betide Al-
Rashid after her, when he should come to her apartment and
find her not; and she plunged into the sea of her solicitude, till
slumber overtook her and soon she slept. Presently she felt a
breath upon her face; whereupon she awoke and found Queen
Kamariyah kissing her, and with her her three sisters, Queen
Jamrah, Queen Wakhímah and Queen Sharárah. So she arose
and kissed their hands and rejoiced in them with the utmost joy
and they ceased not, she and they, to talk and converse, what
while she related to them her history, from the time of her purchase by the Maghrabi to that of her coming to the quarters of
the slave-dealer, where she besought Ishak al-Nadim to buy her,[1]
and how she won union with Al-Rashid, till the moment when
Iblis came to her and brought her to them. They gave not over
talking till the sun declined and yellowed and the hour of its
setting drew near and the day departed, whereupon Tohfah was
urgent in supplication[2] to Allah Almighty, on the occasion of the
sundown-prayer, that he would reunite her with her lord Al-
Rashid. After this, she abode with the four queens, till they
arose and entered the palace, where she found the waxen tapers
lit and ranged in candlesticks of gold and silver, and censing
vessels of silver and gold filled with lign-aloes and ambergris,
and there were the kings of the Jann sitting. So she saluted them
with the salam, kissing the earth before them and doing them
service; and they rejoiced in her and in her sight. Then she
ascended the estrade and sat down upon her chair, whilst King
Al-Shisban and King Al-Muzfir[3] and Queen Lúlúah and other
kings of the Jann sat on chairs, and they brought choice tables,
spread with all manner meats befitting royalties. They ate their
fill; after which the tables were removed and they washed their
hands and wiped them with napkins. Then they brought the
wine-service and set on tasses and cups and flagons and beakers

---

[1] Slaves, male as well as female, are as fond of talking over their sale as European dames
enjoy looking back upon the details of courtship and marriage.

[2] Arab. "Du'á," = supplication, prayer, as opposed to "Salát" = divine worship,
"prayers." For the technical meaning of the latter see vol. iv. 65. I have objected to
Mr. Redhouse's distinction without a difference between Moslem's worship and prayer:
voluntary prayers are not prohibited to them and their praises of the Lord are mingled, as
amongst all worshippers, with petitions.

[3] Al-Muzfir = the Twister; Zafáir al-Jinn = Adiantum capillus veneris. Lúlúah = The
Pearl, or Wild Heifer: see vol. ix. 218.

of gold and silver and bowls of crystal and gold; and they poured
out the wines and they filled the flagons. Then Iblis took the bowl
and signed to Tohfah to sing: and she said, "To hear is to obey!"
So she hent the lute in hand and tuning it, sang these couplets,

"Drink wine, O ye lovers, I rede you alwày, * And praise his worth who loves
    night and day;
'Mid the myrtle, narcissus and lavender, * And the scented herbs that bedeck
    the tray."

So Iblis the Damned drank and said, "Brava, O desire of hearts!
But thou owest me still another aria." Then he filled the cup
and signed to her to sing. Quoth she, "Hearkening and obedience," and chanted these couplets,

"Ye wot, I am whelmed in despair and despight, * Ye dight me blight that
    delights your sight:
Your wone is between my unrest and my eyes; * Nor tears to melt you, nor
    sighs have might.
How oft shall I sue you for justice, and you * With a pining death my dear
    love requite?
But your harshness is duty, your farness near; * Your hate is Union, your
    wrath is delight:
Take your fill of reproach as you will: you claim * All my heart, and I reck
    not of safety or blame."

All present were delighted and the sitting-chamber was moved
like a wave with mirth, and Iblis said, "Brava, O Tohfat al-
Sudur!" Then they left not liquor-bibbintg and rejoicing and
making merry and tambourining and piping till the night waned
and the dawn waxed near; and indeed exceeding delight entered
into them. The most of them in mirth was the Shaykh Iblis,
and for the stress of that which befel him of joyance, he doffed
all that was on him of coloured clothes and cast them over
Tohfah, and among the rest a robe broidered with jewels and
jacinths, worth ten thousand dinars. Then he kissed the earth
and danced and he thrust his finger up his fundament and hending
his beard in hand, said to her, "Sing about this beard and endeavour after mirth and pleasance, and no blame shall betide
thee for this." So she improvised and sang these couplets:—

"Barbe of the olden, the one-eyed goat! * What words shall thy foulness
    o' deed denote?
Be not of our praises so pompous-proud: * Thy worth for a dock-tail dog's I
    wot.

By Allah, to-morrow shall see me drub * Thy nape with a cow-hide[1] and dust
thy coat!"

All those present laughed at her mockery of Iblis and wondered
at the wittiness of her visnomy[2] and her readiness in versifying,
whilst the Shaykh himself rejoiced and said to her, "O Tohfat
al-Sudur, verily, the night be gone; so arise and rest thyself
ere the day; and to-morrow there shall be naught save weal."
Then all the kings of the Jinn departed, together with those who
were present of guards; and Tohfah abode alone, pondering the
case of Al-Rashid and bethinking her of how it went with him
after her going, and of what had betided him for her loss, till the
dawn lightened, when she arose and walked about the palace.
Suddenly she saw a handsome door; so she opened it and found
herself in a flower-garden finer than the first—ne'er saw eyes of
seer a fairer than it. When she beheld this garth, she was moved
to delight and she called to mind her lord Al-Rashid and wept
with sore weeping and cried, "I crave of the bounty of Allah
Almighty that my return to him and to my palace and to my
home may be nearhand!" Then she walked about the parterres
till she came to a pavilion, high-builded of base and wide of space,
never espied mortal nor heard of a grander than it. So she entered
and found herself in a long corridor, which led to a Hammam
goodlier than that aforetime described, and its cisterns were full
of rose-water mingled with musk. Quoth Tohfah, "Extolled be
Allah! Indeed, this[3] is none other than a mighty great king."
Then she pulled off her clothes and washed her body and made
her Ghusl-ablution of the whole person[4] and prayed that which
was due from her of prayer from the evening of the previous day.[5]
When the sun rose upon the gate of the garden and she saw the
wonders thereof, with that which was therein of all manner
blooms and streams, and heard the voices of its birds, she
marvelled at what she beheld of the rareness of its ordinance and
the beauty of its disposition and sat musing over the case of Al-
Rashid and pondering what was come of him after her. Her tears

---

[1] Arab. "Bi jildi 'l-bakar." I hope that captious critics will not find fault with my rendering, as they did in the case of Fals ahmar = a red cent, vol. i. 321.

[2] Arab. "Farásah" = lit. knowing a horse. Arabia abounds in tales illustrating ab-
normal powers of observation. I have noted this in vol. viii. 326.

[3] i.e. the owner of this palace.

[4] She made the Ghusl not because she had slept with a man, but because the impurity
of Satan's presence called for the major ablution before prayer.

[5] i.e. she conjoined the prayers of nightfall with those of dawn.

coursed down her cheeks and the zephyr blew on her; so she slept and knew no more till she suddenly felt a breath on her side-face, whereat she awoke in affright and found Queen Kamariyah kissing her, and she was accompanied by her sisters, who said, "Rise, for the sun hath set." So Tohfah arose and making the Wuzu-ablution, prayed her due of prayers[1] and accompanied the four queens to the palace, where she saw the wax candles lighted and the kings sitting. She saluted them with the salam and seated herself upon her couch; and behold, King Al-Shisban had shifted his semblance, for all the pride of his soul. Then came up Iblis (whom Allah damn!) and Tohfah rose to him and kissed his hands. He also kissed her hand and blessed her and asked, "How deemest thou? Is not this place pleasant, for all its desertedness and desolation?" Answered she, "None may be desolate in this place;" and he cried, "Know that this is a site whose soil no mortal dare tread;" but she rejoined, "I have dared and trodden it, and this is one of thy many favours." Then they brought tables and dishes and viands and fruits and sweetmeats and other matters, whose description passeth powers of mortal man, and they ate their sufficiency; after which the tables were removed and the dessert-trays and platters set on, and they ranged the bottles and flagons and vessels and phials, together with all manner fruits and sweet-scented flowers. The first to raise the bowl was Iblis the Accursed, who said, "O Tohfat al-Sudur, sing over my cup." So she took the lute and touching it, carolled these couplets,

"Wake ye, Ho sleepers all! and take your joy * Of Time, and boons he deignèd to bestow;
Then hail the Wine-bride, drain the wine-ptisane * Which, poured from flagon, flows with flaming glow:
O Cup-boy, serve the wine, bring round the red[2] * Whose draught gives all we hope for here below:
What's worldly pleasure save my lady's face, * Draughts of pure wine and song of musico?"

So Iblis drained his bowl and, when he had made an end of his draught, waved his hand to Tohfah; then, throwing off that which was upon him of clothes, delivered them to her. The suit would have brought ten thousand dinars and with it was a tray full of jewels worth a mint of money. Presently he filled again

---

[1] i.e. Those of midday, mid-afternoon and sunset.
[2] Arab. "Sahbá" red wine preferred for the morning draught.

and gave the cup to his son Al-Shisban, who took it from his hand and kissing it, stood up and sat down again. Now there was before him a tray of roses; so he said to her, "O Tohfah, sing thou somewhat upon these roses." She replied, "Hearkening and obedience," and chanted these two couplets,

"It proves my price o'er all the flowers that I * Seek you each year, yet stay
    but little stound:
And high my vaunt I'm dyèd by my lord * Whom Allah made the best e'er
    trod on ground.[1]"

So Al-Shisban drank off the cup in his turn and said, "Brava, O desire of hearts!" and he bestowed on her that was upon him, to wit, a dress of cloth-of-pearl, fringed with great unions and rubies and purfled with precious gems, and a tray wherein were fifty thousand dinars. Then Maymun the Sworder took the cup and began gazing intently upon Tohfah. Now there was in his hand a pomegranate-flower and he said to her, "Sing thou some-what, O queen of mankind and Jinn-kind upon this pomegranate-flower; for indeed thou hast dominion over all hearts." Quoth she, "To hear is to obey;" and she improvised and sang these couplets,

"Breathes sweet the zephyr on fair partèrre; * Robing lute in the flamings
    that fell from air:
And moaned from the boughs with its cooing rhyme * Voice of ring-doves
    plaining their love and care:
The branch dresses in suit of fine sendal green* And in wine-hues borrowed
    from bloom Gulnare."[2]

Maymun the Sworder drained his bowl and said to her, "Brava, O perfection of qualities!" Then he signed to her and was absent awhile, after which he returned and with him a tray of jewels worth an hundred thousand ducats, which he gave to Tohfah. Thereupon Kamariyah arose and bade her slave-girl open the closet behind the Songstress, wherein she laid all that wealth; and committed the key to her, saying, "Whatso of riches cometh to thee, lay thou in this closet that is by thy side, and after the

---

[1] The Apostle who delighted in women and perfumes. Persian poetry often alludes to the rose which, before white, was dyed red by his sweat.

[2] For the etymology of Julnár — Byron's "Gulnare" — see vol. vii. 268. Here the rhymer seems to refer to its origin; Gul (Arab. Jul) in Persian a rose; and Anár, a pomegranate, which in Arabic becomes Nár = fire.

festivities, it shall be borne to thy palace on the heads of the Jinn." Tohfah kissed her hand and another king, by name Munír,[1] took the bowl and filling it, said to her, "O ferly Fair, sing to me over my bowl somewhat upon the jasmine." She replied with, "Hearkening and obedience," and improvised these couplets,

" 'Twere as though the Jasmine (when self she enrobes * On her boughs) doth
      display to my wondering eyne;
In sky of green beryl, which Beauty enclothes, * Star-groups like studs of the
      silvern mine."

Munir drank off his cup and ordered her eight hundred thousand dinars, whereat Kamariyah rejoiced and rising to her feet, kissed Tohfah on her face and said to her, "Be the world never bereaved of thee, O thou who lordest it over the hearts of Jinn-kind and mankind!" Then she returned to her place and the Shaykh Iblis arose and danced, till all present were confounded; after which the Songstress said, "Verily, thou embellishest my festivities, O thou who commandest men and Jinn and rejoicest their hearts with thy loveliness and the beauty[2] of thy faithfulness to thy lord. All that thy hands possess shall be borne to thee in thy palace and placed at thy service; but now the dawn is nearhand; so do thou rise and rest thee according to thy custom." Tohfah turned and found with her none of the Jinn; so she laid her head on the floor and slept till she had gotten her repose; after which she arose and betaking herself to the lakelet, made the Wuzu-ablution and prayed. Then she sat beside the water awhile and meditated the matter of her lord Al-Rashid and that which had betided him after her loss and wept with sore weeping. Pres-ently, she heard a blowing behind her;[3] so she turned and behold, a Head without a body and with eyes slit endlong: it was of the bigness of an elephant's skull and bigger and had a mouth as it were an oven and projecting canines as they were grapnels, and hair which trailed upon the ground. So Tohfah cried, "I take refuge with Allah from Satan the Stoned!" and recited the Two

---

[1] i.e. "The brilliant," the enlightened.

[2] i.e. the moral beauty.

[3] A phenomenon well known to spiritualists and to "The House and the Haunter." An old Dutch factory near Hungarian Fiume is famed for this mode of "obsession": the in-mates hear the sound of footfalls, etc., behind them, especially upon the stairs, and see nothing.

Preventives;[1] what while the Head drew near her and said, "Peace be with thee, O Princess of Jinn and men and union-pearl of her age and her time! Allah continue thee on life, for all the lapsing of the days, and reunite thee with thy lord the Imam!"[2] She replied, "And upon thee be Peace; O thou whose like I have not seen among the Jann!" Quoth the Head, "We are a folk who may not change their favours and we are hight Ghuls: mortals summon us to their presence, but we cannot present ourselves before them without leave. As for me, I have gotten leave of the Shaykh Abu al-Tawaif to appear before thee and I desire of thy favour that thou sing me a song, so I may go to thy palace and question its Haunters[3] concerning the plight of thy lord after thee and return to thee; and know, O Tohfat al-Sudur, that between thee and thy lord be a distance of fifty years' journey for the bonâ-fide traveller." She rejoined, "Indeed, thou grievest me anent him between whom and me is fifty years' journey;" but the Head[4] cried to her, "Be of good cheer and of eyes cool and clear, for the sovrans of the Jann will restore thee to him in less than the twinkling of an eye." Quoth she, "I will sing thee an hundred songs, so thou wilt bring me news of my lord and that which betided him after me." And quoth the Head, "Do thou favour me and sing me a song, so I may go to thy lord and fetch thee tidings of him, for that I desire, before I go, to hear thy voice, so haply my thirst[5] may be quenched." So she took the lute and tuning it, sang these couplets:—

"They have marched, yet no empty stead left they: * They are gone, nor
   heart grieves me that fled be they:
My heart forebode the bereaval of friends; * Allah ne'er bereave steads wherefrom sped be they!
Though they hid the stations where led were they, * I'll follow till stars fall in
   disarray!

---

[1] The two short Koranic chapters, The Daybreak (cxiii.) and The Men (cxiv. and last) evidently so called from the words which occur in both (versets i., "I take refuge with"). These "Ma'úzatáni," as they are called, are recited as talismans or preventives against evil, and are worn as amulets inscribed on parchment; they are also often used in the five canonical prayers. I have translated them in vol. iii. 222.

[2] The antistes or fugleman at prayer who leads off the orisons of the congregation; and applied to the Caliph as the head of the faith. See vol. ii. 203 and iv. 111.

[3] Arab. " 'Ummár" i.e. the Jinn, the "spiritual creatures" which walk this earth, and other non-humans who occupy it.

[4] A parallel to this bodiless Head is the Giant Face, which appears to travellers (who expect it) in the Lower Valley of the Indus. See Sind Re-visited, ii. 155.

[5] Arab. "Ghalílí" = my yearning.

Ye slumber, but wake shall ne'er fly these lids; * 'Tis I bear what ye never
    bore—well-away!
It had irked them not to farewell who fares * With the parting-fires that my
    heart waylay.
My friends,[1] your meeting to me is much * But more is the parting befel us
    tway:
You're my heart's delight, or you present be * Or absent, with you is my soul
    for aye!"

Thereupon the Head wept exceeding sore and cried, "O my lady,
indeed thou hast solaced my heart, and I have naught but my
life; so take it." She replied, "Nay, an I but knew that thou
wouldst bring me news of my lord Al-Rashid, 'twere fainer to me
than the reign of the world;" and the Head answered her, "It
shall be done as thou desirest." Then it disappeared and returning to her at the last of the night, said, "O my lady, know that I
have been to thy palace and have questioned one of its Haunters
of the case of the Commander of the Faithful and that which
befel him after thee; and he said, 'When the Prince of True
Believers came to Tohfah's apartment and found her not and saw
no sign of her, he buffeted his face and head and rent his raiment.'
Now there was in thy chamber the Castrato, the chief of thy
household, and the Caliph cried out at him, saying, 'Bring me
Ja'afar the Barmaki and his father and brother at this very moment!' The Eunuch went out, bewildered in his wit for fear of
the King, and when he stood in the presence of Ja'afar, he said to
him, 'Come to the Commander of the Faithful, thou and thy
father and thy brother.' So they arose in haste and betaking
themselves to the presence, said, 'O Prince of True Believers what
may be the matter?' Quoth he, 'There is a matter which passeth
description. Know that I locked the door and taking the key
with me, betook myself to my uncle's daughter, with whom I lay
the night; but, when I arose in the morning and came and opened
the door, I found no sign of Tohfah.' Quoth Ja'afar, 'O Commander of the Faithful have patience, for that the damsel hath
been snatched away, and needs must she return, seeing that she
took the lute with her, and 'tis her own lute. The Jinns have
assuredly carried her off, and we trust in Allah Almighty that
she will return.' Cried the Caliph, 'This[2] is a thing which may
nowise be!' And he abode in her apartment, nor eating nor

---

[1] Arab. "Ahbábu-ná" plur. for singular = my beloved.
[2] i.e. her return.

drinking, while the Barmecides besought him to fare forth to the folk; and he weepeth and tarrieth on such fashion till she shall return. This, then, is that which hath betided him after thee." When Tohfah heard his words, they were grievous to her and she wept with sore weeping; whereupon quoth the Head to her, "The relief of Allah the Most High is nearhand; but now let me hear somewhat of thy speech." So she took the lute and sang three songs, weeping the while. The Head exclaimed, "By Allah, thou hast been bountiful to me, the Lord be with thee!" Then it disappeared and the season of sundown came: so she rose and betook herself to her place in the hall; whereupon behold, the candles sprang up from under the earth and kindled themselves. Then the kings of the Jann appeared and saluted her and kissed her hands and she greeted them with the salam. Presently appeared Kamariyah and her three sisters and saluted Tohfah and sat down; whereupon the tables were brought and they ate; and when the tables were removed there came the wine-tray and the drinking-service. So Tohfah took the lute and one of the three queens filled the cup and signed to the Songstress. Now she had in her hand a violet, so Tohfah improvised these couplets: —

"I'm clad in a leaf-cloak of green; * In an honour-robe ultramarine:
I'm a wee thing of loveliest mien * But all flowers as my vassals are seen:
An Rose title her 'Morn-pride,' I ween * Nor before me nor after she's Queen."

The queen drank off her cup and bestowed on Tohfah a dress of cloth-of-pearl, fringed with red rubies, worth twenty thousand ducats, and a tray whereon were ten thousand sequins. All this while Maymun's eye was upon her and presently he said to her, "Harkye, Tohfah! Sing to me." But Queen Zalzalah cried out at him, and said "Desist,[1] O Maymun. Thou sufferest not Tohfah to pay heed to us." Quoth he, "I will have her sing to me:" and many words passed between them and Queen Zalzalah cried aloud at him. Then she shook and became like unto the Jinns and taking in her hand a mace of stone, said to him, "Fie upon thee! What art thou that thou shouldst bespeak us thus?

---

[1] Arab. "Arja'" lit. return! but here meaning to stop. It is much used by donkey-boys from Cairo to Fez in the sense of "Get out of the way." Hence the Spanish arre! which gave rise to arriero = a carrier, a muleteer.

By Allah, but for the respect due to kings and my fear of troubling the session and the festival and the mind of the Shaykh Iblis,
I would assuredly beat the folly out of thy head!" When Maymun heard these her words, he rose, with the fire shooting from
his eyes, and said, "O daughter of Imlák, what art thou that thou
shouldst outrage me with the like of this talk?" Replied she,
"Woe to thee, O dog of the Jinn, knowest thou not thy place?"
So saying, she ran at him, and offered to strike him with the mace,
but the Shaykh Iblis arose and casting his turband on the ground,
cried, "Out on thee, O Maymun! Thou dost always with us on
this wise. Wheresoever thou art present, thou troublest our
pleasure! Canst thou not hold thy peace until thou go forth of
the festival and this bride-feast be accomplished? When the
circumcision is at an end and ye all return to your dwellings, then
do as thou willest. Fie upon thee, O Maymun! Wottest thou
not that Imlak is of the chiefs of the Jinn? But for my good name,
thou shouldst have seen what would have betided thee of hu-
miliation and chastisement; yet on account of the festival none
may speak. Indeed thou exceedest; dost thou not ken that her
sister Wakhimah is doughtier[1] than any of the Jann? Learn to
know thyself: hast thou no regard for thy life?" So Maymun
was silent and Iblis turned to Tohfah and said to her, "Sing to
the kings of the Jinns this day and to-night until the morrow,
when the boy will be circumcised and each shall return to his own
place." Accordingly she took the lute and Kamariyah said to her
(now she had a citron in hand), "O my sister, sing to me somewhat on this citron." Tohfah replied, "To hear is to obey," and
improvising, sang these couplets,

"I'm a dome of fine gold and right cunningly dight; * And my sweetness of
    youth gladdeth every sight:
My wine is ever the drink of kings * And I'm fittest gift to the friendliest
    sprite."

At this Queen Kamariyah rejoiced with joy exceeding and
drained her cup, crying, "Brava! O thou choice Gift of hearts!"
Furthermore, she took off a sleeved robe of blue brocade, fringed
with red rubies, and a necklace of white jewels worth an hundred
thousand ducats, and gave them to Tohfah. Then she passed the
cup to her sister Zalzalah, who hent in her hand herb basil, and

---

[1] Arab. "Afras" lit. = a better horseman.

she said to Tohfah, "Sing to me somewhat on this basil." She replied, "Hearing and obeying," and improvised and sang these couplets,

"I'm the Queen of herbs in the séance of wine * And in Heaven Na'ím are
    my name and sign:
And the best are promised, in garth of Khuld, * Repose, sweet scents and the
    peace divine:[1]
What prizes then with my price shall vie? * What rank even mine, in all
    mortals' eyne?"

Thereat Queen Zalzalah rejoiced with joy exceeding and bidding her treasuress bring a basket, wherein were fifty pairs of bracelets and the same number of earrings, all of gold, crusted with jewels of price, whose like nor mankind nor Jinn-kind possessed, and an hundred robes of vari-coloured brocades and an hundred thousand ducats, gave the whole to Tohfah. Then she passed the cup to her sister Shararah, who had in her hand a stalk of narcissus; so she took it from her and turning to the Songstress, said to her, "O Tohfah, sing to me somewhat on this." She replied, "Hearkening and obedience," and improvised these couplets,

"With the smaragd wand doth my form compare; * 'Mid the finest flowers my
    worth's rarest rare:
My eyes are likened to Beauty's eyne, * And my gaze is still on the bright
    partèrre."

When she had made an end of her song, Shararah was moved to delight exceeding, and drinking off her cup, said to her, "Brava, O thou choice Gift of hearts!" Then she ordered her an hundred dresses of brocade and an hundred thousand ducats and passed the cup to Queen Wakhimah. Now she had in her hand somewhat of Nu'uman's bloom, the anemone; so she took the cup from her sister and turning to the Songstress, said to her, "O Tohfah, sing to me on this." Quoth she, "I hear and I obey," and improvised these couplets,

"I'm a dye was dyed by the Ruthful's might; * And all confess me the good-
    liest sight:
I began in the dust and the clay, but now * On the cheeks of fair women I
    rank by right."

---

[1] A somewhat crippled quotation from Koran lvi. 87-88, "As for him who is of those brought near unto Allah, there shall be for him easance and basil and a Garden of Delights (Na'ím)."

Therewith Wakhimah rejoiced with joy exceeding and drinking
off the cup, ordered her twenty dresses of Roumí brocade and a
tray, wherein were thirty thousand ducats.   Then she gave the
cup to Queen Shu'á'ah,[1] Regent of the Fourth Sea, who took
it and said, "O my lady Tohfah, sing to me on the gillyflower."
She replied, "Hearing and obeying," and improvised these
couplets,

"The time of my presence ne'er draws to a close, * Amid all whose joyance
    with mirth o'erflows;
When topers gather to sit at wine * Or in nightly shade or when morning
    shows,
I filch from the flagon to fill the bowls * And the crystal cup where the wine-
    beam glows."

Queen Shu'a'ah rejoiced with joy exceeding and emptying her
cup, gave Tohfah an hundred thousand ducats.   Then up sprang
Iblis (whom Allah curse!) and cried, "Verily, the dawn lighten-
eth;" whereupon the folk arose and disappeared, all of them, and
there abode not one of them save the Songstress, who went forth
to the garden and entering the Hammam made her Wuzu-ablu-
tions and prayed whatso lacked her of prayers.   Then she sat
down and when the sun rose, behold, there came up to her near an
hundred thousand green birds, which filled the branches of the
trees with their multitudes and they warbled in various voices,
whilst Tohfah marvelled at their fashion.   Suddenly, appeared
eunuchs, bearing a throne of gold, studded with pearls and gems
and jacinths, both white and red, and having four steps of gold,
together with many carpets of sendal and brocade and Coptic
cloth of silk sprigged with gold; and all these they spread in the
centre of the garden and setting up the throne thereon, perfumed
the place with virgin musk, Nadd[2] and ambergris.   After that,
there came a queen; never saw eyes a fairer than she nor than her
qualities; she was robed in rich raiment, broidered with pearls
and gems, and on her head was a crown set with various kinds of
unions and jewels.   About her were five hundred slave-girls,
high-bosomed maids, as they were moons, screening her, right
and left, and she among them like the moon on the night of its

---

[1] i.e. Queen Sunbeam.
[2] See vol. i. 310 for this compound perfume which contains musk, ambergris and other
essences.

full, for that she was the most worthy of them in majesty and dignity. She ceased not walking till she came to Tohfah, whom she found gazing on her in amazement; and when the Songstress saw her turn to her, she rose to her, standing on her feet, and saluted her and kissed ground between her hands. The queen rejoiced in her and putting out her hand to her, drew her to herself and seated her by her side on the couch; whereupon the Songstress kissed her hands and the queen said to her, "Know, O Tohfah, that all which thou treadest of these carpets belongeth not to any of the Jinn, who may never tread them without thy leave,[1] for that I am the queen of them all and the Shaykh Abu al-Tawaif Iblis sought my permission to hold festival[2] and prayed me urgently to be present at the circumcision of his son. So I despatched to him, in my stead, a slave-girl of my slave-girls, namely, Shu'á'ah Queen of the Fourth Sea, who is vice-reine of my reign. When she was present at the wedding and saw thee and heard thy singing, she sent to me, informing me of thee and setting forth to me thy grace and amiability and the beauty of thy breeding and thy courtesy.[3] So I am come to thee, for that which I have heard of thy charms, and hereby I do thee a mighty great favour in the eyes of all the Jann."[4] Thereupon Tohfah ʼrose and kissed the earth and the queen thanked her for this and bade her sit. So she sat down and the queen called for foods when they brought a table of gold, inlaid with pearls and jacinth; and jewels and bearing kinds manifold of birds and viands of various hues, and the queen said, "O Tohfah, in the name of Allah! Let us eat bread and salt together, I and thou." Accordingly the Songstress came forward and ate of those meats and found therein somewhat the like whereof she had never eaten; no, nor aught more delicious than it, while the slave-girls stood around the table, as the white compasseth the black of the eye, and she sat conversing and laughing with the queen. Then said the lady, "O my sister, a slave-girl told me of thee that thou saidst, 'How loathly is what yonder Jinni Maymun eateth!'[5] Tohfah replied, "By Allah, O my lady, I have not any eye that

---

[1] I can hardly see the sequence of this or what the carpets have to do here.

··re, as before, some insertion has been found necessary.

[2] ··   "Dukhúlak" lit. = thy entering, entrance, becoming familiar.

[4] Or "Ant... ... this there shall be to thee great honour over all the Jinn."

[5] Mr. Payne thus amends the text, "How loathly is yonder Genie Meimoun! There is no eating (in his presence);" referring back to p. 61.

can look at him,[1] and indeed I am fearful of him." When the queen heard this, she laughed till she fell backwards and said, "O my sister, by the might of the graving upon the seal-ring of Solomon, prophet of Allah, I am queen over all the Jann, and none dare so much as cast on thee a glance of the eye;" whereat Tohfah kissed her hand. Then the tables were removed and the twain sat talking. Presently up came the kings of the Jinn from every side and kissed ground before the queen and stood in her service; and she thanked them for this, but moved not for one of them.[2] Then appeared the Shaykh Abu al-Tawáif Iblis (Allah curse him!) and kissed the earth before her, saying, "O my lady, may I not be bereft of these steps!"[3] She replied, "O Shaykh Abu al-Tawáif, it behoveth thee to thank the bounty of the Lady Tohfah, who was the cause of my coming." Rejoined he, "Thou sayest sooth," and kissed ground. Then the queen fared on towards the palace and there arose and alighted upon the trees an hundred thousand birds of manifold hues. The Song-stress asked, "How many are these birds?" and Queen Wakhimah answered her, "Know, O my sister, that this queen is hight Queen al-Shahbá[4] and that she is queen over all the Jann from East to West. These birds thou seest are of her host, and unless they appeared in this shape, earth would not be wide enough for them. Indeed, they came forth with her and are present with her presence at this circumcision. She will give thee after the measure of that which hath been given to thee from the first of the festival to the last thereof;[5] and indeed she honoureth us all with her presence." Then the queen entered the palace and sat down on the couch of the circumcision[6] at the upper end of the hall, where-upon Tohfah took the lute and pressing it to her breast, touched its strings suchwise that the wits of all present were bewildered and Shaykh Iblis cried to her, "O my lady Tohfah, I conjure thee,

---

[1] i.e. "I cannot bear to see him!"

[2] This assertion of dignity, which is permissible in royalty, has been absurdly affected by certain "dames" in Anglo-Egypt who are quite the reverse of queenly; and who degrade "dignity" to the vulgarest affectation.

[3] i.e. "May thy visits never fail me!"

[4] i.e. Ash-coloured, verging upon white.

[5] i.e. "She will double thy store of presents."

[6] The Arab boy who, unlike the Jew, is circumcised long after infancy and often in his teens, thus making the ceremony conform after a fashion with our "Confirmation," is displayed before being operated upon, to family and friends; and the seat is a couch covered with the richest tapestry. So far it resembles the bride-throne.

by the life of this noble queen, sing for me and praise thyself,
and cross me not." Quoth she, "To hear is to obey; still, but for
thine adjuration, I had not done this. Say me, doth any praise
himself? What manner thing is this?" Then she improvised
these couplets:

> "In all fêtes I'm Choice Gift[1] to the minstrel-race;
> Folk attest my worth, rank and my pride of place,
> While Fame, merit and praises with honour engrace."

Her verses pleased the kings of the Jann and they cried, "By
Allah, thou sayst sooth!" Then she rose to her feet, hending lute
in hand, and played and sang, whilst the Jinns and the Shaykh
Abu al-Tawáif danced. Presently the Father of the Tribes came
up to her bussing her bosom, and gave her a Bráhmani[2] carbuncle
he had taken from the hidden hoard of Yáfis bin Núh[3] (on whom
be the Peace), and which was worth the reign of the world; its
light was as the sheen of the sun and he said to her, "Take this
and be equitable therewith to the people of the world."[4] She
kissed his hand and rejoiced in the jewel and said, "By Allah, this
befitteth none save the Commander of the Faithful." Now
Queen Al-Shahba laughed with delight at the dancing of Iblís
and she said to him, "By Allah, this is a goodly pavane!" He
thanked her for this and said to the Songstress, "O Tohfah, there
is not on earth's face a skilfuller than Ishak al-Nadim;[5] but thou
art more skilful than he. Indeed, I have been present with him
many a time and have shown him positions[6] on the lute, and there
has betided me with him that which betided. Indeed, the story
of my dealings with him is a long one but this is no time to repeat
it; for now I would show thee a shift on the lute, whereby thou
shalt be exalted over all folk." Quoth she, "Do what seemeth
good to thee." So he took the lute and played thereon a wondrous playing, with rare divisions and marvellous modulations,
and showed her a passage she knew not; and this was goodlier to
her than all that she had gotten. Then she took the lute from him

---

[1] *Tohfah.*

[2] *i.e.* Hindu, Indian.

[3] Japhet, son of Noah.

[4] Mr. Payne translates "Take this and glorify thyself withal over the people of the
world." His reading certainly makes better sense, but I do not see how the text can carry
the meaning. He also omits the bussing of the bosom, probably from artistic reasons.

[5] A skit at Ishák, making the Devil praise him. See vol. vii. 113.

[6] Arab. "Mawázi" (plur. of Mauza') = lit. places, shifts, passages.

and playing thereon, sang and presently returned to the passage
which he had shown her; and he said, "By Allah, thou singest
better than I!" As for Tohfah, it became manifest to her that
her former practice was all of it wrong and that what she had
learnt from the Shaykh Abu al-Tawáif Iblis was the root and
foundation of all perfection in the art and its modes. So she rejoiced in that which she had won of skill in touching the lute far
more than in all that had fallen to her lot of wealth and honour-
robes and kissed the Master's hand. Then said Queen Al-
Shahba, "By Allah, O Shaykh, my sister Tohfah is indeed singular among the folk of her time, and I hear that she singeth upon
all sweet-smelling blooms." Iblis replied, "Yes, O my lady, and
I am in extremest wonderment thereat. But there remaineth
somewhat of sweet-scented flowers, which she hath not besung,
such as myrtle and tuberose and jessamine and the moss-rose and
the like." Then the Shaykh signed to her to sing somewhat upon
the rest of the flowers, that Queen Al-Shahba might hear, and
she said, "Hearing and obeying." So she took the lute and played
thereon in many modes, then returned to the first and sang these
couplets,

"I'm one of the lover-retinue * Whom long pine and patience have doomèd
    rue:
And sufferance of parting from kin and friends * Hath clothed me, O folk, in
    this yellow hue:
Then, after the joyance had passed away, * Heart-break, abasement and cark
    I knew,
Through the long, long day when the lift is light, * Nor, when night is murk,
    my pangs cease pursue:
So, 'twixt fairest hope and unfailing fear, * My bitter tears ever flow anew."

Thereat Queen Al-Shahba rejoiced with joy exceeding and
cried, "Brava, O queen of delight! No one is able to describe
thee. Sing to us on the Apple." Quoth Tohfah, "Hearkening
and obedience." Then she recited these couplets,

"I surpass all forms in my coquetry* For mine inner worth and mine outer
    blee;
Tend me noble hands in the sight of all * And slake with pure waters the
    thirst of me;
My robe is of sendal, and eke my veil * Is of sunlight the Ruthful hath
    bidden be:
When my fair companions are marched afar, * In sorrow fro' home they are
    forced to flee:

But noble hands deign hearten my heart * With beds where I sit in my high
degree;[1]
And where, like full moon at its rise, my light * 'mid the garden-fruits thou
shalt ever see."

Queen Al-Shahba rejoiced in this with exceeding joy and cried
"Brava! By Allah, there is none excelleth thee." Tohfah kissed
the ground, then returned to her place and versified on the
Tuberose, saying,

"I'm a marvel-bloom to be worn on head! * Though a stranger among you
fro' home I fled:
Make use of wine in my company * And flout at Time who in languish sped.
E'en so doth camphor my hue attest, * O my lords, as I stand in my present
stead.
So gar me your gladness when dawneth day, * And to highmost seat in your
homes be I led:
And quaff your cups in all jollity, * And cheer and ease shall ne'er cease to be."

At this Queen Al-Shahba rejoiced with exceeding joy and cried,
"Brava, O queen of delight! By Allah, I know not how I shall
do to give thee thy due! May the Most High grant us the
grace of thy long continuance!" Then she strained her to her
breast and bussed her on the cheek; whereupon quoth Iblis (on
whom be a curse!), "This is a mighty great honour!" Quoth
the queen, "Know that this lady Tohfah is my sister and that her
biddance is my biddance and her forbiddance my forbiddance.
So all of you hearken to her word and render her worshipful
obedience." Therewith the kings rose in a body and kissed
ground before Tohfah, who rejoiced in this. Moreover, Queen
Al-Shahba doffed dress and habited her in a suit adorned with
pearls, jewels and jacinths, worth an hundred thousand ducats,
and wrote for her on a slip of paper[2] a patent appointing her to be
her deputy. So the Songstress rose and kissed ground before the
Queen, who said to her, "Of thy favour, sing to us somewhat
concerning the rest of the sweet-scented flowers and herbs, so I
may hear thy chant and solace myself with witnessing thy skill."
She replied, "To hear is to obey, O lady mine," and, taking the
lute, improvised these couplets,

"My hue excelleth all hues in light, * And I would all eyes should enjoy my
sight:

---

[1] The bed (farsh), is I presume, the straw-spread (?) store-room where the apples are
preserved.
[2] Arab. "Farkh warak", which sounds like an atrocious vulgarism.

My site is the site of fillets and pearls * Where the fairest brows are with
　　jasmine dight:
My light's uprist (and what light it shows!) * Is a silvern zone on the waist
　　of Night."

Then she changed the measure and improvised these couplets,

"I'm the gem of herbs, and in seasons twain * My tryst I keep with my lovers·
　　train:
I stint not union for length of time * Nor visits, though some be of severance
　　fain;
The true one am I and my troth I keep, * And, easy of plucking, no hand
　　disdain."

Then, changing measure and the mode, she played so that she
bewildered the wits of those who were present, and Queen Al·
Shahba, moved to mirth and merriment, cried, "Brava, O queen
of delight!" Presently she returned to the first mode and im·
provised these couplets on Nenuphar,

"I fear me lest freke espy me, * In air when I fain deny me;
So I root me beneath the wave, * And my stalks to bow down apply me."

Hereat Queen Al·Shahba rejoiced with exceeding joy, and cried,
"Brava, O Tohfah! Let me hear more of thy chant." Accord·
ingly, she smote the lute and changing the mode, recited on the
Moss·rose these couplets,

"Look on Nasrín[1] those branchy shoots surround; * With greenest leafery
　　'tis deckt and crowned:
Its graceful bending stem draws every gaze * While beauteous bearing makes
　　their love abound."

Then she changed measure and mode and sang these couplets
on the Water·lily,

"O thou who askest Súsan[2] of her scent, * Hear thou my words and beauty of
　　my lay.
'Emir am I whom all mankind desire' * (Quoth she) 'or present or when
　　ta'en away.' "

When Tohfah had made an end of her song, Queen Al·Shahba
rose and said, "I never heard from any the like of this;" and she

---

[1] The Moss-rose; also the eglantine, or dog-rose, and the sweet-briar, whose leaf, unlike
other roses, is so odorous.

[2] The lily in Heb., derived by some from its six (shash) leaves, and by others from its
vivid cheerful brightness. "His lips are lilies" (Cant. v. 13), not in colour, but in odoriferous
sweetness.

drew the Songstress to her and fell to kissing her. Then she took
leave of her and flew away; and on like wise all the birds took
flight with her, so that they walled the horizon; whilst the rest
of the kings tarried behind. Now as soon as it was the fourth
night, there came the boy who was to be circumcised, adorned
with jewels such as never saw eye nor heard ear of, and amongst
the rest a crown of gold crusted with pearls and gems, the worth
whereof was an hundred thousand sequins. He sat down upon
the couch and Tohfah sang to him, till the chirurgeon[1] came and
they snipped his foreskin in the presence of all the kings, who
showered on him a mighty great store of jewels and jacinths and
gold. Queen Kamariyah bade her Eunuchs gather up all this and
lay it in Tohfah's closet and it was as much in value as all that
had fallen to her, from the first of the festivities to the last thereof.
Moreover, the Shaykh Iblis (whom Allah curse!) bestowed upon
the Songstress the crown worn by the boy and gave the circum-
cisee another, whereat Tohfah's reason took flight. Then the
Jinn departed, in order of rank, whilst Iblis farewelled them,
band after band. Seeing the Shaykh thus occupied with taking
leave of the kings, Maymun seized his opportunity, the place
being empty, and taking up Tohfah on his shoulders, soared aloft
with her to the confines of the lift, and flew away with her. Presently, Iblis came to look for the Songstress and see what she purposed, but found her not and sighted the slave-girls slapping
their faces: so he said to them, "Fie on you! What may be the
matter?" They replied, "O our lord, Maymun hath snatched
up Tohfah and flown away with her." When Iblis heard this, he
gave a cry whereto earth trembled and said, "What is to be
done?" Then he buffetted his face and head, exclaiming, "Woe
to you! This be none other than exceeding insolence. Shall he
carry off Tohfah from my very palace and attaint mine honour?
Doubtless, this Maymun hath lost his wits." Then he cried out
a second time, so that the earth quaked, and rose on his wings
high in air. The news came to the rest of the kings; so they flew
after him and overtaking him, found him full of anxiety and affright, with fire issuing from his nostrils, and said to him, "O
Shaykh al-Tawaif,[2] what is to do?" He replied, "Know ye that

---

[1] The barber is now the usual operator; but all operations began in Europe with the
"barber-surgeon."

[2] *Sic* in text xii. 20. It may be a misprint for Abú al-Tawaif, but it can also mean "O
Shaykh of the Tribes (of Jinns)!"

Maymun hath carried off Tohfah from my palace and attainted mine honour." When they heard this, they cried, "There is no Majesty and there is no Might save in Allah the Glorious, the Great. By God he hath ventured upon a grave matter and verily he destroyeth self and folk!" Then Shaykh Iblis ceased not flying till he fell in with the tribes of the Jann, and they gathered together a world of people, none may tell the tale of them save the Lord of All-might. So they came to the Fortress of Copper and the Citadel of Lead,[1] and the people of the sconces saw the tribes of the Jann issuing from every deep mountain-pass[2] and said, "What be the news?" Then Iblis went in to King Al-Shisban and acquainted him with that which had befallen; whereupon quoth he, "Verily, Allah hath destroyed Maymun and his many! He pretendeth to possess Tohfah, and she is become queen of the Jann! But have patience till we devise that which befitteth in the matter of Tohfah." Iblis asked, "And what befitteth it to do?" And Al-Shisban answered, "We will fall upon him and kill him and his host with cut of brand." Then quoth Shaykh Iblis, " 'Twere better to acquaint Queen Kamariyah and Queen Zalzalah and Queen Shararah and Queen Wakhimah; and when they are assembled, Allah shall ordain whatso He deemeth good in the matter of her release." Quoth Al-Shisban, "Right is thy rede" and thy despatched to Queen Kamariyah an Ifrit hight Salhab who came to her palace and found her sleeping; so he roused her and she said, "What is to do, O Salhab?" Cried he, "O my lady, come to the succour of thy sister the Songstress, for Maymun hath carried her off and attainted thine honour and that of Shaykh Iblis." Quoth she, "What sayst thou?" and she sat up straight and cried out with a great cry. And indeed she feared for Tohfah and said, "By Allah, in very sooth she used to say that he gazed at her and prolonged the gaze; but ill is that whereto his soul hath prompted him." Then she rose in haste and mounting a Sataness of her Satans, said to her, "Fly." So she flew off with her and alighted in the palace of her sister Shararah, whereupon she sent for her sisters Zalzalah and Wakhimah and acquainted them with the tidings, saying, "Know that Maymun hath snatched up Tohfah and flown off with her swiftlier than the blinding leven." Then they all flew off in haste and lighting down in the place where were their father Al-Shisban and their

---

[1] The capital of King Al-Shisban.

[2] Arab "Fajj", the Spanish "Vega" which, however, means a mountain-plain, a plain.

grandfather the Shaykh Abu al-Tawáif, found the folk on the
sorriest of situations. When their grandfather Iblis saw them,
he rose to them and wept, and they all wept for the Songstress.
Then said Iblis to them, "Yonder hound hath attainted mine
honour and taken Tohfah, and I think not other wise[1] but that
she is like to die of distress for herself and her lord Al-Rashid and
saying, 'The whole that they said and did was false.'"[2] Quoth
Kamariyah, "O grandfather mine, nothing is left for it but stratagem and device for her deliverance, for that she is dearer to me
than everything; and know that yonder accursed when he
waxeth ware of your coming upon him, will ken that he hath no
power to cope with you, he who is the least and meanest of the
Jann; but we dread that he, when assured of defeat, will slay
Tohfah; wherefore nothing will serve but that we contrive a
sleight for saving her; else will she perish." He asked, "And
what hast thou in mind of device?" and she answered, "Let us
take him with fair means, and if he obey, all will be well;[3] else
will we practise stratagem against him; and expect not her
deliverance from other than myself." Quoth Iblis, "The affair is
thine; contrive what thou wilt, for that Tohfah is thy sister and
thy solicitude for her is more effectual than that of any other."
So Kamariyah cried out to an Ifrit of the Ifrits and a calamity of
the calamities,[4] by name Al-Asad al-Tayyár, the Flying Lion
and said to him, "Hie with my message to the Crescent Mountain,[5] the wone of Maymun the Sworder, and enter and say to
him, My lady saluteth thee with the salam and asketh thee,
'How canst thou be assured for thyself of safety, after what thou
hast done, O Maymun? Couldst thou find none to maltreat in
thy drunken humour save Tohfah, she too being a queen? But
thou art excused, because thou didst not this deed, but 'twas thy
drink, and the Shaykh Abu al-Tawáif pardoneth thee, because
thou wast drunken. Indeed, thou hast attainted his honour;
but now restore her to her palace, for that she hath done well
and favoured us and rendered us service, and thou wottest that
she is this day our queen. Belike she may bespeak Queen Al-

---

[1] *i.e.* I am quite sure: emphatically.
[2] *i.e.* all the Jinn's professions of affection and promises of protection were mere lies.
[3] In the original this apodosis is wanting: see vol. vi. 203, 239.
[4] Arab. "Dáhiyat al-Dawáhí;" see vol. ii. 87.
[5] Arab. "Al-Jabal al-Mukawwar" = Chaîne de montagnes de forme demi circulaire,
from Kaur, a park, an enceinte.

Shahba, whereupon the matter will become grievous and that wherein there is no good shall betide thee; and thou wilt get no title of gain. Verily, I give thee good counsel, and so the Peace!'" Al-Asad answered "Hearing and obeying," and flew till he came to the Crescent Mountain, when he sought audience of Maymun, who bade admit him. So he entered and kissing ground before him, gave him Queen Kamariyah's message, which when he heard, he cried to the Ifrit, "Return whence thou comest and say to thy mistress, 'Be silent and thou wilt show thy good sense.' Else will I come and seize upon her and make her serve Tohfah; and if the kings of the Jinn assemble together against me and I be overcome by them, I will not leave her to scent the wind of this world and she shall be neither mine nor theirs, for that she is presently my sprite[1] from between my ribs; and how shall any part with his sprite?" When the Ifrit heard Maymun's words, he said to him, "By Allah, O Maymun, art thou a changeling in thy wits, that thou speakest these words of my lady, and thou one of her page-boys?" Whereupon Maymun cried out and said to him, "Woe to thee, O dog of the Jinns! Wilt thou bespeak the like of me with these words?" Then he bade those who were about him bastinado Al-Asad, but he took flight and soaring high in air, betook himself to his mistress and told her the tidings: when she said, "Thou hast done well, O good knight!" Then she turned to her sire and said to him, "Hear that which I shall say to thee." Quoth he, "Say on;" and quoth she, "I rede thee take thy troops and go to him, for when he heareth this, he will in turn levy his many and come forth to thee; whereupon do thou offer him battle and prolong the fight with him and make a show to him of weakness and giving way. Meantime, I will devise me a device for getting at Tohfah and delivering her, what while he is busied with you in battle; and when my messenger cometh to thee and informeth thee that I have gotten possession of Tohfah and that she is with me, return thou upon Maymun forthwith and overthrow him and his hosts, and take him prisoner. But, an my device succeed not with him and we fail to deliver Tohfah, he will assuredly practise to slay her, without recourse, and regret for her will remain in our hearts." Quoth Iblis, "This is the right rede" and bade call a march among the troops, whereupon an hundred

---

[1] Arab. "Rúhí" lit. my breath, the outward sign of life.

thousand knights, doughty wights of war, joined themselves to him and set out for the country of Maymun. As for Queen Kamariyah, she flew off to the palace of her sister Wakhimah, and told her what deed Maymun had done and how he declared that, whenas he saw defeat nearhand, he would slay Tohfah; adding, "And indeed, he is resolved upon this; otherwise had he not dared to work such sleight. So do thou contrive the affair as thou see fit, for in rede thou hast no superior." Then they sent for Queen Zalzalah and Queen Shararah and sat down to take counsel, one with other, concerning what they had best do in the matter. Presently said Wakhimah, " 'Twere advisable we fit out a ship in this our island home and embark therein, dis-guised as Adam's sons, and fare on till we come to anchor under a little island that lieth over against Maymun's palace. There will we sit drinking and smiting the lute and singing; for Tohfah will assuredly be seated there overlooking the sea, and needs must she see us and come down to us, whereupon we will take her by force and she will be under our hands, so that none shall be able to molest her any more. Or, an Maymun be gone forth to do battle with the Jinns, we will storm his stronghold and take Tohfah and raze his palace and slay all therein. When he hears of this, his heart will be broken and we will send to let our father know, whereat he will return upon him with his troops and he will be destroyed and we shall have rest of him." They answered her, saying, "This is a good counsel." Then they bade fit out a ship from behind the mountain,[1] and it was fitted out in less than the twinkling of an eye; so they launched it on the sea and embarking therein, together with four thousand Ifrits, set out, intending for Maymun's palace. They also bade other five thousand Ifrits betake themselves to the island under the Cres-cent Mountain and there lie in wait for them ambushed well. Thus fared it with the kings of the Jann; but as regards Shaykh Abu al-Tawáif Iblis and his son Al-Shisban the twain set out, as we have said, with their troops, who were of the doughtiest of the Jinn and the prowest of them in wing-flying and horse-manship, and fared on till they drew near the Crescent Moun-tain. When the news of their approach reached Maymun, he cried out with a mighty great cry to the troops, who were twenty thousand riders, and bade them make ready for de-

---

[1] *i.e.* Káf.

parture. Then he went in to Tohfah and kissing her, said,
"Know that thou art this day my life of the world, and indeed
the Jinns are gathered together to wage war on me for thy sake.
An I win the day from them and am preserved alive, I will set
all the kings of the Jann under thy feet and thou shalt become
queen of the world." But she shook her head and shed tears;
and he said, "Weep not, for I swear by the virtue of the mighty
inscription borne on the seal-ring of Solomon, thou shalt never
again see the land of men; no, never! Say me, can any one part
with his life? Give ear, then, to my words; else will I slay thee."
So she was silent. And forthright he sent for his daughter, whose
name was Jamrah,[1] and when she came, he said to her, "Harkye,
Jamrah! Know that I am going to fight the clans of Al-Shisban
and Queen Kamariyah and the Kings of the Jann. An I be vouchsafed the victory over them, to Allah be the laud and thou shalt
have of me largesse;[2] but, an thou see or hear that I am worsted
and any come to thee with ill news of me, hasten to kill Tohfah,
so she may fall neither to me nor to them." Then he farewelled
her and mounted, saying, "When this cometh about, pass over to
the Crescent Mountain and take up thine abode there, and await
what shall befal me and what I shall say to thee." And Jamrah
answered "Hearkening and obedience." Now when the Songstress heard these words, she fell to weeping and wailing and
said, "By Allah, naught irketh me but severance from my lord
Al-Rashid; however, when I am dead, let the world be ruined
after me!"[3] And she was certified in herself that she was assuredly lost. Then Maymun set forth with his army and departed in quest of the hosts of the Jinn, leaving none in the
palace save his daughter Jamrah and Tohfah and an Ifrit which
was dear to him. They fared on till they met with the army of
Al-Shisban; and when the two hosts came face to face, they fell
each upon other and fought a fight, a passing sore than which
naught could be more. After a while, Al-Shisban's troops began
to give way, and when Maymun saw them do thus, he despised

---

[1] i.e. A bit of burning charcoal.

[2] Arab. "Al-yad al-bayzá," = lit. The white hand: see vol. iv. 185.

[3] Showing the antiquity of "Après moi le déluge," the fame of all old politicians and
aged statesmen who can expect but a few years of life. These "burning questions" (e.g.
the Bulgarian) may be smothered for a time, but the result is that they blaze forth with
increased violence. We have to thank Lord Palmerston (an Irish landlord) for ignoring
the growth of Fenianism and another aged statesman for a sturdy attempt to disunite the
United Kingdom. An old nation wants young blood at its head.

them and made sure of victory over them. On this wise it befel
them; but as regards Queen Kamariyah and her company they
sailed on without ceasing, till they came under the palace wherein
was Tohfah, to wit, that of Maymun the Sworder; and by the
decree of the Lord of destiny, the Songstress herself was at that
very time sitting on the belvedere of the palace, pondering the
affair of Harun al-Rashid and her own and that which had befallen her and weeping for that she was doomed to death. She
saw the vessel and what was therein of those we have named,
and they in mortal guise, and said, "Alas, my sorrow for this
ship and for the men that be therein!" As for Kamariyah and her
many, when they drew near the palace, they strained their eyes
and seeing the Songstress sitting, cried, "Yonder sitteth Tohfah.
May Allah not bereave us of her!" Then they moored their
craft and, making for the island which lay over against the
palace, spread carpets and sat eating and drinking; whereupon
quoth Tohfah, "Well come and welcome to yonder faces! These
be my kinswomen and I conjure thee by Allah, O Jamrah, that
thou let me down to them, so I may sit with them awhile and
enjoy kindly converse with them and return." Quoth Jamrah,
"I may on no wise do that;" and Tohfah wept. Then the folk
brought out wine and drank, while Kamariyah took the lute and
sang these couplets,

"By Allah, had I never hoped to greet you * Your guide had failed on camel
   to seat you!
Far bore you parting from friend would greet you * Till meseems mine eyes
   for your wone entreat you."

When Tohfah heard this, she cried out so great a cry, that the
folk heard her and Kamariyah said, "Relief is nearhand." Then
the Songstress looked out to them and called to them, saying, "O
daughters of mine uncle, I am a lonely maid, an exile from kin
and country: so for the love of Allah Almighty, repeat that
song!" Accordingly Kamariyah repeated it and Tohfah swooned
away. When she came to herself, she said to Jamrah, "By the
rights of the Apostle of Allah (whom may He save and assain!)
unless thou suffer me go down to them and look on them and sit
with them for a full hour, I will hurl myself headlong from this
palace, for that I am aweary of my life and know that I am slain
to all certainty; wherefore will I kill myself, ere you pass sentence
upon me." And she was instant with her in asking. When

Jamrah heard her words, she knew that, an she let her not down, she would assuredly destroy herself. So she said to her, "O Tohfah, between thee and them are a thousand cubits; but I will bring the women up to thee." The Songstress replied, "Nay, there is no help but that I go down to them and solace me in the island and look upon the sea anear; then will we return, I and thou; for that, an thou bring them up to us, they will be affrighted and there will betide them neither joy nor gladness. As for me, I wish but to be with them, that they may cheer me with their company neither give over their merrymaking, so peradventure I may broaden my breast with them, and indeed I swear that needs must I go down to them; else I will cast myself upon them." And she cajoled Jamrah and kissed her hands, till she said, "Arise and I will set thee down beside them." Then she took Tohfah under her armpit and flying up swiftlier than the blinding leven, set her down with Kamariyah and her company; whereupon she went up to them and accosted them, saying, "Fear ye not: no harm shall befal you; for I am a mortal, like unto you, and I would fain look on you and talk with you and hear your singing." So they welcomed her and kept their places, whilst Jamrah sat down beside them and fell a-snuffing their odours and saying, "I smell the scent of the Jinn![1] Would I wot whence it cometh!" Then said Wakhimah to her sister Kamariyah, "Yonder foul slut smelleth us and presently she will take to flight; so what be this inaction concerning her?" [2] Thereupon Kamariyah put out an arm long as a camel's neck, and dealt Jamrah a buffet on the head, that made it fly from her body and cast it into the sea. Then cried she, "Allah is All-great!"[3] And they uncovered their faces, whereupon Tohfah knew them and said to them, "Protection!" Queen Kamariyah embraced her, as also did Queen Zalzalah and Queen Wakhimah and Queen Shararah, and the first-named said to her, "Receive the good tidings of assured safety, for there abideth no harm for thee; but this is no time for talk." Then they cried out, whereupon up came the Ifrits ambushed in that island,

---

[1] Suggesting the nursery rhyme:

Fee, fo, fum,
I smell the blood of an Englishman.

[2] *i.e.* why not at once make an end of her.
[3] The well-known war-cry.

hending swords and maces in hand, and taking up Tohfah, flew her to the palace and made themselves masters of it, whilst the Ifrit aforesaid, who was dear to Maymun and whose name was Dukhán,[1] fled like an arrow and stinted not flying till he came to Maymun and found him fighting a sore fight with the Jinn. When his lord saw him, he cried out at him, saying, "Fie upon thee! Whom hast thou left in the palace?" Dukhan answered, saying, "And who abideth in the palace? Thy beloved Tohfah they have captured and Jamrah is slain and they have taken the palace, all of it." At these ill tidings Maymun buffeted his face and head and said, "Oh! Out on it for a calamity!" Then he cried aloud. Now Kamariyah had sent to her sire and reported to him the news, whereat the raven of the wold[2] croaked for the foe. So, when Maymun saw that which had betided him (and indeed the Jinn smote upon him and the wings of eternal sever- ance overspread his host), he planted the heel of his lance in the earth and turning its head to his heart, urged his charger thereat and pressed upon it with his breast, till the point came forth gleaming from his back. Meanwhile the messenger had made the friendly host with the news of Tohfah's deliverance, whereat the Shaykh Abu al-Tawáif rejoiced and bestowed on the bringer of lief tidings a sumptuous robe of honour and made him commander over a company of the Jann. Then they charged home upon Maymun's host and wiped them out to the last man; and when they came to Maymun, they found that he had slain himself and was even as we have said. Presently Kamariyah and her sister Wakhimah came up to their grandfather and told him what they had done; whereupon he came to Tohfah and saluted her with the salam and congratulated her on deliverance. Then he made over Maymun's palace to Salhab; and, taking all the rebel's wealth gave it to the Songstress, while the troops encamped upon the Crescent Mountain. Furthermore, the Shaykh Abu al-Tawáif said to Tohfah, "Blame me not," and she kissed his hands; when behold, there appeared to them the tribes of the Jinn, as they were clouds, and Queen Al-Shahba flying in their van, drawn sword in grip. As she came in sight of the folk, they kissed ground between her hands and she said to them, "Tell me

---

[1] Lit. "Smoke" pop. applied, like our word, to tobacco. The latter, however, is not here meant.

[2] Arab. "Ghuráb al-bayn," of the wold or of parting. See vol. vii. 226.

what hath betided Queen Tohfah from yonder dog Maymun
and why did ye not send to me and report to me?" Quoth they,
"And who was this dog that we should send to thee on his account? Indeed he was the least and lowest of the Jinn." Then
they told her what Kamariyah and her sisters had done and how
they had practised upon Maymun and delivered the Songstress
from his hand, fearing lest he should slay her when he found
himself defeated; and she said, "By Allah, the accursed was wont
to lengthen his looking upon her!" And Tohfah fell to kissing
Al-Shahba's hand, whilst the queen strained her to her bosom
and kissed her, saying, "Trouble is past; so rejoice in assurance
of deliverance." Then they rose and went up to the palace
whereupon the trays of food were brought and they ate and
drank; after which quoth Queen Al-Shahba, "O Tohfah, sing to
us, by way of sweetmeat[1] for thine escape, and favour us with
that which shall solace our minds, for that indeed my thoughts
have been occupied with thee." And quoth Tohfah, "Hearkening and obedience, O my lady." So she improvised and sang
these couplets,

"Breeze of East[2] an thou breathe o'er the dear ones' land * Speed, I pray thee,
    my special salute and salam:
And say them I'm pledged to love them and * In pine that passeth all pine
    I am."

Thereat Queen Al-Shahba rejoiced and with her all who were
present; and they admired her speech and fell to kissing her; and
when she had made an end of her song, Queen Kamariyah said to
her, "O my sister, ere thou go to thy palace, I would fain bring
thee to look upon Al-'Anka,[3] daughter of Bahram Júr, whom
Al-'Anka, daughter of the wind, carried off, and her beauty; for
that there is not her fellow on earth's face." And Queen Al-
Shahba said, "O Kamariyah, I also think it were well an I beheld
her." Quoth Kamirayah, "I saw her three years ago; but my
sister Wakhimah seeth her at all times, for she is near to her
people, and she saith that there is not in the world fairer than she.

---

[1] Arab. "Haláwah"; see vol. iv. 60.
[2] Here the vocative particle "Yá" is omitted.
[3] Lit. "The long-necked (bird)" before noticed with the Rukh (Roc) in vol. v. 122. Here
it becomes a Princess, daughter of Bahrám-i-Gúr (Bahram of the Onager, his favourite
game), the famous Persian king in the fifth century, a contemporary of Theodosius the
younger and Honorius. The "Anká" is evidently the Iranian Símurgh.

Indeed, this Queen Al-Anka is become a byword for beauty
and comeliness." And Wakhimah said, "By the mighty inscription on the seal-ring of Solomon, there is not her like for loveliness
here below." Then said Queen Al-Shahba, "An it needs must be
and the affair is as ye say, I will take Tohfah and go with her to
Al-Anka, so she may look upon her!" So they all arose and
repaired to Al-Anka, who abode in the Mountain Kaf. When
she saw them, she drew near to them and saluted them, saying, "O
my ladies, may I not be bereaved of you!" Quoth Wakhimah to
her, "Who is like unto thee, O Anka? Behold, Queen Al-Shahba
is come to thee." So Al-Anka kissed the Queen's feet and lodged
them in her palace; whereupon Tohfah came up to her and fell
to kissing her and saying, "Never saw I seemlier than this semblance." Then she set before them somewhat of food and they
ate and washed their hands; after which the Songstress took
the lute and smote it well; and Al-Anka also played, and they
fell to improvising verses in turns, whilst Tohfah embraced
Al-Anka every moment. Al-Shahba cried, "O my sister, each
kiss is worth a thousand dinars;" and Tohfah replied, "And a
thousand dinars were little therefor;" whereat Al-Anka laughed
and after nighting in her pavilion on the morrow they took leave
of her and went away to Maymun's palace. Here Queen Al-
Shahba farewelled them and taking her troops, returned to her
capital, whilst the kings also went away to their abodes and the
Shaykh Abu al-Tawaif applied himself to diverting Tohfah till
nightfall, when he mounted her on the back of one of the Ifrits
and bade other thirty gather together all that she had gotten of
treasure and raiment, jewels and robes of honour. Then they
flew off, whilst Iblis went with her, and in less than the twinkling of an eye he set her down in her sleepingroom, where he and
those who were with him bade adieu to her and went away.
When Tohfah found herself in her own chamber[1] and on her
couch, her reason fled for joy and it seemed to her as if she had
never stirred thence: then she took the lute and tuned it and
touched it in wondrous fashion and improvised verses and sang.
The Eunuch heard the smiting of the lute within the chamber
and cried, "By Allah, that is the touch of my lady Tohfah!" So

---

[1] "Chamber" is becoming a dangerous word in English. Roars of laughter from the gods
greeted the great actor's declamation, "The bed has not been slept in! Her little chamber
is empty!"

he arose and went, as he were a madman, falling down and rising up, till he came to the Castrato on guard at the gate of the Commander of the Faithful and found him sitting. When his fellow neutral saw him, and he like a madman, slipping down and stumbling up, he asked him, "What aileth thee and what bringeth thee hither at this hour?" The other answered, "Wilt thou not make haste and awaken the Prince of True Believers?" And he fell to crying out at him; whereupon the Caliph awoke and heard them bandying words together and Tohfah's slave crying to the other, "Woe to thee! Awaken the Commander of the Faithful in haste." So quoth he, "O Sawab, what hast thou to say?" and quoth the Chief Eunuch, "O our lord, the Eunuch of Tohfah's lodging hath lost his wits and crieth, 'Awaken the Commander of the Faithful in haste!'" Then said Al-Rashid to one of his slave-girls, "See what may be the matter." Accordingly she hastened to admit the Castrato, who entered at her order; and when he saw the Commander of the Faithful, he salamed not neither kissed ground, but cried in his hurry, "Quick: up with thee! My lady Tohfah sitteth in her chamber, singing a goodly ditty. Come to her in haste and see all that I say to thee! Hasten! She sitteth awaiting thee." The Caliph was amazed at his speech and asked him, "What sayst thou?" He answered, "Didst thou not hear the first of the speech? Tohfah sitteth in the sleeping-chamber, singing and lute-playing. Come thy quickest! Hasten!" Accordingly Al-Rashid sprang up and donned his dress; but he believed not the Eunuch's words and said to him, "Fie upon thee! What is this thou sayst? Hast thou not seen this in a dream?" Quoth the Eunuch, "By Allah, I wot not what thou sayest, and I was not asleep;" and quoth Al-Rashid, "An thy speech be soothfast, it shall be for thy good luck, for I will free thee and give thee a thousand gold pieces; but, an it be untrue and thou have seen this in dream-land, I will crucify thee." The Eunuch said within himself, "O Protector, let me not have seen this in vision!" then he left the Caliph and running to the chamber-door, heard the sound of singing and lute-playing; whereupon he returned to Al-Rashid and said to him, "Go and hearken and see who is asleep." When the Prince of True Believers drew near the door of the sleeping-chamber, he heard the sound of the lute and Tohfah's voice singing; whereat he could not restrain his reason and was like to faint for excess of delight. Then he pulled out the key but his hand refused to draw

the bolt: however, after a while, he took heart and applying himself, opened the door and entered, saying, "Methinks this is none
other than a vision or an imbroglio of dreams." When Tohfah
saw him, she rose and coming to meet him, pressed him to her
breast; and he cried out a cry wherein his sprite was like to
depart and fell down in a fit. She again strained him to her
bosom and sprinkled on him rose-water mingled with musk, and
washed his face, till he came to himself, as he were a drunken man,
and shed tears for the stress of his joy in Tohfah's return to him,
after he had despaired of her returning. Then she took the lute
and smote thereon, after the fashion she had learnt from Shaykh
Iblis, so that Al-Rashid's wit was bewildered for excess of joy and
his understanding was confounded for exultation; after which
she improvised and sang these couplets,

"That I left thee my heart to believe is unlief; * For the life that's in it ne'er
    leaveth; brief,
An thou say 'I went,' saith my heart 'What a fib!' * And I bide 'twixt be-
    lieving and unbelief."

When she had made an end of her verses, Al-Rashid said to her,
"O Tohfah, thine absence was wondrous, yet is thy presence
still more marvellous." She replied, "By Allah, O my lord, thou
sayst sooth;" then, taking his hand, she said to him, "O Commander of the Faithful, see what I have brought with me." So
he looked and spied treasures such as neither words could describe nor registers could document, pearls and jewels and
jacinths and precious stones and unions and gorgeous robes of
honour, adorned with margarites and jewels and purfled with red
gold. There he beheld what he never had beheld all his life long,
not even in idea; and she showed him that which Queen Al-
Shahba had bestowed on her of those carpets, which she had
brought with her, and that throne, the like whereof neither
Kisrà possessed nor Cæsar, and those tables inlaid with pearls and
jewels and those vessels which amazed all who looked on them,
and that crown which was on the head of the circumcised boy,
and those robes of honour, which Queen Al-Shahba and Shaykh
Abu al-Tawaif had doffed and donned upon her, and the trays
wherein were those treasures; brief, she showed him wealth
whose like he had never in his life espied and which the tongue
availeth not to describe and whereat all who looked thereon
were bewildered, Al-Rashid was like to lose his wits for amaze-

ment at this spectacle and was confounded at that he sighted
and witnessed. Then said he to Tohfah, "Come, tell me thy
tale from beginning to end, and let me know all that hath
betided thee, as if I had been present." She answered, "Hearkening and obedience," and acquainting him with all that had betided her first and last, from the time when she first saw the
Shaykh Abu al-Tawaif, how he took her and descended with her
through the side of the Chapel of Ease; and she told him of the
horse she had ridden, till she came to the meadow aforesaid and
described it to him, together with the palace and that was therein
of furniture, and related to him how the Jinn rejoiced in her,
and whatso she had seen of their kings, masculine and feminine,
and of Queen Kamariyah and her sisters and Queen Shu'a'ah,
Regent of the Fourth Sea, and Queen Al-Shahba, Queen of
Queens, and King Al-Shisban, and that which each one of them
had bestowed upon her. Moreover, she recited to him the story
of Maymun the Sworder and described to him his fulsome
favour, which he had not deigned to change, and related to him
that which befel her from the kings of the Jinn, male and female,
and the coming of the Queen of Queens, Al-Shahba, and how she
had loved her and appointed her her vice-reine and how she was
thus become ruler over all the kings of the Jann; and she showed
him the writ of investiture which Queen Al-Shahba had written
her and told him what had betided her with the Ghulish Head,
when it appeared to her in the garden, and how she had despatched it to her palace, beseeching it to bring her news of the
Commander of the Faithful and of what had betided him after
her. Then she described to him the flower-gardens, wherein she
had taken her pleasure, and the Hammam-baths inlaid with
pearls and jewels and told him that which had befallen Maymun
the Sworder, when he bore her off, and how he had slain himself;
in fine, she related to him everything she had seen of wonders and
marvels and that which she had beheld of all kinds and colours
among the Jinn. Then she told him the story of Al-Anka, daughter of Bahram Jur, with Al-Anka, daughter of the wind, and
described to him her dwelling-place and her island, whereupon
quoth Al-Rashid, "O Tohfat al-Sadr,[1] tell me of Al-Anka, daughter of Bahram Jur; is she of the Jinn-kind or of mankind or of the
bird-kind? For this long time have I desired to find one who

---

[1] Choice Gift of the breast (or heart).

should tell me of her." Tohfah replied, " 'Tis well, O Commander of the Faithful. I asked the queen of this and she acquainted me with her case and told me who built her the palace."
Quoth Al-Rashid, "Allah upon thee, tell it me;" and quoth
Tohfah, "I will well," and proceeded to tell him. And he was
amazed at that which he heard from her and what she reported to
him and at that which she had brought back of jewels and jacinths
of various hues and precious stones of many sorts, such as amazed
the beholder and confounded thought and mind. As for this,
Tohfah was the means of the enrichment of the Barmecides and
the Abbasides, and they had endurance in their delight. Then
the Caliph went forth and bade decorate the city: so they deco-
rated it and the drums of glad tidings were beaten; and they
made banquets to the people for whom the tables were spread
seven days. And Tohfah and the Commander of the Faithful
ceased not to enjoy the most delightsome of life and the most
prosperous till there came to them the Destroyer of delights and
the Severer of societies; and this is all that hath come down to
us of their story.

WOMEN'S WILES.[1]

On the following night Dunyazad said to her sister Shahrazad,
"O sister mine, an thou incline not unto sleep, prithee tell us a
tale which shall beguile our watching through the dark hours."
She replied: — With love and gladness.[2] It hath reached me, O
magnificent King, that whilome there was in the city of Baghdad,
a comely youth and a well-bred, fair of favour, tall of stature, and
slender of shape. His name was Alá al-Dín and he was of the
chiefs of the sons of the merchants and had a shop wherein he
sold and bought. One day, as he sat in his shop, there passed by
him a merry girl[3] who raised her head and casting a glance at the

---

[1] From the Calc. Edit. (1814–18), Nights cxcvi.-cc., vol. ii., pp. 367-378. The translation has been compared and collated with that of Langlès (Paris, 1814), appended to his
Edition of the Voyages of Sindbad. The story is exceedingly clever and well deserves
translation.

[2] It is regretable that this formula has not been preserved throughout The Nights: it
affords, I have noticed, a pleasing break to the long course of narrative.

[3] Arab. "Banát-al-hawá," lit. daughters of love, usually meaning an Anonyma, a fille de
joie; but here the girl is of good repute, and the offensive term must be modified to a gay,
frolicsome lass.

young merchant, saw written in a flowing hand on the forehead[1] of his shop door these words, "THERE BE NO CRAFT SAVE MEN'S CRAFT, FORASMUCH AS IT OVERCOMETH WOMEN'S CRAFT." When she beheld this, she was wroth and took counsel with herself, saying, "As my head liveth, there is no help but I show him a marvel-trick of the wiles of women and put to naught this his inscription!" Thereupon she hied her home; and on the morrow she made her ready and donning the finest of dress, adorned herself with the costliest of ornaments and the highest of price and stained her hands with henna. Then she let down her tresses upon her shoulders and went forth, walking with coquettish gait and amorous grace, followed by her slave-girl carrying a parcel, till she came to the young merchant's shop and sitting down under pretext of seeking stuffs, saluted him with the salam and demanded of him somewhat of cloths. So he brought out to her various kinds and she took them and turned them over, talking with him the while. Then said she to him, "Look at the shapeliness of my shape and my semblance! Seest thou in me aught of default?" He replied, "No, O my lady;" and she continued, "Is it lawful in any one that he should slander me and say that I am humpbacked?" Then she discovered to him a part of her bosom, and when he saw her breasts his reason took flight from his head and his heart clave to her and he cried, "Cover it up,[2] so may Allah veil thee!" Quoth she, "Is it fair of any one to decry my charms?" and quoth he, "How shall any decry thy charms, and thou the sun of loveliness?" Then said she, "Hath any the right to say of me that I am lophanded?" and tucking up her sleeves, she showed him forearms as they were crystal; after which she unveiled to him a face, as it were a full moon breaking forth on its fourteenth night, and said to him, "Is it lawful for any to decry me and declare that my face is pitted with smallpox or that I am one-eyed or crop-eared?" and said he, "O my lady, what is it moveth thee to discover unto me that lovely face and those fair limbs, wont to be so jealously veiled and guarded? Tell me the truth of the matter, may I be thy ransom!" And he began to improvise,[3]

---

[1] Arab. "Jabhat," the lintel opposed to the threshold.

[2] Arab. "Ghatti," still the popular term said to a child showing its nakedness, or a lady of pleasure who insults a man by displaying any part of her person.

[3] She is compared with a flashing blade (her face) now drawn from its sheath (her hair) then hidden by it.

"White Fair now drawn from sheath of parted hair, * Then in the blackest
tresses hid from sight,
Flasheth like day irradiating Earth * While round her glooms the murk of
nightliest night."

—— And Shahrazad perceived the dawn of day and ceased to
say her permitted say. Whereupon cried Dunyazad her sister,
"O sister mine, how delectable is this tale and how desirable!"
She replied, saying, "And where is this compared with that which
I will recount to thee next night, Inshallah?"

The Hundred and Ninety-seventh Night.

Now when came the night, quoth Dunyazad to her sister Shahrazad, "O sister mine, an thou incline not unto sleep, prithee
finish thy tale which shall beguile our watching through the dark
hours." She replied: — With love and gladness! It hath
reached me, O auspicious King, that the girl said to the young
merchant, "Know, O my lord, that I am a maid oppressed of my
sire, who speaketh at me and saith to me, Thou art loathly of
looks and semblance and it besitteth not that thou wear rich
raiment; for thou and the slave-girls are like in rank, there is no
distinguishing thee from them. Now he is a richard, having a
mighty great store of money and saith not thus save because he is a
pinchpenny, and grudgeth the spending of a farthing; wherefore
he is loath to marry me, lest he be put to somewhat of expense in
my marriage, albeit Almighty Allah hath been bounteous to him
and he is a man puissant in his time and lacking naught of worldly
weal." The youth asked, "Who is thy father and what is his
condition?" and she answered, "He is the Chief Kazi of the well-
known Supreme Court, under whose hands are all the Kazis who
administer justice in this city." The merchant believed her and
she farewelled him and fared away, leaving in his heart a thousand
regrets, for that the love of her had prevailed over him and he
knew not how he should win to her; wherefore he woned
enamoured, love-distracted, unknowing if he were alive or dead.
As soon as she was gone, he shut up shop and walked straightway to the Court, where he went in to the Chief Kazi and
saluted him. The magistrate returned his salam and treated him
with distinction and seated him by his side. Then said Ala

al-Din to him, "I come to thee seeking thine alliance and desiring the hand of thy noble daughter." Quoth the Kazi, "O my lord merchant, welcome to thee and fair welcome; but indeed my daughter befitteth not the like of thee, neither beseemeth she the goodliness of thy youth and the pleasantness of thy composition and the sweetness of thy speech;" but Ala al-Din replied, "This talk becometh thee not, neither is it seemly in thee; if I be content with her, how should this vex thee?" So the Kazi was satisfied and they came to an accord and concluded the marriage contract at a dower precedent of five purses[1] ready money and a dower contingent of fifteen purses, so it might be hard for him to put her away, her father having given him fair warning, but he would not be warned. Then they wrote out the contract-document and the merchant said, "I desire to go in to her this night." Accordingly they carried her to him in procession that very evening, and he prayed the night-prayer and entered the private chamber prepared for him; but, when he lifted the head-gear from the bride's head and the veil from her face and looked, he saw a foul face and a favour right fulsome; indeed he beheld somewhat whereof may Allah never show thee the like! loathly, dispensing from description, inasmuch as there were reckoned in her all legal defects.[2] So he repented, when repentance availed him naught, and knew that the girl had cheated him. —— And Shahrazad perceived the dawn of day and ceased to say her permitted say. Whereupon cried Dunyazad, her sister, "O sister mine, how delectable is thy story and how sweet!" She replied, saying, "And where is this compared with that which I will recount to thee next night an I be spared and suffered to live by the King, whom Almighty Allah preserve?"

The Hundred and Ninety-eighth Night.

Now whenas came the night, quoth Dunyazad to her sister Shahrazad, "O sister mine, an thou incline not unto sleep, prithee finish thy story which shall beguile our watching through the dark hours, for indeed 'tis a fine tale and a wondrous." She re-

---

[1] The "Muajjalah" or money paid down before consummation was about £25; and the "Mu'ajjalah" or coin to be paid contingent on divorce was about £75. In the Calc. Edit ii. 371, both dowers are £35.

[2] All the blemishes which justify returning a slave to the slave-dealer.

plied: — With love and gladness! It hath reached me, O generous King, that the unhappy merchant carnally knew the loathly bride, sore against the grain, and abode that night troubled in mind, as he were in the prison of Al-Daylam.[1] Hardly had the day dawned when he arose from her side and betaking himself to one of the Hammams, dozed there awhile, after which he made the Ghusl-ablution of ceremonial impurity[2] and donned his everyday dress. Then he went out to the coffee house and drank a cup of coffee; after which he returned to his shop and opening the door, sat down, with concern and chagrin manifest on his countenance. After an hour or so, his friends and intimates among the merchants and people of the market began to come up to him, by ones and twos; to give him joy, and said to him, laughing, "A blessing! a blessing! Where be the sweetmeats? Where be the coffee?[3] 'Twould seem thou hast forgotten us; and nothing made thee oblivious save that the charms of the bride have disordered thy wit and taken thy reason, Allah help thee! We give thee joy, we give thee joy." And they mocked at him whilst he kept silence before them, being like to rend his raiment and shed tears for rage. Then they went away from him, and when it was the hour of noon, up came his mistress, the crafty girl, trailing her skirts and swaying to and fro in her gait, as she were a branch of Ban in a garden of bloom. She was yet more richly dressed and adorned and more striking and cutting[4] in her symmetry and grace than on the previous day, so that she made the passers stop and stand in espalier to gaze upon her. When she came to Ala al-Din's shop, she sat down thereon and said to him, "Blessed be the day to thee, O my lord Ala al-Din! Allah prosper thee and be good to thee and perfect thy gladness and make it a wedding of weal and welfare!" He knitted his brows and frowned in answer to her; then asked her, "Wherein have I failed of thy due, or what have I done to harm thee, that thou shouldst requite me after this fashion?" She answered, "Thou hast been no wise in default; but 'tis yonder inscription written on the door of thy

---

[1] Media: see vol. ii. 94. The "Daylamite prison" was one of many in Baghdad.

[2] See vol. v. 199. I may remark that the practice of bathing after copulation was kept up by both sexes in ancient Rome. The custom may have originated in days when human senses were more acute. I have seen an Arab horse object to be mounted by the master when the latter had not washed after sleeping with a woman.

[3] On the morning after a happy night the bridegroom still offers coffee and Halwá to friends.

[4] i.e. More bewitching.

shop that irketh me and vexeth my heart. An thou have the
courage to change it and write up the contrary thereof, I will
deliver thee from thine evil plight." And he answered, "Thy
requirement is right easy: on my head and eyes!" So saying, he
brought out a sequin[1] and summoning one of his Mamelukes,
said to him, "Get thee to Such-an-one the Scribe and bid him
write us an epigraph, adorned with gold and lapis lazuli, in these
words, There be no craft save women's craft, for indeed
their craft is a mighty craft[2] and overcometh and hum-
bleth the falses of men." And she said to the white slave,
"Fare thee forthright." So he repaired to the Scribe, who wrote
him the scroll, and he brought it to his master, who set it on
the door and asked the damsel, "Is thy heart satisfied?" She
answered, "Yes! Arise forthwith and get thee to the place
before the citadel, where do thou foregather with all the mountebanks and ape-dancers and bear-leaders and drummers and pipers
and bid them come to thee to-morrow early, with their kettle-
drums and flageolets, whilst thou art drinking coffee with thy
father-in-law the Kazi, and congratulate thee and wish thee joy,
saying, 'A blessing, O son of our uncle! Indeed, thou art the vein[3]
of our eye! We rejoice for thee, and if thou be ashamed of us,
verily we pride ourselves upon thee; so, although thou banish us
from thee, know that we will not forsake thee, albeit thou forsake
us.' And do thou fall to throwing dinars and dirhams amongst
them; whereupon the Kazi will question thee, and do thou
answer him, saying, 'My father was an ape-dancer and this is our
original condition; but our Lord opened on us the gate of fortune
and we have gotten us a name amongst the merchants and with
their provost.' Upon this he will say to thee, 'Then thou art an
ape-leader of the tribe of the mountebanks?' and do thou rejoin,
'I may in nowise deny my origin, for the sake of thy daughter and
in her honour.' The Kazi will say, 'It may not be that thou shalt
be given the daughter of a Shaykh who sitteth upon the carpet of
the Law and whose descent is traceable by genealogy to the loins
of the Apostle of Allah,[4] nor is it meet that his daughter be in
the power of a man who is an ape-dancer, a minstrel.' Then do
thou reply, 'Nay, O Efendi, she is my lawful wife, and every hair

---

[1] Arab. "Sharífí" more usually Ashrafi, the Port. Xerafim, a gold coin = 6s.-7s.
[2] The oft-repeated Koranic quotation.
[3] Arab. "'Irk": our phrase is "the apple of the eye."
[4] Meaning that he was a Sayyid or a Sharif.

of her is worth a thousand lives, and I will not put her away though I be given the kingship of the world.' At last be thou persuaded to speak the word of divorce and so shall the marriage be voided and ye be saved each from other." Quoth Ala al-Din, "Right is thy rede," and locking up his shop, betook himself to the place —— And Shahrazad perceived the dawn of day and ceased saying her permitted say. Whereupon cried Dunyazad, her sister, "O sister mine, how goodly is thy story and how sweet!" She replied, saying, "And where is this compared with that which I will recount to thee next night, Inshallah!"

The Hundred and Ninety-ninth Night.

AND whenas came the night, quoth Dunyazad to her sister, "O sister mine, an thou incline not unto sleep, pray finish thy tale which shall beguile our watching through the dark hours." She replied: — With love and gladness! It hath reached me, O generous King, that the young merchant betook himself to the place before the citadel, where he foregathered with the dancers, the drummers and pipers and instructed them how they should do, promising them a mighty fine reward. They received his word with "Hearing and obeying;" and he betook himself on the morrow, after the morning prayer, to the presence of the Judge, who received him with humble courtesy and seated him by his side. Then he addressed him and began questioning him of matters of selling and buying and of the price current of the various commodities which were carried to Baghdad from all quarters, whilst his son-in-law replied to all whereof he was questioned. As they were thus conversing, behold, up came the dancers and drummers with their drums and pipers with their pipes, whilst one of their number preceded them, with a long pennon-like banner in his hand, and played all manner antics with voice and limbs. When they came to the Court-house, the Kazi cried, "I seek refuge with Allah from yonder Satans!" and the young merchant laughed but said naught. Then they entered and saluting his worship the Kazi, kissed Ala al-Din's hands and said, "A blessing on thee, O son of our uncle! Indeed, thou coolest our eyes in whatso thou doest, and we beseech Allah for the enduring greatness of our lord the Kazi, who hath honoured us by admitting thee to his connection and hath allotted to us a portion in his high rank and degree." When the Judge heard this

talk, it bewildered his wit and he was dazed and his face flushed
with rage, and quoth he to his son-in-law, "What words are
these?" Quoth the merchant, "Knowest thou not, O my lord,
that I am of this tribe? Indeed this man is the son of my maternal
uncle and that other the son of my paternal uncle, and if I be
reckoned of the merchants, 'tis but by courtesy!" When the
Kazi heard these words his colour changed —— And Shahrazad
perceived the dawn of day, whereupon cried Dunyazad her sister,
"O sister mine, how delectable is thy story and how desirable!"
She replied, saying, "And where is its first compared with its
last? But I will forthwith relate it to you an I be spared and
suffered to live by the King, whom may Allah the Most High
keep!" Quoth the King within himself, "By the Almighty, I
will not slay her until I hear the end of her tale!"

The Two Hundredth Night.

Now whenas came the night, quoth Dunyazad to her sister, "O
sister mine, an thou incline not unto sleep, prithee finish thy
tale which shall beguile our watching through the dark hours."
She replied: — With love and gladness! It hath reached me,
O auspicious king, that the Kazi's colour changed and he was
troubled and waxed wroth with exceeding wrath and was like
to burst for stress of rage. Then said he to the young merchant,
"Allah forfend that this should last! How shall it be permitted
that the daughter of the Kazi of the Moslems cohabit with a man
of the dancers and vile of origin? By Allah, unless thou repudiate
her forthright, I will bid beat thee and cast thee into prison and
there confine thee till thou die. Had I foreknown that thou
wast of them, I had not suffered thee near me, but had spat in
thy face, for that thou art more ill-omened than a dog or a hog."[1]
Then he kicked him down from his place and commanded him to
divorce; but he said, "Be ruthful to me, O Efendi, for that Allah
is ruthful, and hasten not: I will not divorce my wife, though
thou give me the kingdom of Al-Irak." The Judge was perplexed
and knew that compulsion was not permitted of Holy Law;[2]

---

[1] *i.e.* than a Jew or a Christian. So the Sultan, when appealed to by these religionists,
who were as usual squabbling and fighting, answered, "What matter if the dog tear the
hog or the hog tear the dog"?

[2] The "Sharí'at" forbidding divorce by force.

so he bespake the young merchant fair and said to him, "Veil me,[1] so may Allah veil thee. An thou divorce her not, this dishonour shall cleave to me till the end of time." Then his fury gat the better of his wit and he cried, "An thou divorce her not of thine own will, I will forthright bid strike off thy head and slay myself; Hell-flame but not shame."[2] The merchant bethought himself awhile, then divorced her with a manifest divorce and a public[3] and on this wise he won free from that unwelcome worry. Then he returned to his shop and presently sought in marriage of her father her who had done with him what she did[4] and who was the daughter of the Shaykh of the guild of the blacksmiths. So he took her to wife and they abode each with other and lived the pleasantest of lives and the most delightsome, till the day of death: and praise be to Allah the Lord of the Three Worlds.

NUR AL-DIN ALI OF DAMASCUS AND THE DAMSEL SITT AL-MILAH.[5]

There was one, in days of yore and in ages and times long gone before, a merchant of the merchants of Damascus, by name Abu al-Hasan, who had money and means, slave-blacks and slave-girls, lands and gardens, houses and Hammams in that city; but he was not blessed with boon of child and indeed his age waxed great. So he addressed himself to supplicate[6] Allah Almighty in private and in public and in his bows and his prostrations and at the season of prayer-call, beseeching Him to vouchsafe him, before his decease, a son who should inherit his wealth and possessions. The Lord answered his prayer; his wife conceived and the days of her pregnancy were accomplished and her months and her

---

[1] i.e. protect my honour.

[2] For this proverb see vol. v. 138. I have remarked that "Shame" is not a passion in Europe as in the East; the Western equivalent to the Arab. "Hayá' 'would be the Latin "Pudor."

[3] Arab. "Talákan báinan," here meaning a triple divorce before witnesses, making it irrevocable.

[4] i.e. who had played him that trick.

[5] The Bresl. Edit. (vol. xii. pp. 50-116, Nights dccclviii-dcccclxv.) entitles it "Tale of Abu al-Hasan the Damascene and his son Sídí Nur al-Dín ' Alí." Sídí means simply "my lord," but here becomes part of the name, a practice perpetuated in Zanzibar. See vol. v. 283.

[6] i.e. at the hours of canonical prayers and other suitable times he made an especial orison (du'á) for issue.

nights; and the travail-pangs came upon her and she gave birth to a boy, as he were a slice of Luna. He had not his match for beauty and he put to shame the sun and the resplendent moon; for he had a beaming face and black eyes of Bábilí witchery[1] and aquiline nose and carnelian lips; in fine, he was perfect of attributes, the loveliest of folk of his time, sans dubitation or gainsaying. His father joyed in him with exceeding joy and his heart was solaced and he was at last happy: he made banquets to the folk and he clad the poor and the widows. Presently he named the boy Sídí Nur al-Din Ali and reared him in fondness and delight among the hand-maids and thralls. When he had passed his seventh year, his father put him to school, where he learned the sublime Koran and the arts of writing and reckoning; and when he reached his tenth year, he was taught horseman-ship and archery and to occupy himself with arts and sciences of all kinds, part and parts.[2] He grew up pleasant and polite, winsome and lovesome; a ravishment to all who saw him, and he inclined to companying with brethren and comrades and mixing with merchants and travelled men. From these he heard tell of that which they had witnessed of the wonders of the cities in their wayfare and heard them say, "Whoso journeyeth not en-joyeth naught;[3] especially of the city of Baghdad." So he was concerned with exceeding concern for his lack of travel and dis-closed this to his sire, who said to him, "O my son, why do I see thee chagrined?" Quoth he, "I would fain travel;" and quoth Abu al-Hasan, "O my son, none travelleth save those whose need is urgent and those who are compelled thereto by want. As for thee, O my son, thou enjoyest ample means; so do thou content thyself with that which Allah hath given thee and be bounteous to others, even as He hath been bountiful to thee; and afflict not thyself with the toil and tribulation of travel, for indeed it is said that travel is a piece of Hell-torment."[4] But the youth said, "Needs must I journey to Baghdad, the House of Peace." When his father saw the strength of his resolve to travel he fell in with his wishes and fitted him out with five thousand dinars in cash and the like in merchandise and sent with him two

---

[1] See vol. i. 85, for the traditional witchcraft of Babylonia.

[2] *i.e.* More or less thoroughly.

[3] *i.e.* "He who quitteth not his native country diverteth not himself with a sight of the wonders of the world."

[4] For similar sayings, see vol. ix. 257, and my Pilgrimage i. 127.

serving-men. So the youth fared forth, on the blessing of Allah
Almighty;[1] and his parent went out with him, to take leave of
him, and returned to Damascus. As for Nur al-Din Ali, he
ceased not travelling days and nights till he entered Baghdad
city, and laying up his loads in the Wakálah,[2] made for the Hammam-bath, where he did away that which was upon him of the
soil of the road and doffing his travelling clothes, donned a costly
suit of Yamaní stuff, worth an hundred dinars. Then he loaded
his sleeve with a thousand miskals of gold and sallied forth
a-walking and swaying gracefully as he paced along. His gait
confounded all those who gazed upon him, as he shamed the
branches with his shape and belittled the rose with the redness
of his cheeks and his black eyes of Babilí witchcraft: thou wouldst
deem that whoso looked on him would surely be preserved from
bane and bale;[3] for he was even as saith of him one of his describ-
ers in these couplets: —

"Thy haters and enviers say for jeer * A true say that profits what ears will
hear;
'No boast is his whom the gear adorns; * The boast be his who adorns the
gear!' "

So Sidi Nur al-Din went walking in the highways of the city
and viewing its edifices and its bazars and thoroughfares and
gazing on its folk. Presently, Abú Nowás met him. (Now he
was of those of whom it is said, "They love fair lads," and indeed there is said what is said concerning him.)[4] When he saw
Nur al-Din Ali, he stared at him in amazement and exclaimed,
"Say, I take refuge with the Lord of the Daybreak!" Then he
accosted the youth and saluting him, asked him, "Why do I see
my lord lone and lorn? Meseemeth thou art a stranger and
knowest not this country; so, with leave of my lord, I will put
myself at his service and acquaint him with the streets, for
that I know this city." Nur al-Din answered, "This will be
of thy favour, O nuncle." Abu Nowas rejoiced at this and fared

---

[1] i.e. relying upon, etc.
[2] The Egyptian term for a khan, called in Persia caravanserai (karwán-seráí); and in
Marocco funduk, from the Greek; whence the Spanish "fonda." See vol. i. 92.
[3] Arab. "Baliyah," to jingle with "Bábiliyah."
[4] As a rule whenever this old villain appears in The Nights, it is a signal for an outburst
of obscenity. Here, however, we are quittes pour la peur. See vol. v. 65 for some of his
abominations.

on with him, showing him the streets and bazars, till they came
to the house of a slave-dealer, where he stopped and said to the
youth, "From what city art thou?" "From Damascus," replied
Nur al-Din; and Abu Nowas said, "By Allah, thou art from a
blessed city, even as saith of it the poet in these couplets,

'Now is Damascus a garth adorned * For her seekers, the Houris and Paradise-
　　boys.'"

Sidi Nur al-Din thanked him and the twain entered the mansion
of the slave-merchant. When the people of the house saw Abu
Nowas, they rose to do him reverence, for that which they knew
of his rank with the Commander of the Faithful; and the slave-
dealer himself came up to them with two chairs whereon they
seated themselves. Then the slave-merchant went inside and
returning with a slave-girl, as she were a branch of Ban or a
rattan-cane, clad in a vest of damask silk and tired with a black
and white headdress whose ends fell down over her face, seated
her on a chair of ebony; after which he cried to those who were
present, "I will discover to you a favour as it were a full moon
breaking forth from under a cloud-bank." They replied, "Do
so;" whereupon he unveiled the damsel's face and behold, she
was like the shining sun, with shapely shape and dawn-bright
cheeks and thready waist and heavy hips; brief, she was endowed
with an elegance, whose description is unfound, and was even as
saith of her the poet,[1]

"A fair one, to idolaters if she herself should show, They'd leave their idols
　　and her face for only Lord would know;
And if into the briny sea one day she chanced to spit, Assuredly the salt sea's
　　floods straight fresh and sweet would grow."

The dealer stood at the hand-maid's head and one of the merchants said, "I bid a thousand dinars for her." Quoth another,
"I bid one thousand one hundred dinars;" and a third, "I bid
twelve hundred." Then said a fourth merchant, "Be she mine
for fourteen hundred ducats." And the biddings standing still
at that sum, her owner said, "I will not sell her save with her
consent: an if she desire to be sold, I will sell her to whom she
willeth." The slave-dealer asked him, "What is her name?"

---

[1] The lines are in vols. viii. 279 and ix. 197. I quote Mr. Payne.

Answered the other, "Her name is Sitt al-Miláh;"[1] whereupon
the dealer said to her, "With thy leave, I will sell thee to yonder
merchant for this price of fourteen hundred dinars." Quoth she,
"Come hither to me." So the man-vendor came up to her and
when he drew near, she gave him a kick with her foot and cast
him to the ground, saying, "I will not have that oldster." The
slave-dealer arose, shaking the dust from his dress and head,
and cried, "Who biddeth more of us? Who is desirous?"[2] Said
one of the merchants, "I," and the dealer said to her, "O Sitt
al-Milah, shall I sell thee to this merchant?" She replied, "Come
hither to me;" but he rejoined, "Nay; speak and I will hear
thee from my place, for I will not trust myself to thee nor hold
myself safe when near thee." So she cried, "Indeed I will not
have him." Then the slave-dealer looked at her and seeing her
fix eyes on the young Damascene, for that in very deed he had
fascinated her with his beauty and loveliness, went up to him
and said to him, "O my lord, art thou a looker-on or a buyer?
Tell me." Quoth Nur al-Din, "I am both looker-on and buyer.
Wilt thou sell me yonder slave-girl for sixteen hundred ducats?"
And he pulled out the purse of gold. Hereupon the dealer
returned, dancing and clapping his hands and saying, "So be it,
so be it, or not at all!" Then he came to the damsel and said to
her, "O Sitt al-Milah, shall I sell thee to yonder young Damascene for sixteen hundred dinars?" But she answered, "No," of
bashfulness before her master and the bystanders; whereupon
the people of the bazar and the slave-merchant departed, and Abu
Nowas and Ali Nur al-Din arose and went each his own way,
whilst the damsel returned to her owner's house, full of love for
the young Damascene. When the night darkened on her, she
called him to mind and her heart hung to him and sleep visited
her not; and on this wise she abode days and nights, till she
sickened and abstained from food. So her lord went in to her
and asked her, "O Sitt al-Milah, how findest thou thyself?"
Answered she, "O my lord, dead without chance of deliverance
and I beseech thee to bring me my shroud, so I may look upon it
ere I die." Therewith he went out from her, sore concerned for
her, and betaking himself to the bazar, found a friend of his, a
draper, who had been present on the day when the damsel was

---

[1] Lady or princess of the Fair (ones).
[2] *i.e.* of buying.

cried for sale. Quoth his friend to him, "Why do I see thee troubled?" and quoth he, "Sitt al-Milah is at the point of death and for three days she hath neither eaten nor drunken. I questioned her to-day of her case and she said, 'O my lord, buy me a shroud so I may look upon it ere I die.'" The draper replied, "Methinks naught aileth her but that she is in love with the young Damascene, and I counsel thee to mention his name to her and declare to her that he hath foregathered with thee on her account and is desirous of coming to thy quarters, so he may hear somewhat of her singing. An she say, 'I reck not of him, for there is that to do with me which distracteth me from the Damascene and from other than he,' know that she saith sooth concerning her sickness; but, an she say thee other than this, acquaint me therewith." So the man returned to his lodging and going in to his slave-girl said to her, "O Sitt al-Milah, I went out for thy need and there met me the young man of Damascus, and he saluted me with the salam and saluteth thee; he seeketh to win thy favour and prayed me to admit him as a guest in our dwelling, so thou mayst let him hear somewhat of thy singing." When she heard speak of the young Damascene, she gave a sob, that her soul was like to leave her body, and answered, "He knoweth my plight and how these three days past I have not eaten nor drunken, and I beseech thee, O my lord, by Allah of All-Might, to do thy duty by the stranger and bring him to my lodging and make excuse to him for me." When her master heard this, his reason fled for joy, and he went to his familiar the draper and said to him, "Thou wast right in the matter of the damsel, for that she is in love with the young Damascene; so how shall I manage?" Said the other, "Go to the bazar and when thou seest him, salute him, and say to him, 'Thy departure the other day, without winning thy wish, was grievous to me; so, an thou be still minded to buy the maid, I will abate thee of that which thou badest for her an hundred sequins by way of gaining thy favour; seeing thou be a stranger in our land.' If he say to thee, 'I have no desire for her,' and hold off from thee, be assured that he will not buy; in which case, let me know, so I may devise thee another device; and if he say to thee other than this, conceal not from me aught." So the girl's owner betook himself to the bazar, where he found the youth seated at the upper end of the place where the merchants mostly do meet, selling and buying and taking and giving, as he were the moon on the night of its full, and saluted him.   The young man returned his salam and he said to him, "O my lord, be not offended at the damsel's speech the other day, for her price shall be lowered to the intent that I may secure thy favour.   An thou desire her for naught, I will send her to thee or an thou wouldst have me abate to thee her price, I will well, for I desire nothing save what shall content thee; seeing thou art a stranger in our land and it behoveth us to treat thee hospitably and have consideration for thee."   The youth replied, "By Allah, I will not take her from thee but at an advance on that which I bade thee for her afore; so wilt thou now sell her to me for one thousand and seven hundred dinars?" And the other rejoined, "O my lord, I sell her to thee, may Allah bless thee in her!"   Thereupon the young man went to his quarters and fetching a purse, sent for the girl's owner and weighed out to him the price aforesaid, whilst the draper was between the twain.   Then said he, "Bring her forth;" but the other replied, "She cannot come forth at this present; but be thou my guest the rest of this day and night, and on the morrow thou shalt take thy slave-girl and go in the ward of Allah."   The youth agreed with him on this and he carried him to his house, where, after a little, he bade meat and wine be brought, and they ate and drank.   Then said Nur al-Din to the girl's owner, "I would have thee bring me the damsel, because I bought her not but for the like of this time."   So he arose and going in to the girl, said to her, "O Sitt al-Milah, the young man hath paid down thy price and we have bidden him hither; so he hath come to our quarters and we have entertained him, and he would fain have thee be present with him."   Therewith the damsel rose deftly and doffing her dress, bathed and donned sumptuous apparel and perfumed herself and went out to him, as she were a branch of Ban or a cane of rattan, followed by a black slave-girl, bearing the lute.   When she came to the young man, she saluted him and sat down by his side.   Then she took the lute from the slave-girl and screwing up its pegs,[1] smote thereon in four-and-twenty modes, after which she returned to the first and sang these couplets,

"My joy in this world is to see and sit near thee. * Thy love's my religion;
    thy Union my pleasure.
Attest it these tears when in memory I speer thee, * And unchecked down
    my cheeks pours the flood without measure.

---

[1] Arab. "Azán-hú," = lit. its ears.

By Allah, no rival in love hast to fear thee; * I'm thy slave as I sware, and
    this troth is my treasure.
Be not this our last meeting: by Allah I swear thee * Thy severance to me
    were most bitter displeasure!"

The young man was moved to delight and cried, "By Allah,
thou sayest well, O Sitt al-Milah! Let me hear more." Then
he largessed her with fifty gold pieces and they drank and the
cups made circuit among them; and her seller said to her, "O
Sitt al-Milah, this is the season of farewelling; so let us hear
somewhat thereon." Accordingly she struck the lute and
touching upon that which was in her heart, improvised these
couplets,

"I thole longing, remembrance and sad repine, * Nor my heart can brook woes
    in so lengthened line.
O my lords think not I forget your love; * My case is sure case and cure shows
    no sign.
If creature could swim in the flood of his tears, * I were first to swim in these
    floods of brine:
O Cup-boy withhold cup and bowl from a wretch * Who ne'er ceaseth to
    drink of her tears for wine!
Had I known that parting would do me die, * I had shirked to part, but—'twas
    Fate's design."

Now whilst they were thus enjoying whatso is most delicious of
ease and delight, and indeed the wine was to them sweet and
the talk a treat, behold, there came a knocking at the door. So
the house-master went out, that he might see what might be the
matter, and found ten head of the Caliph's eunuchs at the entrance. When he saw this, he was startled and said, "What is
to do?" "The Commander of the Faithful saluteth thee and
requireth of thee the slave-girl whom thou hast exposed for sale
and whose name is Sitt al-Milah." "By Allah, I have sold her."
"Swear by the head of the Commander of the Faithful that she
is not in thy quarters." The slaver made oath that he had sold
her and that she was no longer at his disposal: yet they paid no
heed to his word and forcing their way into the house, found the
damsel and the young Damascene in the sitting-chamber. So they
laid hands upon her, and the youth said, "This is my slave-girl,
whom I have bought with my money;" but they hearkened not
to his speech and taking her, carried her off to the Prince of True
Believers. Therewith Nur al-Din's pleasure was troubled: he
arose and donned his dress, and his host said, "Whither away

this night, O my lord?" Said he, "I purpose going to my quarters, and tomorrow I will betake myself to the palace of the Commander of the Faithful and demand my slave-girl." The other
replied, "Sleep till the morning, and fare not forth at the like of
this hour." But he rejoined, "Needs must I go;" and the host
said to him, "Go in Allah his safeguard." So the youth went
forth and, drunkenness having got the mastery of his wits, he
threw himself down on a bench before one of the shops. Now
the watchmen were at that hour making their rounds and they
smelt the sweet scent of essences and wine that reeked from him;
so they made for it and suddenly beheld the youth lying on the
bench, without sign of recovering. They poured water upon
him, and he awoke, whereupon they carried him off to the office
of the Chief of Police and he questioned him of his case. He
replied, "O my lord, I am an alien in this town and have been
with one of my friends: I came forth from his house and drunkenness overcame me." The Wali bade carry him to his lodging; but
one of those in attendance upon him, Al-Murádi hight, said to
him, "What wilt thou do? This man is robed in rich raiment
and on his finger is a golden ring, whose bezel is a ruby of great
price; so we will carry him away and slay him and take that
which is upon him of clothes and bring to thee all we get; for
that thou wilt not often see profit the like thereof, especially as
this fellow is a foreigner and there is none to ask after him."[1]
Quoth the Chief, "This wight is a thief and that which he saith
is leasing." Nur al-Din said, "Allah forfend that I should be a
thief!" but the Wali answered, "Thou liest." So they stripped
him of his clothes and taking the seal-ring from his finger, beat
him with a grievous beating, what while he cried out for succour,
but none succoured him, and besought protection, but none
protected him. Then said he to them, "O folk, ye are quit[2] of
that which ye have taken from me; but now restore me to my
lodging." They replied, "Leave this knavery, O rascal! thine
intent is to sue us for thy clothes on the morrow." The youth
cried, "By the truth of the One, the Eternal One, I will not sue
any for them!" but they said, "We find no way to this." And
the Prefect bade them bear him to the Tigris and there slay him

---

[1] Here again the policeman is made a villain of the deepest dye; bad enough to gratify
the intelligence of his deadliest enemy, a lodging-keeper in London.
[2] *i.e.* You are welcome to it and so it becomes lawful (*haláĺ*) to you.

and cast him into the stream. So they dragged him away, while he wept and said the words which shall nowise shame the sayer: "There is no Majesty and there is no Might save in Allah, the Glorious, the Great!" When they came to the Tigris, one of them drew the sword upon him and Al-Muradi said to the sworder, "Smite off his head;" but one of them, hight Ahmad, cried, "O folk, deal softly with this poor wretch and slay him not unjustly and wickedly, for I stand in fear of Allah Almighty, lest He burn me with his fire." Quoth Al-Muradi, "A truce to this talk!" and quoth the Ahmad aforesaid, "An ye do with him aught, I will acquaint the Commander of the Faithful." They asked, "How, then, shall we do with him?" and he answered, "Let us deposit him in prison and I will be answerable to you for his provision; so shall we be quit of his blood, for indeed he is a wronged man." Accordingly they agreed to this and taking him up cast him into the Prison of Blood,[1] and then went their ways. So far as regards them; but returning to the damsel, they carried her to the Commander of the Faithful and she pleased him; so he assigned her a chamber of the chambers of choice. She tarried in the palace, neither eating nor drinking, and weeping sans surcease night and day, till, one night, the Caliph sent for her to his sitting-hall and said to her, "O Sitt al-Milah, be of good cheer and keep thine eyes cool of tear, for I will make thy rank higher than any of the concubines and thou shalt see that which shall rejoice thee." She kissed ground and wept; whereupon the Prince of True Believers called for her lute and bade her sing: so in accordance with that which was in her heart, she sang these improvised couplets,

"By the sheen of thy soul and the sheen of thy smile,[2] * Say, moan'st thou for
    doubt or is't ring-dove's moan?
How many have died who by love were slain! * Fails my patience but blaming
    my blamers wone."

Now when she had made an end of her song, she threw the lute from her hand and wept till she fainted away, whereupon the Caliph bade carry her to her chamber. But he was fascinated by her and loved her with exceeding love; so, after a while, he again commanded to bring her in to the presence, and when she came,

---

[1] Arab. "Sijn al-Dam," the Carcere duro inasprito (to speak Triestine), where men convicted or even accused of bloodshed were confined.

[2] Arab. "Mabásim"; plur. of Mabsim, a smiling mouth which shows the foreteeth.

he ordered her to sing. Accordingly, she took the lute and chanted to it that which was in her heart and improvised these couplets,

"Have I patience and strength to support this despair? * Ah, how couldst thou
　　purpose afar to fare?
Thou art swayed by the spy to my cark and care: * No marvel an branchlet
　　sway here and there![1]
With unbearable load thou wouldst load me, still * Thou loadest with love
　　which I theewards bear."

Then she cast the lute from her hand and fainted away; so she was carried to her sleeping-chamber and indeed passion grew upon her. After a long while, the Prince of True Believers sent for her a third time and commanded her to sing. So she took the lute and chanted these couplets,

"O of piebald wild ye dunes sandy and drear, * Shall the teenful lover 'scape
　　teen and tear?
Shall ye see me joined with a lover, who * Still flies or shall meet we in joyful
　　cheer?
O hail to the fawn with the Houri eye, * Like sun or moon on horizon clear!
He saith to lovers, 'What look ye on?' * And to stony hearts, 'Say, what love
　　ye dear?'[2]
I pray to Him who departed us * With severance-doom, 'Be our union near!' "

When she had made an end of her verse, the Commander of the Faithful said to her, "O damsel, thou art in love." She replied, "Yes;" and he asked, "With whom?" Answered she, "With my lord and sovran of my tenderness, for whom my love is as the love of the earth for rain, or as the desire of the female for the male; and indeed the love of him is mingled with my flesh and my blood and hath entered into the channels of my bones. O Prince of True Believers, whenever I call him to mind my vitals are consumed, for that I have not yet won my wish of him, and but that I fear to die, without seeing him, I had assuredly slain myself." Thereupon quoth he, "Art thou in my presence and durst bespeak me with the like of these words? Forsure I will gar thee forget thy lord." Then he bade take her away; so she was carried to her pavilion and he sent her a concubine, with a casket wherein were three thousand ducats and a collar of gold set with seed-pearls and great unions, and jewels, worth other

---

[1] The branchlet, as usual, is the youth's slender form.
[2] *Subaudi*, "An ye disdain my love."

three thousand, saying to her, "The slave-girl and that which is with her are a gift from me to thee." When she heard this, she cried, "Allah forfend that I be consoled for the love of my lord and my master, though with an earth-full of gold!" And she improvised and recited these couplets,

"By his life I swear, by his life I pray; * For him fire I'd enter unful dismay!
'Console thee (cry they) with another fere * Thou lovest!' and I, 'By 's life, nay, NAY!'
He's moon whom beauty and grace array; * From whose cheeks and brow shineth light of day."

Then the Commander of the Faithful summoned her to his presence a fourth time and said, "O Sitt al-Milah, sing." So she recited and sang these couplets,

"The lover's heart by his beloved is oft disheartenèd * And by the hand of sickness eke his sprite dispiritèd,
One asked, 'What is the taste of love?'[1] and I to him replied, * 'Love is a sweet at first but oft in fine unsweetenèd.'
I am the thrall of Love who keeps the troth of love to them[2] * But oft they proved themselves 'Urkúb[3] in pact with me they made.
What in their camp remains? They bound their loads and fared away; * To other feres the veilèd Fairs in curtained litters sped;
At every station the beloved showed all of Joseph's charms: * The lover wone with Jacob's woe in every shift of stead."

When she had made an end of her song, she threw the lute from her hand and wept herself a-swoon. So they sprinkled on her musk-mingled rose-water and willow-flower water; and when she came to her senses, Al-Rashid said to her, "O Sitt al-Milah, this is not just dealing in thee. We love thee and thou lovest another." She replied, "O Commander of the Faithful, there is no help for it." Thereupon he was wroth with her and cried,"By the virtue of Hamzah[4] and 'Akíl[5] and Mohammed, Prince of the Apostles, an thou name in my presence one other than I, I will assuredly order strike off thy head!" Then he bade return her to her chamber, whilst she wept and recited these couplets,

---

[1] In the text "sleep."
[2] "Them" and "him" for "her."
[3] 'Urkúb, a Jew of Yathrib or Khaybar, immortalised in the A.P. (i. 454) as "more promise-breaking than 'Urkúb."
[4] Uncle of Mohammed. See vol. viii. 172.
[5] First cousin of Mohammed. See ib.

" 'Oh brave!' I'd cry an I my death could view; * My death were better than
    these griefs to rue,
Did sabre hew me limb by limb; this were * Naught to affright a lover leal-
    true."

Then the Caliph went in to the Lady Zubaydah, complexion-
altered with anger, and she noted this in him and said to him,
"How cometh it that I see the Commander of the Faithful
changed of colour?" He replied, "O daughter of my uncle, I
have a beautiful slave-girl, who reciteth verses by rote and telleth
various tales, and she hath taken my whole heart; but she loveth
other than myself and declareth that she affecteth her former lord;
so I have sworn a great oath that, if she come again to my sitting-
hall and sing for other than for me, I will assuredly shorten her
highest part by a span."[1] Quoth Zubaydah, "Let the Commander
of the Faithful favour me by presenting her, so I may look on her
and hear her singing." Accordingly he bade fetch her and she
came, upon which the Lady Zubaydah withdrew behind the curtain,[2] where the damsel saw her not, and Al-Rashid said to her,
"Sing to us." So she took the lute and tuning it, recited these
couplets,

"O my lord! since the day when I lost your sight, * My life was ungladdened,
    my heart full of teen;
The memory of you kills me every night; * And by all the worlds is my trace
    unseen;
All for love of a Fawn who hath snared my sprite * By his love and his brow
    as the morning sheen.
Like a left hand parted from brother right * I became by parting thro' Fortune's
    spleen.
On the brow of him Beauty deigned indite * 'Blest be Allah, whom best of
    Creators I ween!'
And Him I pray, who could disunite * To re-unite us. Then cry 'Ameen!' "[3]

When Al-Rashid heard the end of this, he waxed exceeding
wroth and said, "May Allah not reunite you twain in gladness!"
Then he summoned the headsman, and when he presented himself, he said to him, "Strike off the head of this accursed slave-
girl." So Masrur took her by the hand and led her away; but,
when she came to the door, she turned and said to the Caliph,

---

[1] This threat of "'Orf with her 'cad" shows the Caliph's lordliness.
[2] Arab. "Al-Bashkhánah."
[3] i.e. Amen. See vol. ix. 131.

"O Commander of the Faithful, I conjure thee, by thy fathers and forefathers, behead me not until thou give ear to that I shall say!" Then she improvised and recited these couplets,

"Emir of Justice, be to lieges kind * For Justice ever guides thy generous mind;
And, oh, who blamest love to him inclining! * Are lovers blamed for lâches undesigned?
By Him who gave thee rule, deign spare my life * For rule on earth He hath to thee assigned."

Then Masrur carried her to the other end of the sitting-hall and bound her eyes and making her sit, stood awaiting a second order: whereupon quoth the Lady Zubaydah, "O Prince of True Believers, with thy permission, wilt thou not vouchsafe this damsel a portion of thy clemency? An thou slay her, 'twere injustice." Quoth he, "What is to be done with her?" and quoth she, "Forbear to slay her and send for her lord. If he be as she describeth him in beauty and loveliness, she is excused, and if he be not on this wise then kill her, and this shall be thy plea against her."[1] Al-Rashid replied, "No harm in this rede;" and caused return the damsel to her chamber, saying to her, "The Lady Zubaydah saith thus and thus." She rejoined, "God requite her for me with good! Indeed, thou dealest equitably, O Commander of the Faithful, in this judgment." And he retorted, "Go now to thy place, and to-morrow we will bid them bring thy lord." So she kissed ground and recited these couplets,

' I indeed will well for whom love I will: * Let chider chide and let blamer blame:
All lives must die at fixt tide and term * But I must die ere my life-term came:
Then Oh whose love hath afflicted me * Well I will but thy presence in haste I claim."

Then she arose and returned to her chamber. Now on the morrow, the Commander of the Faithful sat in his hall of audience and his Wazir Ja'afar bin Yahya the Barmecide came in to him; whereupon he called to him, saying, "I would have thee bring me a youth who is lately come to Baghdad, hight Sidi Nur al-Din Ali the Damascene." Quoth Ja'afar, "Hearing and obeying," and going forth in quest of the youth, sent to the bazars and Wakalahs and Khans for three successive days, but discovered

---

[1] When asked, on Doomsday, his justification for having slain her.

no trace of him, neither happened upon the place of him. So on the fourth day he presented himself before the Caliph and said to him, "O our lord, I have sought him these three days, but have not found him." Said Al-Rashid, "Make ready letters to Damascus. Peradventure he hath returned to his own land." Accordingly Ja'afar wrote a letter and despatched it by a dromedary-courier to the Damascus-city; and they sought him there and found him not. Meanwhile, news was brought that Khorasan had been conquered;[1] whereupon Al-Rashid rejoiced and bade decorate Baghdad and release all in the gaol, giving each of them a ducat and a dress. So Ja'afar applied himself to the adornment of the city and bade his brother Al-Fazl ride to the prison and robe and set free the prisoners. Al-Fazl did as his brother commanded and released all save the young Damascene, who abode still in the Prison of Blood, saying, "There is no Majesty, and there is no Might save in Allah, the Glorious, the Great! Verily, we are God's and to Him are we returning." Then quoth Al-Fazl to the gaoler, "Is there any left in the prison?" Quoth he, "No," and Al-Fazl was about to depart, when Nur al-Din called out to him from within the prison, saying, "O our lord, tarry awhile, for there remaineth none in the prison other than I and indeed I am wronged. This is a day of pardon and there is no disputing concerning it." Al-Fazl bade release him; so they set him free and he gave him a dress and a ducat. Thereupon the young man went out, bewildered and unknowing whither he should wend, for that he had sojourned in the gaol a year or so and indeed his condition was changed and his favour fouled, and he abode walking and turning round, lest Al-Muradi come upon him and cast him into another calamity. When Al-Muradi learnt his release, he betook himself to the Wali and said, "O our lord, we are not assured of our lives from that youth, because he hath been freed from prison and we fear lest he complain of us." Quoth the Chief, "How shall we do?" and quoth Al-Muradi, "I will cast him into a calamity for thee." Then he ceased not to follow the Damascene from place to place till he came up with him in a narrow stead and cul-de-sac; whereupon he accosted him and casting a cord about his neck, cried out, "A thief!" The folk flocked to him from all sides and fell to beating and abusing

---

[1] Khorasan which included our Afghanistan, turbulent then as now, was in a chronic state of rebellion during the latter part of Al-Rashid's reign.

Nur al-Din,[1] whilst he cried out for aidance but none aided him, and Al-Muradi kept saying to him, "But yesterday the Commander of the Faithful released thee and to-day thou robbest!" So the hearts of the mob were hardened against him and again Al-Muradi carried him to the Chief of Police, who bade hew off his hand. Accordingly, the hangman took him and bringing out the knife, proceeded to cut off his hand, while Al-Muradi said to him, "Cut and sever the bone and fry[2] not in oil the stump for him, so he may lose all his blood and we be at rest from him." But Ahmad, he who had before been the cause of his deliverance, sprang up to him and cried, "O folk, fear Allah in your action with this youth, for that I know his affair, first and last, and he is clear of offence and guiltless: he is of the lords of houses,[3] and unless ye desist from him, I will go up to the Commander of the Faithful and acquaint him with the case from beginning to end and that the youth is innocent of sin or crime." Quoth Al-Muradi, "Indeed, we are not assured from his mischief;" and quoth Ahmad, "Set him free and commit him to me and I will warrant you against his doings, for ye shall never see him again after this." So they delivered Nur al-Din to him and he took him from their hands and said to him, "O youth, have ruth on thyself, for indeed thou hast fallen into the hands of these folk twice and if they prevail over thee a third time, they will make an end of thee; and I in doing thus with thee, aim at reward for thee and recompense in Heaven and answer of prayer."[4] So Nur al-Din fell to kissing his hand and blessing him said, "Know that I am a stranger in this your city and the completion of kindness is better than its commencement; wherefore I pray thee of thy favour that thou make perfect to me thy good offices and generosity and bring me to the city-gate. So will thy beneficence be accomplished unto me and may God Almighty requite thee for me with good!" Ahmad replied, "No harm shall betide thee:

---

[1] The brutality of a Moslem mob on such occasions is phenomenal: no fellow-feeling makes them decently kind. And so at executions even women will take an active part in insulting and tormenting the criminal, tearing his hair, spitting in his face and so forth. It is the instinctive brutality with which wild beasts and birds tear to pieces a wounded companion.

[2] The popular way of stopping hæmorrhage by plunging the stump into burning oil which continued even in Europe till Ambrose Paré taught men to take up the arteries.

[3] i.e. folk of good family.

[4] i.e. the result of thy fervent prayers to Allah for me.

go; I will bear thee company till thou come to thy place of
safety."   And he left him not till he brought him to the city-gate
and said to him, "O youth, go in Allah's guard and return not to
the city, for, an they fall in with thee again, they will make an
end of thee."   Nur al-Din kissed his hand and going forth the city,
gave not over walking till he came to a mosque that stood in one
of the suburbs of Baghdad and entered therein with the night.
Now he had with him naught wherewith he might cover himself;
so he wrapped himself up in one of the mats of the mosque and
thus abode till dawn, when the Muezzins came and finding him
seated in such case, said to him, "O youth, what is this plight?"
Said he, "I cast myself on your protection, imploring this defence
from a company of folk who seek to slay me unjustly and wrongously, without cause."   And one of the Muezzins said, "I will
protect thee; so be of good cheer and keep thine eyes cool of
tear."   Then he brought him old clothes and covered him therewith; he also set before him somewhat of victual and seeing upon
him signs of fine breeding, said to him, "O my son, I grow old
and desiring help from thee, I will do away thy necessity."   Nur
al-Din replied, "To hear is to obey;" and abode with the old
man, who rested and took his ease, while the youth did his service
in the mosque, celebrating the praises of Allah and calling the
Faithful to prayer and lighting the lamps and filling the spout-
pots[1] and sweeping and cleaning out the place of worship. On this-
wise it befel the young Damascene; but as regards Sitt al-Milah,
the Lady Zubaydah, the wife of the Commander of the Faithful,
made a banquet in her palace and assembled her slave-girls. And
the damsel came, weeping-eyed and heavy-hearted, and those
present blamed her for this, whereupon she recited these couplets,

"Ye blame the mourner who weeps his woe; * Needs must the mourner sing,
     weeping sore;
An I see not some happy day I'll weep * Brine-tears till followed by gouts of
     gore."

When she had made an end of her verses, the Lady Zubaydah
bade each damsel sing a song, till the turn came round to
Sitt al-Milah, whereupon she took the lute and tuning it, carolled

---

[1] Arab. "Al-Abárík" plur. of Ibrík, an ewer containing water for the Wuzu-ablution.
I have already explained that a Moslem wishing to be ceremonially pure, cannot wash as
Europeans do, in a basin whose contents are fouled by the first touch.

thereto four-and-twenty carols in four-and-twenty modes; then she returned to the first and sang these couplets,

"The World hath shot me with all her shafts * Departing friends parting-grief
    t' aby:
So in heart the burn of all hearts I bear * And in eyes the tear-drops of every
    eye."

When she had made an end of her song, she wept till she garred the bystanders weep and the Lady Zubaydah condoled with her and said to her, "Allah upon thee, O Sitt al-Milah, sing us somewhat, so we may hearken to thee." The damsel replied, "Hearing and obeying," and sang these couplets,

"People of passion, assemble ye! * This day be the day of our agony:
The Raven o' severance croaks at our doors; * Our raven which nigh to us
    aye see we.
The friends we love have appointed us * The grievousest parting-dule to dree.
Rise, by your lives, and let all at once * Fare to seek our friends where their
    sight we see."

Then she threw the lute from her hand and shed tears till she drew tears from the Lady Zubaydah who said to her, "O Sitt al-Milah, he whom thou lovest methinks is not in this world, for the Commander of the Faithful hath sought him in every place, but hath not found him." Whereupon the damsel arose and kissing the Princess's hands, said to her, "O my lady, an thou wouldst have him found, I have this night a request to make whereby thou mayst win my need with the Caliph." Quoth the Lady, "And what is it?" and quoth Sitt al-Milah, " 'Tis that thou get me leave to fare forth by myself and go round about in quest of him three days, for the adage saith, Whoso keeneth for herself is not like whoso is hired to keen![1] An if I find him, I will bring him before the Commander of the Faithful, so he may do with us what he will, and if I find him not, I shall be cut off from hope of him and the heat of that which is with me will be cooled." Quoth the Lady Zubaydah, "I will not get thee leave from him but for a whole month; so be of good cheer and eyes cool and clear." Whereat Sitt al-Milah rejoiced and rising, kissed ground before her once more and went away to her own place, and right

---

[1] Arab. "Náihah," the præfica or myriologist. See vol. i. 311. The proverb means, "If you want a thing done, do it yourself."

glad was she. As for Zubaydah, she went in to the Caliph and
talked with him awhile; then she fell to kissing him between the
eyes and on his hands and asked him for that which she had
promised to Sitt al-Milah, saying, "O Commander of the Faithful,
I doubt me her lord is not found in this world; but, an she go
about seeking him and find him not, her hopes will be cut off and
her mind will be set at rest and she will sport and laugh; and
indeed while she nourisheth hope, she will never take the right
direction." And she ceased not cajoling him till he gave Sitt al-
Milah leave to fare forth and make search for her lord a month's
space and ordered a riding-mule and an eunuch to attend her and
bade the privy purse give her all she needed, were it a thousand
dirhams a day or even more. So the Lady Zubaydah arose and
returning to her palace bade summon Sitt al-Milah and, as soon
as she came, acquainted her with that which had passed; whereupon she kissed her hand and thanked her and called down blessings on her. Then she took leave of the Princess and veiling her
face with a mask,[1] disguised herself;[2] after which she mounted
the she-mule and sallying forth, went round about seeking her
lord in the highways of Baghdad three days' space, but happed
on no tidings of him; and on the fourth day, she rode forth without the city. Now it was the noon-hour and fierce was the heat,
and she was aweary and thirst came upon her. Presently, she
reached the mosque of the Shaykh who had lodged the young
Damascene, and dismounting at the door, said to the old Muezzin,
"O Shaykh, hast thou a draught of cold water? Verily, I am
overcome with heat and thirst." Said he, " 'Tis with me in my
house." So he carried her up into his lodging and spreading her
a carpet, seated her; after which he brought her cold water and
she drank and said to her eunuch, "Go thy ways with the mule
and to-morrow come back to me here." Accordingly he went
away and she slept and rested herself. When she awoke, she
asked the old man, "O Shaykh, hast thou aught of food?" and he
answered, "O my lady, I have bread and olives." Quoth she,
"That be food which befitteth only the like of thee. As for me,
I will have naught save roast lamb and soups and reddened fowls

---

[1] Arab. "Burka'," the face veil of Egypt, Syria, and Arabia with two holes for the eyes,
and the end hanging to the waist, a great contrast with the "Lithám" or coquettish fold
of transparent muslin affected by modest women in Stambul.

[2] i.e. donned petticoat-trousers and walking boots other than those she was wont to wear.

right fat and ducks farcis with all manner stuffing of pistachio-nuts and sugar." Quoth the Muezzin, "O my lady, I have never heard of this chapter¹ in the Koran, nor was it revealed to our lord Mohammed, whom Allah save and assain!"² She laughed and said, "O Shaykh, the matter is even as thou sayest; but bring me pen-case and paper." So he brought her what she sought and she wrote a note and gave it to him, together with a seal-ring from her finger, saying, "Go into the city and enquire for Such-an-one the Shroff and give him this my note." Accordingly the oldster betook himself to the city, as she bade him, and asked for the money-changer, to whom they directed him. So he gave him ring and writ, seeing which, he kissed the letter and breaking it open, read it and apprehended its contents. Then he repaired to the bazar and buying all that she bade him, laid it in a porter's crate and made him go with the Shaykh. The old man took the Hammál and went with him to the mosque, where he relieved him of his burden and carried the rich viands in to Sitt al-Milah. She seated him by her side and they ate, he and she, of those dainty cates, till they were satisfied, when the Shaykh rose and removed the food from before her. She passed that night in his lodging and when she got up in the morning, she said to him, "O elder, may I not lack thy kind offices for the breakfast! Go to the Shroff and fetch me from him the like of yesterday's food." So he arose and betaking himself to the money-changer, acquainted him with that which she had bidden him. The Shroff brought him all she required and set it on the heads of Hammals; and the Shaykh took them and returned with them to the damsel, when she sat down with him and they ate their sufficiency, after which he removed the rest of the meats. Then she took the fruits and the flowers and setting them over against herself, wrought them into rings and knots and writs, whilst the Shaykh looked on at a thing whose like he had never in his life seen and rejoiced in the sight. Presently said she to him, "O elder, I would fain drink." So he arose and brought her a gugglet of water; but she cried to

---

¹ "Surah" (Koranic chapter) may be a clerical error for "Súrah" (with a Sád) = sort, fashion (of food).

² This is solemn religious chaff; the Shaykh had doubtless often dipped his hand abroad in such dishes; but like a good Moslem, he contented himself at home with wheaten scones and olives, a kind of sacramental food like bread and wine in southern Europe. But his retort would be acceptable to the True Believer who, the strictest of conservatives, prides himself on imitating in all points, the sayings and doings of the Apostle.

him, "Who said to thee, Fetch that?" Quoth he, "Saidst thou not to me, I would fain drink?" and quoth she, "I want not this; nay, I want wine, the solace of the soul, so haply, O Shaykh, I may refresh myself therewith." Exclaimed the old man, "Allah forfend that strong drink be drunk in my house, and I a stranger in the land and a Muezzin and an Imam, who leadeth the True Believers in prayer, and a servant of the House of the Lord of the three Worlds!" "Why wilt thou forbid me to drink thereof in thy house?" "Because 'tis unlawful." "O elder, Allah hath for-bidden only the eating of blood and carrion[1] and hog's flesh: tell me, are grapes and honey lawful or unlawful?" "They are lawful." "This is the juice of grapes and the water of honey." "Leave this thy talk, for thou shalt never drink wine in my house." "O Shaykh, people eat and drink and enjoy themselves and we are of the number of the folk and Allah is indulgent and merciful." [2] "This is a thing that may not be." "Hast thou not heard what the poet saith?" And she recited these couplets,

"Cease thou to hear, O Sim'án-son,[3] aught save the say of me; * How bitter
   'twas to quit the monks and fly the monast'ry!
When, on the Fête of Palms there stood, amid the hallowed fane,[4] * A pretty
   Fawn whose lovely pride garred me sore wrong to dree.
May Allah bless the night we spent when he to us was third, * While Moslem,
   Jew, and Nazarene all sported fain and free.
Quoth he, from out whose locks appeared the gleaming of the morn, * 'Sweet
   is the wine and sweet the flowers that joy us comrades three.
The garden of the garths of Khuld where roll and rail amain, * Rivulets 'neath
   the myrtle shade and Bán's fair branchery;
And birds make carol on the boughs and sing in blithest lay, * Yea, this indeed
   is life, but, ah! how soon it fades away.'"

She then asked him, "O Shaykh, an Moslems and Jews and Nazarenes drink wine, who are we that we should reject it?"

---

[1] *i.e.* animals that died without being ceremonially killed.

[2] Koran ii. 168. This is from the Chapter of the Cow where "that which dieth of itself (carrion), blood, pork, and that over which other name but that of Allah (*i.e.* idols) hath been invoked" are forbidden. But the verset humanely concludes: "Whoso, however, shall eat them by constraint, without desire, or as a transgressor, then no sin shall be upon him."

[3] *i.e.* son of Simeon = a Christian.

[4] Arab. and Heb. "Haykal," suggesting the idea of large space, a temple, a sanctuary, a palace which bear a suspicious likeness to the Accadian É-kal or Great House == the old Egyptian Perao (Pharaoh?), and the Japanese "Mikado."

Answered he, "By Allah, O my lady, spare thy pains, for this be a thing whereto I will not hearken." When she knew that he would not consent to her desire, she said to him, "O Shaykh, I am of the slave-girls of the Commander of the Faithful and the food waxeth heavy on me and if I drink not, I shall die of in-digestion, nor wilt thou be assured against the issue of my case.[1] As for me, I acquit myself of blame towards thee, for that I have bidden thee beware of the wrath of the Commander of the Faithful, after making myself known to thee." When the Shaykh heard her words and that wherewith she threatened him, he sprang up and went out, perplexed and unknowing what he should do, and there met him a Jewish man, which was his neighbour, and said to him, "How cometh it that I see thee, O Shaykh, strait of breast? Eke, I hear in thy house a noise of talk, such as I am unwont to hear with thee." Quoth the Muezzin, " 'Tis of a damsel who declareth that she is of the slave-girls of the Commander of the Faithful, Harun al-Rashid; and she hath eaten meat and now would drink wine in my house, but I forbade her. However she asserteth that unless she drink thereof, she will die, and indeed I am bewildered concerning my case." Answered the Jew, "Know, O my neighbour, that the slave-girls of the Commander of the Faithful are used to drink wine, and when they eat and drink not, they die; and I fear lest happen some mishap to her, when thou wouldst not be safe from the Caliph's fury." The Shaykh asked, "What is to be done?" and the Jew answered, "I have old wine that will suit her." Quoth the Shaykh, "By the right of neighbourship, deliver me from this descent[2] of calamity and let me have that which is with thee!" Quoth the Jew, "Bismillah, in the name of Allah," and passing to his quarters, brought out a glass flask of wine, where-with the Shaykh returned to Sitt al-Milah. This pleased her and she cried to him, "Whence hadst thou this?" He replied, "I got it from the Jew, my neighbour: I set forth to him my case with thee and he gave me this." Thereupon Sitt al-Milah filled a cup and emptied it; after which she drank a second and a third. Then she crowned the cup a fourth time and handed it to the

---

[1] Wine, carrion and pork being lawful to the Moslem if used to save life. The former is also the sovereignest thing for inward troubles, flatulence, indigestion, etc. See vol. v. 2, 24.

[2] Arab. "Názilah," i.e., a curse coming down from Heaven.

Shaykh, but he would not accept it from her. However, she conjured him, by her own head and that of the Prince of True Believers, that he take the cup from her, till he received it from her hand and kissed it and would have set it down; but she sware him by her life to smell it. Accordingly he smelt it and she said to him, "How deemest thou?" Said he, "I find its smell is sweet;" and she conjured him by the Caliph's life to taste thereof. So he put it to his mouth and she rose to him and made him drink; whereupon quoth he, "O Princess of the Fair,[1] this is none other than good." Quoth she, "So deem I: hath not our Lord promised us wine in Paradise?" He answered, "Yes! The Most High saith, 'And rivers of wine, delicious to the drinkers.'[2] And we will drink it in this world and in the next world." She laughed and emptying the cup, gave him to drink, and he said, "O Princess of the Fair, indeed thou art excusable in thy love for this." Then he hent in hand from her another and another, till he became drunken and his talk waxed great and his prattle. The folk of the quarter heard him and assembled under the window; and when the Shaykh was ware of them, he opened the window and said to them, "Are ye not ashamed, O pimps? Every one in his own house doth whatso he willeth and none hindereth him; but we drink one single day and ye assemble and come, panders that ye are! To-day, wine, and to-morrow business;[3] and from hour to hour cometh relief." So they laughed together and dispersed. Then the girl drank till she was drunken, when she called to mind her lord and wept, and the Shaykh said to her, "What maketh thee weep, O my lady?" Said she, "O elder, I am a lover and a separated." He cried, "O my lady, what is this love?" Cried she, "And thou, hast thou never been in love?" He replied, "By Allah, O my lady, never in all my life heard I of this thing, nor have I ever known it! Is it of the sons of Adam or of the Jinn?" She laughed and said, "Verily, thou art even as those of whom the poet speaketh, in these couplets,

---

[1] Here and below, a translation of her name.

[2] "A picture of Paradise which is promised to the God-fearing! Therein are rivers of water which taint not; and rivers of milk whose taste changeth not; and rivers of wine, etc." — Koran xlvii. 16.

[3] Let us have wine and women, mirth and laughter,
Sermons and soda-water the day after.

Don Juan ii. 178.

"How oft shall they admonish and ye shun this nourishment; * When e'en the
    shepherd's bidding is obeyèd by his flocks?
I see you like in shape and form to creatures whom we term * Mankind, but
    in your acts and deeds you are a sort of ox "[1]

The Shaykh laughed at her speech and her verses pleased him.
Then cried she to him, "I desire of thee a lute." So he arose and
brought her a bit of fuel.[2] Quoth she, "What is that?" and
quoth he "Didst thou not say: Bring me fuel?" Said she, "I do
not want this," and said he, "What then is it that is hight fuel,
other than this?" She laughed and replied, "The lute is an instrument of music, whereunto I sing." Asked he, "Where is this
thing found and of whom shall I get it for thee?" and answered
she, "Of him who gave thee the wine." So he arose and betaking
himself to his neighbour the Jew, said to him "Thou favouredst
us before with the wine; so now complete thy favours and look
me out a thing hight lute, which be an instrument for singing;
for she seeketh this of me and I know it not." Replied the Jew,
"Hearkening and obedience," and going into his house, brought
him a lute. The old man carried it to Sitt al-Milah, whilst the
Jew took his drink and sat by a window adjoining the Shaykh's
house, so he might hear the singing. The damsel rejoiced, when
the old man returned to her with the lute, and taking it from him,
tuned its strings and sang these couplets,

"Remains not, after you are gone, or trace of you or sign, * But hope to see
    this parting end and break its lengthy line:
You went and by your wending made the whole world desolate; * And none
    may stand this day in stead to fill the yearning eyne.
Indeed, you've burdened weakling me, by strength and force of you * With
    load no hill hath power t'upheave nor yet the plain low li'en:
And I, whenever fain I scent the breeze your land o'erbreathes, * Lose all my
    wits as though they were bemused with heady wine.
O folk no light affair is Love for lover woe to dree * Nor easy 'tis to satisfy its
    sorrow and repine.
I've wandered East and West to hap upon your trace, and when * Spring-
    camps I find the dwellers cry, 'They've marched, those friends o' thine!'
Never accustomed me to part these intimates I love; * Nay, when I left them
    all were wont new meetings to design."

---

[1] The ox (Bakar) and the bull (Taur, vol. i. 16) are the Moslem emblems of stupidity, as
with us are the highly intelligent ass and the most sagacious goose.
[2] In Arab. " 'Ud" means primarily wood; then a lute. See vol. ii. 100. The Muezzin,
like the schoolmaster, is popularly supposed to be a fool.

Now when she had ended her song, she wept with sore weeping, till presently sleep overcame her and she slept. On the morrow, she said to the Shaykh, "Get thee to the Shroff and fetch me the ordinary;" so he repaired to the money-changer and delivered him the message, whereupon he made ready meat and drink, according to his custom, with which the old man returned to the damsel and they ate their sufficiency. When she had eaten, she sought of him wine and he went to the Jew and fetched it. Then the twain sat down and drank; and when she waxed drunken, she took the lute and smiting it, fell a-singing and chanted these couplets,

"How long ask I the heart, the heart drowned, and eke * Refrain my complaint
    while I my tear-floods speak?
They forbid e'en the phantom to visit me, * (O marvel!) her phantom my
    couch to seek."[1]

And when she had made an end of her song, she wept with sore weeping. All this time, the young Damascene was listening, and now he likened her voice to the voice of his slave-girl and then he put away from him this thought, and the damsel had no knowledge whatever of his presence. Then she broke out again into song and chanted these couplets,

"Quoth they, 'Forget him! What is he?' To them I cried, * 'Allah forget me
    when forget I mine adored!'
Now in this world shall I forget the love o' you? * Heaven grant the thrall
    may ne'er forget to love his lord!
I pray that Allah pardon all except thy love * Which, when I meet Him may
    my bestest plea afford."

After ending this song she drank three cups and filling the old man other three, improvised these couplets,

"His love he hid which tell-tale tears betrayed; * For burn of coal that 'neath
    his ribs was laid:
Giv'n that he seek his joy in spring and flowers * Some day, his spring's the
    face of dear-loved maid.
O ye who blame me for who baulks my love! * What sweeter thing than boon
    to man denayed?
A sun, yet scorcheth he my very heart! * A moon, but riseth he from breasts
    a-shade!"

---

[1] I have noticed that among Arab lovers it was the fashion to be jealous of the mistress's nightly phantom which, as amongst mesmerists, is the lover's embodied will.

When she had made an end of her song, she threw the lute from her hand and wept, whilst the Shaykh wept for her weeping. Then she fell down in a fainting fit and presently recovering, crowned the cup and drinking it off, gave the elder to drink, after which she took the lute and breaking out into song, chanted these couplets,

"Thy parting is bestest of woes to my heart, * And changed my case till all sleep it eschewed:
The world to my being is desolate; * Then Oh grief! and O lingering solitude!
Maybe The Ruthful incline thee to me * And join us despite what our foes have sued!"

Then she wept till her voice rose high and her wailing was discovered to those without; after which she again began to drink and plying the Shaykh with wine, sang these couplets,

"An they hid thy person from eyen-sight, * They hid not thy name fro' my mindful sprite:
Or meet me; thy ransom for meeting I'll be[1] * Or fly me; and ransom I'll be for thy flight!
Mine outer speaks for mine inner case, * And mine inner speaks for mine outer plight."

When she had made an end of her verses, she threw the lute from her hand and wept and wailed. Then she slept awhile and presently awaking, said, "O Shaykh, say me, hast thou what we may eat?" He replied, "O my lady, I have the rest of the food;" but she cried, "I will not eat of the orts I have left. Go down to the bazar and fetch us what we may eat." He rejoined, "Excuse me, O my lady, I cannot rise to my feet, because I am bemused with wine; but with me is the servant of the mosque, who is a sharp youth and an intelligent. I will call him, so he may buy thee whatso thou wantest." Asked she, "Whence hast thou this servant?" and he answered, "He is of the people of Damascus." When she heard him say "of the people of Damascus," she sobbed such a sob that she swooned away; and when she came to herself, she said, "Woe is me for the people of Damascus and for those who are therein! Call him, O Shaykh, that he may do our need." Accordingly, the old man put his head forth of the window and called the youth, who came to him from the mosque

---

[1] i.e. I will lay down my life to save thee from sorrow — a common-place hyperbole of love.

and sought leave to enter. The Muezzin bade him come in, and when he appeared before the damsel, he knew her and she knew him; whereupon he turned back in bewilderment and would have fled at hap-hazard; but she sprang up to him and held him fast, and they embraced and wept together, till they fell to the floor in a fainting fit. When the Shaykh saw them in this con-dition, he feared for himself and fared forth in fright, seeing not the way for drunkenness. His neighbour the Jew met him and asked him, "How is it that I behold thee astounded?" Answered the old man, "How should I not be astounded, seeing that the damsel who is with me is fallen in love with the mosque servant and they have embraced and slipped down in a swoon? Indeed, I fear lest the Caliph come to know of this and be wroth with me; so tell me thou what is thy device for that wherewith I am afflicted in the matter of this damsel." Quoth the Jew, "For the present, take this casting-bottle of rose-water and go forthright and sprinkle them therewith: an they be aswoon for this their union and embrace, they will recover, and if otherwise, then take to flight." The Shaykh snatched the casting-bottle from the Jew and going up to the twain, sprinkled their faces, whereupon they came to themselves and fell to relating each to other that which they had suffered, since both had been parted, for the pangs of severance. Nur al-Din also acquainted Sitt al-Milah with that which he had endured from the folk who would have killed[1] him and utterly annihilated him; and she said to him, "O my lord, let us for the nonce leave this talk and praise Allah for reunion of loves, and all this shall cease from us." Then she gave him the cup and he said, "By Allah, I will on no wise drink it, whilst I am in this case!" So she drank it off before him and taking the lute, swept the strings and sang these couplets,

"O absent fro' me and yet present in place, * Thou art far from mine eyes and yet ever nigh!
Thy farness bequeathed me all sorrow and care * And my troublous life can no joy espy:
Lone, forlorn, weeping-eyelidded, miserablest, * I abide for thy sake as though banisht I:
Then (ah grief o' me!) far thou hast fared from sight * Yet canst no more depart me than apple of eye!"

---

1 Arab. "Katl." I have noticed the Hibernian "kilt" which is not a bull but, like most provincialisms and Americanisms, a survival, an archaism. In the old Frisian dialect, which agrees with English in more words than "bread, butter and cheese," we find the

When she had made an end of her verse, she wept and the young man of Damascus, Nur al-Din, wept also. Then she took the lute and improvised these couplets,

"Well Allah wots I never naměd you * But tears o'erbrimming eyes in floods
        outburst;
And passion raged and pine would do me die, * Yet my heart rested wi' the
        thought it nurst;
O eye-light mine, O wish and O my hope! * Your face can never quench mine
        eyes' hot thirst."

When Nur al-Din heard these his slave-girl's verses, he fell a-weeping, while she strained him to her bosom and wiped away his tears with her sleeve and questioned him and comforted his mind. Then she took the lute and sweeping its strings, played thereon with such performing as would move the staidest to delight and sang these couplets,

"Indeed, what day brings not your sight to me, * That day I rem'mber not as
        dight to me!
And, when I vainly long on you to look, * My life is lost, Oh life and light o'
        me!"

After this fashion they fared till the morning, tasting not the nourishment of sleep;[1] and when the day lightened, behold the eunuch came with the she-mule and said to Sitt al-Milah, "The Commander of the Faithful calleth for thee." So she arose and taking by the hand her lord, committed him to the Shaykh, saying, "This is the deposit of Allah, then thy deposit,[2] till this eunuch cometh to thee; and indeed, O elder, my due to thee is the white hand of favour such as filleth the interval betwixt heaven and earth." Then she mounted the mule and repairing to the palace of the Commander of the Faithful, went in to him and kissed ground before him. Quoth he to her, as who should make mock of her, "I doubt not but thou hast found thy lord;" and quoth she, "By thy felicity and the length of thy continuance on life, I have indeed found him!" Now Al-Rashid was leaning back; but, when he heard this, he sat upright and said to her,

---

primary meaning of terms which with us have survived only in their secondary senses, *e.g.*
killen = to beat and slagen = to strike. Here is its great value to the English philologist.
When the Irishman complains that he is "kilt" we know through the Frisian what he
really means.
    [1] The decency of this description is highly commendable and I may note that the Bresl.
Edit. is comparatively free from erotic pictures.
    [2] *i.e.* "I commit him to thy charge under God."

"By my life, true?" She replied, "Ay, by thy life!" He said,
"Bring him into my presence, so I may see him;" but she said,
"O my lord, there have happened to him many hardships and his
charms are changed and his favour faded; and indeed the Prince
of True Believers vouchsafed me a month; wherefore I will tend
him the rest of the month and then bring him to do his service to
the Commander of the Faithful." Quoth Al-Rashid, "Sooth
thou sayest: the condition certainly was for a month; but tell me
what hath betided him." Quoth she, "O my lord (Allah prolong
thy continuance and make Paradise thy place of returning and
thine asylum and the fire the abiding-place of thy foes!), when he
presenteth himself to serve thee, he will assuredly expound to
thee his case and will name to thee his wrong-doers; and indeed
this is an arrear that is due to the Prince of True Believers, by
whom may Allah fortify the Faith and vouchsafe him the victory
over rebel and froward wretch!" Thereupon he ordered her a fine
house and bade furnish it with carpets and vessels of choice and
commanded them to give all she needed. This was done during
the rest of the day, and when the night came, she sent the eunuch
with a suit of clothes and the mule, to fetch Nur al-Din from the
Muezzin's lodging. So the young man donned the dress and
mounting, rode to the house, where he abode in comfort and
luxury a full-told month, while she solaced him with four things,
the eating of fowls and the drinking of wine and the sleeping
upon brocade and the entering the bath after horizontal refreshment.[1] Furthermore, she brought him six suits of linen stuffs and
took to changing his clothes day by day; nor was the appointed
time of delay accomplished ere his beauty and loveliness returned
to him; nay, his favour waxed tenfold fairer and he became a
seduction to all who looked upon him. One day of the days Al-
Rashid bade bring him to the presence; so his slave-girl changed
his clothes and robing him in sumptuous raiment, mounted him on
the she-mule. Then he rode to the palace and presenting himself
before the Caliph, saluted him with the goodliest of salutations
and bespake him with Truchman's[2] speech eloquent and deep-
thoughted. When Al-Rashid saw him, he marvelled at the
seemliness of his semblance and his loquence and eloquence and

---

[1] This is an Americanism, but it translates passing well "Al-iláj" == insertion.

[2] Arab. (and Heb.) "Tarjumán" == a dragoman, for which see vol. i. 100. In the next
tale it will occur with the sense of polyglottic.

asking of him, was told that he was Sitt al-Milah's lord; whereupon quoth he, "Indeed, she is excusable in her love for him, and if we had put her to death wrongfully, as we were minded to do, her blood would have been upon our heads." Then he accosted the young man and entering into discourse with him, found him well-bred, intelligent, clever, quick-witted, generous, pleasant, elegant, excellent. So he loved him with exceeding love and questioned him of his native city and of his sire and of the cause of his journey to Baghdad. Nur al-Din acquainted him with that which he would know in the goodliest words and concisest phrases; and the Caliph asked him, "And where hast thou been absent all this while? Verily, we sent after thee to Damascus and Mosul and all other cities, but happened on no tidings of thee." Answered the young man, "O my lord, there betided thy slave in thy capital that which never yet betided any." Then he acquainted him with his case, first and last, and told him that which had befallen him of evil from Al-Muradi and the Chief of Police. Now when Al-Rashid heard this, he was chagrined with sore chagrin and waxed wroth with exceeding wrath and cried, "Shall this thing happen in a city wherein I am?" And the Háshimí vein[1] started out between his eyes. Then he bade fetch Ja'afar, and when he came between his hands, he acquainted him with the adventure and said to him, "Shall this thing come to pass in my city and I have no news of it?" Thereupon he bade Ja'afar fetch all whom the young Damascene had named, and when they came, he bade smite their necks: he also summoned him whom they called Ahmad and who had been the means of the young man's deliverance a first time and a second, and thanked him and showed him favour and bestowed on him a costly robe of honour and made him Chief of Police in his city.[2] Then he sent for the Shaykh, the Muezzin, and when the messenger came to him and told him that the Commander of the Faithful summoned him, he feared the denunciation of the damsel and walked with him to the palace, farting for fear as he went, whilst all who passed him by laughed at him. When he came into the presence of the Commander of the Faithful, he fell a-trembling and his tongue was tied,[3] so that he could not speak. The Caliph smiled at him

---

[1] See vol. i. p. 35.
[2] After putting to death the unjust Prefect.
[3] Arab. "Lujlaj." See vol. ix. 322.

and said, "O Shaykh, thou hast done no offence; so why fearest thou?" Answered the old man (and indeed he was in the sorest of that which may be of fear), "O my lord, by the virtue of thy pure forefathers, indeed I have done naught, and do thou enquire of my manners and morals." The Caliph laughed at him and ordering him a thousand dinars, bestowed on him a costly robe of honour and made him headman of the Muezzins in his mosque. Then he called Sitt al-Milah and said to her, "The house wherein thou lodgest with all it containeth is a largesse to thy lord: so do thou take him and depart with him in the safeguard of Allah Almighty; but absent not yourselves from our presence." Accordingly she went forth with the young Damascene and when she came to the house, she found that the Prince of True Believers had sent them gifts galore and good things in store. As for Nur al-Din, he sent for his father and mother and appointed for himself agents in the city of Damascus, to receive the rent of the houses and gardens and Wakalahs and Hammams; and they occupied themselves with collecting that which accrued to him and sending it to him every year. Meanwhile, his father and mother came to him, with that which they had of monies and merchandise of price and, foregathering with their son, found that he was become of the chief officers and familiars of the Commander of the Faithful and of the number of his sitting-companions and nightly entertainers, wherefore they rejoiced in reunion with him and he also rejoiced in them. The Caliph assigned them solde and allowances; and as for Nur al-Din, his father brought him those riches and his wealth waxed and his estate was stablished, till he became the richest of the folk of his time in Baghdad and left not the presence of the Commander of the Faithful or by night or by day. He was vouchsafed issue by Sitt al-Milah, and he ceased not to live the goodliest of lives, he and she and his father and his mother, a while of time, till Abu al-Hasan sickened of a sore sickness and departed to the mercy of Allah Almighty. Presently, his mother also died and he carried them forth and shrouded them and buried and made them expiations and funeral ceremonies.[1] In due course his children grew up and became like moons, and he reared them in splendour and affection, while his wealth waxed and his case never waned. He ceased not to pay frequent visits to the Commander of the Faithful, he and his

---

[1] Arab. "Mawálid" lit. = nativity festivals (plur. of Maulid). See vol. ix. 289.

children and his slave-girl Sitt al-Milah, and they abode in all
solace of life and prosperity till there came to them the Destroyer
of delights and the Sunderer of societies; and laud to the Abiding,
the Eternal! This is all that hath come down to us of their story.

TALE OF KING INS BIN KAYS AND HIS DAUGHTER WITH THE SON OF KING AL-'ABBAS.[1]

THERE was once, in days of yore and in ages and times long gone
before, in the city of Baghdad, the House of Peace, a king mighty
of estate, lord of understanding and beneficence and generosity
and munificence, and he was strong of sultanate and endowed
with might and majesty and magnificence. His name was Ins bin
Kays bin Rabí' al-Shaybání,[2] and when he took horse, there rode
about him riders from the farthest parts of the two Iraks.[3] Almighty Allah decreed that he should take to wife a woman hight
'Afífah, daughter of Asad al-Sundúsi, who was endowed with
beauty and loveliness and brightness and perfect grace and
symmetry of shape and stature; her face was like the crescent
moon and she had eyes as they were gazelle's eyes and an aquiline
nose like Luna's cymb. She had learned cavalarice and the use of
arms and had mastered the sciences of the Arabs; eke she had
gotten by heart all the dragomanish[4] tongues and indeed she was
a ravishment to mankind. She abode with Ins bin Kays twelve
years, during which time he was not blessed with children by her;
so his breast was straitened by reason of the failure of lineage, and
he besought his Lord to vouchsafe him a son. Accordingly the
queen conceived, by permission of Allah Almighty; and when
the days of her pregnancy were accomplished, she gave birth to a
maid-child, than whom never saw eyes fairer, for that her face was
as it were a pearl pure-bright or a lamp raying light or a candle

---

[1] Bresl. Edit., vol. xii. pp. 116–237, Nights dccclxvi–dcccclxxix. Mr. Payne entitles
it "El Abbas and the King's Daughter of Baghdad."

[2] "Of the Shaybán tribe." I have noticed (vol. ii. 1) how loosely the title Malik (King)
is applied in Arabic and in mediæval Europe. But it is ultra-Shakespearean to place a
Badawi King in Baghdad, the capital founded by the Abbasides and ruled by those
Caliphs till their downfall.

[3] i.e. Irák Arabí (Chaldæa) and 'Ajami (Western Persia). For the meaning of Al-Irák,
which always, except in verse, takes the article, see vol. ii. 132.

[4] See supra, p. 135. Mr. Payne suspects a clerical error for "Turkumániyah" = Turco-
manish; but this is hardly acceptable.

gilt with gold or a full moon breaking cloudy fold, extolled be
He who her from vile water dight and made her to the beholders
a delight! When her father saw her in this fashion of loveliness,
his reason fled for joy, and when she grew up, he taught her
writing and *belles-lettres* and philosophy and all manner of
tongues. So she excelled the folk of her time and surpassed her
peers; and the sons of the kings heard of her and all of them
longed to look upon her. The first who sought her to wife was
King Nabhán[1] of Mosul, who came to her with a great company,
bringing an hundred she-camels, laden with musk and lign-aloes
and ambergris and five score loaded with camphor and jewels
and other hundred laden with silver monies and yet other hundred loaded with raiment of silken stuffs, sendal and brocade,
besides an hundred slave-girls and a century of choice steeds of
swift and generous breeds, completely housed and accoutred, as
they were brides; and all this he had laid before her father, de-
manding her of him in wedlock. Now King Ins bin Kays had
bound himself by an oath that he would not marry his daughter
save to him whom she should choose; so, when King Nabhan
sought her in marriage, her father went in to her and consulted
her concerning his affair. She consented not and he repeated to
Nabhan that which she said, whereupon he departed from him.
After this came King Bahrám, lord of the White Island, with
treasures richer than the first; but she accepted not of him and he
returned disappointed; nor did the kings cease coming to her sire,
on her account, one after other, from the farthest of the lands
and the climes, each glorying in bringing more than those who
forewent him; but she heeded not any one of them. Presently,
Al-'Abbás, son of King Al-'Azíz, lord of the land of Al-Yaman
and Zabídún[2] and Meccah (which Allah increase in honour
and brightness and beauty!) heard of her; and he was of the
great ones of Meccah and Al-Hijáz[3] and was a youth without
hair on his side-face. So he presented himself one day in his sire's
assembly, whereupon the folk made way for him and the king
seated him on a chair of red gold, crusted with pearls and gems.
The Prince sat, with his head bowed groundwards, and spake not

---

[1] As fabulous a personage as "King Kays."
[2] Possibly a clerical error for Zabíd, the famous capital of the Tahámah or lowlands of
Al-Yaman.
[3] The Moslem's Holy Land whose capital is Meccah.

to any: whereby his father knew that his breast was straitened and bade the cup-companions and men of wit relate marvellous histories, such as beseem the sessions of kings; nor was there one of them but spoke forth the goodliest of that which was with him; but Al-'Abbás still abode with his head bowed down. Then the king bade his sitting-companions withdraw, and when the chamber was private, he looked at his son and said to him, "By Allah, thou cheerest me with thy coming in to me and chagrinest me for that thou payest no heed to any of the familiars nor of the cup-companions. What is the cause of this?" Answered the Prince, "O my papa, I have heard tell that in the land of Al-Irák is a woman of the daughters of the kings, and her father is called King Ins bin Kays, lord of Baghdad; she is famed for beauty and loveliness and brightness and perfect grace, and indeed many of the kings have sought her in marriage; but her soul consented not unto any one of them. Wherefore my thought prompteth me to travel herwards, for that my heart cleaveth to her, and I beseech thee suffer me to go to her." His sire replied, "O my son, thou knowest that I have none other than thyself of children and thou art the coolth of mine eyes and the fruit of my vitals; nay, I cannot brook to be parted from thee a single hour and I purpose to seat thee on the throne of the kingship and espouse thee to one of the daughters of the kings, who shall be fairer than she." Al-Abbas gave ear to his father's word and dared not gainsay him; wherefore he abode with him awhile, whilst the love-fire raged in his vitals. Then the king took rede with himself to build his son a Hammam and adorn it with various paintings, so he might display it to him and divert him with the sight thereof, to the intent that his body might be solaced thereby and that the accident of travel might cease from him and he be turned from his purpose of removal from his parents. Presently he addressed himself to the building of the bath and assembling architects and artisans from all his cities and citadels and islands, assigned them a foundation-site and marked out its boundaries. Then the workmen occupied themselves with the building of the Hammam and the ordinance and adornment of its cabinets and roofs. They used paints and precious minerals of all kinds, according to the contrast of their colours, red and green and blue and yellow and what not else of all manner tincts; and each artisan wrought at his craft and each painter at his art, whilst the rest of the folk busied themselves with

transporting thither vari-coloured stones. One day, as the
Master-painter wrought at his work, there came in to him a
poor man, who looked long upon him and observed his mystery;
whereupon quoth the artist to him, "Knowest thou aught of
painting?" Quoth the stranger, "Yes;" so he gave him tools and
paints and said to him, "Limn for us a rare semblance." Accordingly the pauper stranger entered one of the bath-chambers and
drew on its walls a double border, which he adorned on both
sides, after a fashion than which eyes never saw a fairer. Moreover, amiddlemost the chamber he limned a picture to which
there lacked but the breath,[1] and it was the portraiture of
Máriyah, daughter to the king of Baghdad. Then, when he had
finished the portrait, he went his way and told none of what he
had done, nor knew any wight the chambers and doors of the
bath and the adornment and ordinance thereof. Presently the
chief artisan came to the palace and sought audience of the king
who bade admit him. So he entered and kissing the earth, saluted
him with a salam beseeming Sultans and said, "O king of the
time and lord of the age and the tide, may prosperity endure to
thee and acceptance and eke thy degree over all the kings both
morning and evening[2] exalted be! The work of the bath is accomplished, by the king's fair fortune and the purity of his
purpose, and indeed, we have done all that behoved us and there
remaineth but that which behoveth the king." Al-Aziz ordered
him a costly robe of honour and expended monies galore, giving
unto each who had wroughten after the measure of his work.
Then he assembled in the Hammam all the Lords of his realm,
Emirs and Wazirs and Chamberlains and Nabobs, and the chief
officers of his kingdom and household, and sending for his son
Al-Abbas, said to him, "O my son, I have builded thee a bath,
wherein thou mayst take thy pleasance; so enter that thou mayst
see it and divert thyself by gazing upon it and viewing the beauty
of its ordinance and decoration." "With love and gladness,"
replied the Prince and entered the bath, he and the king and the
folk about them, so they might divert themselves with viewing
that which the workmen's hands had worked. Al-Abbas went
in and passed from place to place and chamber to chamber, till

---

[1] A hinted protest against making a picture or a statue which the artist cannot quicken;
as this process will be demanded of him on Doomsday. Hence also the Princess is called
Máriyah (Maria, Mary), a non-Moslem name.

[2] i.e. day and night, for ever.

he came to the room aforesaid and espied the portrait of Mariyah, whereupon he fell down in a fainting-fit and the workmen went to his father and said to him, "Thy son Al-Abbas hath swooned away." So the king came and finding his son cast down, seated himself at his head and bathed his face with rose-water. After awhile he revived and the king said to him, "I seek refuge with Allah for thee, O my son! What accident hath befallen thee?" The Prince replied, "O my father, I did but look on yonder picture and it bequeathed me a thousand qualms and there befel me that which thou beholdest." Therewith the king bade fetch the Master-painter, and when he stood before him, he said to him, "Tell me of yonder portrait and what girl is this of the daughters of the kings; else I will take thy head." Said the painter, "By Allah, O king, I limned it not, neither know I who she is; but there came to me a poor man and looked hard at me. So I asked him, Knowest thou the art of painting? and he answered, Yes. Whereupon I gave him the gear and said to him, Limn for us a rare semblance. Accordingly he painted yonder portrait and went away and I wot him not neither have I ever set eyes on him save that day." Hearing this, the king ordered all his officers to go round about in the thoroughfares and colleges and to bring before him all strangers they found there. So they went forth and brought him much people, amongst whom was the pauper who had painted the portrait. When they came into the presence, the Sultan bade the crier make public proclamation that whoso wrought the portrait should discover himself and have whatso he wished. Thereupon the poor man came forward and kissing the ground before the king, said to him, "O king of the age, I am he who limned yonder likeness." Quoth Al-Aziz, "And knowest thou who she is?" and quoth the other, "Yes, this is the portrait of Mariyah, daughter of the king of Baghdad." The king ordered him a robe of honour and a slave-girl and he went his way. Then said Al-Abbas, "O my papa, give me leave to seek her, so I may look upon her: else shall I farewell the world, withouten fail." The king his father wept and answered, "O my son, I builded thee a Hammam, that it might turn thee from leaving me, and behold, it hath been the cause of thy going forth; but the behest of Allah is a determinate decree."[1] Then he wept again

---

[1] Koran xxxiii. 38; this concludes a "revelation" concerning the divorce and marriage to Mohammed of the wife of his adopted son Zayd. Such union, superstitiously held in-

and Al-Abbas said to him, "Fear not for me, for thou knowest my prowess and puissance in returning answers in the assemblies of the land and my good breeding and accomplishments together with my skill in rhetoric; and indeed for him whose father thou art and whom thou hast reared and bred and in whom thou hast united praiseworthy qualities, the repute whereof hath traversed the East and the West, thou needest not fear aught, more especially as I purpose but to seek pleasuring and return to thee, an it be the will of Allah Almighty." Quoth the king, "Whom wilt thou take with thee of attendants and what of monies?" Replied Al-Abbas, "O my papa, I have no need of horses or camels or weapons, for I purpose not warfare, and I will have none go forth with me save my page 'Amir and no more." Now as he and his father were thus engaged in talk, in came his mother and caught hold of him; and he said to her, "Allah upon thee, let me gang my gait and strive not to divert me from what purpose I have purposed, for needs must I go." She replied, "O my son, if it must be so and there be no help for it, swear to me that thou wilt not be absent from me more than a year." And he sware to her. Then he entered his father's treasuries and took therefrom what he would of jewels and jacinths and everything weighty of worth and light of load: he also bade his servant Amir saddle him two steeds and the like for himself, and whenas the night beset his back,[1] he rose from his couch and mounting his horse, set out for Baghdad, he and Amir, whilst the page knew not whither he intended.[2] He gave not over going and the journey was joyous to him, till they came to a goodly land, abounding in birds and wild beasts, whereupon Al-Abbas started a gazelle and shot it with a shaft. Then he dismounted and cutting its throat, said to his servant, "Alight thou and skin it and carry it to the water." Amir answered him with "Hearkening and obedience" and going down to the water, built a fire and broiled the gazelle's flesh. Then they ate their fill and drank of the water, after which they mounted again and fared on with diligent faring, and Amir still

cestuous by all Arabs, was a terrible scandal to the rising Faith, and could be abated only by the "Commandment of Allah." It is hard to believe that a man could act honestly after such fashion; but we have seen in our day a statesman famed for sincerity and uprightness honestly doing things the most dishonest possible. Zayd and Abu Lahab (chap. cxi. i.) are the only contemporaries of Mohammed named in the Koran.

[1] *i.e.* darkened behind him.

[2] Here we have again, as so common in Arab romances, the expedition of a modified Don Quixote and Sancho Panza.

unknowing whither Al-Abbas was minded to wend. So he said to him, "O my lord, I conjure thee by Allah of All-might, wilt thou not tell me whither thou intendest?" Al-Abbas looked at him and in reply improvised these couplets,

"In my vitals are fires of desire and repine; * And naught I reply when they
    flare on high:
Baghdad-wards I hie me on life-and-death work, * Loving one who distorts my
    right judgment awry:
A swift camel under me shortcuts the wold * And deem it a cloud all who
    nearhand espy:
O 'Ámir make haste after model of her * Who would heal mine ill and Love's
    cup drain dry:
For the leven of love burns the vitals of me; * So with me seek my tribe and
    stint all reply."

When Amir heard his lord's verses, he knew that he was a slave of love and that she whom he loved abode in Baghdad. Then they fared on night and day, traversing plain and stony way, till they sighted Baghdad and lighted down in its environs[1] and there lay their night. When they arose in the morning, they removed to the bank of the Tigris where they encamped and sojourned a second day and a third. As they abode thus on the fourth day, behold, a company of folk giving their beasts the rein and crying aloud and saying, "Quick! Quick! Haste to our rescue, Ho thou the King!" Therewith the King's chamberlains and officers accosted them and said, "What is behind you and what hath betided you?" Quoth they, "Bring us before the King." So they carried them to Ins bin Kays; and when they saw him, they said to him, "O king, unless thou succour us, we are dead men; for that we are a folk of the Banú Shaybán,[2] who have taken up our abode in the parts of Bassorah, and Hodhayfah the wild Arab hath come down on us with his steeds and his men and hath slain our horse-men and carried off our women and children; nor was one saved of the tribe but he who fled; wherefore we crave help first by Allah Almighty, then by thy life." When the king heard their speech, he bade the crier proclaim in the highways of the city that the troops should busk them to march and that the horsemen should mount and the footmen fare forth; nor was it but the twinkling of the eye ere the kettle-drums beat and the trumpets

---

[1] Arab. "Arzi-há" = in its earth, its outlying suburbs.
[2] The king's own tribe.

blared; and scarce was the forenoon of the day passed when the
city was blocked with horse and foot.   Presently, the king re-
viewed them and behold, they were four-and-twenty thousand in
number, cavalry and infantry. He bade them go forth to the
enemy and gave the command of them to Sa'ad ibn al-Wákidí,
a doughty cavalier and a dauntless champion; so the horsemen
set out and fared on along the Tigris-bank. Al-Abbas, son of
King Al-Aziz, looked at them and saw the flags flaunting and the
standards stirring and heard the kettle-drums beating; so he
bade his page saddle him a blood-steed and look to the surcingles
and bring him his harness of war, for indeed horsemanship[1] was
rooted in his heart. Quoth Amir, "And indeed I saw Al-Abbas,
his eyes waxed red and the hair of his hands on end." So he
mounted his charger, whilst Amir also bestrode a destrier, and
they went forth with the commando and fared on two days.
On the third day, after the hour of the mid-afternoon prayer, they
came in sight of the foe and the two armies met and the two ranks
joined in fight. The strife raged amain and sore was the strain,
whilst the dust rose in clouds and hung in vaulted shrouds, so
that all eyes were blinded; and they ceased not from the battle
till the night overtook them,[2] when the two hosts drew off from
the mellay and passed the night, perplexed concerning themselves.
When Allah caused the morning to morrow, the two hosts were
aligned in line and their thousands fixed their eyne and the
troops stood looking one at other.   Then sallied forth Al-Háris
ibn Sa'ad between the two lines and played with his lance and
cried out and improvised these couplets,

"You are in every way this day our prey; * And ever we prayèd your sight
    to see:
The Ruthful drave you Hodhayfah-wards * To the Brave, the Lion who sways
    the free:
Say, amid you's a man who would heal his ills, * With whose lust of battle
    shrewd blows agree?
Then by Allah meet me who come to you * And whoso is wronged shall the
    wronger be."[3]

Thereupon there sallied forth to him Zuhayr bin Habíb, and

---

[1] *i.e.* he was always "spoiling for a fight."
[2] In the text the two last sentences are spoken by Amir and the story-teller suddenly
resumes the third person.
[3] Mr. Payne translates this "And God defend the right" (of plunder according to the
Arabs).

they wheeled about and wiled a while, then they exchanged
strokes. Al-Haris forewent his foe in smiting and stretched him
weltering in his gore; whereupon Hodhayfah cried out to him,
"Gifted of Allah[1] art thou, O Haris! Call out another of them."
So he cried aloud, "I say, who be a champion?" But they of
Baghdad held back from him; and when it appeared to Al-Haris
that consternation was amongst them, he charged down upon
them and overrolled the first of them upon the last of them and
slew of them twelve men. Then the evening caught him and the
Baghdadis began addressing themselves to flight. No sooner had
the morning morrowed than they found themselves reduced to a
fourth part of their number and there was not one of them had
dismounted from his horse. Wherefore they made sure of destruction and Hodhayfah rushed out between the two lines
(now he was reckoned good for a thousand knights)and cried out,
"Harkye, my masters of Baghdad! Let none come forth to me
but your Emir, so I may talk with him and he with me; and he
shall meet me in combat singular and I will meet him, and may
he who is clear of offence come off safe." Then he repeated his
words and said, "How is it I see your Emir refuse me a reply?"
But Sa'ad, the Emir of the army of Baghdad, answered him not,
and indeed his teeth chattered in his mouth, when he heard him
summon him to the duello. Now when Al-Abbas heard Hodhayfah's challenge and saw Sa'ad in this case, he came up to the
Emir and asked him, "Wilt thou suffer me to answer him and I
will be thy substitute in replying him and in monomachy with
him and will make my life thy sacrifice?" Sa'ad looked at him and
seeing knighthood shining from between his eyes, said to him,
"O youth, by the virtue of Mustafà the Chosen Prophet (whom
Allah save and assain), tell me who thou art and whence thou
comest to bring us victory."[2] Quoth the Prince, "This is no
place for questioning;" and quoth Sa'ad to him, "O Knight, up
and at Hodhayfah! Yet, if his Satan prove too strong for thee,
afflict not thyself on thy youth."[3] Al-Abbas cried, "Allah is

---

[1] Arab. "Lilláhi darruk"; see vol. iv. 20. Captain Lockett (p. 28) justly remarks that
"it is a sort of encomiastic exclamation of frequent occurrence in Arabic and much easier to
comprehend than translate." Darra signifies flowing freely (as milk from the udder) and
was metaphorically transferred to bounty and to indoles or natural capacity. Thus the
phrase means "your flow of milk is by or through Allah." i.e., of unusual abundance.

[2] The words are euphemistic: we should say "comest thou to our succour."

[3] i.e. If his friend the Devil be overstrong for thee, flee him rather than be slain; as

He of whom help is to be sought;"[1] and, taking his arms, fortified his purpose and went down into the field, as he were a fort of the forts or a mountain's contrefort.   Thereupon Hodhayfah cried out to him, saying, "Haste thee not, O youth! Who art thou of the folk?"   He replied, "I am Sa'ad ibn al-Wakidi, commander of the host of King Ins, and but for thy pride in challenging me, I had not come forth to thee; for thou art no peer for me to front nor as mine equal dost thou count nor canst thou bear my brunt. Wherefore get thee ready for the last march[2] seeing that there abideth but a little of thy life."   When Hodhayfah heard this speech, he threw himself backwards,[3] as if in mockery of him, whereat Al-Abbas was wroth and called out to him, saying, "O Hodhayfah, guard thyself against me."   Then he rushed upon him, as he were a swooper of the Jinn,[4] and Hodhayfah met him and they wheeled about a long while.   Presently, Al-Abbas cried out at Hodhayfah a cry which astounded him and struck him a stroke, saying, "Take this from the hand of a brave who feareth not the like of thee."   Hodhavfah met the sabre-sway with his shield, thinking to ward it off from him; but the blade shore the target in sunder and descending upon his shoulder, came forth gleaming from the tendons of his throat and severed his arm at the armpit; whereupon he fell down, wallowing in his blood, and Al-Abbas turned upon his host; not had the sun departed the dome of the welkin ere Hodhayfah's army was in full flight before Al-Abbas and the saddles were empty of men. Quoth Sa'ad, "By the virtue of Mustafa the Chosen Prophet, whom Allah save and assain, I saw Al-Abbas with the blood upon his saddle-pads, in clots like camels' livers, smiting with the sword right and left, till he scattered them abroad in every gorge and wold; and when he hied him back to the camp, the men of Baghdad were fearful of him."   But as soon as they saw this victory which had betided them over their foes, they turned back and gathering together the weapons and treasures and horses of those

---

He who fights and runs away
Shall live to fight another day.

[1] *i.e.* I look to Allah for said (and keep my powder dry).

[2] *i.e.* to the next world.

[3] This falling backwards in laughter commonly occurs during the earlier tales; it is, however, very rare amongst the Badawin.

[4] *i.e.* as he were a flying Jinni, swooping down and pouncing falcon-like upon a mortal from the upper air.

they had slain, returned to Baghdad, victorious, and all by the
knightly valour of Al-Abbas. As for Sa'ad, he foregathered with
his lord, and they fared on in company till they came to the place
where Al-Abbas had taken horse, whereupon the Prince dismounted from his charger and Sa'ad said to him, "O youth, wherefore alightest thou in other than thy place? Indeed, thy rights be
incumbent upon us and upon our Sultan; so go thou with us to
the dwellings, that we may ransom thee with our souls." Replied
Al-Abbas, "O Emir Sa'ad, from this place I took horse with thee
and herein is my lodging. So, Allah upon thee, mention not me
to the king, but make as if thou hadst never seen me because I
am a stranger in the land." So saying, he turned away from him
and Sa'ad fared on to his palace, where he found all the courtiers
in attendance on the king and recounting to him that which had
betided them with Al-Abbas. Quoth the king, "Where is he?"
and quoth they, "He is with the Emir Sa'ad." So, when the
Emir entered, the king looked, but found none with him; and
Sa'ad, seeing at a glance that he longed to look upon the youth,
cried out to him, saying, "Allah prolong the king's days! Indeed,
he refuseth to present himself before thee, without order or
leave." Asked the king, "O Sa'ad, whence cometh this man?"
and the Emir answered, "O my lord, I know not; but he is a
youth fair of favour, amiable of aspect, accomplished in address,
ready of repartee, and valour shineth from between his eyes."
Quoth the king, "O Sa'ad, fetch him to me, for indeed thou
describest to me at full length a mighty matter."[1] And he answered, saying, "By Allah, O my lord, hadst thou but seen our
case with Hodhayfah, when he challenged me to the field of fight
and the stead of cut-and-thrust and I held back from doing battle
with him! Then, as I thought to go forth to him, behold, a knight
gave loose to his bridle-rein and called out to me, saying, 'O Sa'ad,
wilt thou suffer me to be thy substitute in waging war with him
and I will ransom thee with myself?' And quoth I, 'By Allah,
O youth, whence comest thou?' and quoth he, 'This be no time
for thy questions, while Hodhayfah standeth awaiting thee.'"
Thereupon he repeated to the king all that had passed between
himself and Al-Abbas from first to last; whereat cried Ins bin
Kays, "Bring him to me in haste, so we may learn his tidings and

---

[1] This may be (reading Imraan = man, for Amran = matter) "a masterful man"; but
I can hardly accept it.

question him of his case." " 'Tis well," replied Sa'ad, and going forth of the king's presence, repaired to his own house, where he doffed his war-harness and took rest for himself. On this wise fared it with the Emir Sa'ad, but as regards Al-Abbas, when he dismounted from his destrier, he doffed his war-gear and reposed himself awhile; after which he brought out a body-dress of Venetian[1] silk and a gown of green damask and donning them, bound about his head a turband of Damietta stuff and zoned his waist with a kerchief. Then he went out a-walking in the highways of Baghdad and fared on till he came to the bazar of the traders. There he found a merchant, with chess before him; so the Prince stood watching him, and presently the other looked up at him and asked him, "O youth, what wilt thou bet upon the game?" He answered, "Be it thine to decide." Said the merchant, "Then be it an hundred dinars," and Al-Abbas consented to him; whereupon quoth he, "Produce the money, O youth, so the game may be fairly stablished." Accordingly Al-Abbas brought out a satin purse, wherein were a thousand dinars, and laid down an hundred dinars therefrom on the edge of the carpet, whilst the merchant produced the like, and indeed his reason fled for joy when he saw the gold in possession of Al-Abbas. The folk flocked about them, to divert themselves with watching the play, and they called the bystanders to witness the wager and after the stakes were duly staked, the twain fell a-playing. Al-Abbas forebore the merchant, so he might lead him on, and dallied with him a full hour; and the merchant won and took of him the hundred dinars. Then said the Prince, "Wilt thou play another partie?" and the other said, "O youth, I will not play again, save for a thousand dinars." Quoth the youth, "Whatsoever thou stakest, I will match thy stake with its like." So the merchant brought out a thousand dinars and the Prince covered them with other thousand. Then the game began, but Al-Abbas was not long with him ere he beat him in the house of the elephant,[2] nor did he cease to do thus till he had beaten him four times and won of him four thousand dinars. This was all the merchant had of money; so he said, "O youth, I will play thee another game for

---

[1] Arab. "Bunduki," the adj. of Bunduk, which the Moslems evidently learned from Slav sources; Venedik being the Dalmatian corruption of Venezia. See Dubrovenedik in vol. ii. 219.

[2] i.e. the castle's square.

the shop." Now the value of the shop was four thousand dinars; so they played and Al-Abbas beat him and won his shop, with whatso was therein; upon which the other arose, shaking his clothes,[1] and said to him, "Up, O youth, and take thy shop." Accordingly Al-Abbas arose and repairing to the shop, took possession thereof, after which he returned to the place where he had left his servant 'Amir, and found there the Emir Sa'ad, who was come to bid him to the presence of the king. The Prince consented to this and accompanied him till they came before King Ins bin Kays, whereupon he kissed the ground and saluted him and exaggerated[2] the salutation. So the king asked him, "Whence comest thou, O youth, and whither goest thou?" and he answered, "I come from Al-Yaman." Then said the king, "Hast thou a need we may fulfil to thee; for indeed thou hast strong claims to our favour after that which thou didst in the matter of Hodhayfah and his folk." And he commanded to cast over him a mantle of Egyptian satin, worth an hundred dinars. He also bade his treasurer give him a thousand dinars and said to him, "O youth, take this in part of that which thou deservest of us; and if thou prolong thy sojourn with us, we will give thee slaves and serv-ants." Al-Abbas kissed ground and said, "O king, Allah grant thee abiding weal, I deserve not all this." Then he put his hand to his pouch and pulling out two caskets of gold, in each of which were rubies whose value none could estimate, gave them to the king, saying, "O king, Allah cause thy welfare to endure, I con-jure thee by that which the Almighty hath vouchsafed thee, heal my heart by accepting these two caskets, even as I have accepted thy present." So the king accepted the two caskets and Al-Abbas took his leave and went away to the bazar. Now when the merchants saw him, they accosted him and said, "O youth, wilt thou not open thy shop?" As they were addressing him, up came a woman, having with her a boy bare of head, and stood looking at Al-Abbas, till he turned to her, when she said to him, "O youth, I conjure thee by Allah, look at this boy and have ruth on him, for that his father hath forgotten his skull-cap in the shop he lost to thee; so, an thou see fit to give it him, thy reward be with Allah! For indeed the child maketh our hearts ache

---

[1] In sign of quitting possession. Chess in Europe is rarely played for money, with the exception of public matches: this, however, is not the case amongst Easterns, who are also for the most part as tricky as an old lady at cribbage rightly named.

[2] *i.e.* he was as eloquent and courtly as he could be.

with his excessive weeping, and the Lord be witness for us that,
had they left us aught wherewith to buy him a cap in its stead,
we had not sought it of thee." Replied Al-Abbas, "O adornment of womankind,[1] indeed, thou bespeakest me with thy fair
speech and supplicatest me with thy goodly words! But bring
me thy husband." So she went and fetched the merchant, whilst
a crowd collected to see what Al-Abbas would do. When the
man came, he returned him the gold he had won of him, art and
part, and delivered him the keys of the shop, saying, "Requite us
with thy pious prayers." Therewith the woman came up to him
and kissed his feet, and in like fashion did the merchant her husband: and all who were present blessed him, and there was no
talk but of Al-Abbas. Thus fared it with him; but as for the
merchant, he bought him a head of sheep[2] and slaughtering it,
roasted it and dressed birds and other meats of various kinds and
colours and purchased dessert and sweetmeats and fresh fruits;
then he repaired to Al-Abbas and conjured him to accept of his
hospitality and visit his home and eat of his provaunt. The Prince
consented to his wishes and went with him till they came to his
house, when the merchant bade him enter: so Al-Abbas went in
and saw a goodly house, wherein was a handsome saloon, with a
vaulted ceiling. When he entered the saloon, he found that the
merchant had made ready food and dessert and perfumes, such
as may not be described; and indeed he had adorned the table with
sweet-scented flowers and sprinkled musk and rose-water upon
the food; and he had smeared the saloon walls with ambergris
and had burned aloes-wood therein and Nadd. Presently, Al-
Abbas looked out of the window of the saloon and saw by its side
a house of goodly ordinance, tall of base and wide of space, with
rooms manifold and two upper stories crowning the whole; but
therein was no sign of inhabitants. So he said to the merchant,
"Verily, thou exaggeratest in doing us honour; but, by Allah,
I will not eat of thy meat until thou tell me what hath caused
the voidance of yonder house." Said he, "O my lord, that was
Al-Ghitrif's house and he passed away to the mercy of the Almighty and left no heir save myself; whereupon the mansion
became mine, and by Allah, an thou have a mind to sojourn in

---

[1] Arab. "Ya Zínat al-Nisá," which may either be a P. N. or a polite address as *Bella fi*
(Handsome woman) is to any feminine in Southern Italy.
[2] Arab. "Raas Ghanam": this form of expressing singularity is common to Arabic and
the Eastern languages, which it has influenced.

Baghdad, take up thine abode in this house, whereby thou mayst be in my neighbourhood; for that verily my heart inclineth unto thee with affection and I would have thee never absent from mine eyes, so I may still have my fill of thee and hearken to thy speech." Al-Abbas thanked him and said to him, "By Allah, thou art indeed friendly in thy converse and thou exaggeratest in thy discourse, and needs must I sojourn in Baghdad. As for the house, if it please thee to lodge me, I will abide therein; so accept of me its price." Therewith he put hand to his pouch and bringing out from it three hundred dinars, gave them to the merchant, who said in himself, "Unless I take his dirhams, he will not darken my doors." So he pocketed the monies and sold him the mansion, taking witnesses against himself of the sale. Then he arose and set food before Al-Abbas and they sat down to his good things; after which he brought him dessert and sweetmeats whereof they ate their sufficiency, and when the tables were removed they washed their hands with musked rose-water and willow-water. Then the merchant brought Al-Abbas a napkin scented with the smoke of aloes-wood, on which he wiped his right hand, and said to him, "O my lord, the house is become thy house; so bid thy page transport thither the horses and arms and stuffs." The Prince did this and the merchant rejoiced in his neighbourhood and left him not night nor day,[1] so that Al-Abbas said to him, "By the Lord, we distract thee from thy livelihood." He replied, "Allah upon thee, O my lord, name not to me aught of this, or thou wilt break my heart, for the best of traffic art thou and the best of livelihood." So there befel straight friendship between them and all ceremony was laid aside. Meanwhile[2] the king said to his Wazir, "How shall we do in the matter of yonder youth, the Yamáni, on whom we thought to confer gifts, but he hath gifted us with tenfold our largesse and more, and we know not an he be a sojourner with us or not?" Then he went into the Harim and gave the rubies to his wife Afifah, who asked him, "What is the worth of these with thee and with other of the kings?" Quoth he, "They are not to be found save with the greatest of sovrans

---

[1] This most wearisome form of politeness is common in the Moslem world, where men fondly think that the more you see of them the more you like of them. Yet their Proverbial Philosophy ("the wisdom of many and the wit of one") strongly protests against the practice: I have already quoted Mohammed's saying, "Zur ghibban, tazid Hibban"—visits rare keep friendship fair.

[2] This clause in the text is evidently misplaced (vol. xii. 144).

nor can any price them with monies." Quoth she, "Whence gottest thou them?" So he recounted to her the story of Al-Abbas from beginning to end, and she said, "By Allah, the claims of honour are imperative on us and the King hath fallen short of his devoir; for that we have not seen him bid the youth to his assembly, nor hath he seated him on his left hand." When the king heard his wife's words, it was as if he had been asleep and awoke; so he went forth the Harim and bade kill poultry and dress meats of every kind and colour. Moreover, he assembled all his courtiers and let bring sweetmeats and dessert and all that beseemeth the tables of kings. Then he adorned his palace and despatched after Al-Abbas a man of the chief officers of his household, who found him coming forth of the Hammam, clad in a jerkin[1] of fine goats' hair and over it a Baghdádi scarf; his waist was girt with a Rustaki[2] kerchief and on his head he wore a light turband of Damietta[3] stuff. The messenger wished him joy of the bath and exaggerated in doing him honour: then he said to him, "The king biddeth thee in weal."[4] "To hear is to obey," quoth Al-Abbas and accompanied the officer to the king's palace. Now Afifah and her daughter Mariyah were behind the curtain, both looking at him; and when he came before the sovran he saluted him and greeted him with the greeting of kings, whilst all present gazed at him and at his beauty and loveliness and perfect grace. The king seated him at the head of the table; and when Afifah saw him and considered him straitly, she said, "By the virtue of Mohammed, prince of the Apostles, this youth is of the sons of the kings and cometh not to these parts save for some noble purpose!" Then she looked at Mariyah and saw that her favour was changed, and indeed her eye-balls were as dead in her face and she turned not her gaze from Al-Abbas a twinkling of the eyes, for that the love of him had sunk deep into her heart. When the queen saw what had befallen her daughter, she feared for her from reproach concerning Al-Abbas; so she

---

[1] Arab. Dara' or Dira'=armour, whether of leather or metal; here the coat worn under the mail.

[2] Called from Rustak, a quarter of Baghdad. For Rusták town see vol. vi. 289.

[3] From Damietta comes our "dimity." The classical name was Tamiáthis apparently Coptic græcised: the old town on the shore famed in Crusading times was destroyed in A. H. 648 = 1251.

[4] Easterns are always startled by a sudden summons to the presence either of King or Kazi: here the messenger gives the youth to understand that it is in kindness, not in anger.

shut the casement-wicket that the Princess might not look upon him any more. Now there was a pavilion set apart for Mariyah, and therein were boudoirs and bowers, balconies and lattices, and she had with her a nurse, who served her as is the fashion with the daughters of the Kings. When the banquet was ended and the folk had dispersed, the King said to Al-Abbas, "I would fain have thee abide with me and I will buy thee a mansion, so haply we may requite thee for thy high services; and indeed imperative upon us is thy due and magnified in our eyes is thy work; and soothly we have fallen short of thy deserts in the matter of distance."[1] When the youth heard the king's speech, he rose and sat down[2] and kissing ground, returned thanks for his bounty and said, "I am the King's thrall, wheresoever I may be, and under his eye." Then he told him the tale of the merchant and the manner of the buying of the house, and the king said, "In very truth I would fain have had thee in my neighbourhood and by side of me." Presently Al-Abbas took leave of the king and went away to his own house. Now it chanced that he passed under the palace of Mariyah, the king's daughter, and she was sitting at a casement. He happened to look round and his eyes met those of the Princess, whereupon his wit departed and he was ready to swoon away, whilst his colour changed, and he said, "Verily, we are Allah's and unto Him are we returning!" But he feared for himself lest severance betide him; so he concealed his secret and discovered not his case to any of the creatures of Allah Almighty. When he reached his quarters, his page Amir said to him, "I seek refuge for thee with Allah, O my lord, from change of colour! Hath there betided thee a pain from the Lord of All-might or aught of vexation? In good sooth, sickness hath an end and patience doeth away trouble." But the Prince returned him no answer. Then he brought out ink-case[3] and paper and wrote these couplets: —

I cry (and mine's a frame that pines alwày), * A mind which fires of passion e'er waylay;
And eyeballs never tasting sweets of sleep; * Yet Fortune spare its cause I ever pray!

---

[1] *i.e.* in not sending for thee to court instead of allowing thee to live in the city without guest-rite.

[2] In sign of agitation: the phrase has often been used in this sense and we find it also in Al-Mas'udi.

[3] I would remind the reader that the "Dawát" (ink-case) contains the reed-pens.

While from world-perfidy and parting I * Like Bishr am with Hind,[1] that well-
   loved may; —
Yea, grown a bye-word 'mid the folk but aye * Spend life unwinning wish or
   night or day.
"Ah say, wots she my love when her I spied * At the high lattice shedding
   sunlike ray?"
Her glances, keener than the brand when bared * Cleave soul of man nor ever
   'scapes her prey:
I looked on her in lattice pierced aloft * When bare her cheat of veil that
   slipped away;
And shot me thence a shaft my liver pierced * When thrall to care and dire
   despair I lay
Knowst thou, O Fawn o' the palace, how for thee * I fared from farness o'er
   the lands astray?
Then read my writ, dear friends, and show some ruth * To wight who wones
   black-faced, distraught, sans stay!

And when he ended inditing, he folded up the letter. Now the
merchant's wife aforesaid, who was the nurse of the king's
daughter, was watching him from a window, unknown of him,
and when she saw him writing and reciting, she knew that some
rare tale attached to him; so she went in to him and said, "Peace
be with thee, O afflicted wight, who acquaintest not leach with
thy plight! Verily, thou exposest thy life to grievous blight. I
conjure thee by the virtue of Him who hath afflicted thee and
with the constraint of love-liking hath stricken thee, that thou
acquaint me with thine affair and disclose to me the truth of thy
secret; for that indeed I have heard from thee verses which
trouble the mind and melt the body." Accordingly he acquainted
her with his case and enjoined her to secrecy, whereof she consented, saying, "What shall be the recompense of whoso goeth
with thy letter and bringeth thee its reply?" He bowed his
head for shame before her and was silent; and she said to him,
"Raise thy head and give me thy writ": so he gave her the
letter and she hent it and carrying it to the Princess, said to her,
"Take this epistle and give me its answer." Now the dearest of
all things to Mariyah was the recitation of poesy and verses and
linked rhymes and the twanging of lute-strings, and she was
versed in all tongues; wherefore she took the writ and opening
it, read that which was therein and understood its purport.
Then she threw it to the ground and cried, "O nurse, I have no

---

1 Two well-known lovers.

answer to make to this letter." Quoth the nurse, "Indeed, this
is weakness in thee and a reproach to thee, for that the people of
the world have heard of thee and commend thee for keenness of
wit and understanding; so do thou return him an answer, such
as shall trick his heart and tire his soul." Quoth she, "O nurse,
who may be the man who presumeth upon me with this correspondence? Haply 'tis the stranger youth who gave my father
the rubies." The woman said, "It is himself," and Mariyah
said, "I will answer his letter in such fashion that thou shalt not
bring me other than it." Cried the nurse, "So be it."[1] Thereupon the Princess called for ink-case and paper and wrote these
couplets: —

Thou art bold in the copy thou sentest! May be * 'Twill increase the dule
    foreign wight must dree!
Thou hast spied me with glance that bequeaths thee woe * Ah! far is thy hope,
    a mere foreigner's plea!
Who art thou, poor freke, that wouldst win my love * Wi' thy verse? What
    seeks thine insanity?
An thou hope for my favours and greed therefor; * Where find thee a leach
    for such foolish gree?
Then rhyme-linking leave and fool-like be not * Hanged to Cross at the
    doorway of ignomy!
Deem not that to thee I incline, O youth! * 'Mid the Sons of the Path[2] is no
    place for me.
Thou art homeless waif in the wide wide world; * So return thee home where
    they keen for thee:[3]
Leave verse-spouting, O thou who a-wold dost wone, * Or minstrel shall name
    thee in lay and glee:
How many a friend who would meet his love * Is baulked when the goal is
    right clear to see!
So begone and ne'er grieve for what canst not win * Albe time be near, yet
    thy grasp 'twill flee.
Now such is my say and the tale I'd tell; * So master my meaning and — fare
    thee well!

When Mariyah had made an end of her verses, she folded the
letter and delivered it to the nurse, who hent it and went with it
to Al-Abbas. When she gave it to him, he took it and breaking
it open, read it and comprehended its contents; and when he
reached the end of it, he swooned away. After awhile, he came

---

[1] On such occasions the old woman (and Easterns are hard de dolo vetularum) always
assents to the sayings of her prey, well knowing what the doings will inevitably be.
[2] Travellers, Nomads, Wild Arabs.
[3] Whither they bear thee back dead with the women crying and keening.

to himself and cried, "Praise be to Allah who hath caused her
return a reply to my writ! Canst thou carry her another missive,
and with Allah Almighty be thy requital?"   Said she, "And
what shall letters profit thee, seeing that such is her reply;" but
he said, "Peradventure, she may yet be softened."   Then he
took ink-case and paper and wrote these couplets: —

Reached me the writ and what therein didst write, * Whence grew my pain
    and bane and blight:
I read the marvel-lines made wax my love * And wore my body out till slight-
    est slight.[1]
Would Heaven ye wot the whole I bear for love * Of you, with vitals clean for
    you undight!
And all I do t' outdrive you from my thought * 'Vails naught and 'gainst th'
    obsession loses might:
Couldst for thy lover feel 'twould ease his soul; * E'en thy dear Phantom
    would his sprite delight!
Then on my weakness lay not coyness-load * Nor in such breach of troth be
    traitor-wight:
And, weet ye well, for this your land I fared * Hoping to 'joy the union-boon
    forthright:
How many a stony wold for this I spanned; * How oft I waked when men
    kept watch o'night!
To fare fro' another land for sight of you * Love bade, while length of way for-
    bade my sprite:
So by His name[2] who molt my frame, have ruth, * And quench the flames thy
    love in me did light:
Thou fillest, arrayed with glory's robes and rays, * Heaven's stars with joy and
    Luna with despight.
Then who dare chide or blame me for my love * Of one that can all Beauty's
    boons unite?

When Al-Abbas had made an end of his verses, he folded the
letter and delivering it to the nurse, charged her keep the secret.
So she took it and carrying it to Mariyah, gave it to her.   The
Princess broke it open and read it and apprehended its purport;
then cried she, "By Allah, O nurse, my heart is chagrined with
exceeding chagrin, never knew I a sorer, because of this correspondence and of these verses."   And the nurse made answer to
her, "O my lady, thou art in thy dwelling and thy palace and thy
heart is void of care; so return to him a reply and reck not."
Accordingly, the Princess called for ink-case and paper and wrote
these couplets: —

---

[1] Arab. Aznání = emaciated me.
[2] Either the Deity or the Love-god.

Ho thou who wouldst vaunt thee of cark and care; * How many love-molten, tryst-craving be there?

An hast wandered the wold in the murks of night * Bound afar and anear on the tracks to fare,

And to eyne hast forbidden the sweets of sleep, * Borne by Devils and Marids to dangerous lair;

And beggest my boons, O in tribe-land[1] homed * And to urge thy wish and desire wouldst dare;

Now, woo Patience fair, an thou bear in mind * What The Ruthful promised to patient prayer![2]

How many a king for my sake hath vied, * Craving love and in marriage with me to pair.

Al-Nabhán sent, when a-wooing me, * Camels baled with musk and Nadd scenting air.

They brought camphor in boxes and like thereof * Of pearls and rubies that countless were;

Brought pregnant lasses and negro-lads, * Blood steeds and arms and gear rich and rare;

Brought us raiment of silk and of sendal sheen, * And came courting us but no bride he bare:

Nor could win his wish, for I 'bode content * To part with far parting and love forswear;

So for me greed not, O thou stranger wight * Lest thou come to ruin and dire despair!

When she had made an end of her verses, she folded the letter and delivered it to the nurse, who took it and carried it to Al-Abbas. He broke it open and read it and comprehended its contents; then took ink-case and paper and wrote these improvised couplets:—

Thou hast told me the tale of the Kings, and of them * Each was rending lion, a furious foe:

And thou stolest the wits of me, all of them * And shotst me with shaft of thy magic bow:

Thou hast boasted of slaves and of steeds and wealth; * And of beauteous lasses ne'er man did know;

How presents in mighty store didst spurn, * And disdainedst lovers both high and low:

Then I follow'd their tracks in desire for thee, * With naught save my scymitar keen of blow;

Nor slaves nor camels that run have I; * Nor slave-girls the litters enveil, ah, no!

But grant me union and soon shalt sight * My trenchant blade with the foeman's woe;

---

[1] Arab. "Himà" = the tribal domain, a word which has often occurred.

[2] "O ye who believe! seek help through patience and prayer: verily, Allah is with the patient." Koran ii. 148. The passage refers to one of the battles, Bedr or Ohod.

Shalt see the horsemen engird Baghdad * Like clouds that wall the whole
   world below,
Obeying behests which to them I deal * And hearing the words to the foes I
   throw.
An of negro chattels ten thousand head * Wouldst have, or Kings who be
   proud and prow,
Or chargers led for thee day by day * And virgin girls high of bosom, lo!
Al-Yaman land my command doth bear * And my biting blade to my foes I
   show.
I have left this all for the sake of thee, * Left Aziz and my kinsmen for ever-
   mo'e;
And made Al-Irák making way to thee * Under nightly murks over rocks
   arow;
When the couriers brought me account of thee * Thy beauty, perfection, and
   sunny glow,
Then I sent thee verses whose very sound * Burns the heart of shame with a
   fiery throe;
Yet the world with falsehood hath falsèd me, * Though Fortune was never so
   false as thou,
Who dubbest me stranger and homeless one * A witless fool and a slave-girl's
   son!

Then he folded the letter and committed it to the nurse and gave
her five hundred dinars, saying, "Accept this from me, for by
Allah thou hast indeed wearied thyself between us." She replied,
"By Allah, O my lord, my aim is to bring about forgathering
between you, though I lose that which my right hand possesseth." And he said, "May the Lord of All-might requite thee
with good!" Then she carried the letter to Mariyah and said to
her, "Take this letter; haply it may be the end of the correspondence." So she took it and breaking it open, read it, and when she
had made an end of it, she turned to the nurse and said to her,
"This one foisteth lies upon me and asserteth unto me that he
hath cities and horsemen and footmen at his command and sub-
mitting to his allegiance; and he wisheth of me that which he
shall not win; for thou knowest, O nurse, that kings' sons have
sought me in marriage, with presents and rarities; but I have
paid no heed unto aught of this; how, then, shall I accept of this
fellow, who is the ignoramus of his time and possesseth naught
save two caskets of rubies, which he gave to my sire, and indeed
he hath taken up his abode in the house of Al-Ghitrif and abideth
without silver or gold? Wherefore, Allah upon thee, O nurse,
return to him and cut off his hope of me." Accordingly the nurse
rejoined Al-Abbas, without letter or answer; and when she
came in to him, he looked at her and saw that she was troubled,

and he noted the marks of anger on her face; so he said to her,
"What is this plight?" Quoth she, "I cannot set forth to thee
that which Mariyah said; for indeed she charged me return to
thee without writ or reply." Quoth he, "O nurse of kings, I
would have thee carry her this letter and return not to her without it." Then he took ink-case and paper and wrote these
couplets: —

My secret now to men is known though hidden well and true * By me: enough
 is that I have of love and love of you:
I left familiars, friends, and kin to weep the loss of me * With floods of tears
 which like the tide aye flowed and flowed anew:
Then, left my home myself I bore to Baghdad-town one day, * When parting
 drave me there his pride and cruelty to rue:
I have indeed drained all the bowl whose draught repression[1] was * Handed
 by friend who bitter gourd[2] therein for drinking threw.
And, oft as strove I to enjoin the ways of troth and faith, * So often on
 refusal's path he left my soul to sue.
Indeed my body molten is with care I'm doomèd dree; * And yet I hoped
 relenting and to win some grace, my due.
But wrong and rigour waxed on me and changed to worse my case; * And
 love hath left me weeping-eyed for woes that aye pursue.
How long must I keep watch for you throughout the nightly gloom? * How
 many a path of pining pace and garb of grief endue?
And you, what while you joy your sleep, your restful pleasant sleep, * Reck
 naught of sorrow and of shame that to your friend accrue:
For wakefulness I watched the stars before the peep o' day, * Praying that
 union with my dear in bliss my soul imbrue;
Indeed the throes of long desire laid waste my frame and I * Rise every morn
 in weaker plight with hopes e'er fewer few:
"Be not" (I say) "so hard of heart!" for did you only deign * In phantom guise
 to visit me 'twere joy enough to view.
But when ye saw my writ ye grudged to me the smallest boon * And cast
 adown the flag of faith though well my troth ye knew;
Nor aught of answer you vouchsafe, albe you wot full well * The words
 therein address the heart and pierce the spirit through.
You deemed yourself all too secure for changes of the days * And of the far
 and near alike you ever careless grew.
Hadst thou (dear maid) been doomed like me to woes, forsure hadst felt *
 The lowe of love and Lazá-hell which paring doth enmew;
Yet soon shalt suffer torments such as those from thee I bear * And storm of
 palpitation-pangs in vitals thine shall brew:
Yea, thou shalt taste the bitter smack of charges false and foul, * And public
 make the privacy best hid from meddling crew;

---

[1] Arab. "Sirr" (a secret) and afterwards "Kitmán" (concealment) i.e. Keeping a
lover down-hearted.
[2] Arab. "'Alkam" = the bitter gourd, colocynth; more usually "Hanzal."

And he thou lovest shall approve him hard of heart and soul * And heedless
 of the shifts of Time thy very life undo.
Then hear the fond Salam I send and wish thee every day * While swayeth
 spray and sparkleth star all good thy life ensue!

When Al-Abbas had made an end of his verses, he folded the
scroll and gave it to the nurse, who took it and carried it to
Mariyah. When she came into the Princess's presence, she
saluted her; but Mariyah returned not her salutation and she
said, "O my lady, how hard is thy heart that thou grudgest to
return the salam! Accept this letter, because 'tis the last that
shall come to thee from him." Quoth Mariyah, "Take my warning and never again enter my palace, or 'twill be the cause of thy
destruction; for I am certified that thou purposest my disgrace.
So get thee gone from me." And she bade beat the nurse who
went forth fleeing from her presence, changed of colour and
'wildered of wits, and gave not over going till she came to the
house of Al-Abbas. When the Prince saw her in this plight, he
became like a sleeper awakened and cried to her, "What hath
befallen thee? Acquaint me with thy case." She replied,
"Allah upon thee, nevermore send me to Mariyah, and do thou
protect me, so the Lord protect thee from the fires of Gehenna!"
Then she related to him that which had betided her with Mariyah which when Al-Abbas heard, there took him the pride and
high spirit of the generous and this was grievous to him. The
love of Mariyah fled forth of his heart and he said to the nurse,
"How much hadst thou of Mariyah every month?" Quoth she,
"Ten dinars" and quoth he, "Be not concerned." Then he put
hand to pouch and bringing out two hundred ducats, gave them
to her and said, "Take this wage for a whole year and turn not
again to serve anyone of the folk. When the twelvemonth shall
have passed away, I will give thee a two years' wage, for that
thou hast wearied thyself with us and on account of the cutting
off the tie which bound thee to Mariyah." Also he gifted her
with a complete suit of clothes and raising his head to her, said,
"When thou toldest me that which Mariyah had done with
thee, Allah uprooted the love of her from out my heart, and
never again will she occur to my thought; so extolled be He who
turneth hearts and eyes! 'Twas she who was the cause of my
coming out from Al-Yaman, and now the time is past for which
I engaged with my folk and I fear lest my father levy his forces
and ride forth in quest of me, for that he hath no child other than

myself nor can he brook to be parted from me; and in like way 'tis with my mother." When the nurse heard his words, she asked him, "O my lord, and which of the kings is thy sire?" He answered, saying, "My father is Al-Aziz, lord of Al-Yaman, and Nubia and the Islands[1] of the Banu Kahtán, and the Two Sanctuaries[2] (Allah of All-might have them in His keeping!), and whenever he taketh horse, there ride with him an hundred and twenty and four thousand horsemen, each and every smiters with the sword, besides attendants and servants and followers, all of whom give ear to my word and obey my bidding." Asked the nurse, "Why, then, O my lord, didst thou conceal the secret of thy rank and lineage and passedst thyself off for a foreigner and a wayfarer? Alas for our disgrace before thee by reason of our shortcoming in rendering thee thy due! What shall be our excuse with thee, and thou of the sons of the kings?" But he rejoined, "By Allah, thou hast not fallen short! Indeed, 'tis incumbent on me to requite thee, what while I live, though from thee I be far distant." Then he called his man Amir and said to him, "Saddle the steeds." When the nurse heard his words and indeed she saw that Amir brought him the horses and they were resolved upon departure, the tears ran down upon her cheeks and she said to him, "By Allah, thy separation is saddening to me, O coolth of the eye!" Then quoth she, "Where is the goal of thine intent, so we may know thy news and solace ourselves with thy report?" Quoth he, "I go hence to visit 'Akíl, the son of my paternal uncle, for that he hath his sojourn in the camp of Kundah bin Hishám, and these twenty years have I not seen him nor hath he seen me; so I purpose to repair to him and discover his news and return. Then will I go hence to Al-Yaman, Inshallah!" So saying, he took leave of the nurse and her husband and set out, intending for 'Akíl, the son of his father's brother. Now there was between Baghdad and 'Akíl's abiding-place forty days' journey; so Al-Abbas settled himself on the back of his steed and his servant Amir mounted also and they fared forth on their way. Presently, Al-Abbas turned right and left and recited these couplets,

---

[1] "For Jazírah" = insula, island, used in the sense of "peninsula," see vol. i. 2.

[2] Meccah and Al-Medinah. Pilgrimage i. 338 and ii. 57, used in the proverb "Sharr fi al-Haramayn" = wickedness in the two Holy Places.

"I'm the singular knight and my peers I slay! * I lay low the foe and his whole
   array:
I fare me to visit my friend Al-Akíl, * And in safety and Allah-lauds[1] shorten
   the way;
And roll up the width of the wold while still * Hears 'Amir my word or in
   earnest or play.[2]
I spring with the spring of a lynx or a pard * Upon whoso dareth our course
   to stay;
O'erthrow him in ruin and abject shame, * Make him drain the death-cup in
   fatal fray.
My lance is long with its steely blade; * A brand keen-grided, thin-edged I
   sway:
With a stroke an it fell on a towering hill * Of the hardest stone, this would
   cleave in twain:
I lead no troops, nor seek aid save God's, * The creating Lord (to whom laud
   alwày!)
On Whom I rely in adventures all * And Who pardoneth lâches of freeman
   and thrall."

Then they fell a-faring night and day, and as they went, behold,
they sighted a camp of the camps of the Arabs. So Al-Abbas
enquired thereof and was told that it was the camp of the Banu
Zohrah. Now there were around them herds and flocks, such as
filled the earth, and they were enemies to Al-Akil, the cousin of
Al-Abbas, upon whom they made daily raids and took his cattle,
wherefore he used to pay them tribute every year because he
lacked power to cope with them. When Al-Abbas came to the
skirts of the camp, he dismounted from his destrier and his servant Amir also dismounted; and they set down the provaunt and
ate their sufficiency and rested an hour of the day. Then said
the Prince to his page, "Fetch water from the well and give the
horses to drink and draw up a supply for us in thy bag,[3] by way
of provision for the road." So Amir took the water-skin and
made for the well; but, when he came there, behold, two young
men slaves were leading gazelles, and when they saw him, they
said to him, "Whither wendest thou, O youth, and of which of
the Arabs art thou?" Quoth he, "Harkye, lads, fill me my water-
skin, for that I am a stranger astray and a farer of the way, and
I have a comrade who awaiteth me." Quoth the thralls, "Thou

---

[1] Arab. Al-hamd (o li'llah).
[2] i.e. play, such as the chase, or an earnest matter, such as war, etc.
[3] Arab. "Mizwad," or Mizwád = lit. provision-bag, from Zád = viaticum; afterwards
called Kirbah (pron. Girbah, the popular term), and Sakl. The latter is given in the Dic-
tionaries as Askálah = scala, échelle, stage, plank.

art no wayfarer, but a spy from Al-Akíl's camp." Then they
took him and carried him to their king Zuhayr bin Shabíb; and
when he came before him, he said to him, "Of which of the
Arabs art thou?" Quoth Amir, "I am a wayfarer." So Zuhayr
said, "Whence comest thou and whither wendest thou?" and
Amir replied, "I am on my way to Al-Akíl." When he named
Al-Akíl, those who were present were excited; but Zuhayr
signed to them with his eyes and asked him, "What is thine
errand with Al-Akíl?" and he answered, "We would fain see
him, my friend and I." As soon as Zuhayr heard his words, he
bade smite his neck;[1] but his Wazir said to him, "Slay him not,
till his friend be present." So he commanded the two slaves to
fetch his friend; whereupon they repaired to Al-Abbas and
called to him, saying, "O youth, answer the summons of King
Zuhayr." He enquired, "What would the king with me?" and
they replied, "We know not." Quoth he, "Who gave the king
news of me?" and quoth they, "We went to draw water, nad
found a man by the well. So we questioned him of his case,
but he would not acquaint us therewith, wherefore we carried
him willy-nilly to King Zuhayr, who asked him of his adventure
and he told him that he was going to Al-Akíl. Now Al-Akíl
is the king's enemy and he intendeth to betake himself to his
camp and make prize of his offspring, and cut off his traces."
Said Al-Abbas, "And what hath Al-Akíl done with King
Zuhayr?" They replied, "He engaged for himself that he would
bring the King every year a thousand dinars and a thousand
she-camels, besides a thousand head of thoroughbred steeds and
two hundred black slaves and fifty hand-maids; but it hath
reached the king that Al-Akíl purposeth to give naught of this;
wherefore he is minded to go to him. So hasten thou with us,
ere the King be wroth with thee and with us." Then said Al-
Abbas to them, "O youths, sit by my weapons and my stallion
till I return." But they said, "By Allah, thou prolongest discourse with that which beseemeth not of words! Make haste,
or we will go with thy head, for indeed the King purposeth

---

[1] Those blood-feuds are most troublesome to the traveller, who may be delayed by them
for months: and, until a peace be patched up, he will never be allowed to pass from one
tribe to their enemies. A quarrel of the kind prevented my crossing Arabia from Al-
Medinah to Maskat (Pilgrimage, ii. 297), and another in Africa from visiting the head of
the Tanganyika Lake. In all such journeys the traveller who has to fight against Time is
almost sure to lose.

to slay thee and to slay thy comrade and take that which is
with you." When the Prince heard this, his skin bristled with
rage and he cried out at them with a cry which made them
tremble. Then he sprang upon his horse and settling himself
in the saddle, galloped till he came to the King's assembly, when
he shouted at the top of his voice, saying, "To horse, O horsemen!" and couched his spear at the pavilion wherein was Zuhayr.
Now there were about the King a thousand smiters with the
sword; but Al-Abbas charged home upon them and dispersed
them from around him; and there abode none in the tent save
Zuhayr and his Wazir. Then Al-Abbas came up to the door of
the tent wherein were four-and-twenty golden doves; so he took
them, after he had tumbled them down with the end of his lance.
Then he called out saying, "Ho, Zuhayr! Doth it not suffice
thee that thou hast abated Al-Akil's repute, but thou art minded
to abate that of those who sojourn round about him? Knowest
thou not that he is of the lieutenants of Kundah bin Hisham
of the Banu Shayban, a man renowned for prowess? Indeed,
greed of his gain hath entered into thee and envy of him hath
gotten the mastery of thee. Doth it not suffice thee that thou
hast orphaned his children[1] and slain his men? By the virtue
of Mustafa, the Chosen Prophet, I will make thee drain the cup
of death!" So saying, he bared his brand and smiting Zuhayr
on his shoulder-blade caused the steel issue gleaming from his
throat tendons; then he smote the Wazir and clove his crown
asunder. As he was thus, behold, Amir called out to him and
said, "O my lord, come help me, or I be a dead man!" So
Al-Abbas went up to him guided by his voice, and found him cast
down on his back and chained with four chains to four pickets
of iron.[2] He loosed his bonds and said to him, "Go in front
of me, O Amir." So he fared on before him a little, and presently
they looked, and, behold, horsemen were making to Zuhayr's
succour, and they numbered twelve thousand riders led by
Sahl bin Ka'ab bestriding a coal-black steed. He charged upon
Amir, who fled from him, then upon Al-Abbas, who said, "O
Amir, hold fast to my horse and guard my back." The page
did as he bade him, whereupon Al-Abbas cried out at the folk

---

[1] i.e. his fighting-men.
[2] The popular treatment of a detected horse-thief, for which see Burckhardt, Travels
in Arabia (1829), and Notes on the Bedouins and Wahabys (1830).

and falling upon them, overthrew their braves and slew of them some two thousand riders, whilst not one of them knew what was to do nor with whom he fought. Then said one of them to other, "Verily, the King is slain; so with whom do we wage war? Indeed ye flee from him; but 'twere better ye enter under his banners, or not one of you will be saved." Thereupon all dismounted and doffing that which was upon them of war-gear, came before Al-Abbas and proffered him allegiance and sued for his protection. So he withheld his brand from them and bade them gather together the spoils. Then he took the riches and the slaves and the camels, and they all became his lieges and his retainers, to the number (according to that which is reported) of fifty thousand horses. Furthermore, the folk heard of him and flocked to him from all sides; whereupon he divided the loot amongst them and gave largesse and dwelt thus three days, and there came gifts to him. After this he bade march for Al-Akil's abiding place; so they fared on six days and on the seventh they sighted the camp. Al-Abbas bade his man Amir precede him and give Al-Akil the good news of his cousin's coming; so he rode on to the camp and, going in to Al-Akil, acquainted him with the glad tidings of Zuhayr's slaughter and the conquest of his clan.[1] Al-Akil rejoiced in the coming of Al-Abbas and the slaughter of his enemy and all in his camp rejoiced also and cast robes of honour upon Amir; while Al-Akil bade go forth to meet Al-Abbas, and commanded that none, great or small, freeman or slave, should tarry behind. So they did his bidding and going forth all, met Al-Abbas at three parasangs' distance from the camp; and when they met him, they dismounted from their horses and Al-Akil and he embraced and clapped palm to palm.[2] Then rejoicing in the coming of Al-Abbas and the killing of their foeman, they returned to the camp, where tents were pitched for the new-comers and skin-rugs spread and game slain and beasts slaughtered and royal guest-meals spread; and after this fashion they abode twenty days in the enjoyment of all delight of life. On this wise fared it with Al-Abbas and his cousin Al-Akil; but as regards King Al-Aziz, when his son left him, he was desolated for him with exceeding desolation, both he and his mother; and when tidings of him tarried long and the tryst-time passed

---

[1] Arab "Ashírah": see vol. vii. 121.
[2] Arab. "Musáfahah": see vol. vi. 287.

without his returning, the king caused public proclamation to be made, commanding all his troops to get ready to mount and ride forth in quest of his son Al-Abbas, at the end of three days, after which no cause of hindrance or excuse would be admitted to any. So on the fourth day, the king bade muster the troops who numbered four-and-twenty thousand horse, besides servants and followers. Accordingly, they reared the standards and the kettle-drums beat the general and the king set out with his power intending for Baghdad; nor did he cease to press forward with all diligence, till he came within half a day's journey of the city, when he bade his army encamp on the Green Meadow. There they pitched the tents, till the lowland was straitened with them, and set up for the king a pavilion of green brocade, purfled with pearls and precious stones. When Al-Aziz had sat awhile, he summoned the Mamelukes of his son Al-Abbas, and they were five-and-twenty in number besides ten slave-girls, as they were moons, five of whom the king had brought with him and other five he had left with the prince's mother. When the Mamelukes came before him, he cast over each and every of them a mantle of green brocade and bade them mount similar horses of one and the same fashion and enter Baghdad and ask after their lord Al-Abbas. So they rode into the city and passed through the market-streets and there remained in Baghdad nor old man nor boy but came forth to gaze on them and divert himself with the sight of their beauty and loveliness and the seemliness of their semblance and the goodliness of their garments and horses, for all were even as moons. They gave not over going till they came to the palace,[1] where they halted, and the king looked at them and seeing their beauty and the brilliancy of their apparel and the brightness of their faces, said, "Would Heaven I knew of which of the tribes these are!" And he bade the Eunuch bring him news of them. The castrato went out to them and questioned them of their case, whereto they replied, "Return to thy lord and enquire of him concerning Prince Al-Abbas, an he have come unto him, for that he left his sire King Al-Aziz a full-told year ago, and indeed longing for him troubleth the King and he hath levied a division of his army and his guards and is come forth in quest of his son, so haply he may light upon tidings of him." Quoth the Eunuch, "Is there amongst you a brother of his or a son?" and quoth they, "Nay,

---

[1] In the text, "To the palace of the king's daughter."

by Allah, but we are all his Mamelukes and the purchased of his money, and his sire Al-Aziz hath sent us to make enquiry of him. Do thou go to thy lord and question him of the Prince and return to us with that which he shall answer thee." Asked the Eunuch, "And where is King Al-Aziz?" and they answered, "He is encamped in the Green Meadow."[1] The Eunuch returned and told the king, who said, "Indeed we have been unduly negligent with regard to Al-Abbas. What shall be our excuse with the King? By Allah, my soul suggested to me that the youth was of the sons of the kings!" His wife, the Lady Afifah, saw him lamenting for his neglect of Al-Abbas, and said to him, "O King, what is it thou regrettest with this mighty regret?" Quoth he, "Thou knowest the stranger youth, who gifted us with the rubies?" Quoth she, "Assuredly;" and he, "Yonder youths, who have halted in the palace court, are his Mamelukes, and his father, King Al-Aziz, lord of Al-Yaman, hath pitched his camp on the Green Meadow; for he is come with his army to seek him, and the number of his troops is four-and-twenty thousand horsemen." Then he went out from her, and when she heard his words, she wept sore for him and had compassion on his case and sent after him, counselling him to summon the Mamelukes and lodge them in the palace and entertain them. The king hearkened to her rede and despatching the Eunuch for the Mamelukes, assigned unto them a lodging and said to them, "Have patience, till the King give you tidings of your lord Al-Abbas." When they heard his words, their eyes ran over with a rush of tears, of their mighty longing for the sight of their lord. Then the King bade the Queen enter the private chamber opening upon the throne-room and let down the curtain before the door, so she might see and not be seen. She did this and he summoned them to his presence; and, when they stood before him, they kissed ground to do him honour, and showed forth their courtly breeding and magnified his dignity. He ordered them to sit, but they refused, till he conjured them by their lord Al-Abbas: accordingly they sat down and he bade set before them food of various kinds and fruits and sweetmeats. Now within the Lady Afifah's palace was a souterrain communicating with the pavilion of the

---

[1] Arab. "Marj Salí' " = cleft meadow (here and below). Mr. Payne suggests that this may be a mistranscription for Marj Salí' (with a Sád) = a treeless champaign. It appears to me a careless blunder for the Marj akhzar (green meadow) before mentioned.

Princess Mariyah: so the Queen sent after her and she came to
her, whereupon she made her stand behind the curtain and gave
her to know that Al-Abbas was son to the King of Al-Yaman and
that these were his Mamelukes: she also told her that the Prince's
father had levied his troops and was come with his army in quest
of him and that he had pitched his camp on the Green Meadow
and had despatched these Mamelukes to make enquiry of their
lord. Then Mariyah abode looking upon them and upon their
beauty and loveliness and the goodliness of their raiment, till they
had eaten their fill of food and the tables were removed; whereupon the King recounted to them the story of Al-Abbas and they
took leave of him and went their ways. So fortuned it with the
Mamelukes; but as for the Princess Mariyah, when she returned
to her palace, she bethought herself concerning the affair of
Al-Abbas, repenting her of what she had done; and the love of
him took root in her heart. And, when the night darkened upon
her, she dismissed all her women and bringing out the letters,
to wit, those which Al-Abbas had written her, fell to reading
them and weeping. She left not weeping her night long, and when
she arose in the morning, she called a damsel of her slave-girls,
Shafikah by name, and said to her, "O damsel, I purpose to
discover to thee mine affair and I charge thee keep my secret,
which is that thou betake thyself to the house of the nurse, who
used to serve me, and fetch her to me, for that I have grave
need of her." Accordingly, Shafikah went out and repairing to
the nurse's house, entered and found her clad in clothing other
and richer than what she had whilome been wont to wear. So
she saluted her and asked her, "Whence hadst thou this dress,
than which there is no goodlier?" Answered the nurse, "O
Shafikah, thou deemest that I have seen no good save of thy
mistress; but, by Allah, had I endeavoured for her destruction,
I had acted righteously, seeing that she did with me what she did
and bade the Eunuch beat me, without offence by me offered:
so tell her that he, on whose behalf I bestirred myself with her,
hath made me independent of her and her humours, for he hath
habited me in this habit and given me two hundred and fifty
dinars and promised me the like every year and charged me
to serve none of the folk." Quoth Shafikah, "My mistress hath a
need for thee; so come thou with me and I will engage to restore
thee to thy dwelling in safety and satisfaction." But quoth the
nurse, "Indeed her palace is become unlawful and forbidden to

me[1] and never again will I enter therein, for that Allah (extolled and exalted be He!) of His favour and bounty hath rendered me independent of her." Presently Shafikah returned to her mistress and acquainted her with the nurse's words and that wherein she was of prosperity; whereupon Mariyah confessed her unmannerly dealing with her and repented when repentance profited her not; and she abode in that her case days and nights, whilst the fire of longing flamed in her heart. On this wise happened it to her; but as regards Al-Abbas, he tarried with his cousin Al-Akil twenty days, after which he made ready for the journey to Baghdad and bidding bring the booty he had taken from King Zuhayr, divided it between himself and his cousin. Then he sent out a-marching Baghdad-wards and when he came within two days' journey of the city, he summoned his servant Amir and said to him, "Mount thy charger and forego me with the caravan and the cattle." So Amir took horse and fared on till he came to Baghdad, and the season of his entering was the first of the day; nor was there in the city little child or old greybeard but came forth to divert himself with gazing on those flocks and herds and upon the beauty of those slave-girls; and their wits were wildered at what they saw. Soon afterwards the news reached the king that the young man Al-Abbas, who had gone forth from him, was come back with booty and rarities and black slaves and a conquering host and had taken up his sojourn without the city, whilst his servant Amir was presently come to Baghdad, so he might get ready for his lord dwelling-places wherein he should take up his abode. When the King heard these tidings of Amir, he sent for him and caused bring him before him; and when he entered his presence, he kissed the ground and saluted with the salam and showed his fine breeding and greeted him with the goodliest of greetings. The King bade him raise his head and, this done, questioned him of his lord Al-Abbas; whereupon he acquainted him with his adventures and told him that which had betided him with King Zuhayr and of the army that was become at his command and of the spoil he had secured. He also gave him to know that Al-Abbas was to arrive on the morrow, and with him more than fifty thousand cavaliers, obedient to his orders. When the king heard his words, he bade decorate

---

[1] The palace, even without especial and personal reasons, not being the place for a religious and scrupulous woman.

Baghdad and commanded the citizens to equip themselves with the richest of their apparel, in honour of the coming of Al-Abbas. Furthermore, he sent to give King Al-Aziz the glad tidings of his son's return and informed him of all which he had heard from the Prince's servant. When the news reached King Al-Aziz, he joyed with exceeding joy in the approach of his son and straightway took horse, he and all his host, while the trumpets blared and the musicians played, so that the earth quaked and Baghdad also trembled, and it was a notable day. When Mariyah beheld all this, she repented in all possible penitence of that which she had done against Al-Abbas and the fires of desire raged in her vitals. Meanwhile, the troops[1] sallied forth of Baghdad and went out to meet those of Al-Abbas, who had halted in a garth called the Green Island. When he espied the approaching host, he strained his sight and, seeing horsemen coming and troops and footmen he knew not, said to those about him, "Among yonder troops are flags and banners of various kinds; but, as for the great green standard that ye see, 'tis the standard of my sire, the which is reserved to him and never displayed save over his head, and thus I know that he himself is come out in quest of me." And he was certified of this, he and his troops. So he fared on towards them and when he drew near them, he knew them and they knew him; whereupon they lighted down from their horses and saluting him, gave him joy of his safety and the folk flocked to him. When he came to his father, they embraced and each greeted other a long time, whilst neither of them could utter a word, for the greatness of that which betided them of joy in reunion. Then Al-Abbas bade the folk take horse; so they mounted and his Mamelukes surrounded him and they entered Baghdad on the most splendid wise and in the highest honour and glory. Now the wife of the shopkeeper, that is, the nurse, came out, with the rest of those who flocked forth, to divert herself with gazing upon the show, and when she saw Al-Abbas and beheld his beauty and the beauty of his host and that which he had brought back with him of herds and slave-girls, Mamelukes and negroes, she improvised and recited these couplets,

"Al-Abbás from the side of Akíl is come; * Caravans and steeds he hath
    plunderèd:

---

[1] "*i.e.* those of El Aziz, who had apparently entered the city or passed through it on their way to the camp of El Abbas." This is Mr. Payne's suggestion.

Yea; horses he brought of pure blood, whose necks * Ring with collars like
    anklets wher'er they are led.
With domèd hoofs they pour torrent-like, * As they prance through dust on
    the level stead:
And bestriding their saddles come men of war, * Whose fingers play on the
    kettle drum's head:
And couched are their lances that bear the points * Keen grided, which fill
    every soul with dread:
Who wi' them would fence draweth down his death * For one deadly lunge
    soon shall do him dead:
Charge, comrades, charge ye and give me joy, * Saying, 'Welcome to thee,
    O our dear comràde!'
And who joys at his meeting shall 'joy delight * Of large gifts when he from
    his steed shall 'light."

When the troops entered Baghdad, each of them alighted in his
tent, whilst Al-Abbas encamped apart on a place near the Tigris
and issued orders to slaughter for the soldiers, each day, that
which should suffice them of oxen and sheep and to bake them
bread and spread the tables: so the folk ceased not to come to him
and eat of his banquet. Furthermore, all the country-people
flocked to him with presents and rarities and he requited them
many times the like of their gifts, so that the lands were filled with
his renown and the fame of him was bruited abroad among the
habitants of wold and town. Then, as soon as he rode to the
house he had bought, the shopkeeper and his wife came to him
and gave him joy of his safety; whereupon he ordered them three
head of swift steeds and thoroughbred and ten dromedaries and
an hundred head of sheep and clad them both in costly robes of
honour. Presently he chose out ten slave-girls and ten negro
slaves and fifty mares and the like number of she-camels and three
hundred of sheep, together with twenty ounces of musk and as
many of camphor, and sent all this to the King of Baghdad. When
the present came to Ins bin Kays, his wit fled for joy and he was
perplexed wherewith to requite him. Al-Abbas also gave gifts
and largesse and bestowed robes of honour upon noble and
simple, each after the measure of his degree, save only Mariyah;
for to her indeed he sent nothing. This was grievous to the
Princess and it irked her sore that he should not remember her;
so she called her slave-girl Shafikah and said to her, "Hie thee to
Al-Abbas and salute him and say to him, 'What hindereth thee
from sending my lady Mariyah her part of thy booty?'" So
Shafikah betook herself to him and when she came to his door,
the chamberlains refused her admission, until they should have

got for her leave and permission. When she entered, Al-Abbas
knew her and knew that she had somewhat of speech with him;
so he dismissed his Mamelukes and asked her, "What is thine
errand, O hand-maid of good?"   Answered she, "O my lord, I
am a slave-girl of the Princess Mariyah, who kisseth thy hands
and offereth her salutation to thee.   Indeed, she rejoiceth in thy
safety and blameth thee for that thou breakest her heart, alone
of all the folk, because thy largesse embraceth great and small,
yet hast thou not remembered her with anything of thy plunder,
as if thou hadst hardened thy heart against her."   Quoth he,
"Extolled be He who turneth hearts! By Allah, my vitals were
consumed with the love of her; and, of my longing after her I
came forth to her from my mother-land and left my people and my
home and my wealth, and it was with her that began the hard-
heartedness and the cruelty.   Natheless, for all this, I bear her no
malice and there is no help but that I send her somewhat whereby she may remember me; for that I sojourn in her country but a
few days, after which I set out for the land of Al-Yaman."   Then
he called for a chest and thence bringing out a necklace of Greek
workmanship, worth a thousand dinars, wrapped it in a mantle
of Greek silk, set with pearls and gems and purfled with red gold,
and joined thereto a couple of caskets containing musk and ambergris.   He also put off upon the girl a mantle of Greek silk, striped
with gold, wherein were divers figures and portraitures de-
pictured, never saw eyes its like.   Therewithal the girl's wit fled
for joy and she went forth from his presence and returned to her
mistress.   When she came in to her, she acquainted her with
that which she had seen of Al-Abbas and that which was with
him of servants and attendants and set out to her the loftiness
of his station and gave her that which was with her.   Mariyah
opened the mantle, and when she saw that necklace (and indeed
the place was illumined with the lustre thereof), she looked at
her slave-girl and said to her, "By Allah, O Shafikah, one look
at him were dearer to me than all that my hand possesseth! Oh,
would Heaven I knew what I shall do, when Baghdad is empty
of him and I hear of him no news!"   Then she wept and calling
for ink-case and paper and pen of brass, wrote these couplets:

Longsome my sorrows are; my liver's fired with ecstasy; * And severance-
    shaft hath shot me through whence sorest pangs I dree:
And howso could my soul forget the love I bear to you? * You-wards my will
    perforce returns nor passion sets me free:

I 'prison all desires I feel for fear of spies thereon * Yet tears that streak my
 cheek betray for every eye to see.
No place of rest or joy I find to bring me life-delight; * No wine tastes well,
 nor viands please however savoury:
Ah me! to whom shall I complain of case and seek its cure * Save unto thee
 whose Phantom deigns to show me sight of thee?
Then name me not or chide for aught I did in passion-stress, * With vitals
 gone and frame consumed by yearning-malady!
Secret I keep the fire of love which aye for severance burns; * Sworn slave[1]
 to Love who robs my rest and wakes me cruelly:
And ceaseth not my thought to gaze upon your ghost by night, * Which falsing
 comes and he I love still, still unloveth me.
Would Heaven ye wist the blight that I for you are doomed to bear * For love
 of you, which tortures me with parting agony!
Then read between the lines I wrote, and mark and learn their sense * For such
 my tale, and Destiny made me an outcast be:
Learn eke the circumstance of Love and lover's woe nor deign * Divulge its
 mysteries to men nor grudge its secrecy.

Then she folded the scroll and giving it to her slave-girl, bade her
bear it to Al-Abbas and bring back his reply. So Shafikah took
the letter and carried it to the Prince, after the doorkeeper had
sought leave of him to admit her. When she came in to him, she
found with him five damsels, as they were moons, clad in rich
raiment and ornaments; and when he saw her, he said to her,
"What is thy need, O hand-maid of good?" Presently she put out
her hand to him with the writ, after she had kissed it, and he bade
one of his slave-girls receive it from her.[2] Then he took it from
the girl and breaking the seal, read it and comprehended its contents; whereupon he cried, "Verily, we be Allah's and unto Him
we shall return!" and calling for ink-case and paper, wrote these
improvised couplets:—

I wonder seeing how thy love to me * Inclined, while I in heart from love
 declined:
Eke wast thou wont to say in verseful writ, * "Son of the Road[3] no road to
 me shall find!
How oft kings flocked to me with mighty men * And bales on back of Bukhti[4]
 beast they bind:
And noble steeds of purest blood and all * They bore of choicest boons to me
 consigned;

---

[1] Arab "Hátif"; gen. = an ally.
[2] Not wishing to touch the hand of a strange woman.
[3] i.e. a mere passer-by, a stranger; alluding to her taunt.
[4] The Bactrian or double-humped dromedary. See vol. iii. 67. Al-Mas'udi (vii. 169)
calls it "Jamal fálij," lit. = the palsy-camel.

Yet won no favour!" Then came I to woo * And the long tale o' love I had
    designed,
I fain set forth in writ of mine, with words * Like strings of pearls in goodly
    line aligned: —
Set forth my sev'rance, griefs, tyrannic wrongs, * And ill device ill-suiting
    lover-kind.
How oft love-claimant, craving secrecy, * How oft have lovers 'plained as sore
    they pined,
How many a brimming bitter cup I've quaffed, * And wept my woes when
    speech was vain as wind!
And thou: — "Be patient, 'tis thy bestest course * And choicest medicine for
    mortal mind!"
Then unto patience worthy praise cleave thou; * Easy of issue and be lief
    resigned:
Nor hope thou aught of me lest ill alloy * Or aught of dross affect my blood
    refined:
Such is my speech. Read, mark, and learn my say! * To what thou deemest
    ne'er I'll tread the way.

Then he folded the scroll and sealing it, entrusted it to the damsel, who took it and bore it to her mistress. When the Princess
read the letter and mastered its meaning, she said, "Meseemeth
he recalleth bygones to me." Then she called for pens, ink, and
paper, and wrote these couplets:

Love thou didst show me till I learnt its woe * Then to the growth of grief
    didst severance show:
I banisht joys of slumber after you * And e'en my pillow garred my wake to
    grow.
How long in parting shall I pine with pain * While severance-spies[1] through
    night watch every throe?
I've left my kingly couch and self withdrew * Therefrom, and taught mine eye-
    lids sleep t'unknow:
'Twas thou didst teach me what I ne'er can bear: * Then didst thou waste
    my frame with parting-blow.
By oath I swear thee, blame and chide me not: * Be kind to mourner Love
    hath stricken low!
For parting-rigours drive him nearer still * To narrow home, ere clad in
    shroud for clo':
Have ruth on me, since Love laid waste my frame, * 'Mid thralls enrolled me
    and lit fires that flame.

Mariyah rolled up the letter and gave it to Shafikah, bidding her
bear it to Al-Abbas. Accordingly she took it and going with it
to his door, proceeded to enter; but the chamberlains and serving-

---

[1] i.e. Stars and planets.

men forbade her, till they had obtained her leave from the Prince. When she went into him, she found him sitting in the midst of the five damsels before mentioned, whom his father had brought for him; so she gave him the letter and he tare it open and read it. Then he bade one of the damsels, whose name was Khafífah and who came from the land of China, tune her lute and sing anent separation. Thereupon she came forward and tuning her lute, played thereon in four-and-twenty modes: after which she returned to the first and sang these couplets,

"Our friends, when leaving us on parting-day, * Drave us in wolds of
      severance-grief to stray:
When bound the camels' litters bearing them, * And cries of drivers urged
      them on the way,
Outrusht my tears, despair gat hold of me * And sleep betrayed mine eyes to
      wake a prey.
The day they went I wept, but showed no ruth * The severance-spy and
      flared the flames alway:
Alas for lowe o' Love that fires me still! * Alack for pine that melts my heart
      away!
To whom shall I complain of care, when thou * Art gone, nor fain a-pillow
      head I lay?
And day by day Love's ardours grow on me, * And far's the tent that holds
      my fondest may:
O Breeze o' Heaven, bear for me a charge * (Nor traitor-like my troth in love
      betray!),
Whene'er thou breathest o'er the loved one's land * Greet him with choice
      salam fro' me, I pray:
Dust him with musk and powdered ambergris * While time endures! Such is
      my wish for aye."

When the damsel had made an end of her song, Al-Abbas swooned away and they sprinkled on him musked rose-water, till he recovered from his fainting-fit, when he called another damsel (now there was on her of linen and raiment and ornaments that which undoeth description, and she was a model of beauty and brightness and loveliness and symmetry and perfect grace, such as shamed the crescent moon, and she was a Turkish girl from the land of the Roum and her name was Háfizah) and said to her, "O Hafizah, close thine eyes and tune thy lute and sing to us upon the days of severance." She answered him, "To hear is to obey" and taking the lute, tightened its strings and cried out from her head,[1] in a plaintive voice, and sang these couplets,

---

[1] i.e. Sang in tenor tones which are always in falsetto.

"My friends! tears flow in painful mockery, * And sick my heart from parting
   agony:
My frame is wasted and my vitals wrung * And love-fires grow and eyes set
   tear-floods free:
And when the fire burns high beneath my ribs * With tears I quench it as sad
   day I see.
Love left me wasted, baffled, pain-begone, * Sore frighted, butt to spying
   enemy:
When I recal sweet union wi' their loves * I chase dear sleep from the sick
   frame o' me.
Long as our parting lasts the rival joys * And spies with fearful prudence gain
   their gree.
I fear me for my sickly, langourous frame * Lest dread of parting slay me
   incont'nently."

When Hafizah had ended her song, Al-Abbas cried to her,
"Brava! Verily, thou quickenest hearts from griefs." Then he
called another maiden of the daughters of Daylam by name
Marjánah, and said to her, "O Marjanah, sing to me upon the
days of parting." She said, "Hearing and obeying," and recited
these couplets,

" 'Cleave to fair Patience! Patience 'gendereth weal': * Such is the rede to us
   all sages deal:
How oft I plained the lowe of grief and love * Mid passions cast my soul in
   sore unheal.
How oft I waked and drained the bitter cup * And watched the stars, nor
   sleep mine eyes would seal!
Enough it were an deal you grace to me * In writ a-morn and garred no
   hope to feel.
But Thoughts which probed its depths would sear my heart * And start from
   eye-brows streams that ever steal:
Nor cease I suffering baleful doom and nights * Wakeful, and heart by sorrows
   rent piece-meal:
But Allah purged my soul from love of you * When all knew secrets cared I
   not reveal.
I march to-morrow from your country and * Haply you'll speed me nor fear
   aught unweal;
And, when in person you be far from us, * Would heaven we knew who
   shall your news reveal.
Who kens if home will e'er us two contain * In dearest life with union naught
   can stain!"

When Marjanah had made an end of her song, the Prince said
to her, "Brava, O damsel! Indeed, thou sayest a thing which had
occurred to my mind and my tongue was near to speaking it."
Then he signed to the fourth damsel, who was a Cairene, by name

Sitt al-Husn, and bade her tune her lute and sing to him upon the
same theme. So the Lady of Beauty tuned her lute and sang
these couplets,

"Patience is blest for weal comes after woe * And all things stated time and
  ordinance show;
 Haps the Sultan, hight Fortune, prove unjust * Shifting the times, and man
  excuse shall know:
 Bitter ensueth sweet in law of change * And after crookedness things
  straightest grow.
 Then guard thine honour, nor to any save * The noble knowledge of the
  hid bestow:
 These be vicissitudes the Lord commands * Poor men endure, the sinner and
  the low."

When Al-Abbas heard her make an end of her verses, they
pleased him and he said to her, "Brava, O Sitt al-Husn! Indeed,
thou hast done away with anxiety from my heart and hast banished the things which had occurred to my thought." Then he
sighed and signing to the fifth damsel, who was from the land of
the Persians and whose name was Marzíyah (now she was the
fairest of them all and the sweetest of speech and she was like
unto a lustrous star, a model of beauty and loveliness and perfection and brightness and justness of shape and symmetric
grace and had a face like the new moon and eyes as they were
gazelle's eyes) and said to her, "O Marzíyah, come forward and
tune thy lute and sing to us on the same theme, for indeed we are
resolved upon faring to the land of Al-Yaman." Now this
maiden had met many of the monarchs and had foregathered
with the great; so she tuned her lute and sang these couplets,

"Friend of my heart why leave thou lone and desolate these eyne? * Fair union
  of our lots ne'er failed this sitting-stead of mine!
 And ah! who dwellest singly in the heart and sprite of me, * (Be I thy
  ransom!) desolate for loss of friend I pine!
 By Allah! O thou richest form in charms and loveliness, * Give alms to lover
  who can show of patience ne'er a sign!
 Alms of what past between us tway (which ne'er will I divulge) * Of privacy between us tway that man shall ne'er divine:
 Grant me approval of my lord whereby t' o'erwhelm the foe * And let my
  straitness pass away and doubtful thoughts malign:
 Approof of thee (an gained the meed) for me high rank shall gain * And show
  me robed in richest weed to eyes of envy fain."

When she had ended her song, all who were in the assembly
wept for the daintiness of her delivery and the sweetness of her

speech and Al-Abbas said to her, "Brava, O Marzíyah! Indeed, thou bewilderest the wits with the beauty of thy verse and the polish of thy speech."[1] All this while Shafikah abode gazing about her, and when she beheld the slave-girls of Al-Abbas and considered the charms of their clothing and the subtlety of their senses and the delicacy of their delivery her reason flew from her head. Then she sought leave of Al-Abbas and returning to her mistress Mariyah, sans letter or reply, acquainted her with what she had espied of the damsels and described to her the condition wherein he was of honour and delight, majesty, venerance and loftiness of rank. Lastly, she enlarged upon what she had seen of the slave-girls and their case and that which they had said and how they had incited Al-Abbas anent returning to his own country by the recitation of songs to the sound of the strings. When the Princess heard this her slave-girl's report, she wept and wailed and was like to leave the world. Then she took to her pillow and said, "O Shafikah, I will inform thee of a something which is not hidden from Allah the Most High, and 'tis that thou watch over me till the Almighty decree the accomplishment of His destiny, and when my days are ended, take thou the necklace and the mantle with which Al-Abbas gifted me and return them to him. I deem not he will survive me, and if the Lord of All-might determine against him and his days come to an end, do thou give one charge to shroud us and entomb us both in one tomb." Then her case changed and her colour waxed wan; and when Shafikah saw her mistress in this plight, she repaired to her mother and told her that the lady Mariyah refused meat and drink. Asked the Queen, "Since when hath this befallen her?" and Shafikah answered, "Since yesterday's date;" whereat the mother was confounded and betaking herself to her daughter, that she might inquire into her case, lo and behold! found her as one dying. So she sat down at her head and Mariyah opened her eyes and seeing her mother sitting by her, sat up for shame before her. The Queen questioned her of her case and she said, "I entered the Hammam and it stupefied me and prostrated me and left in my head an exceeding pain; but I trust in Allah Almighty that it will cease." When her mother went out from her, Mariyah took to chiding the damsel for that which she had

---

[1] Arab. Tahzíb = reforming morals, amending conduct, chastening style.

done and said to her, "Verily, death were dearer to me than this; so discover thou not my affair to any and I charge thee return not to the like of this fashion." Then she fainted and lay swooning for a whole hour, and when she came to herself, she saw Shafikah weeping over her; whereupon she pluckt the necklace from her neck and the mantle from her body and said to the damsel, "Lay them in a damask napkin and bear them to Al-Abbas and acquaint him with that wherein I am for the stress of severance and the strain of forbiddance." So Shafikah took them and carried them to Al-Abbas, whom she found in readiness to depart, being about to take horse for Al-Yaman. She went in to him and gave him the napkin and that which was therein, and when he opened it and saw what it contained, namely, the mantle and the necklace, his chagrin was excessive and his eyes turned in his head[1] and his rage shot out of them. When Shafikah saw that which betided him, she came forward and said to him, "O bountiful lord, verily my mistress returneth not the mantle and the necklace for despite; but she is about to quit the world and thou hast the best right to them." Asked he, "And what is the cause of this?" and Shafikah answered, "Thou knowest. By Allah, never among the Arabs nor the Ajams nor among the sons of the kings saw I a harder of heart than thou! Can it be a slight matter to thee that thou troublest Mariyah's life and causest her to mourn for herself and quit the world for the sake of thy youth?[2] Thou wast the cause of her acquaintance with thee and now she departeth this life on thine account, she whose like Allah Almighty hath not created among the daughters of the kings." When Al-Abbas heard from the damsel these words, his heart burned for Mariyah and her case was not light to him, so he said to Shafikah, "Canst thou bring me in company with her; so haply I may discover her concern and allay whatso aileth her?" Said she, "Yes, I can do that, and thine will be the bounty and the favour." So he arose and followed her, and she preceded him, till they came to the palace. Then she opened and locked behind them four-and-twenty doors and made them fast with padlocks; and when he came to Mariyah, he found her as she were the

---

[1] *i.e.* so as to show only the whites, as happens to the "mesmerised."
[2] *i.e.* for love of and longing for thy youth.

downing sun, strown upon a Táif rug of perfumed leather,[1] surrounded by cushions stuffed with ostrich down, and not a limb of her quivered. When her maid saw her in this state, she offered to cry out; but Al-Abbas said to her, "Do it not, but have patience till we discover her affair; and if Allah (be He extolled and exalted!) have decreed her death, wait till thou have opened the doors to me and I have gone forth. Then do what seemeth good to thee." So saying, he went up to the Princess and laying his hand upon her bosom, found her heart fluttering like a doveling and the life yet hanging to her breast.[2] So he placed his hand on her cheek, whereat she opened her eyes and beckoning to her maid, said to her by signs, "Who is this that treadeth my carpet and transgresseth against me?"[3] "O my lady," cried Shafikah, "this is Prince Al-Abbas, for whose sake thou forsakest the world." When Mariyah heard speak of Al-Abbas, she raised her hand from under the coverlet and laying it upon his neck, inhaled awhile his scent. Then she sat up and her complexion returned to her and they abode talking till a third part of the night was past. Presently, the Princess turned to her handmaid and bade her fetch them somewhat of food, sweetmeats, and fruits, fresh and dry. So Shafikah brought what she desired and they ate and drank and abode on this wise without lewdness, till night went and light came. Then said Al-Abbas, "Indeed, the morn breaketh. Shall I hie to my sire and bid him go to thy father and seek thee of him in wedlock for me, in accordance with the book of Allah Almighty and the practice of His Apostle (whom may He save and assain!) so we may not enter into transgression?" And Mariyah answered, saying, "By Allah, 'tis well counselled of thee!" So he went away to his lodging and naught befel between them; and when the day lightened, she recited these couplets,

"O friends, morn-breeze with Morn draws on amain: * A Voice[4] bespeaks us,
    gladding us with 'plain.
Up to the convent where our friend we'll sight * And wine more subtile than
    the dust[5] we'll drain;

---

[1] *i.e.* leather from Al-Táif: see vol. viii. 303. The text has by mistake Tálifi.

[2] *i.e.* she was at her last breath, when cured by the magic of love.

[3] *i.e.* violateth my private apartment.

[4] The voice (Sházz) is left doubtful: it may be girl's, nightingale's, or dove's.

[5] Arab. "Hibá" partly induced by the rhyme. In desert countries the comparison will be appreciated: in Sind the fine dust penetrates into a closed book.

Whereon our friend spent all the coin he owned * And made the nursling in
his cloak contain;[1]

And, when we oped the jar, light opalline * Struck down the singers in its
search waylain.

From all sides flocking came the convent-monks * Crying at top o' voices,
'Welcome fain!'

And we carousing sat, and cups went round, * Till rose the Venus-star o'er
Eastern plain.

No shame in drinking wine, which means good cheer * And love and promise
of prophetic strain![2]

Ho thou, the Morn, our union sundering, * These joyous hours to fine thou
dost constrain.

Show grace to us until our pleasures end, * And latest drop of joy fro' friends
we gain:

You have affection candid and sincere * And Love and Joy are best of Faiths
for men."

Such was the case with Mariyah; but as regards Al-Abbas, he
betook himself to his father's camp, which was pitched on the
Green Meadow, by the Tigris-side, and none might thread his
way between the tents, for the dense network of the tent ropes.
When the Prince reached the first of the pavilions, the guards
and servants came out to meet him from all sides and walked in
his service till he drew near the sitting-place of his sire, who
knew of his approach. So he issued forth his marquee and coming
to meet his son, kissed him and made much of him. Then they
returned together to the royal pavilion and when they had seated
themselves therein and the guards had taken up their station in
attendance on them, the King said to Al-Abbas, "O my son, get
ready thine affair, so we may go to our own land, for that the
lieges in our absence are become as they were sheep lacking shepherd." Al-Abbas looked at his father and wept till he fainted,
and when he recovered from his fit, he improvised and recited
these couplets,

"I embraced him,[3] and straight I waxt drunk wi' the smell * Of a fresh young
branch wont in wealth to dwell.

Yea, drunken, but not by the wine; nay, 'twas * By draughts from his lips
that like wine-cups well:

For Beauty wrote on his cheek's fair page * 'Oh, his charms! take refuge fro'
danger fell!'[4]

---

[1] *i.e.* he smuggled it in under his 'Abá-cloak: perhaps it was a better brand than that
made in the monastery.

[2] *i.e.* the delights of Paradise promised by the Prophet.

[3] Again, "he" for "she," making the lover's address more courtly and delicate.

[4] *i.e.* take refuge with Allah from the evil eye of her charms.

Mine eyes, be easy, since him ye saw; * Nor mote nor blearness with you
    shall mell:
In him Beauty showeth fro' first to fine * And bindeth on hearts bonds un-
    frangible:
An thou kohl thyself with his cheek of light * Thou'll find but jasper and or
    in stelle:[1]
The chiders came to reproach me when * For him longing and pining my
    heart befel:
But I fear not, I end not, I turn me not * From his life, let tell-tale his tale
    e'en tell:
By Allah, forgetting ne'er crossed my thought * While by life-tie bound, or
    when ends my spell:
An I live I will live in his love, an I die * Of love and longing, I'll cry, ' 'Tis
    well!' "

Now when Al-Abbas had ended his verses, his father said to
him, "I seek refuge for thee with Allah, O my son! Hast thou
any want thou art powerless to win, so I may endeavour for thee
therein and lavish my treasures in its quest." Cried Al-Abbas,
"O my papa, I have, indeed, an urgent need, on whose account
I came forth of my mother-land and left my people and my home
and affronted perils and horrors and became an exile, and I trust
in Allah that it may be accomplished by thy magnanimous endeavour." Quoth the King, 'And what is thy want?" and
quoth Al-Abbas, "I would have thee go and ask for me to wife
Mariyah, daughter of the King of Baghdad, for that my heart is
distracted with love of her." Then he recounted to his father
his adventure from first to last. When the King heard this from
his son, he rose to his feet and calling for his charger of parade,
took horse with four-and-twenty Emirs of the chief officers of his
empire. Then he betook himself to the palace of the King of
Baghdad who, when he saw him coming, bade his chamberlains
open the doors to them and going down himself to meet them,
received him with all honour and hospitality and carried him
and his into the palace; then causing make ready for them carpets and cushions, sat down upon his golden throne and seated
the guest by his side upon a chair of gold, framed in juniper-wood
set with pearls and jewels. Presently he bade bring sweetmeats
and confections and scents and commanded to slaughter four
and-twenty head of sheep and the like of oxen and make ready

---

[1] *i.e.* an thou prank or adorn thyself: I have translated literally, but the couplet
strongly suggests "nonsense verses."

geese and chickens and pigeons stuffed and boiled, and spread the tables; nor was it long before the meats were served up in vessels of gold and silver. So they ate their sufficiency and when they had eaten their fill, the tables were removed and the wine-service set on and the cups and flagons ranged in ranks, whilst the Mamelukes and the fair slave-girls sat down, with zones of gold about their waists, studded with all manner pearls, diamonds, emeralds, rubies and other jewels. Moreover, the king bade fetch the musicians; so there presented themselves before him twenty damsels with lutes and psalteries[1] and viols, and smote upon instruments of music playing and performing on such wise that they moved the assembly to delight. Then said Al-Aziz to the King of Baghdad, "I would fain speak a word to thee; but do thou not exclude from us those who are present. An thou consent unto my wish thine is ours and on thee shall be whatso is on us;[2] and we will be to thee a mighty forearm against all unfriends and foes." Quoth Ins bin Kays, "Say what thou wilt, O King, for indeed thou excellest in speech and in whatso thou sayest dost hit the mark." So Al-Aziz said to him, "I desire that thou marry thy daughter Mariyah to my son Al-Abbas, for thou knowest what he hath of beauty and loveliness, brightness and perfect grace and his frequentation of the valiant and his constancy in the stead of cut-and-thrust." Said Ins bin Kays, "By Allah, O King, of my love for Mariyah, I have appointed her mistress of her own hand; accordingly, whomsoever she chooseth of the folk, to him will I wed her." Then he arose to his feet and going in to his daughter, found her mother with her; so he set out to them the case and Mariyah said, "O my papa, my wish followeth thy word and my will ensueth thy will; so whatsoever thou chooseth, I am obedient to thee and under thy dominion." Therewith the King knew that Mariyah inclined to Al-Abbas; he therefore returned forthright to King Al-Aziz and said to him, "May Allah amend the King! Verily, the wish is won and there is no opposition to that thou commandest." Quoth Al-Aziz, "By Allah's leave are wishes won. How deemest

---

[1] Arab. "Santír:" Lane (M. E., chapt. xviii.) describes it as resembling the Kanún (dulcimer or zither) but with two oblique peg-pieces instead of one and double chords of wire (not treble strings of lamb's gut) and played upon with two sticks instead of the little plectra. Dozy also gives Santir from ψαλτήριον, the Psaltrún of Daniel.

[2] i.e. That which is ours shall be thine, and that which is incumbent on thee shall be incumbent on us = we will assume thy debts and responsibilities.

thou, O King, of fetching Al-Abbas and documenting the marriage-contract between Mariyah and him?" and quoth Ins bin Kays, "Thine be the rede." So Al-Aziz sent after his son and acquainted him with that which had passed; whereupon Al-Abbas called for four-and-twenty mules and ten horses and as many camels and loaded the mules with fathom-long pieces of silk and rugs of leather and boxes of camphor and musk and the camels and horses with chests of gold and silver. Eke, he took the richest of the stuffs and wrapping them in wrappers of gold-purfled silk, laid them on the heads of porters,[1] and they fared on with the treasures till they reached the King of Baghdad's palace, whereupon all who were present dismounted in honour of Al-Abbas and escorting him in a body to the presence of Ins bin Kays, displayed to the King all that they had with them of things of price. The King bade carry all this into the store rooms of the Harim and sent for the Kazis and the witnesses, who wrote out the contract and married Mariyah to Al-Abbas, whereupon the Prince commanded slaughter one thousand head of sheep and five hundred buffaloes. So they spread the bride-feast and bade thereto all the tribes of the Arabs, men of tents and men of towns, and the banquet continued for the space of ten days. Then Al-Abbas went into Mariyah in a commendable and auspicious hour and lay with her and found her a pearl unthridden and a goodly filly no rider had ridden;[2] wherefore he rejoiced and was glad and made merry, and care and sorrow ceased from him and his life was pleasant and trouble departed and he ceased not abiding with her in most joyful case and in the most easeful of life, till seven days were past, when King Al-Aziz resolved to set out and return to his realm and bade his son seek leave of his father-in-law to depart with his wife to his own country. So Al-Abbas spoke of this to King Ins, who granted him the permission he sought; whereupon he chose out, a red camel,[3] taller and more valuable than the rest of the camels,

---

[1] This passage is sadly disjointed in the text: I have followed Mr. Payne's ordering.

[2] The Arab of noble tribe is always the first to mount his own mare: he also greatly fears her being put out to full speed by a stranger, holding that this should be reserved for occasions of life and death; and that it can be done to perfection only once during the animal's life.

[3] The red (Ahmar) dromedary like the white-red (Sahab) were most valued because they are supposed best to bear the heats of noon; and thus "red camels" is proverbially used for wealth. When the head of Abu Jahl was brought in after the Battle of Bedr, Mahommed exclaimed, " 'Tis more acceptable to me than a red camel!"

and loading it with apparel and ornaments, mounted Mariyah
in a litter thereon. Then they spread the ensigns and the standards, whilst kettle-drums beat and the trumpets blared, and set
out upon the homewards way. The King of Baghdad rode
forth with them and companied them three days' journey on
their route, after which he farewelled them and returned with
his troops to Baghdad. As for King Al-Aziz and his son, they
fared on night and day and gave not over going till there remained but three days' journey between them and Al-Yaman,
when they despatched three men of the couriers to the Prince's
mother to report that they were bringing with them Mariyah,
the King's daughter of Baghdad, and returning safe and laden
with spoil. When the Queen-mother heard this, her wit took
wings for joy and she adorned the slave-girls of Al-Abbas after
the finest fashion. Now he had ten hand-maids, as they were
moons, whereof his father had carried five with him to Baghdad,
as hath erst been set forth, and the remaining five abode with his
mother. When the dromedary-posts[1] came, they were certified of
the approach of Al-Abbas, and when the sun easted and their
flags were seen flaunting, the Prince's mother came out to meet
her son; nor on that day was there great or small, boy or greybeard, but went forth to greet the king. Then the kettle-drums
of glad tidings beat and they entered in the utmost of pomp and
the extreme of magnificence; so that the tribes and the towns-
people heard of them and brought them the richest of gifts and
the rarest of presents and the Prince's mother rejoiced with joy
exceeding. They butchered beasts and spread mighty bride-
feasts for the people and kindled fires,[2] that it might be visible

---

[1] *i.e.* Couriers on dromedaries, the only animals used for sending messages over long
distances.

[2] These guest-fires are famous in Arab poetry. So Al-Hariri (Ass. of Banu Haram)
sings:—

> A beacon fire I ever kindled high;

i.e. on the hill-tops near the camp, to guide benighted travellers. Also the Lamíyat al-
Ajam says:—

> The fire of hospitality is ever lit on the high stations.

This natural telegraph was used in a host of ways by the Arabs of The Ignorance; for
instance, when a hated guest left the camp they lighted the "Fire of Rejection," and cried,
"Allah, bear him far from us!" Nothing was more ignoble than to quench such fire:
hence in obloquy of the Fazár tribe it was said:—

> Ne'er trust Fazár with an ass, for they
> Once roasted ass-pizzle, the rabble rout:

afar to townsman and tribesman that this was the house of hospitality and the stead of the wedding-festival, to the intent that,
if any passed them by, it should be of his own sin against himself.
So the folk came to them from all districts and quarters and in this
way they abode days and months. Presently the Prince's mother
bade fetch the five slave-girls to that assembly; whereupon they
came and the ten damsels met. The queen seated five of them
on her son's right hand and the other five on his left and the folk
gathered about them. Then she bade the five who had remained
with her speak forth somewhat of poesy, so they might entertain
therewith the séance and that Al-Abbas might rejoice thereat.
Now she had clad them in the costliest of clothes and adorned
them with trinkets and ornaments and moulded work of gold and
silver and collars of gold, wrought with pearls and gems. So
they paced forward, with harps and lutes and zithers and re-
corders and other instruments of music before them, and one of
them, a damsel who came from the land of China and whose
name was Bá'úthah, advanced and screwed up the strings of her
lute. Then she cried out from the top of her head and recited
these couplets,

"Indeed your land returned, when you returned, * To whilom light which
    overgrew its gloom:
Green grew the land that was afore dust-brown. * And fruits that failed
    again showed riping bloom:
And clouds rained treasures after rain had lacked, * And plenty poured from
    earth's re-opening womb.
Then ceased the woes, my lords, that garred us weep, * With tears like
    dragons' blood, our severance-doom,
Whose length, by Allah, made me yearn and pine, * Would Heaven, O lady
    mine, I were thy groom!"

When she had ended her song, all who were present were delighted and Al-Abbas rejoiced in this. Then he bade the second
damsel sing somewhat on the same theme. So she came forward
and tightening the strings of her harp, which was of balass ruby,[1]
raised her voice in a plaintive air and improvised these couplets,

"Brought the Courier glad news of our absentees,[2] * To please us through
    those who had wrought us unease:

      And, when sight they guest, to their dams they say,
        "Piss quick on the guest-fire and put it out!"
(Al-Mas'údi vi. 140.)

[1] i.e. of rare wood, set with rubies.
[2] i.e. whose absence pained us.

Cried I, 'My life ransom thee, messenger man, * Thou hast kept thy faith
   and thy boons are these.'
An the nightlets of union in you we joyed * When fared you naught would
   our grief appease;
You sware that folk would to folk be true, * And you kept your oaths as good
   faith decrees.
To you made I oath true lover am I * Heaven guard me when sworn from
   all perjuries:
I fared to meet you and loud I cried, * 'Aha, fair welcome when come you
   please!'
And I joyed to meet you and when you came, * Deckt all the dwelling with
   tapestries,
And death in your absence to us was dight, * But your presence bringeth
   us life and light."

When she had made an end of her verse, Al-Abbas bade the third
damsel (who came from Samarkand of Ajam-land and whose name
was Rummánah) sing, and she answered, "To hear is to obey."
Then she took the zither and crying out from the midst of her
head, recited and sang these couplets,[1]

"My watering mouth declares thy myrtle-cheek my food to be * And cull my
   lips thy side-face rose, who lily art to me!
And twixt the dune and down there shows the fairest flower that blooms *
   Whose fruitage is granado's fruit with all granado's blee.[2]
Forget my lids of eyne their sleep for magic eyes of him; * Naught since he
   fared but drowsy charms and languorous air I see.[3]
He shot me down with shaft of glance from bow of eyebrow sped: * What
   Chamberlain[4] betwixt his eyes garred all my pleasure flee?

---

[1] Mr. Payne and I have long puzzled over these enigmatical and possibly corrupt lines:
he wrote to me in 1884, "This is the first piece that has beaten me." In the couplet above
(vol. xii. 230) "Rayhání" may mean "my basil-plant" or "my food" (the latter Koranic),
"my compassion," etc.; and Súsání is equally ancipitous "My lilies" or "my sleep": see
Bard al-Susan = les douceurs du sommeil in Al-Mas'údi vii. 168.

[2] The "Niká" or sand hill is the swell of the throat: the Ghaur or lowland is the fall of
the waist: the flower is the breast anent which Mr. Payne appropriately quotes the well-
known lines of Fletcher:

> "Hide, O hide those hills of snow,
> That thy frozen bosom bears,
> *On whose tops the pinks that grow*
> Are of those that April wears."

[3] Easterns are right in regarding a sleepy languorous look as one of the charms of
women, and an incitement to love because suggestive only of bed. Some men also find the
same pleasure in a lacrymose expression of countenance, seeming always to call for consolation: one of the most successful women I know owes her exceptional good fortune to
this charm.

[4] Arab. "Hájib," eyebrow or chamberlain; see vol. iii. 233. The pun is classical used by
a host of poets including Al-Haríri.

Haply shall heart of me seduce his heart by weakness' force * E'en as his own
    seductive grace garred me love-ailment dree.
For an by him forgotten be our pact and covenant * I have a King who never
    will forget my memory.
His sides bemock the bending charms of waving Tamarisk,[1] * And in his
    beauty-pride he walks as drunk with coquetry:
His feet and legs be feather-light whene'er he deigns to run * And say, did
    any ride the wind except 'twere Solomon?"[2]

Therewith Al-Abbas smiled and her verses pleased him. Then
he bade the fourth damsel come forward and sing (now she was
from the Sundown-land[3] and her name was Balakhshá); so she
came forward and taking the lute and the zither, tuned the strings
and smote them in many modes; then she returned to the first and
improvising, sang these couplets,

"When to the séance all for pleasure hied * Thy lamping eyes illumined its
    every side;
While playing round us o'er the wine-full bowl * Those necklace-pearls old
    wine with pleasure plied,[4]
Till wits the wisest drunken by her grace * Betrayed for joyance secrets sages
    hide;
And, seen the cup, we bade it circle round * While sun and moon spread
    radiance side and wide.
We raised for lover veil of love perforce * And came glad tidings which new
    joys applied:
Loud sang the camel-guide; won was our wish * Nor was the secret by the
    spy espied:
And, when my days were blest by union-bliss * And to all-parting Time was
    aid denied,
Each 'bode with other, clear of meddling spy * Nor feared we hate of foe or
    neighbour-pride.
The sky was bright, friends came and severance fared * And Love-in-union
    rained boons multiplied:
Saying, 'Fulfil fair union, all are gone * Rivals and fears lest shaming foe
    deride:'

---

[1] Arab. "Tarfah." There is a Tarfia Island in the Guadalquivir and in Gibraltar a
"Tarfah Alto" opposed to "Tarfah bajo." But it must not be confounded with Tarf = a
side, found in the Maroccan term for "The Rock" Jabal al-Tarf = Mountain of the Point
(of Europe).
[2] For Solomon and his flying carpet see vol. iii. 267.
[3] Arab. "Bilád al-Maghrib (al-Aksa," in full) = the Farthest Land of the setting Sun,
shortly called Al-Maghrib and the people "Maghribi." The earliest occurrence of our
name Morocco or Marocco I find in the "Marákiyah" of Al-Mas'udi (iii. 241), who apparently applies it to a district whither the Berbers migrated.
[4] The necklace-pearls are the cup-bearer's teeth.

Friends now conjoinèd are: wrong passed away * And meeting-cup goes
   round and joys abide:
On you be Allah's Peace with every boon * Till end the dooming years and
   time and tide."

When Balakhshá had ended her verse, all present were moved to
delight and Al-Abbas said to her, "Brava, O damsel!"   Then he
bade the fifth damsel come forward and sing (now she was from
the land of Syria and her name was Rayhánah; she was passing
of voice and when she appeared in an assembly, all eyes were
fixed upon her), so she came forward and taking the viol (for she
was used to play upon all instruments) recited and sang these
couplets,

"Your me-wards coming I hail to sight; * Your look is a joy driving woe from
   sprite:
With you love is blest, pure and white of soul; * Life's sweet and my planet
   grows green and bright:
By Allah, you-wards my pine ne'er ceased * And your like is rare and right
   worthy hight.
Ask my eyes an e'er since the day ye went * They tasted sleep, looked on
   lover-wight:
My heart by the parting-day was broke * And my wasted body betrays my
   plight:
Could my blamers see in what grief am I, * They had wept in wonder my
   loss, my blight!
They had joined me in shedding torrential tears * And like me a-morn had
   shown thin and slight:
How long for your love shall your lover bear * This weight o'er much for the
   hill's strong height?
By Allah what then for your sake was doomed * To my heart, a heart by its
   woes turned white!
An showed I the fires that aye flare in me, * They had 'flamed Eastern world
   and earth's Western site.
But after this is my love fulfilled * With joy and gladness and mere delight;
And the Lord who scattered hath brought us back * For who doeth good
   shall of good ne'er lack."

When King Al-Aziz heard the damsel's song, both words and
verses pleased him and he said to Al-Abbas, "O my son, verily
long versifying hath tired these damsels, and indeed they make us
yearn after the houses and the homesteads with the beauty of
their songs. These five have adorned our meeting with the charm
of their melodies and have done well in that which they have said
before those who are present; so we counsel thee to free them for
the love of Allah Almighty."   Quoth Al-Abbas, "There is no
command but thy command;" and he enfranchised the ten dam-

sels in the assembly; whereupon they kissed the hands of the
King and his son and prostrated themselves in thanksgiving to the
Lord of All-might.   Then they put off that which was upon them
of ornaments and laying aside the lutes and other instruments of
music, kept to their houses like modest women and veiled, and
fared not forth.[1]   As for King Al-Aziz, he lived after this seven
years and was removed to the mercy of Almighty Allah; when
his son Al-Abbas bore him forth to burial as beseemeth kings and
let make for him perlections and professional recitations of the
Koran.   He kept up the mourning for his father during four successive weeks, and when a full-told month had elapsed he sat
down on the throne of the kingship and judged and did justice
and distributed silver and gold.   He also loosed all who were in
the jails and abolished grievances and customs dues and righted
the oppressed of the oppressor; so the lieges prayed for him and
loved him and invoked on him endurance of glory and continuance of kingship and length of life and eternity of prosperity
and happiness.   The troops submitted to him, and the hosts from
all parts of the kingdom, and there came to him presents from each
and every land: the kings obeyed him and many were his war-
riors and his grandees, and his subjects lived with him the most
easeful of lives and the most delightsome.   Meanwhile, he
ceased not, he and his beloved, Queen Mariyah, in the most
enjoyable of life and the pleasantest, and he was vouchsafed
by her children; and indeed there befel friendship and affection
between them and the longer their companionship was prolonged,
the more their love waxed, so that they became unable to endure
each from other a single hour, save the time of his going forth to
the Divan, when he would return to her in the liveliest that might
be of longing.   And after this fashion they abode in all solace of
life and satisfaction till there came to them the Destroyer of
delights and the Severer of societies.   So extolled be the Eternal
whose sway endureth for ever and aye, who never unheedeth
neither dieth nor sleepeth!   This is all that hath come down to
us of their tale, and so the Peace!

---

[1] In these unregenerate days they would often be summoned to the houses of the royal
family; but now they had "got religion" and, becoming freed women, were resolved to
be "respectable."   In not a few Moslem countries men of wealth and rank marry professional singers who, however loose may have been their artistic lives, mostly distinguish
themselves by decency of behaviour often pushed to the extreme of rigour.   Also jeune
coquette, vieille dévote, is a rule of the world, Eastern and Western.

SHAHRAZAD AND SHAHRYAR.[1]

KING SHAHRYAR marveled at this history[2] and said, "By Allah,
verily, injustice slayeth its folk!"[3] And he was edified by that,
wherewith Shahrazad bespoke him and sought help of Allah the
Most High. Then said he to her, "Tell me another of thy tales,
O Shahrazad; supply me with a pleasant story and this shall be
the completion of the story-telling." Shahrazad replied, "With
love and gladness! It hath reached me, O auspicious King, that a
man once declared to his mates, 'I will set forth to you a means
of security against annoy.' A friend of mine once related to me
and said, 'We attained to security against annoy, and the origin
of it was other than this; that is, it was the following'"[4]

TALE OF THE TWO KINGS AND THE WAZIR'S
DAUGHTERS.[5]

I OVERTRAVELLED whilome lands and climes and towns and
visited the cities of high renown and traversed the ways of
dangers and hardships. Towards the last of my life, I entered
a city of the cities of China,[6] wherein was a king of the Chosroës
and the Tobbas[7] and the Cæsars.[8] Now that city had been
peopled with its inhabitants by means of justice and equity; but
its then king was a tyrant dire who despoiled lives and souls
at his desire; in fine, there was no warming oneself at his fire,[9]

---

[1] Bresl. Edit., vol. xii p. 383 (Night mi). The king is called as usual "Shahrbán," which
is nearly synonymous with Shahryár.

[2] *i.e.* the old Sindibad-Námeh (see vol. vi. 122), or "The Malice of Women" which the
Bresl. Edit. entitles, "Tale of the King and his Son and his Wife and the Seven Wazirs."
Here it immediately follows the Tale of Al-Abbas and Mariyah and occupies pp. 237-383
of vol. xii. (Nights dcccclxxix-m).

[3] *i.e.* Those who commit it.

[4] The connection between this pompous introduction and the story which follows is not
apparent. The "Tale of the Two Kings and the Wazir's Daughters" is that of Shahrazad
told in the third person, in fact a rechauffé of the Introduction. But as some three years
have passed since the marriage, and the dénouement of the plot is at hand, the Princess is
made, with some art I think, to lay the whole affair before her husband in her own words,
the better to bring him to a "sense of his duty."

[5] Bresl. Edit. vol. xii. pp. 384-412.

[6] This clause is taken from the sequence, where the elder brother's kingdom is placed
in China.

[7] For the Tobbas = "Successors" or the Himyaritic kings, see vol.. i. 216.

[8] Kayásirah, opp. to Akásirah, here and in many other places.

[9] See vol. ii. 77. King Kulayb ("little dog") al-Wá'il, a powerful chief of the Banu Ma'ad

for that indeed he oppressed the believing band and wasted the land. Now he had a younger brother, who was king in Sarma-kand of the Persians, and the two kings sojourned a while of time, each in his own city and stead, till they yearned unto each other and the elder king despatched his Wazir to fetch his younger brother. When the Minister came to the King of Samarkand and acquainted him with his errand, he submitted himself to the bidding of his brother and answered, "To hear is to obey." Then he equipped himself and made ready for wayfare and brought forth his tents and pavilions. A while after midnight, he went in to his wife, that he might farewell her, and found with her a strange man, lying by her in one bed. So he slew them both and dragging them out by the feet, cast them away and set forth on his march. When he came to his brother's court, the elder king rejoiced in him with joy exceeding and lodged him in the pavilion of hospitality beside his own palace. Now this pavilion overlooked a flower-garden belonging to the elder brother and there the younger abode with him some days. Then he called to mind that which his wife had done with him and remembered her slaughter and bethought him how he was a king, yet was not exempt from the shifts of Time; and this affected him with exceeding affect, so that it drave him to abstain from meat and drink, or, if he ate anything, it profited him naught. When his brother saw him on such wise, he deemed that this had betided him by reason of severance from his folk and family, and said to him, "Come, let us fare forth a-coursing and a-hunting." But he refused to go with him; so the elder brother went to the chase, whilst the younger abode in the pavilion aforesaid. Now, as he was diverting himself by looking out upon the flower-garden from the latticed window of the palace, behold, he saw his brother's wife and with her ten black slaves and ten slave-girls. Each slave laid hold of a damsel and another slave came forth and did the like with the queen; and when they had their wills one of other they all returned whence they came. Hereat there

---

in the Kasín district of Najd, who was connected with the war of Al-Basús. He is so called because he lamed a pup (kulayb) and tied it up in the midst of his Himà (domain, place of pasture and water), forbidding men to camp within sound of its bark or sight of his fire. Hence "more masterful than Kulayb," A. P. ii. 145, and Al-Hariri Ass. xxvi. (Chenery, p. 448). This angry person came by his death for wounding in the udder a trespassing camel (Sorab) whose owner was a woman named Basús. Her friend (Jasús) slew him; and thus arose the famous long war between the tribes Wá'il Bakr and Taghlib. It gave origin to the saying, "Die thou and be an expiation for the shoe-latchet of Kulayb."

betided the King of Samarkand exceeding surprise and solace
and he was made whole of his malady, little by little. After a
few days, his brother returned, and finding him cured of his
complaint, said to him, "Tell me, O my brother, what was the
cause of thy sickness and thy pallor, and what is the reason of the
return of health to thee and of rosiness to thy face after this?"
So he acquainted him with the whole case and this was grievous
to him; but they hid their affair and agreed to leave the kingship
and fare forth a-pilgrimaging and adventuring at hap-hazard, for
they deemed that there had befallen none the like of what had
befallen them. Accordingly, they went forth and as they journeyed, they saw by the way a woman imprisoned in seven chests,
whereon were five padlocks, and sunken deep in the midst of the
salt sea, under the guardianship of an Ifrit; yet for all this that
woman issued out of the ocean and opened those padlocks and
coming forth of those chests, did what she would with the two
brothers, after she had practised upon the Ifrit. When the two
kings saw that woman's fashion and how she circumvented the
Ifrit, who had lodged her in the abyss of the main, they turned
back to their kingdoms and the younger betook himself to Samarkand, whilst the elder returned to China and contrived for himself a custom in the slaughter of damsels, which was, his Wazir
used to bring him every night a girl, with whom he lay that
night, and when he arose in the morning, he gave her to the
Minister and bade him do her die. After this fashion he abode
a long time, whilst the folk murmured and God's creatures were
destroyed and the commons cried out by reason of that grievous
affair into which they were fallen and feared the wrath of Allah
Almighty, dreading lest He destroy them by means of this. Still
the king persisted in that practice and in his blameworthy intent
of the killing of damsels and the despoilment of maidens concealed by veils,[1] wherefore the girls sought succour of the Lord of
All-might, and complained to Him of the tyranny of the king
and of his oppression. Now the king's Wazir had two daughters,
sisters german, the elder of whom had read the books and made
herself mistress of the sciences and studied the writings of the
sages and the stories of the cup-companions,[2] and she was a

---

[1] Arab. "Mukhaddarát, maidens concealed behind curtains and veiled in the Harem.
[2] i.e. The professional Ráwis or tale-reciters who learned stories by heart from books
like "The Arabian Nights." See my Terminal Essay, vol. x. 144.

maiden of abundant lore and knowledge galore and wit than which naught can be more. She heard that which the folk suffered from that king in his misusage of their children; whereupon ruth for them gat hold of her and jealousy and she besought Allah Almighty that He would bring the king to renounce that his new and accursed custom,[1] and the Lord answered her prayer. Then she consulted her younger sister and said to her, "I mean to devise a device for freeing the children of folk; to wit, I will go up to the king and offer myself to marry him, and when I come to his presence, I will send to fetch thee. When thou comest in to me and the king hath had his carnal will of me, do thou say to me, 'O my sister, let me hear a story of thy goodly stories, wherewith we may beguile the waking hours of our night, till the dawn, when we take leave each of other; and let the king hear it likewise!' " The other replied, " 'Tis well; forsure this contrivance will deter the king from this innovation he practiseth and thou shalt be requited with favour exceeding and recompense abounding in the world to come, for that indeed thou perilest thy life and wilt either perish or win to thy wish." So she did this and Fortune favoured her and the Divine direction was vouchsafed to her and she discovered her design to her sire, the Wazir, who thereupon forbade her, fearing her slaughter. However, she repeated her words to him a second time and a third, but he consented not. Then he cited to her a parable, which should deter her, and she cited to him a parable of import contrary to his, and the debate was prolonged between them and the adducing of instances, till her father saw that he was powerless to turn her from her purpose and she said to him, "There is no help but that I marry the King, so haply I may be a sacrifice for the children of the Moslems: either I shall turn him from this his heresy or I shall die." When the Minister despaired of dissuading her, he went up to the king and acquainted him with the case, saying, "I have a maiden daughter and she desireth to give herself in free gift to the King." Quoth the King, "How can thy soul consent to this, seeing that thou knowest I abide but a single night with a girl and when I arise on the morrow, I do her dead, and 'tis thou who slayest her, and again and again thou hast done this?"

---

[1] Arab. "Bid'ah," lit. = an innovation, a new thing, an invention, any change from the custom of the Prophet and the universal practice of the Faith, whether it be in the cut of the beard or a question of state policy. Popularly the word = heterodoxy, heresy; but theologically it is not necessarily used in a bad sense. See vol. v. 167.

Quoth the Wazir, "Know, O king, that I have set forth all this to her, yet consented she not to aught, but needs must she have thy company and she chooseth to come to thee and present her-self before thee, albeit I have cited to her the sayings of the sages; but she hath answered me with more than that which I said to her and contrariwise." Then quoth the king, "Suffer her visit me this night and to-morrow morning come thou and take her and kill her; and by Allah, an thou slay her not, I will slay thee and her also!" The Minister obeyed the king's bidding and going out from the presence returned home. When it was night, he took his elder daughter and carried her up to the king; and when she came before him she wept;[1] whereupon he asked her, "What causeth thee weep? indeed, 'twas thou who willedst this." She answered, "I weep not but of longing after my little sister; for that, since we grew up, I and she, I have never been parted from her till this day; so, an it please the King to send for her, that I may look on her, and listen to her speech and take my fill of her till the morning, this were a boon and an act of kindness of the King." So he bade fetch the damsel and she came. Then there befel that which befel of his union with the elder sister,[2] and when he went up to his couch, that he might sleep, the younger sister said to her elder, "Allah upon thee, O my sister, an thou be not asleep, tell us a tale of thy goodly tales, wherewith we may beguile the watches of our night, ere day dawn and parting." Said she, "With love and gladness;" and fell to relating to her, whilst the king listened. Her story was goodly and delectable, and whilst she was in the midst of telling it, the dawn brake. Now the king's heart clave to the hearing of the rest of the story; so he respited her till the morrow; and, when it was the next night, she told him a tale concerning the marvels of the lands and the won-ders of Allah's creatures which was yet stranger and rarer than the first. In the midst of the recital, appeared the day and she was silent from the permitted say. So he let her live till the following night, that he might hear the end of the history and after that slay her. On this wise it fortuned with her; but as regards the people of the city, they rejoiced and were glad and blessed the Wazir's daughters, marvelling for that three days had

---

[1] About three parts of this sentence have been supplied by Mr. Payne, the careless scribe having evidently omitted it.

[2] Here, as in the Introduction (vol. i. 24), the king consummates his marriage in presence of his virgin sister-in-law, a process which decency forbids amongst Moslems.

passed and that the king had not put his bride to death and exulting in that he had returned to the ways of righteousness and would never again burthen himself with blood-guilt against any of the maidens of the city.   Then, on the fourth night, she related to him a still more extraordinary adventure, and on the fifth night she told him anecdotes of Kings and Wazirs and Notables.   Brief, she ceased not to entertain him many days and nights, while the king still said to himself, "Whenas I shall have heard the end of the tale, I will do her die," and the people redoubled their marvel and admiration.   Also, the folk of the circuits and cities heard of this thing, to wit, that the king had turned from his custom and from that which he had imposed upon himself and had renounced his heresy, wherefor they rejoiced and the lieges returned to the capital and took up their abode therein, after they had departed thence; and they were constant in prayer to Allah Almighty that He would stablish the king in his present stead." "And this," said Shahrazad, "is the end of that which my friend related to me."   Quoth Shahryar,[1] "O Shahrazad, finish for us the tale thy friend told thee, inasmuch as it resembleth the story of a King whom I knew; but fain would I hear that which betided the people of this city and what they said of the affair of the King, so I may return from the case wherein I was."   She replied, "With love and gladness!"   Know, O auspicious king and lord of right rede and praiseworthy meed and prowest of deed, that, when the folk heard how the king had put away from him his malpractice and returned from his unrighteous wont, they rejoiced in this with joy exceeding and offered up prayers for him. Then they talked one with other of the cause of the slaughter of the maidens, and the wise said, "Women are not all alike, nor are the fingers of the hand alike."   Now when King Shahryar heard this story he came to himself and awakening from his drunkenness,[2] said, "By Allah, this story is my story and this case is my case, for that indeed I was in reprobation and danger of judgment till thou turnedst me back from this into the right way, extolled be the Causer of causes and the Liberator of necks!" presently adding, "Indeed, O Shahrazad, thou hast awakened me to many things and hast aroused me from mine ignorance of the right."

---

[1] Al-Mas'udi (vol. iv. 213) uses this term to signify viceroy in "Shahryár Sajastán."
[2] i.e. his indifference to the principles of right and wrong, which is a manner of moral intoxication.

Then said she to him, "O chief of the kings, the wise say, 'The
kingship is a building, whereof the troops are the base, and when
the foundation is strong, the building endureth;' wherefore it
behoveth the king to strengthen the foundation, for that they
say, 'Whenas the base is weak, the building falleth.' In like
fashion it besitteth the king to care for his troops and do justice
among his lieges, even as the owner of the garden careth for his
trees and cutteth away the weeds that have no profit in them;
and so it befitteth the king to look into the affairs of his Ryots and
fend off oppression from them. As for thee, O king, it behoveth
thee that thy Wazir be virtuous and experienced in the require-
ments of the people and the peasantry; and indeed Allah the
Most High hath named his name[1] in the history of Musà (on
whom be the Peace!) when he saith, 'And make me a Wazir of my
people, Aaron.' Now could a Wazir have been dispensed withal,
Moses son of Imrán had been worthier than any to do without a
Minister. As for the Wazir, the Sultan discovereth unto him his
affairs, private and public; and know, O king, that the likeness of
thee with the people is that of the leach with the sick man; and
the essential condition of the Minister is that he be soothfast in
his sayings, reliable in all his relations, rich in ruth for the folk
and in tenderness of transacting with them. Verily, it is said, O
king, that good troops be like the druggist; if his perfumes reach
thee not, thou still smellest the fragrance of them; and bad en-
tourage be like the blacksmith; if his sparks burn thee not, thou
smellest his evil smell. So it befitteth thee take to thyself a
virtuous Wazir, a veracious counsellor, even as thou takest unto
thee a wife displayed before thy face, because thou needest the
man's righteousness for thine own right directing, seeing that,
if thou do righteously, the commons will do right, and if thou do
wrongously, they also will do wrong." When the King heard
this, drowsiness overcame him and he slept and presently
awaking, called for the candles; so they were lighted and he sat
down on his couch and seating Shahrazad by him, smiled in her
face. She kissed the ground before him and said, "O king of the
age and lord of the time and the years, extolled be the Forgiving,
the Bountiful, who hath sent me to thee, of His grace and good
favour, so I have incited thee to longing after Paradise; for verily
this which thou wast wont do was never done of any of the

---

[1] *i.e.* hath mentioned the office of Wazir (in Koran xx. 30).

kings before thee. Then laud be to the Lord who hath directed
thee into the right way, and who from the paths of frowardness
hath diverted thee! As for women, Allah Almighty maketh
mention of them also when He saith in His Holy Book, 'Truly,
the men who resign themselves to Allah[1] and the women who
resign themselves, and the true-believing men and the true-
believing women and the devout men and the devout women and
truthful men and truthful women, and long-suffering men and
long-suffering women, and the humble men and the humble
women, and charitable men and charitable women, and the men
who fast and the women who fast, and men who guard their
privities and women who guard their privities, and men who are
constantly mindful of Allah and women who are constantly
mindful, for them Allah hath prepared forgiveness and a rich
reward.'[2] As for that which hath befallen thee, verily, it hath
befallen many kings before thee and their women have falsed
them, for all they were more majestical of puissance than thou,
and mightier of kingship and had troops more manifold. If I
would, I could relate unto thee, O king, concerning the wiles of
women, that whereof I should not make an end all my life long;
and indeed, in all these my nights that I have passed before thee,
I have told thee many tales of the wheedling of women and of
their craft; but soothly the things abound on me;[3] so, an thou
please, O king, I will relate to thee somewhat of that which befel
olden kings of perfidy from their women and of the calamities
which overtook them by reason of these deceivers." Asked the
king, "How so? Tell on;" and she answered, "Hearkening and
obedience. It hath been told me, O king, that a man once related
to a company the following tale:"

THE CONCUBINE AND THE CALIPH.[4]

ONE day of the days, as I stood at the door of my house, and the
heat was excessive, behold, I saw a fair woman approaching, and
with her a slave-girl carrying a parcel. They gave not over going

---

[1] *i.e.* Moslems, who practise the Religion of Resignation.

[2] Koran xxxiii. 35. This is a proemium to the "revelation" concerning Zayd and Zaynab.

[3] *i.e.* I have an embarras de richesse in my repertory.

[4] The title is from the Bresl. Edit. (vol. xii. pp. 398-402). Mr. Payne calls it "The
Favourite and her Lover."

till they came up to me, when the woman stopped and asked me,
"Hast thou a draught of water?" Answered I, "Yes, enter the
vestibule, O my lady, so thou mayst drink." Accordingly she
came in and I went up into the house and fetched two gugglets
of earthenware, smoked with musk[1] and full of cold water. She
took one of them and discovered her face, the better to drink;
whereupon I saw that she was as the rising moon or the resplendent sun and said to her, "O my lady, wilt thou not come up into
the house, so thou mayst rest thyself till the air cool and afterwards fare thee to thine own place?" Quoth she, "Is there none
with thee?" and quoth I, "Indeed I am a bachelor and have none
belonging to me, nor is there a wight in the site;[2] whereupon she
said, "An thou be a stranger, thou art he in quest of whom I was
going about." So she went up into the house and doffed her
walking-dress and I found her as she were the full moon. I
brought her what I had by me of food and drink and said to her,
"O my lady, excuse me: this is all that is ready;" and said she,
"This is right good[3] and indeed 'tis what I sought." Then she
ate and gave the slave-girl that which was left; after which I
brought her a casting-bottle of musked rose-water, and she
washed her hands and abode with me till the season of mid-
afternoon prayer, when she brought out of the parcel she had
with her a shirt and trousers and an upper garment[4] and a gold-
worked kerchief and gave them to me; saying, "Know that I am
one of the concubines of the Caliph, and we be forty concubines,
each of whom hath a cicisbeo who cometh to her as often as she
would have him; and none is without a lover save myself, wherefore I came forth this day to get me a gallant and now I have
found thee. Thou must know that the Caliph lieth each night
with one of us, whilst the other nine-and-thirty concubines take
their ease with the nine-and-thirty masculines, and I would have
thee company with me on such a day, when do thou come up to
the palace of the Caliph and sit awaiting me in such a place, till a
little eunuch come out to thee and say to thee a certain watch-
word which is, 'Art thou Sandal?' Answer 'Yes,' and wend thee

---

[1] The practice of fumigating gugglets is universal in Egypt (Lane, M. E., chapt. v.);
but I never heard of musk being so used.

[2] Arab. "Laysa fi 'l-diyári dayyár—a favourite jingle.

[3] Arab. "Khayr Kathír" (pron. Katír) which also means "abundant kindness."

[4] Dozy says of "Hunayní" (Haíní), Il semble être le nom d'un vêtement. On which we
may remark, Connu!

with him." Then she took leave of me and I of her, after I had strained her to my bosom and thrown my arms round her neck and we had exchanged kisses awhile. So she fared forth and I abode patiently expecting the appointed day, till it came, when I arose and went out, intending for the trysting-place; but a friend of mine met me by the way and made me go home with him. I accompanied him and when I came up into his sitting-chamber he locked the door on me and walked out to fetch what we might eat and drink. He was absent until midday, then till the hour of mid-afternoon prayer, whereat I was chagrined with sore concern. Then he was missing till sundown, and I was like to die of vexation and impatience; and indeed he returned not and I passed my night on wake, nigh upon death, for the door was locked on me, and my soul was like to depart my body on account of the assignation. At daybreak, my friend returned and opening the door, came in, bringing with him meat-pudding[1] and fritters and bees' honey, and said to me, "By Allah, thou must needs excuse me, for that I was with a company and they locked the door on me and have let me go but this very moment." I returned him no reply; however, he set before me that which was with him and I ate a single mouthful and went out running at speed so haply I might overtake the rendezvous which had escaped me. When I came to the palace, I saw over against it eight-and-thirty gibbets set up, whereon were eight-and-thirty men crucified, and under them eight-and-thirty[2] concubines as they were moons. So I asked the cause of the crucifixion of the men and concerning the women in question, and it was said unto me, "The men thou seest crucified the Caliph found with yonder damsels, who be his bed-fellows." When I heard this, I prostrated myself in thanksgiving to Allah and said, "The Almighty requite thee with all good, O my friend!" For had he not invited me and locked me up in his house that night, I had been crucified with these men, wherefore Alhamdolillah—laud to the Lord! "On this wise" (continued Shahrazad), "none is safe from the calamities of the world and the vicissitudes of Time, and in proof

---

[1] Arab. Harísah: see vol. i. 131. Westerns make a sad mess of this dish when they describe it as une sorte d'*olla podrida* (the hotch-pot), une pâtée de viandes, de froment et de légumes secs (Al-Mas'udi viii. 438). Whenever I have eaten it, it was always a meat-pudding, for which see vol. i. 131.

[2] Evidently one escaped because she was sleeping with the Caliph and a second because she had kept her assignation.

of this, I will relate unto thee yet another story still rarer and stranger than this. Know, O king, that one said to me: A friend of mine, a merchant, told me the following tale:"

THE CONCUBINE OF AL-MAAMUN.[1]

As I sat one day in my shop, there came up to me a fair woman, as she were the moon at its rising, and with her a hand-maid. Now I was a handsome man in my time; so that lady sat down on my shop[2] and buying stuffs of me, paid the price and went her ways. I asked the girl anent her and she answered, "I know not her name." Quoth I, "Where is her abode?" Quoth she, "In heaven;" and I, "She is presently on the earth; so when doth she ascend to heaven and where is the ladder by which she goeth up?"[3] The girl retorted, "She hath her lodging in a palace between two rivers,[4] that is, in the palace of Al-Maamún al-Hákim bi-Amri 'llah."[5] Then said I, "I am a dead man, without a doubt;" but she replied, "Have patience, for needs must she return to thee and buy other stuffs of thee." I asked, "And how cometh it that the Commander of the Faithful trusteth her to go out?" and she answered, "He loveth her with exceeding love and is wrapped up in her and crosseth her not." Then the slave-girl went away, running after her mistress; whereupon I left the shop and followed them, so I might see her abiding-place. I kept them in view all the way, till she disappeared from mine eyes, when I returned to my place, with heart a-fire. Some days after, she came to me again and bought stuffs of me: I refused to take the price and she cried, "We have no need of thy goods." Quoth I, "O my lady, accept them from me as a gift;" but quoth she,

---

[1] Mr. Payne entitles it, "The Merchant of Cairo and the Favourite of the Khalif el Mamoun el Hakim bi Amrillah."

[2] See my Pilgrimage (i. 100): the seat would be on the same bit of boarding where the master sits or on a stool or bench in the street.

[3] This is true Cairene chaff, give and take; and the stranger must accustom himself to it before he can be at home with the people.

[4] *i.e.* In Rauzah-Island: see vol. v. 169.

[5] There is no historical person who answers to these names, "The Secure, the Ruler by Commandment of Allah." The cognomen applies to two soldans of Egypt, of whom the later Abu al-Abbas Ahmad the Abbaside (A. D. 1261-1301) has already been mentioned in The Nights (vol. v. 86). The tale suggests the earlier Al-Hakim (Abu Ali al-Mansúr, the Fatimite, A. D. 995-1021), the God of the Druze "persuasion;" and the tale-teller may have purposely blundered in changing Mansúr to Maamún for fear of offending a sect which has been most dangerous in the matter of assassination and which is capable of becoming so again.

"Wait till I try thee and make proof of thee." Then she brought
out of her pocket a purse and gave me therefrom a thousand
dinars, saying, "Trade with this till I return to thee." So I took
the purse and she went away and returned not till six months
had passed. Meanwhile, I traded with the money and sold and
bought and made other thousand dinars profit on it. At last she
came to me again and I said to her, "Here is thy money and I
have gained with it other thousand ducats;"and she,"Let it lie by
thee and take these other thousand dinars. As soon as I have
departed from thee, go thou to Al-Rauzah, the Garden-holm,
and build there a goodly pavilion, and when the edifice is accomplished, give me to know thereof." So saying, she left me and
went away. As soon as she was gone, I betook myself to Al-
Rauzah and fell to building the pavilion, and when it was
finished, I furnished it with the finest of furniture and sent to tell
her that I had made an end of the edifice; whereupon she sent
back to me, saying, "Let him meet me to-morrow about daybreak at the Zuwaylah gate and bring with him a strong ass."
I did as she bade and, betaking myself to the Zuwaylah gate, at
the appointed time, found there a young man on horseback,
awaiting her, even as I awaited her. As we stood, behold, up she
came, and with her a slave-girl. When she saw that young man,
she asked him, "Art thou here?" and he answered, "Yes, O my
lady." Quoth she, "To-day I am invited by this man: wilt thou
wend with us?" and quoth he, "Yes." Then said she, "Thou
hast brought me hither against my will and parforce. Wilt thou
go with us in any case?" [1] He cried, "Yes, yes," and we fared on,
all three, till we came to Al-Rauzah and entered the pavilion.
The dame diverted herself awhile with viewing its ordinance
and furniture, after which she doffed her walking-dress and sat
down with the young man in the goodliest and chiefest place.
Then I fared forth and brought them what they should eat at the
first of the day; presently I again went out and fetched them
what they should eat at the last of the day and brought for the
twain wine and dessert and fruits and flowers. After this fashion
I abode in their service, standing on my feet, and she said not
unto me, "Sit," nor "Take, eat" nor "Take, drink," while she
and the young man sat toying and laughing, and he fell to kissing

---

[1] Arab. " 'Alà kulli hál" == "whatever may betide," or "willy-nilly." The phrase is
still popular.

her and pinching her and hopping over the ground[1] and laughing.
They remained thus awhile and presently she said, "Hitherto we
have not become drunken; let me pour out." So she took the
cup, and crowning it, gave him to drink and plied him with wine,
till he lost his wits, when she took him up and carried him into a
closet. Then she came out, with the head of that youth in her
hand, while I stood silent, fixing not mine eyes on her eyes
neither questioning her of the case; and she asked me, "What
be this?" "I wot not," answered I; and she said, "Take it and
throw it into the river." I accepted her commandment and she
arose and stripping herself of her clothes, took a knife and cut the
dead man's body in pieces, which she laid in three baskets, and
said to me, "Throw them into the river." I did her bidding and
when I returned, she said to me, "Sit, so I may relate to thee
yonder fellow's case, lest thou be affrighted at what accident
hath befallen him. Thou must know that I am the Caliph's
favourite concubine, nor is there any higher in honour with him
than I; and I am allowed six nights in each month, wherein I go
down into the city and tarry with my whilome mistress who
reared me; and when I go down thus, I dispose of myself as I will.
Now this young man was the son of certain neighbours of my
mistress, when I was a virgin girl. One day, my mistress was
sitting with the chief officers of the palace and I was alone in the
house, and as the night came on, I went up to the terrace-roof in
order to sleep there, but ere I was ware, this youth came up from
the street and falling upon me knelt on my breast. He was armed
with a dagger and I could not get free of him till he had taken my
maidenhead by force; and this sufficed him not, but he mustneeds
disgrace me with all the folk for, as often as I came down from
the palace, he would stand in wait for me by the way and fut-
tered me against my will and follow me whithersoever I went.
This, then, is my story, and as for thee, thou pleasest me and thy
patience pleaseth me and thy good faith and loyal service, and
there abideth with me none dearer than thou." Then I lay with
her that night and there befel what befel between us till the
morning, when she gave me abundant wealth and took to meeting
me at the pavilion six days in every month. After this wise we
passed a whole year, at the end of which she cut herself off from
me a month's space, wherefore fire raged in my heart on her

---

[1] The dulce desipere of young lovers, he making a buffoon of himself to amuse her.

account. When it was the next month, behold, a little eunuch presented himself to me and said, "I am a messenger to thee from Such-an-one, who giveth thee to know that the Commander of the Faithful hath ordered her to be drowned, her and those who are with her, six-and-twenty slave-girls, on such a day at Dayr al-Tin,[1] for that they have confessed of lewdness, one against other and she sayeth to thee, 'Look how thou mayst do with me and how thou mayst contrive to deliver me, even an thou gather together all my money and spend it upon me, for that this be the time of manhood.' "[2] Quoth I, "I know not this woman; belike it is other than I to whom this message is sent; so beware, O Eunuch, lest thou cast me into a cleft." Quoth he, "Behold, I have told thee that I had to say," and went away, leaving me in sore concern on her account. Now when the appointed day came, I arose and changing my clothes and favour, donned sailor's apparel; then I took with me a purse full of gold and buying a right good breakfast, accosted a boatman at Dayr al-Tin and sat down and ate with him; after which I asked him, "Wilt thou hire me thy boat?" Answered he, "The Commander of the Faithful hath commanded me to be here;" and he told me the tale of the concubines and how the Caliph purposed to drown them that day. When I heard this from him, I brought out to him ten gold pieces and discovered to him my case, whereupon he said to me, "O my brother, get thee empty gourds, and when thy mistress cometh, give me to know of her and I will contrive the trick." So I kissed his hand and thanked him and, as I was walking about, waiting, up came the guards and eunuchs escorting the women, who were weeping and shrieking and farewelling one another. The Castratos cried out to us, whereupon we came with the boat, and they said to the sailor, "Who be this?" Said he, "This be my mate whom I have brought to help me, so one of us may keep the boat, whilst another doth your service." Then they brought out to us the women, one by one, saying, "Throw them in by the Island;" and we replied, " 'Tis well." Now each of them was shackled and they had made fast about her neck a jar of sand. We did as the neutrals bade us and ceased not to take the women, one after other, and cast them in, till they gave us my mistress and I winked to my mate. So

---

[1] "The convent of Clay," a Coptic monastery near Cairo.
[2] i.e. this is the time to show thyself a man.

we took her and carried her out and cast her into mid-stream, where I threw to her the empty gourds[1] and said to her, "Wait for me at the mouth of the Canal."[2] Now there remained one woman after her: so we took her and drowned her and the eunuchs went away, whilst we dropped down the river till we came to where I saw my mistress awaiting me. We haled her into the canoe and returned to our pavilion. Then I rewarded the sailor and he took his boat and went away; whereupon quoth she to me, "Thou art indeed the friend ever faithful found for the shifts of Fortune."[3] And I sojourned with her some days; but the shock wrought upon her so that she sickened and fell to wasting away and redoubled in weakness till she died. I mourned for her and buried her; after which I removed all that was in the pavilion and abandoned the building. Now she had brought to that pavilion a little coffer of copper and laid it in a place whereof I knew not; so, when the Inspector of Inheritances[4] came, he rummaged the house and found the coffer. Presently he opened it and seeing it full of jewels and seal-rings, took it, and me with it, and ceased not to put me to the question with beating and torment till I confessed the whole affair. Thereupon they carried me to the Caliph and I told him all that had passed between me and her; and he said to me, "O man, depart this city, for I release thee on account of thy courage and because of thy constancy in keeping thy secret and thy daring in exposing thyself to death." So I arose forthwith and fared from his city; and this is what befel me.

---

[1] The Eastern succedaneum for swimming corks and other "life-preservers." The practice is very ancient: we find these gourds upon the monuments of Egypt and Babylonia.

[2] Arab. "Al-Khalíj," the name, still popular, of the Grand Canal of Cairo, whose banks, by-the-by, are quaint and picturesque as anything of the kind in Holland.

[3] We say more laconically "A friend in need."

[4] Arab. "Názir al-Mawárís," the employé charged with the disposal of legacies and seizing escheats to the Crown when Moslems die intestate. He is usually a prodigious rascal as in the text. The office was long kept up in Southern Europe, and Camoens was sent to Macao as "Provedor dos defuntos e ausentes."

END OF VOLUME XII.

VARIANTS AND ANALOGUES

OF

SOME OF THE TALES ·

IN

VOLUMES XI. AND XII.

By W. A. CLOUSTON.

AUTHOR OF "POPULAR TALES AND FICTIONS: THEIR MIGRATIONS

AND TRANSFORMATIONS, ' ETC.

Appendix.

——❖——

VARIANTS AND ANALOGUES OF SOME OF THE TALES IN VOLUMES XI AND XII.

By W. A. Clouston.

———

THE SLEEPER AND THE WAKER.—Vol. XI. p. 1.

Few of the stories in the "Arabian Nights" which charmed our marvelling boyhood were greater favourites than this one, under the title of "Abou Hassan; or, the Sleeper Awakened." What recked we in those days whence it was derived?—the *story*—the story was the thing! As Sir R. F. Burton observes in his first note, this is "the only one of the eleven added by Galland, whose original has been discovered in Arabic;" [1] and it is probable that Galland heard it recited in a coffee-house during his residence in Constantinople. The plot of the Induction to Shakspeare's comedy of "The Taming of the Shrew" is similar to the adventure of Abú al-Hasan the Wag, and is generally believed to have been adapted from a story entitled "The Waking Man's Fortune" in Edward's collection of comic tales, 1570, which were retold somewhat differently in Goulart's "Admirable and Memorable Histories," 1607; both versions are reprinted in Mr. Hazlitt's "Shakspeare Library," vol. iv., part I, pp. 403-414. In Percy's "Reliques of Ancient English Poetry" we find the adventure told in a ballad entitled "The Frolicksome Duke; or, the Tinker's Good Fortune," from the Pepys collection: "whether it may be thought to have suggested the hint to Shakspeare or is not rather of later date," says Percy, "the reader must determine:"

> Now as fame does report, a young duke keeps a court,
> One that pleases his fancy with frolicksome sport:
> But amongst all the rest, here is one, I protest,
> Which will make you to smile when you hear the true jest:
> A poor tinker he found lying drunk on the ground,
> As secure in a sleep as if laid in a swownd.

———

[1] Sir R. F. Burton has since found two more of "Galland's" tales in an Arabic text of The Nights, namely, Aladdin and Zeyn al-Asnam.

VOL. XII.

The duke said to his men, William, Richard, and Ben,
Take him home to my palace, we'll sport with him then.
O'er a horse he was laid, and with care soon convey'd
To the palace, altho' he was poorly arrai'd;
Then they stript off his cloaths, both his shirt, shoes, and hose,
And they put him in bed for to take his repose.

Having pull'd off his shirt, which was all over durt,
They did give him clean holland, this was no great hurt:
On a bed of soft down, like a lord of renown,
They did lay him to sleep the drink out of his crown.
In the morning when day, then admiring[1] he lay,
For to see the rich chamber both gaudy and gay.

Now he lay something late, in his rich bed of state,
Till at last knights and squires they on him did wait;
And the chamberling bare, then did likewise declare,
He desired to know what apparel he'd ware:
The poor tinker amaz'd, on the gentleman gaz'd,
And admired how he to this honour was rais'd.

Tho' he seem'd something mute, yet he chose a rich suit,
Which he straitways put on without longer dispute;
With a star on his side, which the tinker offt ey'd,
And it seem'd for to swell him no little with pride;
For he said to himself, Where is Joan my sweet wife?
Sure she never did see me so fine in her life.

From a convenient place, the right duke his good grace
Did observe his behaviour in every case.
To a garden of state, on the tinker they wait,
Trumpets sounding before him: thought he this is great:
Where an hour or two, pleasant walks he did view,
With commanders and squires in scarlet and blew.

A fine dinner was drest, both for him and his guests,
He was placed at the table above all the rest,
In a rich chair, or bed, lin'd with fine crimson red,
With a rich golden canopy over his head:
As he sat at his meat, the musick play'd sweet,
With the choicest of singing his joys to compleat.

While the tinker did dine, he had plenty of wine.
Rich canary with sherry and tent superfine,
Like a right honest soul, faith, he took off his bowl,
Till at last he began for to tumble and roul
From his chair to the floor, where he sleeping did snore,
Being seven times drunker than ever before.

Then the duke did ordain, they should strip him amain,
And restore him his old leather garments again:

---

[1] *i.e.* wondering; thus Lady Macbeth says:
    "You have displaced the mirth, broke the good meeting,
    With most *admired* disorder."—*Macbeth*, iii. 4.

'Twas a point next the worst, yet perform it they must,
And they carry'd him strait, where they found him at first;
Then he slept all the night, as indeed well he might,
But when he did waken, his joys took their flight.

For his glory to him so pleasant did seem,
That he thought it to be but a meer golden dream;
Till at length he was brought to the duke, where he sought
For a pardon as fearing he had set him at nought;
But his highness he said, Thou'rt a jolly bold blade,
Such a frolick before I think never was plaid.

Then his highness bespoke him a new suit and cloak,
Which he gave for the sake of this frolicksome joak;
Nay, and five hundred pound, with ten acres of ground
Thou shalt never, said he, range the counteries round,
Crying old brass to mend, for I'll be thy good friend,
Nay, and Joan thy sweet wife shall my duchess attend.

Then the tinker reply'd, What! must Joan my sweet bride
Be a lady in chariots of pleasure to ride?
Must we have gold and land ev'ry day at command?
Then I shall be a squire I well understand;
Well I thank your good grace, and your love I embrace,
I was never before in so happy a case.

The same story is also cited in the "Anatomy of Melancholy," part 2, sec. 2, memb. 4, from Ludovicus Vives in Epist.[1] and Pont. Heuter in Rerum Burgund., as follows: "It is reported of Philippus Bonus, that good Duke of Burgundy, that the said duke, at the marriage of Eleonora, sister to the King of Portugal, at Bruges in Flanders, which was solemnized in the deep of winter, when as by reason of the unseasonable (!) weather he could neither hawk nor hunt, and was now tyred with cards, dice, &c., and such other domestical sports, or to see ladies dance, with some of his courtiers, he would in the evening walk disguised all about the town. It so fortuned as he was walking late one night, he found a country fellow dead drunk, snorting on a bulk; he caused his followers to bring him to his palace, and there stripping him of his old clothes, and attiring him after the court fashion, when he waked, he and they were all ready to attend upon his excellency, persuading him that he was some great duke. The poor fellow, admiring how he came there, was served in state all the day long; after supper he saw them dance, heard musick, and the rest of those court-like pleasures; but late at night, when he was well tipled, and again fast asleep they put on his old robes, and so conveyed him to the place where they first found him. Now the fellow had not made them so good sport the day before, as he did when he returned to himself; all the jest was to see how he looked upon it. In conclusion, after some little admiration, the poor man told his friends he had seen a vision, constantly beleeved it, would not otherwise be perswaded; and so the jest ended."
I do not think that this is a story imported from the East: the adventure is just as likely to have happened in Bruges as in Baghdád; but the exquisite humour of the Arabian tale is wanting—even Shakspeare's Christopher Sly is not to be compared with honest Abú al-Hasan the Wag.

This story of The Sleeper and the Waker recalls the similar device practised by the Chief of the Assassins—that formidable, murderous association, the terror of the Crusaders—on

---

[1] Ludovicus Vives, one of the most learned of Spanish authors, was born at Valentia in 1492 and died in 1540.

promising novices. Von Hammer, in his "History of the Assassins," end of Book iv., gives a graphic description of the charming gardens into which the novices were carried while insensible from hashish:

In the centre of the Persian as well as of the Assyrian territory of the Assassins, that is to say, both at Alamut and Massiat, were situated, in a space surrounded by walls, splendid gardens—true Eastern paradises. There were flower-beds and thickets of fruit-trees, intersected by canals, shady walks, and verdant glades, where the sparkling stream bubbled at every step; bowers of roses and vineyards; luxurious halls and porcelain kiosks, adorned with Persian carpets and Grecian stuffs, where drinking-vessels of gold, silver, and crystal glittered on trays of the same costly materials; charming maidens and handsome boys of Muhammed's Paradise, soft as the cushions on which they reposed, and intoxicating as the wine which they presented. The music of the harp was mingled with the songs of birds, and the melodious tones of the songstress harmonized with the murmur of the brooks. Everything breathed pleasure, rapture, and sensuality. A youth, who was deemed worthy by his strength and resolution to be initiated into the Assassin service, was invited to the table and conversation of the grand master, or grand prior; he was then intoxicated with hashish and carried into the garden, which on awaking he believed to be Paradise; everything around him, the houris in particular, contributing to confirm the delusion. After he had experienced as much of the pleasures of Paradise, which the Prophet has promised to the faithful, as his strength would admit; after quaffing enervating delight from the eyes of the houris and intoxicating wine from the glittering goblets; he sank into the lethargy produced by debility and the opiate, on awakening from which, after a few hours, he again found himself by the side of his superior. The latter endeavoured to convince him that corporeally he had not left his side, but that spiritually he had been wrapped into Paradise and had there enjoyed a foretaste of the bliss which awaits the faithful who devote their lives to the service of the faith and the obedience of their chiefs.

THE TEN WAZIRS; OR, THE HISTORY OF KING ÁZÁDBAKHT AND HIS SON.—Vol. XI. p. 37.

THE precise date of the Persian original of this romance ("Bakhtyár Náma") has not been ascertained, but it was probably composed before the beginning of the fifteenth century, since there exists in the Bodleian Library a unique Turkí version, in the Uygur language and characters, which was written in 1434. Only three of the tales have hitherto been found in other Asiatic storybooks. The Turkí version, according to M. Jaubert, who gives an account of the MS. and a translation of one of the tales in the *Journal Asiatique*, tome x. 1827, is characterised by "great sobriety of ornament and extreme simplicity of style, and the evident intention on the part of the translator to suppress all that may not have appeared to him sufficiently probable, and all that might justly be taxed with exaggeration;" and he adds that "apart from the interest which the writing and phraseology of the work may possess for those who study the history of languages, it is rather curious to see how a Tátár translator sets to work to bring within the range of his readers stories embellished in the original with descriptions and images familiar, doubtless, to a learned and refined nation like the Persians, but foreign to shepherds."

At least three different versions are known to the Malays—different in the frame, or leading story, if not in the subordinate tales. One of those is described in the second volume of Newbold's work on Malacca, the frame of which is similar to the Persian original and its Arabian derivative, excepting that the name of the king is Zádbokhtin and that of the minister's daughter (who is nameless in the Persian) is Mahrwat. Two others are described in Van den Berg's account of Malay, Arabic, Javanese and other MSS. published at Batavia, 1877: p. 21, No. 132 is entitled "The History of Ghulám, son of Zádbukhtán,

King of Adán, in Persia," and the frame also corresponds with our version, with the important difference that the robber-chief who had brought up Ghulám, "learning that he had become a person of consequence, came to his residence to visit him, but finding him imprisoned, he was much concerned, and asked the king's pardon on his behalf, telling him at the same time how he had formerly found Ghulám in the jungle; from which the king knew that Ghulám was his son." The second version noticed by Van den Berg (p. 32, No. 179), though similar in title to the Persian original, "History of Prince Bakhtyár," differs very materially in the leading story, the outline of which is as follows: This prince, when his father was put to flight by a younger brother, who wished to dethrone him, was born in a jungle, and abandoned by his parents. A merchant named Idrís took charge of him and brought him up. Later on he became one of the officers of state with his own father, who had in the meanwhile found another kingdom, and decided with fairness, the cases brought before him. He was, however, put in prison, on account of a supposed attempt on the king's life, and would have been put to death had he not stayed the execution by telling various beautiful stories. Even the king came repeatedly to listen to him. At one of these visits Bakhtyár's foster-father Idrís was present, and related to his adopted son how he had found him in the jungle. The king, on hearing this, perceived that it was his son who had been brought up by Idrís, recognised Bakhtyár as such, and made over to him the kingdom."—I have little doubt that this romance is of Indian extraction.

STORY OF KING DADBIN AND HIS WAZIRS.—Vol. XI. p. 68.

This agrees pretty closely with the Turkí version of the same story (rendered into French by M. Jaubert), though in the latter the names of the characters are the same as in the Persian, King Dádín and the Wazírs Kámgár and Kárdár. In the Persian story, the damsel is tied hands and feet and placed upon a camel, which is then turned into a dreary wilderness. "Here she suffered from the intense heat and from thirst; but she resigned herself to the will of Providence, conscious of her own innocence. Just then the camel lay down, and on the spot a fountain of delicious water suddenly sprang forth; the cords which bound her hands and feet dropped off; she refreshed herself by a draught of the water, and fervently returned thanks to Heaven for this blessing and her wonderful preservation." This two-fold miracle does not appear in the Turkí and Arabian versions. It is not the cameleer of the King of Persia, but of King Dádín, who meets with the pious damsel in the wilderness. He takes her to his own house and one day relates his adventure to King Dádín, who expresses a wish to see such a prodigy of sanctity. The conclusion of the Persian story is quite dramatic: The cameleer, having consented, returned at once to his house, accompanied by the king, who waited at the door of the apartment where the daughter of Kámgár was engaged in prayer. When she had concluded he approached, and with astonishment recognised her. Having tenderly embraced her, he wept, and entreated her forgiveness. This she readily granted, but begged that he would conceal himself in the apartment while she should converse with Kárdár, whom she sent for. When he arrived, and beheld her with a thousand expressions of fondness, he inquired how she had escaped, and told her that on the day the king banished her into the wilderness, he had sent people to seek her and bring her to him. "How much better would it have been," he added, "had you followed my advice, and agreed to my proposal of poisoning the king, who, I said, would one day destroy you as he had done your father! But you rejected my advice, and declared yourself ready to submit to whatever Providence should decree. Hereafter you will pay more attention to my words. But now let us not think of what is past. I am your slave, and you are dearer to me than my own eyes." So saying, he attempted to clasp the daughter of Kámgár in his arms, when the king, who was concealed behind the hangings, rushed furiously on him and put him to death. After this he conducted the damsel to his palace, and constantly lamented his precipitancy in having killed her father.—This tale seems to have been taken from the Persian "Túti Náma," or Parrot-book, composed by Nahkshabí about the year 1306;[1] it occurs in the 51st Night of the India Office MS.2573, under the title of "Story of the Daughter of the Vazír Khássa, and how she found safety through the blessing of her piety:" the name of the king is Bahram, and the Wazírs are called Khássa and Khalássa.

STORY OF AYLAN SHAH AND ABÚ TAMMÁM.—Vol. XI p. 82.

THE catastrophe of this story forms the subject of the Lady's 37th tale in the text of the Turkish "Forty Vezírs," translated by Mr. E. J. W. Gibb. This is how it goes:

In the palace of the world there was a king, and that king had three vezírs, but there was rivalry between them. Two of them day and night incited the king against the third, saying, "He is a traitor." But the king believed them not. At length they promised two pages much gold, and instructed them thus: "When the king has lain down, ere he yet fall asleep, do ye feign to think him asleep, and while talking with each other, say at a fitting time,'I have heard from such a one that yon vezír says this and that concerning the king, and that he hates him; many people say that vezír is an enemy to our king.'" So they did this, and when the king heard them, he said in his heart, "What those vezírs said is then true; when the very pages have heard somewhat it must indeed have some foundation. Till now, I believed not those vezírs, but it is then true." And the king executed that vezír. The other vezírs were glad and gave the pages the gold they had promised. So they took it and went to a private place, and while they were dividing it one of them said, "I spake first; I want more." The other said, "If I had not said he was an enemy to our king, the king would not have killed him; I shall take more." And while they were quarrelling with one another the king passed by there, and he listened attentively to their words, and when he learned of the matter, he said, "Dost thou see, they have by a trick made us kill that hapless vezír." And he was repentant.

STORY OF KING SULAYMAN SHAH AND HIS NIECE.—Vol. XI. p. 97.

THE Persian original has been very considerably amplified by the Arabian translator. In the "Bakhtyár Náma" there is not a word about the two brothers and their fair cousin, the attempted murder of the infant, and the adventures of the fugitive young prince. This story has also been taken from the "Túti Náma" of Nakhshabí, Night the 50th of the India Office MS. 2573, where, under the title of "Story of the Daughter of the Kaysar of Roum, and her trouble by reason of her son," it is told somewhat as follows:

In former times there was a great king, whose army was numerous and whose treasury was full to overflowing; but, having no enemy to contend with, he neglected to pay his soldiers, in consequence of which they were in a state of destitution and discontent. At length one day the soldiers went to the prime minister and made their condition known to him. The vazír promised that he would speedily devise a plan by which they should have employment and money. Next morning he presented himself before the king, and said that it was widely reported the Kaysar of Roum had a daughter unsurpassed for beauty— one who was fit only for such a great monarch as his Majesty; and suggested that it would

---

[1] There was an older "Túti Náma," which Nakhshabí modernised, made from a Sanskrit story-book, now lost, but its modern representative is the "Suka Saptatí," or Seventy (Tales) of a Parrot in which most of Nakhshabí's tales are found.

be advantageous if an alliance were formed between two such great potentates. The notion pleased the king well, and he forthwith despatched to Roum an ambassador with rich gifts, and requested the Kaysar to grant him his daughter in marriage. But the Kaysar waxed wroth at this, and refused to give his daughter to the king. When the ambassador returned thus unsuccessful, the king, enraged at being made of no account, resolved to make war upon the Kaysar; so, opening the doors of his treasury, he distributed much money among his troops, and then, "with a woe-bringing host, and a blood-drinking army, he trampled Roum and the folk of Roum in the dust." And when the Kaysar was become powerless, he sent his daughter to the king, who married her according to the law of Islam.

Now that princess had a son by a former husband, and the Kaysar had said to her before she departed, "Beware that thou mention not thy son, for my love for his society is great, and I cannot part with him." [1] But the princess was sick at heart for the absence of her son, and she was ever pondering how she should speak to the king about him, and in what manner she might contrive to bring him to her. It happened one day the king gave her a string of pearls and a casket of jewels. She said, "With my father is a slave who is well skilled in the science of jewels." The king replied, "If I should ask that slave of thy father, would he give him to me?" "Nay," said she, "for he holds him in the place of a son. But if the king desire him, I will send a merchant to Roum, and I myself will give him a token, and with pleasant wiles and fair speeches will bring him hither." Then the king sent for a clever merchant who knew Arabic eloquently and the language of Roum, and gave him goods for trading and sent him to Roum with the object of procuring that slave. But the daughter of the Kaysar said privily to the merchant, "That slave is my son; I have, for a good reason, said to the king that he is a slave; so thou must bring him as a slave, and let it be thy duty to take care of him." In due course the merchant brought the youth to the king's service; and when the king saw his fair face, and discovered in him many pleasing and varied accomplishments, he treated him with distinction and favour, and conferred on the merchant a robe of honour and gifts. His mother saw him from afar, and was pleased with receiving a secret salutation from him.

One day the king had gone to the chase, and the palace remained void of rivals; so the mother called in her son, kissed his fair face, and told him the tale of her great sorrow. A chamberlain became aware of the secret, and another suspicion fell upon him, and he said to himself, "The harem of the king is the sanctuary of security and the palace of protection. If I speak not of this, I shall be guilty of treachery and shall have wrought unfaithfulness." When the king returned from the chase, the chamberlain related to him what he had seen, and the king was angry and said, "This woman hath deceived me with words and deeds, and has brought hither her desire by craft and cunning. This conjecture must be true, else why did she play such a trick? And why did she hatch such a plot? And why did she send the merchant?" Then the king, enraged, went into the harem, and the queen saw from his countenance that the occurrence of the night before had become known to him, and she said, "Be it not that I see the king angry?" He said, "How should I not be angry? Thou, by craft, and trickery, and intrigue, and plotting, hast brought thy desire from Roum—what wantonness is this that thou hast done?" And then he thought to slay her, but he forebore, because of his great love for her. But he ordered the chamberlain to carry the youth to some obscure place, and straightway sever his head from his body. When the poor mother saw this, she well-nigh fell on her face, and her soul was near leaving her body. But she knew that sorrow would not avail, and so she restrained herself.

And when the chamberlain took the youth into his own house, he said to him, "O youth, knowest thou not that the harem of the king is the sanctuary of security? What great treachery is this that thou hast perpetrated?" The youth replied, "That queen is my mother, and I am her true son. Because of her natural delicacy, she said not to the king

---

[1] According to Lescallier's French translation of the "Bakhtyár Náma," made from two MSS. = "She had previously had a lover, with whom, *unknown to her father*, she had intimate relations, and had given birth to a beautiful boy, whose education she secretly confided to some trusty servants."

that she had a son by another husband. And when yearning came over her, she contrived to bring me here from Roum; and while the king was engaged in the chase, maternal love stirred in her, and she called me to her and embraced me." On hearing this, the chamberlain said to himself, "What is passing in his mother's breast? What I have not done I can yet do, and it were better that I preserve this youth some days, for such a rose may not be wounded through idle words, and such a bough may not be broken by a breath. For some day the truth of the matter will be disclosed, and it will become known to the king when repentance may be of no avail." So he went before the king and said, "That which was commanded have I fulfilled." On hearing this the king's wrath was to some extent removed but his trust in the Kaysar's daughter was departed; while she, poor creature, was grieved and dazed at the loss of her son.

Now in the palace-harem there was an old woman, who said to the queen, "How is it that I find thee sorrowful?" And the queen told the whole story, concealing nothing. This old woman was a heroine in the field of craft, and she answered, "Keep thy mind at ease; I will devise a stratagem by which the heart of the king will be pleased with thee, and every grief he has will vanish from his heart." The queen said that, if she did so, she should be amply rewarded. One day the old woman, seeing the king alone, said to him, "Why is thy former aspect altered? And why are traces of care and anxiety visible on thy countenance?" The king then told her all. Then said the old woman, "I have an amulet of the charms of Sulayman, in the Syriac language, and in the writing of the jinn (genii). When the queen is asleep, do thou place it on her breast, and whatever it may be, she will tell the truth of it. But take care, fall not thou asleep, but listen well to what she says." The king wondered at this and said, "Give me that amulet, that the truth of this matter may be learned." So the old woman gave him the amulet, and then went to the queen and explained what she had done, and said, "Do thou feign to be asleep, and relate the whole of thy story faithfully."

When a watch of the night was past, the king laid the amulet upon his wife's breast, and she thus began: "By a former husband I had a son, and when my father gave me to this king, I was ashamed to say I had a tall son. When my yearning passed all bounds, I brought him here by an artifice. One day that the king was gone to the chase I called him into the house, when, after the way of mothers, I took him in my arms and kissed him. This reached the king's ears; he unwittingly gave it another construction, and cut off the head of that innocent boy, and withdrew from me his own heart. Alike is my son lost to me and the king angry." When the king heard these words he kissed her and exclaimed, "O my life, what an error is this thou hast committed! Thou hast brought calumny upon thyself, and hast given such a son to the winds, and hast made me ashamed!" Straightway he called the chamberlain, and said, "That boy whom thou hast killed is the son of my beloved and the darling of my beauty! Where is his grave, that we may make there a guest-house?" The chamberlain said, "That youth is yet alive. When the king commanded his death, I was about to kill him, but he said, 'That queen is my mother. Through modesty before the king, she revealed not the secret that she has a tall son. Kill me not; it may be that some day the truth will become known, and repentance profiteth not, and regret is useless.'" The king commanded them to bring the youth; so they brought him forthwith. And when the mother saw the face of her son, she thanked God and praised the Most High, and became one of the Muslims, and from the sect of unbelievers came into the faith of Islam. And the king favoured the chamberlain in the highest degree, and they passed the rest of their lives in comfort and ease.

FIRUZ AND HIS WIFE.—Vol. XI. p. 125.

This tale, as Sir R. F. Burton remarks, is a rechauffé of that of the King and the Wazír's Wife in the "Malice of Women," or the Seven Wazírs (vol. vi. 129); and at p. 308 we have yet another variant.[1] It occurs in all the Eastern texts of the Book of Sindibád, and it is commonly termed by students of that cycle of stories "The Lion's Track," from the parabolical manner in which the husband justifies his conduct before the king. I have cited some versions in the Appendix to my edition of the Book of Sindibád (p. 256 ff.), and to these may be added the following Venetian variant, from Crane's "Italian Popular Tales," as an example of how a story becomes garbled in passing orally from one generation unto another generation:

A king, averse from marriage, commanded his steward to remain single. The latter, however, one day saw a beautiful girl named Vigna and married her secretly. Although he kept her closely confined in her chamber, the king became suspicious, and sent the steward on an embassy. After his departure the king entered the apartment occupied by him, and saw his wife asleep. He did not disturb her, but in leaving the room accidentally dropped one of his gloves on the bed. When the husband returned he found the glove, but kept a discreet silence, ceasing, however, all demonstration of affection, believing his wife had been unfaithful. The king, desirous to see again the beautiful woman, made a feast and ordered the steward to bring his wife. He denied that he had one, but brought her at last, and while every one else was talking gaily at the feast she was silent. The king observed it and asked the cause of her silence, and she answered with a pun on her own name, "Vineyard I was, and Vineyard I am. I was loved and no longer am. I know not for what reason the Vineyard has lost its season." Her husband, who heard this, replied, "Vineyard thou wast, and Vineyard thou art: the Vineyard lost its season, for the lion's claw." The king, who understood what he meant, answered, "I entered the Vineyard; I touched the leaves; but I swear by my crown that I have not tasted the fruit." Then the steward understood that his wife was innocent, and the two made peace, and always after lived happy and contented.

So far as I am aware, this tale of "The Lion's Track" is not popularly known in any European country besides Italy; and it is not found in any of the Western versions of the Book of Sindibád, generally known under the title of the "History of the Seven Wise Masters;" how, then, did it reach Venice, and become among the people "familiar in their mouths as household words?" I answer, that the intimate commercial relations which long existed between the Venetian Republic and Egypt and Syria are amply sufficient to account for the currency of this and scores of other Eastern tales in Italy. This is not one of those fictions introduced into the south of Europe through the Ottomans, since Boccaccio has made use of the first part of it in his "Decameron," Day I. nov. 5; and it is curious to observe that the garbled Venetian popular version has preserved the chief characteristic of the Eastern story—the allegorical reference to the king as a lion and his assuring the husband that the lion had done no injury to his "Vineyard."

KING SHAH BAKHT AND HIS WAZIR AL-RAHWAN. Vol. XI. p. 127.

WHILE the frame-story of this interesting group is similar to that of the Ten Wazírs (vol. i. p. 37), insomuch as in both a king's favourite is sentenced to death in consequence of the false accusations of his enemies, and obtains a respite from day to day by relating stories to the king, there is yet a very important difference: Like those of the renowned Shahrazád, the stories which Al-Rahwan tells have no particular, at least no uniform, "purpose," his sole object being to prolong his life by telling the king an entertaining story, promising, when he has ended his recital, to relate one still "stranger" the next night, if the king will spare his life another day. On the other hand, Bakhtyár, while actuated by the same

---

[1] There is a slight mistake in the passage in p. 313 supplied from the story in vol. vi. It is not King Shah Bakht, but the other king, who assures his chamberlain that "the lion" has done him no injury.

motive, appeals to the king's reason, by relating stories distinctly designed to exhibit the evils of hasty judgments and precipitate conduct—in fact, to illustrate the maxim,

> Each order given by a reigning king,
>   Should after long reflection be expressed;
> For it may be that endless woe will spring
>   From a command he paused not to digest.

And in this respect they are consistent with the circumstances of the case, like the tales of the Book of Sindibád, from which the frame of the Ten Wazírs was imitated, and in which the Wazírs relate stories showing the depravity and profligacy of women and that no reliance should be placed on their unsupported assertions, and to these the lady opposes equally cogent stories setting forth the wickedness and perfidy of men. Closely resembling the frame-story of the Ten Wazírs, however, is that of a Tamil romance entitled "Alakeswara Kathá," a copy of which, written on palm leaves, was in the celebrated Mackenzie collection, of which Dr. H. H. Wilson published a descriptive catalogue; it is "a story of the Rájá of Alakepura and his four ministers, who, being falsely accused of violating the sanctity of the inner apartments, vindicate their innocence and disarm the king's wrath by relating a number of stories." Judging by the specimen given by Wilson, the well-known tale of the Lost Camel, it seems probable that the ministers' stories, like those of Bakhtyár, are suited to their own case and illustrate the truth of the adage that "appearances are often deceptive." Whether in the Siamese collection "Nonthuk Pakkaranam" (referred to in vol. i. p. 127) the stories related by the Princess Kankras to the King of Pataliput (Palibothra), to save her father's life, are similarly designed, does not appear from Benfeys' notice of the work in his paper in "Orient und Occident," iii. 171 ff. He says that the title of the book, "Nonthuk Pakkaranam," is taken from the name of a wise ox, Nonthuk, that plays the principal part in the longest of the tales, which are all apparently translated from the Sanskrit, in which language the title would be Nandaka Prakaranam, the History of Nandaka.

Most of the tales related by the wazír Al-Rahwan are not only in themselves entertaining, but are of very considerable importance from the story-comparer's point of view, since in this group occur Eastern forms of tales which were known in Italy in the 14th century, and some had spread over Europe even earlier. The reader will have seen from Sir R. F. Burton's notes that not a few of the stories have their parallels or analogues in countries far apart, and it is interesting to find four of them which properly belong to the Eastern texts of the Book of Sindibad, with the frame-story of which that of this group has so close an affinity.

THE ART OF ENLARGING PEARLS.—Vol. XI. p. 131.

"Quoth she, I have a bangle; sell it and buy seed pearls with the price; then round them and fashion them into great pearls."

FOR want of a more suitable place, I shall here reproduce an account of the "Method of making false pearls" (nothing else being meant in the above passage), cited, from Postl. Com. Dict., in vol. xxvi. of "Rees' Cyclopædia," London, 1819:

"Take of thrice distilled vinegar two pounds, Venice turpentine one pound, mix them together into a mass and put them into a cucurbit, fit a head and receiver to it, and after you have luted the joints set it when dry on a sand furnace, to distil the vinegar from it; do not give it too much heat, lest the stuff swell up. After this put the vinegar into another glass cucurbit in which there is a quantity of seed pearls wrapped in a piece of thin silk, but so as not to touch the vinegar; put a cover or head upon the cucurbit, lute it well and put it in bal. Mariæ, where you may let it remain a fortnight. The heat of the balneum will raise the fumes of the vinegar, and they will soften the pearls in the silk and bring them to the consistence of a paste, which being done, take them out and mould them to what bigness, form, and shape you please. Your mould must be of fine silver, the inside gilt; you must also refrain from touching the paste with your fingers, but use silver-gilt utensils, with which fill your moulds. When they are moulded, bore them through with a hog's bristle or gold wire, and then tread them again on gold wire, and put them into a glass, close it up, and set them in the sun to dry. After they are thoroughly dry, put them in a glass matrass into a stream of running water and leave them there twenty days; by that time they will contract the natural hardness and solidity of pearls. Then take them out of the matrass and hang them in mercurial water, where they will moisten, swell, and assume their Oriental beauty; after which shift them into a matrass hermetically closed to prevent any water coming to them, and let it down into a well, to continue there about eight days. Then draw the matrass up, and in opening it you will find pearls exactly resembling Oriental ones." (Here follows a *recipe* for making the mercurial water used in the process, with which I need not occupy more space.)

A similar formula, "To make of small pearls a necklace of large ones," is given in the "Lady's Magazine" for 1831, vol. iv., p. 119, which is said to be extracted from a scarce old book. Thus, whatever mystery may surround the art in Asiatic countries there is evidently none about it in Europe. The process appears to be somewhat tedious and complicated, but is doubtless profitable.

In Philostratus' Life of Apollonius there is a curious passage about pearl-making which has been generally considered as a mere "traveller's tale": Apollonious relates that the inhabitants of the shores of the Red Sea, after having calmed the water by means of oil, dived after the shell-fish, enticed them with some bait to open their shells, and having pricked the animals with a sharp-pointed instrument, received the liquor that flowed from them in small holes made in an iron vessel, in which it hardened into real pearls. — It is stated by several reputable writers that the Chinese do likewise at the present day. And Sir R. F. Burton informs me that when he was on the coast of Midian he found the Arabs were in the habit of "growing" pearls by inserting a grain of sand into the shells. ·

THE SINGER AND THE DRUGGIST. — *Vol. XI. p.* 136.

THE diverting adventures related in the first part of this tale should be of peculiar interest to the student of Shakspeare as well as to those engaged in tracing the genealogy of popular fictions. Jonathan Scott has given — for reasons of his own — a meagre abstract of a similar tale which occurs in the "Bahár-i-Dánish" (vol. iii. App., p. 291), as follows:

PERSIAN VERSION.

A YOUNG MAN, being upon business in a certain city, goes on a hunting excursion, and, fatigued with the chase, stops at a country house to ask refreshment. The lady of the mansion receives him kindly, and admits him as her lover. In the midst of their dalliance the husband comes home, and the young man had no recourse to escape discovery but to jump into a basin which was in the court of the house, and stand with head in a hollow gourd that luckily happened to be in the water. The husband, surprised to see the gourd stationary in the water, which was itself agitated by the wind, throws a stone at it, when the lover slips from beneath it and holds his breath till almost suffocated. Fortunately the husband presently retires with his wife into an inner room of the house, and thus the young man was enabled to make good his escape.

The next day he relates his adventure before a large company at a coffee-house. The husband happens to be one of the audience, and, meditating revenge, pretends to admire the gallantry of the young man and invites him to his house. The lover accompanies him, and on seeing his residence is overwhelmed with confusion; but, recovering himself, resolves to abide all hazards, in hopes of escaping by some lucky stratagem. His host introduces him to his wife, and begs him to relate his merry adventure before her, having resolved, when he should finish, to put them both to death. The young man complies, but with an artful presence of mind exclaims at the conclusion, "Glad was I when I awoke from so alarming a dream." The husband upon this, after some questions, is satisfied that he had only told his dream, and, having entertained him nobly, dismisses him kindly.

The story is told in an elaborate form by Ser Giovanni Fiorentino, in "Il Pecorone" (The Big Sheep, or, as Dunlop has it, The Dunce), which was begun in 1378 but not published till 1554 (at Milan). It is the second novel of the First Day and has been thus translated by Roscoe:

SER GIOVANNI'S VERSION.

THERE were once two very intimate friends, both of the family of Saveli, in Rome; the name of one of whom was Bucciolo; that of the other, Pietro Paolo, both of good birth and easy circumstances. Expressing a mutual wish to study for a while together at Bologna they took leave of their relatives and set out. One of them attached himself to the study of the civil law, the other to that of the canon law, and thus they continued to apply themselves for some length of time. But the subject of Decretals takes a much narrower range than is embraced by the common law, so Bucciolo, who pursued the former, made greater progress than did Pietro Paolo, and, having taken a licentiate's degree, he began to think of returning to Rome. "You see, my dear fellow student," he observed to his friend Paolo, "I am now a licentiate, and it is time for me to think of moving homewards." "Nay, not so," replied his companion; "I have to entreat you will not think of leaving me here this winter. Stay for me till spring, and we can return together. In the meantime you may pursue some other study, so that you need not lose any time;" and to this Bucciolo at length consented, promising to await his relative's own good time.

Having thus resolved, he had immediate recourse to his former tutor, informing him of his determination to bear his friend company a little longer, and entreating to be employed in some pleasant study to beguile the period during which he had to remain. The professor begged him to suggest something he should like, as he should be very happy to assist him in its attainment. "My worthy tutor," replied Bucciolo, "I think I should like to learn the way in which one falls in love, and the best manner to begin." "O very good!" cried the tutor, laughing. "You could not have hit upon anything better, for you must know that, if such be your object, I am a complete adept in the art. To lose no time, in the first place go next Sunday to the church of the Frati Minori [Friars Minor of St. Francis], where all the ladies will be clustered together, and pay proper attention during service in order to discover if any one of them in particular happens to please you. When you have done this, keep your eye upon her after service, to see the way she takes to her residence, and then come back to me. And let this be the first lesson — the first part — of that in which it is my intention to instruct you." Bucciolo went accordingly, and taking his station the next Sunday in the church, as he had been directed, his eyes, wandering in every direction, were fixed upon all the pretty women in the place, and upon one in particular, who pleased him above all the rest. She was by far the most beautiful and attractive lady he could discover, and on leaving church he took care to obey his master and follow her until he had made himself acquainted with her residence. Nor was it long before the young lady began to perceive that the student was smitten with her; upon which Bucciolo returned to his master and informed him of what he had done. "I have," said he, "learned as much as you ordered me, and have found somebody I like very well." "So far, good," cried the professor, not a little amused at the sort of science to which his pupil had thus seriously devoted himself — "so far, good! And now observe what I have next to say to you: Take care to walk two or three times a day very respectfully before her house, casting your eyes about you in such a way that no one may catch you staring in her face; look in a modest and becoming manner, so that she cannot fail to notice and be struck with it. And then return to me; and this, sir, will be the second lesson in this gay science."

So the scholar went and promenaded with great discretion before the lady's door, who observed that he appeared to be passing to and fro out of respect to one of the inhabitants.

This attracted her attention, for which Bucciolo very discreetly expressed his gratitude by looks and bows, which being as often returned, the scholar began to be aware that the lady liked him. He immediately went and told the professor all that had passed, who replied, "Come, you have done very well. I am hitherto quite satisfied. It is now time for you to find some way of speaking to her, which you may easily do by means of those gipsies who haunt the streets of Bologna, crying ladies' veils, purses, and other articles for sale. Send word by her that you are the lady's most faithful, devoted servant, and that there is no one in the world you so much wish to please. In short, let her urge your suit, and take care to bring the answer to me as soon as you have received it. I will then tell you how you are to proceed."

Departing in all haste, he soon found a little old pedlar woman, quite perfect in the trade, to whom he said he should take it as a particular favour if she would do one thing, for which he would reward her handsomely. Upon this she declared her readiness to serve him in anything he pleased. "For you know," she added, "it is my business to get money in every way I can." Bucciolo gave her two florins, saying, "I wish you to go for me to-day as far as the Via Maccarella, where resides a young lady of the name of Giovanna, for whom I have the very highest regard. Pray tell her so, and recommend me to her most affection-ately, so as to obtain for me her good graces by every means in your power. I entreat you to have my interest at heart, and to say such pretty things as she cannot refuse to hear." "O leave that to me, sir," said the little old woman, "I will not fail to say a good word for you at the proper time." "Delay not," said Bucciolo, "but go now, and I will wait for you here;" and she set off at once, taking her basket of trinkets under her arm. On approach-ing the place, she saw the lady before the door, enjoying the air, and curtseying to her very low, "Do I happen to have anything here you would fancy?" she said, displaying her wares. "Pray take something, madam — whatever pleases you best." Veils, stays, purses, and mirrors were now spread in the most tempting way before the lady's eyes. Out of all these things her attention seemed to be most attracted by a beautiful purse, which, she observed, if she could afford, she should like to purchase. "Nay, madam," exclaimed the crone, "do not think anything about the price — take anything you please, since they are all paid for already, I assure you." Surprised at hearing this, and perceiving the very respectful manner of the speaker, the lady rejoined, "Do you know what you are saying? What do you mean by that?" The old woman, pretending now to be much affected, said, "Well, madam, if it must be so, I shall tell you. It is very true that a young gentleman of the name of Bucciolo sent me hither; one who loves you better than all the world besides. There is nothing he would not do to please you, and indeed he appears so very wretched because he cannot speak to you, and he is so very good, that it is quite a pity. I think it will be the death of him, and then he is such a fine — such an elegant — young man, the more is the pity!" On hearing this, the lady, blushing deeply, turned sharply round upon the little old woman, exclaiming, "O you wicked creature! were it not for the sake of my own reputation, I would give you such a lesson that you should remember it to the latest day of your life! A pretty story to come before decent people with! Are you not ashamed of yourself to let such words come out of your mouth?" Then seizing an iron bar that lay across the doorway, "Ill betide you, little wretch!" she cried, as she brandished it. "If you ever come this way again, depend upon it, you will never go back alive!" The trembling old trot, quickly bundling up her wares, scampered off, in dread of feeling that cruel weapon on her shoulders, nor did she think of stopping till she had reached the place where Bucciolo stood waiting her return. Eagerly inquiring the news and how she had succeeded, "O very badly — very badly," answered the crone. "I never was in such a fright in all my life. Why, she will neither see nor listen to you, and if I had not run away, I should have felt the weight of a great iron bar upon my shoulders. For my own part, I shall go there no more; and I advise you, signor, to look to yourself how you proceed in such affairs in future."

Poor Bucciolo became quite disconsolate, and returned in all haste to acquaint the professor with this unlucky result. But the professor, not a whit cast down, consoled him, saying, "Do not despair; a tree is not levelled at a single stroke, you know. I think you must have a repetition of your lesson to-night. So go and walk before her door as usual; notice how she eyes you, and whether she appears angry or not, and then come back again to me." Bucciolo accordingly proceeded without delay to the lady's house. The moment she perceived him she called her maid and said to her, "Quick, quick — hasten after the young man — that is he, and tell him from me that he must come and speak with me this evening without fail — without fail." The girl soon came up with Bucciolo, and thus addressed him: "My lady, signor, my lady, Giovanna, would be glad of your company this evening, she would be very glad to speak with you." Greatly surprised at this, Bucciolo replied, "Tell your lady I shall be most happy to wait upon her," so saying, he set off once more to the professor, and reported the progress of the affair. But this time the master looked a little more serious; for, from some trivial circumstances put together, he began to entertain suspicions that the lady was (as it really turned out) no other than his own wife. So he rather anxiously inquired of Bucciolo whether he intended to accept the invitation. "To be sure I do," replied his pupil. "Then," said the professor, "promise that you will come here before you set off." "Certainly I will," answered Bucciolo readily, and took his leave.

Now Bucciolo was far from suspecting that the lady bore so near a relationship to his respected tutor, although the latter began to be rather uneasy as to the result, feeling some twinges of jealousy which were by no means pleasant. For he passed most of his winter evenings at the college where he gave lectures, and not unfrequently remained there for the night. "I should be sorry," said he to himself, "if this young gentleman were learning these things at my expense, and I must therefore know the real state of the case." In the evening his pupil called according to promise, saying, "Worthy master, I am now ready to go." "Well, go," replied the professor; "but be wise, Signor Bucciolo — be wise, and think more than once what you are about." "Trust me for that," said the scholar, a little piqued: "I shall go well provided, and not walk into the mouth of danger unarmed." And away he went, furnished with a good cuirass, a rapier, and a stiletto in his belt. He was no sooner on his way than the professor slipped out quietly after him, dogging his steps closely, until, trembling with rage, he saw him stop at his own house-door, which, on a smart tap being given, was quickly opened by the lady herself and the pupil admitted. When the professor saw that it was indeed his own wife, he was quite overwhelmed and thought, "Alas, I fear this young fellow has learned more than he confesses at my expense;" and vowing to be revenged, he ran back to the college, where arming himself with sword and dagger, he then hastened to his house in a terrible passion. Arriving at his own door, he knocked loudly, and the lady, sitting before the fire with Bucciolo, instantly knew it was her husband, so taking hold of Bucciolo, she concealed him hurriedly under a heap of damp clothes lying on a table near the window ready for ironing, which done, she ran to the door and inquired who was there. "Open quickly," exclaimed the professor. "You vile woman, you shall soon know who is here!" On opening the door, she beheld him with a drawn sword, and cried in well-affected alarm, "O my dearest life, what means this?" "You know very well what it means," said he. "The villain is now in the house." "Good Heaven! what is that you say?" exclaimed the lady. "Are you gone out of your wits? Come and search the house, and if you find anybody, I will give you leave to kill me on the spot. What! do you think I should now begin to misconduct myself as I never before did — as none of my family ever did before? Beware lest the Evil One should be tempting you, and, suddenly depriving you of your senses, draw you to perdition!" But the professor, calling for candles, began to search the house from the cellar upwards — among the tubs and casks — in every place but the right place — running his sword through the beds and under the beds, and into every inch of the bedding — leaving no corner or crevice of the whole house untouched. The lady accompanied him with a candle in her hand, frequently interrupting him with, "Say your beads — say your beads, good signor; it is certain that the Evil One is dealing with you, for were I half so bad as you esteem me, I would kill myself with my own hands. But I entreat you not to give way to this evil suggestion: oppose the adversary while you can." Hearing these virtuous observations of his wife, and not being able to discover any one after the strictest search, the professor began to think that he must, after all, be possessed, and presently extinguished the lights and returned to the college. The lady, on shutting the door after him, called out to Bucciolo to come from his hiding place, and then, stirring the fire, began to prepare a fine capon for supper, with some delicious wines and fruits. And thus they regaled themselves, highly entertained with each other, nor was it their least satisfaction that the professor had just left them, apparently convinced that they had learned nothing at his expense.

Proceeding to the college next morning, Bucciolo, without the least suspicion of the truth, informed his master that he had something for his ear which he was sure would make him laugh. "How so?" demanded the professor. "Why," said his pupil, "you must know that last night, just as I had entered the lady's house, who should come in but her husband, and in such a rage! He searched the whole house from top to bottom, without being able to find me. I lay under a heap of newly-washed clothes, which were not half dry. In short, the lady played her part so well that the poor gentlemen forthwith took his leave, and we afterwards ate a fine capon for supper and drank such wines — and with such zest! It was really one of the pleasantest evenings I ever spent in my life. But I think I'll go and take a nap, for I promised to return this evening about the same hour." "Then be sure before you go," said the professor, trembling with suppressed rage, "be sure to come and tell me when you set out." "O certainly," responded Bucciolo, and away he went. Such was now the unhappy tutor's condition as to render him incapable of delivering a single lecture during the whole day, and such was his extreme vexation and eagerness for evening, that he spent his time in arming himself with sword and dagger and cuirass, meditating only upon deeds of blood. At the appointed time came Bucciolo, with the utmost innocence, saying, "My dear master, I am going now." "Yes, go," replied the professor, "and come back to-morrow morning, if you can, and tell me how you have fared." "I intend doing so," said Bucciolo, and departed at a brisk pace for the house of the lady.

Armed *cap-à-pie*, the professor ran out after him, keeping pretty close to his heels, with the intention of catching him just as he entered. But the lady, being on the watch, opened the door suddenly for the pupil and shut it in her husband's face. The professor began to knock and to call out with a furious noise. Extinguishing the light in a moment, the lady placed Bucciolo behind the door, and throwing her arms round her husband's neck as he entered, motioned to her lover while thus she held his enemy to make his escape, and he, upon the husband's rushing forward, slipped out from behind the door unperceived. She then began to scream as loud as she could, "Help! help! the professor has gone mad! Will nobody help me?" for he was in an ungovernable rage, and she clung faster to him than before. The neighbours running to her assistance and seeing the peaceable professor armed with deadly weapons, and his wife crying out, "Help, for the love of Heaven! — too much study hath driven him mad!" they readily believed such to be the fact. "Come, good signor," they said, "what is all this about? Try to compose yourself — nay, do not struggle so hard, but let us help you to your couch." "How can I rest, think you," he replied, "while this wicked woman harbours paramours in my house? I saw him come in with my own eyes." "Wretch that I am!" cried his wife. "Inquire of all my friends and neighbours whether any one of them ever saw anything the least unbecoming in my conduct." The whole party with one voice entreated the professor to lay such thoughts aside, for there was not a better lady breathing, or one who set a higher value upon her reputation. "But how can that be," said he, "when I saw him enter the house, and he is in it now?" In the meanwhile the lady's two brothers arrived, when she began to weep bitterly, exclaiming, "O my dear brothers, my poor husband has gone mad, quite mad — and he even says there is a man in the house. I believe he would kill me if he could; but you know me too well to listen for a moment to such a story," and she continued to weep.

The brothers then accosted the professor in no gentle terms: "We are surprised, signor — we are shocked to find that you dare bestow such epithets on our sister. What can have led you, after living so amicably together, to bring these charges against her now?" "I can only tell you," answered the professor, "that there is a man in the house. I saw him enter." "Then come, and let us find him. Show him to us," retorted the incensed brothers, "for we will sift this matter to the bottom. Show us the man, and we will then punish her in such a way as will satisfy you." One of the brothers, taking his sister aside, said, "First tell me, have you really got any one hidden in the house? Tell the truth." "Heavens!" cried his sister, "I tell you, I would rather suffer death. Should I be the first to bring a scandal on our house? I wonder you are not ashamed to mention such a thing." Rejoiced to hear this, the brothers, directed by the professor, at once commenced a search. Half frantic, he led them at once to the great bundle of linen, which he pierced through and through with his sword, firmly believing that he was killing Bucciolo, all the while taunting him at every blow. "There! I told you," cried his wife, "that he was mad. To think of destroying our own property thus! It is plain he did not help to get them up," she continued, whimpering — "all my best clothes!"

Having now sought everywhere in vain, one of the brothers observed, "He is indeed mad," to which the other agreed, while he again attacked the professor in the bitterest terms: "You have carried matters too far, signor; your conduct to our sister is shameful, and nothing but insanity can excuse it." Vexed enough before, the professor upon this flew into a violent passion, and brandished his naked sword in such a way that the others were obliged to use their sticks, which they did so very effectively that, after breaking them over his head, they chained him down like a maniac upon the floor, declaring he had lost his wits by excessive study, and taking possession of his house, they remained with their sister all night. Next morning they sent for a physician, who ordered a couch to be placed as near as possible to the fire, that no one should be allowed to speak or reply to the patient, and that he should be strictly dieted until he recovered his wits; and this regimen was diligently enforced.[1]

A report immediately spread through Bologna that the good professor had become insane, which caused very general regret, his friends observing to each other, "It is indeed a bad business; but I suspected yesterday how it was — he could scarcely get a word out as he was delivering his lecture, did you not perceive?" "Yes," said another, "I saw him change colour, poor fellow." And by everybody, everywhere, it was decided that the professor was mad. In this situation numbers of his scholars went to see him, and among the rest Bucciolo, knowing nothing of what had happened, agreed to accompany them to the college, desirous of acquainting his master with last night's adventure. What was his surprise to learn that he had actually taken leave of his senses, and being directed on leaving the college to the professor's house, he was almost panic-struck on approaching the place, beginning to comprehend the whole affair. Yet, in order that no one might be led to suspect the real truth, he walked into the house along with the rest, and on reaching a certain apartment which he knew, he beheld his poor tutor almost beaten to a mummy, and chained down upon his bed, close to the fire. His pupils were standing round condoling with him and lamenting his piteous case. At length it came to Bucciolo's turn to say something to him, which he did as follows: "My dear master, I am as truly concerned for you as if you were my own father, and if there is anything in which I can be of service to you, command me as your own son." To this the poor professor only replied, "No, Bucciolo, depart in peace, my pupil; depart, for you have learned much, very much, at my expense." Here his wife interrupted him: "You see how he wanders — heed not what he says — pay no attention to him, signor." Bucciolo, however, prepared to depart, and taking a hasty leave of the professor, he proceeded to the lodging of his friend Pietro Paolo, and said to him, "Fare you well. God bless you, my friend. I must away; and I have lately learned so much at other people's expense that I am going home." So saying, he hurried away, and in due course arrived in safety at Rome.

The affliction of the professor of Giovanni's sprightly tale will probably be considered by most readers as well-merited punishment; the young gallant proved an apt scholar in the art of love, and here was the inciter to evil repaid with the same coin!

---

[1] Such was formerly the barbarous manner of treating the insane.

Straparola also tells the story, but in a different form, in his "Pleasant Nights" (Piacevoli Notti), First Day, second novella; and his version is taken into a small collection entitled "Tarlton's Newes out of Purgatorie," first published in or before 1590 — a catchpenny tract in which, of course, Dick Tarlton had never a hand, any more than he had in the collection of jests which goes under his name.

STRAPAROLA'S VERSION.[1]

In Pisa, a famous cittie of Italye, there lived a gentleman of good lineage and landes, feared as well for his wealth, as honoured for his vertue, but indeed well thought on for both; yet the better for his riches. This gentleman had one onelye daughter, called Margaret, who for her beauty was liked of all, and desired of many. But neither might their sutes nor her owne prevaile about her father's resolution, who was determyned not to marrye her, but to such a man as should be able in abundance to maintain the excellency of her beauty. Divers yong gentlemen proffered large feoffments, but in vaine, a maide shee must bee still: till at last an olde doctor in the towne, that professed phisicke, became a sutor to her, who was a welcome man to her father, in that he was one of the welthiest men in all Pisa; a tall stripling he was and a proper youth, his age about foure score, his heade as white as milke, wherein for offence sake there was left never a tooth. But it is no matter, what he wanted in person he had in the purse, which the poore gentlewoman little regarded, wishing rather to tie herself to one that might fit her content, though they lived meanely, then to him with all the wealth in Italye. But shee was yong, and forcst to follow her father's direction, who, upon large covenants, was content his daughter should marry with the doctor, and whether she likte him or no, the match was made up, and in short time she was married. The poore wench was bound to the stake, and had not onely an olde impotent man, but one that was so jealous, as none might enter into his house without suspition, nor shee doo any thing without blame; the least glance, the smallest countenance, any smile was a manifest instance to him that shee thought of others better than himselfe. Thus he himselfe lived in a hell, and tormented his wife in as ill perplexitie.

At last it chaunced that a young gentleman of the citie, comming by her house, and seeing her looke out at her window, noting her rare and excellent proportion, fell in love with her, and that so extreamelye, as his passions had no meanes till her favour might mittigate his heart sicke discontent. The yong man that was ignorant in amorous matters, and had never beene used to courte anye gentlewoman, thought to reveale his passions to some one freend that might give him counsaile for the winning of her love, and thinking experience was the surest maister, on a daye seeing the olde doctor walkinge in the churche that was Margaret's husband, little knowing who he was, he thought this the fittest man to whom he might discover his passions, for that hee was olde and knew much, and was a phisition that with his drugges might helpe him forward in his purposes; so that seeing the olde man walke solitary, he joinde unto him, and after a curteous salute, tolde him that he was to impart a matter of great import to him, wherein, if hee would not onely be secrete, but indevour to pleasure him, his pains should bee every way to the full considered. You must imagine, gentleman, quoth Mutio, for so was the doctor's name, that men of our profession are no blabs, but hold their secrets in their hearts bottome, and therefore reveale what you please, it shall not onely be concealed, but cured, if either my art or counsaile may doo it. Upon this, Lyonell, so was the young gentleman called, told and discourst unto him from point to point, how he was falne in love with a gentlewoman that was married to one of his profession, discovered her dwelling and the house, for that he was unacquainted with the woman, and a man little experienced in love matters, he required his favour to further him with his advice. Mutio at this motion was stung to the hart, knowing it was his wife hee was fallen in love withall, yet to conceale the matter, and to experience his wive's chastity, and that if she plaide false, he might be revenged on them

---

[1] From "Tarlton's Newes out of Purgatorie."

both, he dissembled the matter, and answered that he knewe the woman very well, and commended her highly: but said she had a churle to her husband, and therefore he thought shee would bee the more tractable: Trye her, man, quoth hee, fainte harte never wonne faire lady, and if shee will not be brought to the bent of your bowe, I will provide such a potion as shall dispatch all to your owne content: and to give you further instructions for oportunitie, knowe that her husband is foorth every after-noone from three till sixe. Thus farre I have advised you, because I pitty your passions, as my selfe being once a lover, but now I charge thee reveale it to none whomsoever, least it doo disparage my credit to meddle in amorous matters.

The yong gentleman not onely promised all carefull secrecy, but gave him harty thanks for his good counsell, promising to meete him there the next day, and tell him what newes. Then hee left the old man, who was almost mad for feare his wife any way should play false: he saw by experience brave men came to besiege the castle, and seeing it was in woman's custodie, and had so weeke a governor as himselfe, he doubted it would in time be delivered up: which feare made him almost franticke, yet he drivde of the time great torment, till he might heare from his rival. Lionello he hastes him home and sutes him in his braverye, and goes downe toward the house of Mutio, where he sees her at the windowe whome he courted with a passionate looke, with such humble salute as shee might perceive how the gentleman was affectionate. Margaretta, looking earnestlye upon him, and noting the perfection of his proportion, accounted him in her eye the flower of all Pisa, thinkte her-selfe fortunate if shee might have him for her freend, to supply those defaultes that she found in Mutio. Sundry times that afternoone he past by her window, and he cast not up more loving lookes, than he received gratious favours, which did so incourage him that the next daye betweene three and sixe hee went to her house, and knocking at the doore, de-sired to speake with the mistris of the house, who hearing by her maid's description what he was, commaunded him to come in, where she intertained him with all courtesie.

The youth that never before had given the attempt to court a ladye, began his *exordium* with a blushe; and yet went forward so well, that hee discourst unto her howe hee loved her, and that if it might please her to accept of his service, as of a freende ever vowde in all dutye to bee at her commaunde, the care of her honour should bee deerer to him than his life, and hee would be ready to prise her discontent with his bloud at all times. The gentlewoman was a little coye, but, before they part, they concluded that the next daye at foure of the clock hee should come thither and eate a pound of cherries, which was resolved on with a *succado des labras*, and so with a loath to depart they tooke their leaves. Lionello as joyfull a man as might be, hyed him to the church to meete his olde doctor, where he found him in his olde walke: What newes, syr, quoth Mutio, how have you sped? Even as I can wishe, quoth Lionello, for I have been with my mistrisse, and have found her so tractable, that I hope to make the olde peasant, her husband, looke broadheaded by a paire of browantlers. How deepe this strooke into Mutio's hart, let them imagine that can conjecture what jelousie is; insomuch that the olde doctor askte when should be the time. Marry, quoth Lionello, tomorrow, at foure of the clocke in the afternoone, and then Maister Doctor, quoth hee, will I dub the old squire knight of the forked order.

Thus they past on in that, till it grew late, and then Lyonello went home to his lodging and Mutio to his house, covering all his sorrowes with a merrye countenance, with full resolution to revenge them both the next day with extremitie. He past the night as patiently as he could, and the next daye, after dinner, awaye hee went, watching when it should bee foure of the clocke. At the hour justly came Lyonello and was intertained with all curtesie; but scarce had they kist, ere the maide cryed out to her mistresse that her maister was at the doore; for he hasted, knowing that a horne was but a litle while in grafting. Margaret, at this alarum, was amazed, and yet for a shift chopt Lionello into a great driefatte[1] full of feathers,[2] and sat her downe close to her woorke. By that came

---

[1] A basket.
[2] In the *fabliau* "De la Dame qui atrappa un Prêtre, un Prévôt, et un Forestier" (or Constant du Hamel), the lady, on the pretext that her husband is at the door, stuffs her

Mutio in blowing, and as though hee came to looke somewhat in haste, called for the keyes of his chamber, and looked in everye place, searching so narrowlye in everye corner of the house, that he left not the very privie unsearcht. Seeing he could not finde him, hee saide nothing, but fayning himselfe not well at ease, staide at home; so that poor Lionello was faine to staye in the drifatte till the olde churle was in bed with his wife; and then the maide let him out at a backe doore, who went home with a flea in his eare to his lodging.

Well, the next day he went againe to meete his doctor, whome he found in his wonted walke. What newes? quoth Mutio, how have you sped? A poxe of the olde slave, quoth Lyonello; I was no sooner in, and had given my mistresse one kisse, but the jelous asse was at the doore; the maide spied him, and cryed her maister; so that the poore gentle-woman, for very shifte, was faine to put me in a driefatte of feathers that stoode in an olde chamber, and there I was faine to tarry while[1] he was in bed and a-sleepe, and then the maide let me out, and I departed. But it is no matter; 'twas but a chaunce, and I hope to crye quittance with him ere it be long. As how? quoth Mutio. Marry, thus, quoth Lion-ello: shee sent me woord by her maide this daye that upon Thursday next the olde churle suppeth with a patient of his a mile out of Pisa, and then I feare not but to quitte[2] him for all. It is well, quoth Mutio; fortune bee your frende. I thanke you, quoth Lionello: and so, after a little more prattle, they departed.

To bee shorte, Thursdaye came, and about sixe of the clocke, foorth goes Mutio no further than a freendes house of his, from whence he might descrye who went into his house; straight hee sawe Lionello enter in, and after goes hee, insomuche that hee was scarcelye sitten downe, before the mayde cryed out againe, my maister comes. The good-wife, that before had provided for after-claps,[3] had found out a privie place betweene two seelings of a plauncher,[4] and there she thrust Lionello, and her husband came sweting. What news, quoth shee, drives you home againe so soone, husband? Marry, sweete wife, quoth he, a fearfull dreame that I had this night, which came to my remembrance, and that was this: me thought there was a villaine that came secretlye into my house, with a naked poinard in his hand, and hid himselfe, but I could not finde the place; with that mine nose bled, and I came back; and, by the grace of God, I will seeke every corner in the house for the quiet of my minde. Marry, I pray you doo, husband, quoth she. With that he lockt in all the doors, and began to search every chamber, every hole, every chest, every tub, the very well; he stabd every feather bed through, and made havocke like a mad man, which made him thinke all was in vaine; and hee began to blame his eies that thought they saw that which they did not. Upon this he rest halfe lunaticke, and all night he was very wakefull, that towards the morning he fell into a dead sleepe, and then was Lionello conveighed away.

In the morning when Mutio wakened, hee thought how by no meanes hee should be able to take Lionello tardy: yet he laid in his head a most dangerous plot; and that was this: Wife, quoth he, I must the next Monday ride to Vycensa, to visit an olde patient of mine; till my returne, which will be some ten dayes, I will have thee staye at our little graunge house in the countrey. Marry, very well content, husband, quoth she. With that he kist her, and was verye pleasant, as though he had suspected nothing, and away hee flings to the church, where he meetes Lionello. What, sir, quoth he, what news? is your mistresse yours in possession? No, a plague of the olde slave, quoth hee. I think he is either a witch, or els woorkes by magick; for I can no sooner enter into the doores, but he is at my backe, and so he was againe yesternight; for I was not warm in my seate before the maide cryed, my maister comes; and then was the poore soule faine to conveigh me betweene two seelings of a chamber, in a fit place for the purpose, wher I laught hartely to myself too see how he sought every corner, ransakt every tub, and stabd every feather bed, but in vaine; I was safe enough till the morning, and then, when he was fast asleepe,

---

lovers, as they arrive successively, unknown to each other, into a large tub full of feathers and afterwards exposes them to public ridicule.

[1] Until.   [3] Accidents.

[2] Requite.   [4] A boarding.

I lept out. Fortune frownes on you, quoth Mutio. I,[1] but I hope, quoth Lionello, this is the last time, and now shee wil begin to smile; for on Monday next he rides to Vicensa, and his wife lyes at the grange house a little [out] of the towne, and there in his absence I will revenge all forepast misfortunes. God send it be so, quoth Mutio; and so took his leave.

These two lovers longd for Monday, and at last it came. Early in the morning Mutio horst himselfe and his wife, his maide and a man, and no more, and away he rides to his grange house, wher, after he had brok his fast, he took his leave, and away towards Vicensa. He rode not far ere, by a false way, he returned into a thicket, and there, with a company of cuntry peasants, lay in an ambuscade to take the young gentleman. In the afternoon comes Lionello galloping, and as soon as he came within sight of the house, he sent back his horse by his boy, and went easily afoot, and there, at the very entry, was entertained by Margaret, who led him up the staires, and convaid him into her bedchamber, saying he was welcome into so mean a cottage. But, quoth she, now I hope fortun shall not envy the purity of our loves. Alas! alas! mistris, cried the maid, heer is my maister, and 100 men with him, with bils and staves. We are betraid, quoth Lionel, and I am but a dead man. Feare not, quoth she, but follow me: and straight she carried him downe into a low parlor, where stoode an olde rotten chest full of writinges; she put him into that, and covered him with olde papers and evidences, and went to the gate to meet her husband.

Why, Signor Mutio, what meanes this hurly burly? quoth she. Vile and shameless strumpet as thou art, thou shalt know by and by, quoth he. Where is thy love? All we have watcht him and seen him enter in. Now, quoth he, shall neither thy tub of feathers or thy seeling serve, for perish he shall with fire, or els fall into my handes. Doo thy worst, jealous foole, quoth she, I ask thee no favour. With that, in a rage, he beset the house round, and then set fire on it. Oh, in what perplexitie was poore Lionello in that he was shut in a chest, and the fire about his eares! and how was Margaret passionat, that knew her lover was in such danger! Yet she made light of the matter, and, as one in a rage, called her maid to her and said: Come on, wench, seeing thy maister, mad with jelousie, hath set the house and al my living on fire, I will be revengd on him: help me heer to lift this old chest where all his writings and deeds are; let that burne first, and as soon as I see that on fire I will walke towards my freends, for the old foole will be beggard, and I will refuse him. Mutio, that knew al his obligations and statutes lay there, puld her back and bad two of his men carry the chest into the field, and see it were safe, himselfe standing by and seeing his house burned downe sticke and stone. Then, quieted in his mind, he went home with his wife and began to flatter her, thinking assuredly that he had burnt her paramour, causing his chest to be carried in a cart to his house in Pisa. Margaret, impatient, went to her mother's and complained to her and her brethren of the jealousie of her husband, who maintaned her it to be true, and desired but a daies respite to proove it.

Wel, hee was bidden to supper the next night at her mother's, she thinking to make her daughter and him freends againe. In the meane time he to his woonted walk in the church, and there, *præter expectationem*, he found Lionello walking. Wondring at this, he straight enquires what newes. What newes, Maister Doctor, quoth he, and he fell in a great laughing; in faith yesterday, I scapt a scouring, for syrrha, I went to the grange-house, where I was appointed to come, and I was no sooner gotten up the chamber, but the magicall villeine, her husband, beset the house with bils and staves, and that he might be sure no seeling nor corner should throwde me, he set the house on fire, and so burnt it downe to the ground. Why, quoth Mutio, and how did you escape? Alas, quoth he, wel fare a woman's wit; she conveighed me into an old chest full of writings, which she knew her husband durst not burne, and so I was saved and brought to Pisa, and yesternight, by her maide, let home to my lodging. This, quoth he, is the pleasantest jest that ever I heard; and upon this I have a sute to you: I am this night bidden foorth to supper, you shall be my guest, onely I will crave so much favour, as after supper for a pleasant sporte, to make relation what successe you have had in your loves. For that I will not sticke, quoth he,

---

[1] The letter I is very commonly substituted for "ay" in 16th century English books.

and so he conveyed Lionello to his mother-in-law's house with him, and discovered to his wive's brethren who he was, and how at supper he would disclose the whole matter; For, quoth he, he knowes not that I am Margaret's husband. At this all the brethren bad him welcome, and so did the mother to, and Margaret, she was kept out of sight. Supper time being come they fell to their victals, and Lionello was carrowst unto by Mutio, who was very pleasant, to drawe him into a merry humour, that he might to the ful discourse the effect and fortunes of his love. Supper being ended, Mutio requested him to tel to the gentlemen what had hapned between him and his mistresse. Lionello, with a smiling countenance, began to describe his mistresse, the house and street where she dwelt, how he fell in love with her, and how he used the councell of this doctor, who in all his affaires was his secretarye. Margaret heard all this with a great feare, and when he came to the last point, she caused a cup of wine to be given him by one of her sisters, wherein was a ring that he had given Margaret. As he had told how he had escapt burning, and was ready to confirme all for a troth, the gentlewoman drunke to him, who taking the cup and seeing the ring, having a quick wit and a reaching head, spide the fetch, and perceived that all this while this was his lover's husband to whome hee had revealed these escapes; at this drinking the wine and swallowing the ring into his mouth he went forward. Gentlemen, quoth he, how like you of my loves and my fortunes? Wel, quoth the gentlemen; I pray you is it true? As true, quoth he, as if I would be so simple as to reveal what I did to Margaret's husband; for, know you, gentlemen, that I knew this Mutio to be her husband whom I notified to be my lover; and for that he was generally known through Pisa to be a jealous fool, therefore, with these tales I brought him into paradice, which are follies of mine owne bralne; for, trust me, by the faith of a gentleman, I never spake to the woman, was never in her companye, neyther doo I know her if I see her. At this they all fell in a laughing at Mutio, who was ashamde that Lionello had so scoft him. But all was well; they were made friends; but the jest went so to his hart that he shortly after died, and Lionello enjoyed the ladye.

Ser Giovanni's story, Roscoe observes, is "curious as having through the medium of translation suggested the idea of those amusing scenes in which the renowned Falstaff acquaints Master Ford, disguised under the name of Brooke, with his progress in the good graces of Mrs. Ford. The contrivances likewise by which he eludes the vengeance of the jealous husband are similar to those recounted in the novel, with the addition of throwing the unweildy knight into the river. Dunlop says that the same story has been translated in a collection entitled 'The Fortunate, Deceived, and Unfortunate Lovers,' and that Shakspeare may probably also have seen it in 'Tarlton's Newes out of Purgatorie,' where the incidents related in the Lovers of Pisa are given according to Straparola's story. Molière made a happy use of it in his 'Ecole des Femmes,' where the humour of the piece turns upon a young gentleman confiding his progress in the affections of a lady to the ear of her guardian, who believed he was on the point of espousing her himself." Two other French plays were based upon the story, one of which was written by La Fontaine under the title of "La Maitre en Droit." Readers of "Gil Blas" will also recollect how Don Raphael confides to Balthazar the progress of his amour with his wife, and expresses his vexation at the husband's unexpected return.

It is much to be regretted that nothing is known as to the date and place of the composition of the Breslau edition of The Nights, which alone contains this and several other tales found in the collections of the early Italian novelists.

THE KING WHO KENNED THE QUINTESSENCE OF THINGS.—Vol. XI. p. 142.

ALTHOUGH we may find, as already stated, the direct source of this tale in the forty-sixth chapter of Al-Mas'údi's "Meadows of Gold and Mines of Gems," which was written about A.D. 943, yet there exists a much older version — if not the original form — in a Sanskrit collection entitled, "Vetálapanchavinsatí," or Twenty-five Tales of a Vampyre. This ancient work is incorporated with the "Kathá Sarit Ságara," or Ocean of the Streams of Story, composed in Sanskrit verse by Somadeva in the 11th century, after a similar work, now apparently lost, entitled "Vrihat Kathá," or Great Story, written by Gunadhya, in the 6th century.[1] In the opinion of Benfey all the Vampyre Tales are of Buddhist extraction (some are unquestionably so), and they probably date from before our era. As a separate work they exist, more or less modified, in many of the Indian vernaculars; in Hindí, under the title of "Baital Pachísí"; in Tamil, "Vedala Kadai"; and there are also versions in Telegu, Mahratta, and Canarese. The following is from Professor C. H. Tawney's complete translation of the "Kathá Sarit Ságara" (it is the 8th recital of the Vetála):

INDIAN VERSION.

THERE is a great tract of land assigned to Bráhmans in the country of Anga, called Vrikshaghata. In it there lived a rich sacrificing Bráhman named Vishnusvámin. And he had a wife equal to himself in birth. And by her he had three sons born to him, who were distinguished for preternatural acuteness. In course of time they grew up to be young men. One day, when he had begun a sacrifice, he sent those three brothers to the sea to fetch a turtle. So off they went, and when they had found a turtle, the eldest said to his two brothers, "Let one of you take the turtle for our father's sacrifice; I cannot take it, as it is all slippery with slime." When the eldest brother said this, the two younger ones answered him, "If you hesitate about taking it, why should not we?" When the eldest heard that, he said, "You two must take the turtle; if you do not, you will have obstructed your father's sacrifice, and then you will certainly sink down to hell." When he told the younger brothers this, they laughed and said to him, "If you see our duty so clearly, why do you not see that your own is the same?" Then the eldest said, "What, do you not know how fastidious I am? I am very fastidious about eating, and I cannot be expected to touch what is repulsive." The middle brother, when he heard this speech of his, said to his brother, "Then I am a more fastidious person than you, for I am a most fastidious connoisseur of the fair sex." When the middle one said this, the eldest went on to say, "Then let the younger of you two take the turtle." Then the youngest brother frowned, and in his turn said to the two elder, "You fools, I am very fastidious about beds; so I am the most fastidious of the lot."

So the three brothers fell to quarrelling with one another, and being completely under the dominion of conceit, they left that turtle, and went off immediately to the court of the king of that country, whose name was Prasenajit, and who lived in a city named Vitankapura, in order to have the dispute decided. There they had themselves announced by the warder, and went in, and gave the king a circumstantial account of their case. The king said, "Wait here, and I will put you all in turn to the proof;" so they agreed and remained there. And at the time that the king took his meal, he had them conducted to a seat of honour, and given delicious food fit for a king, possessing all the six flavours. And while all were feasting around him, the Bráhman who was fastidious about eating alone of all the company did not eat, but sat there with his face puckered up with disgust. The king himself asked the Bráhman why he did not eat his food, though it was sweet and fragrant, and he slowly answered him, "I perceive in this food an evil smell of the reek from corpses, so I cannot bring myself to eat it, however delicious it may be." When he said this before the assembled multitude, they all smelled it by the king's orders, and said, "This food is prepared from white rice and is good and fragrant." But the Bráhman who was so fastidious about eating would not touch it, but stopped his nose. Then the king reflected, and proceeded to inquire into the matter, and found out from his officers that the food had been

---

[1] Oesterley mentions a Sanskrit redaction of the Vampyre Tales attributed to Sivadása, and another comprised in the "Kathárnava."

made from rice which had been grown in a field near the burning *ghát* of a certain village. Then the king was much astonished, and, being pleased, he said to him, "In truth you are very particular as to what you eat; so eat of some other dish."

And after they had finished their dinner, the king dismissed the Bráhmans to their apartments, and sent for the loveliest lady of his court. And in the evening he sent that fair one, all whose limbs were of faultless beauty, splendidly adorned, to the second Bráhman, who was so squeamish about the fair sex. And that matchless kindler of Cupid's flame, with a face like the full moon of midnight, went, escorted by the king's servants, to the chamber of the Bráhman. But when she entered, lighting up the chamber with her brightness, that gentleman who was so fastidious about the fair sex felt quite faint, and stopping his nose with his left hand, said to the king's servants, "Take her away; if you do not, I am a dead man: a smell comes from her like that of a goat." When the king's servants heard this, they took the bewildered fair one to their sovereign, and told him what had taken place. And the king immediately had the squeamish gentleman sent for, and said to him, "How can this lovely woman, who has perfumed herself with sandal-wood, camphor, black aloes, and other splendid scents, so that she diffuses exquisite fragrance through the world, smell like a goat?" But though the king used this argument to the squeamish gentleman he stuck to his point; and then the king began to have his doubts on the subject, and at last, by artfully framed questions, he elicited from the lady herself that, having been separated in her childhood from her mother and nurse, she had been brought up on goat's milk.

Then the king was much astonished, and praised highly the discernment of the man who was fastidious about the fair sex, and immediately had given to the third Bráhman, who was fastidious about beds, in accordance with his taste, a bed composed of seven mattresses placed upon a bedstead. White smooth sheets and coverlets were laid upon the bed, and the fastidious man slept upon it in a splendid room. But, before half a watch of the night had passed, he rose up from that bed, with his hand pressed to his side, screaming in an agony of pain. And the king's officers, who were there, saw a red crooked mark on his side, as if a hair had been pressed deep into it. And they went and told the king, and the king said to them, "Look and see if there is not something under the mattress." So they went and examined the bottom of the mattresses one by one, and they found a hair in the middle of the bedstead underneath them all. And they took it and showed it to the king, and they also brought the man who was fastidious about beds, and when the king saw the state of his body, he was astonished. And he spent the whole night in wondering how a hair could make so deep an impression on his skin through seven mattresses.[1]

And the next morning the king gave three hundred thousand gold pieces to those three fastidious men, because they were persons of wonderful discernment and refinement. And they remained in great comfort in the king's court, forgetting all about the turtle, and little did they reck of the fact that they had incurred sin by obstructing their father's sacrifice.[2]

---

[1] And well might his sapient majesty "wonder"! The humour of this passage is exquisite.

[2] In the Tamil version (Babington's translation of the "Vedála Kadai") there are but two brothers, one of whom is fastidious in his food, the other in beds; the latter lies on a bed stuffed with flowers, deprived of their stalks. In the morning he complains of pains all over his body, and on examining the bed one hair is found amongst the flowers. In the Hindí version, the king asks him in the morning whether he had slept comfortably. "O great King," he replied; "I did not sleep all night." "How so?" quoth he. "O great King, in the seventh fold of the bedding there is a hair, which pricked me in the back, therefore I could not sleep." The youth who was fastidious about the fair sex had a lovely damsel laid beside him, and he was on the point of kissing her, but on smelling her breath he turned away his face, and went to sleep. Early in the morning the king (who had observed through a lattice what passed) asked him, "Did you pass the night pleasantly?" He replied that he did not, because the smell of a goat proceeded from the girl's mouth, which made him very uneasy. The king then sent for the procuress and ascertained that the girl had been brought up on goat's milk.

The story of the brothers who were so very "knowing" is common to most countries, with occasional local modifications. It is not often we find the knowledge of the "quintessence of things" concentrated in a single individual, as in the case of the ex-king of our tale, but we have his exact counterpart—and the circumstance is significant—in No. 2 of the "Cento Novelle Antiche," the first Italian collection of short stories, made in the 13th century, where a prisoner informs the king of Greece that a certain horse has been suckled by a she-ass, that a jewel contains a flaw, and that the king himself is a baker. Mr. Tawney, in a note on the Vetála story, as above, refers also to the decisions of Hamlet in Saxo Grammaticus, 1839, p. 138, in Simrock's "Quellen des Shakespeare," I, 81-85; 5, 170; he lays down that some bread tastes of blood (the corn was grown on a battlefield); that some liquor tastes of iron (the malt was mixed with water taken from a well, in which some rusty swords had lain); that some bacon tastes of corpses (the pig had eaten a corpse); lastly, that the king is a servant and his wife a serving-maid. But in most versions of the story three brothers are the gifted heroes.

In "Mélusine"[1] for 5 Nov. 1885, M. René Basset cites an interesting variant (in which, as is often the case, the "Lost Camel" plays a part, but we are not concerned about it at present) from Radloff's "Proben der Volksliteratur der türkischen Stamme des Sud-Siberiens," as follows:

SIBERIAN VERSION.

MEAT and bread were set before the three brothers, and the prince went out. The eldest said, "The prince is a slave;" the second, "This is dog's flesh;" the youngest, "This bread has grown over the legs of a dead body." The prince heard them. He took a knife and ran to find his mother. "Tell me the truth," cried he—"were you unfaithful to my father during his absence? A man who is here has called me a slave." "My son," replied she, "If I don't tell the truth, I shall die; if I tell it, I shall die. When thy father was absent, I gave myself up to a slave." The prince left his mother and ran to the house of the shepherd: "The meat which you have cooked to-day—what is it? Tell the truth, otherwise I'll cut your head off." "Master, if I tell it, I shall die; if I don't, I shall die. I will be truthful. It was a lamb whose mother had no milk; on the day of its birth, it was suckled by a bitch: that is to-day's ewe." The prince left the shepherd and ran to the house of the husbandman: "Tell the truth, or else I'll cut off your head. Three young men have come to my house. I have placed bread before them, and they say that the grain has grown over the limbs of a dead man." "I will be frank with you. I ploughed with my plough in a place where were [buried] the limbs of a man; without knowing it, I sowed some wheat, which grew up." The prince quitted his slave and returned to his house, where were seated the strangers. He said to the first, "Young man, how do you know that I am a slave?" "Because you went out as soon as the repast was brought in." He asked the second, "How do you know that the meat which was served to-day was that of a dog?" "Because it has a disagreeable taste like the flesh of a dog." Then to the third: "How come you to know that this bread was grown over the limbs of a dead person?" "What shall I say? It smells of the limbs of a dead body; that is why I recognised it. If you do not believe me, ask your slave; he will tell you that what I say is true."

In the same paper (col. 516) M. René Basset cites a somewhat elaborate variant, from Stier's "Ungarische Sagen und Märchen," in which, once more, the knowledge of the "quintessence of things" is concentrated in a single individual:

HUNGARIAN VERSION.

A CLEVER Magyar is introduced with his companions in disguise into the camp of the King of the Tátárs, who is menacing his country. The prince, suspicious, causes him to be

---

[1] Mélusine: Revue de Mythologie, Littérature Populaire, Traditions, et Usages. Dirigée par H. Gaidoz et E. Rolland. — Paris.

carefully watched by his mother, a skilful sorceress. They brought in the evening's repast. "What good wine the prince has!" said she. "Yes," replied one, "but it contains human blood." The sorceress took note of the bed from whence these words proceeded, and when all were asleep, she deftly cut a lock of hair from him who had spoken, crept stealthily out of the room, and brought this mark to her son. The strangers started up, and when our hero discovered what had been done to him, he cut a lock from all, to render his detection impossible. When they came to dinner, the king knew not from whom the lock had been taken. The following night the mother of the prince again slipped into the room, and said, "What good bread has the prince of the Tátárs!" "Very good," replied one, "it is made with the milk of a woman." When all were asleep, she cut a little off the moustache of him who was lying in the bed from which the voice proceeded. This time the Magyars were still more on the alert, and when they were apprised of the matter, they all cut a little from their moustaches, so that next morning the prince found himself again foiled. The third night the old lady hid herself, and said in a loud voice, "What a handsome man is the prince of the Tátárs!" "Yes," replied one, "but he is a bastard." When all were asleep, the old lady made a mark on the visor of the helmet of the one from whence had come the words, and then acquainted her son of what she had done. In the morning the prince perceived that all the helmets were similarly marked.[1] At length he refrained, and said, "I see that there is among you a master greater than myself; that is why I desire very earnestly to know him. He may make himself known; I should like to see and know this extraordinary man, who is more clever and more powerful than myself." The young man started up from his seat and said, "I have not wished to be stronger or wiser than yourself. I have only wished to find out what you had preconcerted for us. I am the person who has been marked three nights." "It is well, young man. But prove now your words: How is there human blood in the wine?" "Call your butler and he will tell you." The butler came in trembling all over, and confessed that when he corked the wine he had cut his finger with the knife, and a drop of blood had fallen into the cask. "But how is there woman's milk in the bread?" asked the king. "Call the bakeress," he replied, "and she will tell it you." When they questioned her, she confessed that she was kneading the bread and at the same time suckling her baby, and that on pressing it to her breast some milk flowed and was mixed with the bread. The sorceress, the mother of the king, when they came to the third revelation of the young man, confessed in her turn that the king was illegitimate.

Mr. Tawney refers to the Chevalier de Mailly's version of the Three Princes of Serendip (Ceylon): The three are sitting at table, and eating a leg of lamb, sent with some splendid wine from the table of the emperor Bahrám. The eldest maintains that the wine was made of grapes that grew in a cemetery; the second, that the lamb was brought up on dog's milk; while the third asserts that the emperor had put to death the son of the wazír, and that the latter is bent on vengeance. All these statements turn out to be well-grounded. Mr. Tawney also refers to parallel stories in the Breslau edition of The Nights; namely, in Night 458, it is similarly conjectured that the bread was baked by a sick woman; that the kid was suckled by a bitch, and that the sultan is illegitimate; and in Night 459, a gem-cutter guesses that a jewel has an internal flaw, a man skilled in the pedigrees of horses divines that a horse is the offspring of a female buffalo, and a man skilled in human pedigrees that the mother of the favourite queen was a rope-dancer. Similar incidents occur in "The Sultan of Yemen and his Three Sons," one of the Additional Tales translated by Scott, from the Wortley-Montague MS., now in the Bodleian Library, and comprised in vol. vi. of his edition of "The Arabian Nights Entertainments," published at London in 1811.

An analogous tale occurs in Mr. E. J. W. Gibb's recently-published translation of the "History of the Forty Vezírs" (the Lady's Fourth Story, p. 69 ff.), the *motif* of which is that "all things return to their origin:"

---

[1] The trick of the clever Magyar in marking all the other sleepers as the king's mother had marked herself occurs in the folk-tales of most countries, especially in the numerous

TURKISH ANALOGUE.

THERE was in the palace of the world a king who was very desirous of seeing Khizr[1] (peace on him!), and he would even say, "If there be any one who will show me Khizr, I will give him whatsoever he may wish." Now there was at that time a man poor of estate, and from the stress of his poverty he said to himself, "Let me go and speak to the king, that if he provide for me during three years, either I shall be dead, or the king will be dead, or he will forgive me my fault, or I shall on somewise win to escape, and in this way shall I make merry for a time." So he went to the king and spake these words to him.[2] The king said, "An thou show him not, then I will kill thee," and that poor man consented. Then the king let give him much wealth and money, and the poor man took that wealth and money and went to his house. Three years he spent in merriment and delight, and he rested at ease till the term was accomplished. At the end of that time he fled and hid himself in a trackless place and he began to quake for fear. Of a sudden he saw a personage with white raiment and shining face, who saluted him. The poor man returned the salutation, and the radiant being asked, "Why art thou thus sad?" But he gave no answer. Again the radiant being asked him and sware to him, saying, "Do indeed tell to me thy plight, that I may find thee some remedy." So that hapless one narrated his story from its beginning to its end, and the radiant being said, "Come, I will go with thee to the king, and I will answer for thee." So they arose.

Now the king wanted that hapless one, and while they were going some of the king's officers who were seeking met them, and they straightway seized the poor man and brought him to the king. Quoth the king, "Lo, the three years are accomplished; come now, and show me Khizr." The poor man said, "My king, grace and bounty are the work of kings—forgive my sin." Quoth the king, "I made a pact; till I have killed thee, I shall not have fulfilled it." And he looked to his chief vezír and said, "How should this be done?" Quoth the vezír, "This man should be hewn in many pieces and then hung up on butchers' hooks, that others may see and lie not before the king." Said that radiant being, "True spake the vezír;—all things return to their origin." Then the king looked to the second vezír and said, "What sayest thou?" He replied, "This man should be boiled in a cauldron." Said that radiant being, "True spake the vezír;—all things return to their origin." The king looked to the third vezír and said, "What sayest thou?" The vezír replied, "This man should be hewn in small pieces and baked in an oven." Again said that elder, "True spake the vezír;—all things return to their origin." Then quoth the king to the fourth vezír, "Let us see what sayest thou?" The vezír replied, "O king, the wealth thou gavest this poor creature was for the love of Khizr (peace on him!) He, thinking to find him, accepted it; now that he has not found him he seeks pardon. This were befitting, that thou set free this poor creature for the love of Khizr." Said that elder, "True spake the vezír;—all things return to their origin." Then the king said to the elder, "O elder, my vezírs have said different things contrary the one to the other, and thou hast said concerning each of them, 'True spake the vezír;—all things return to their origin.' What is the reason thereof?" That elder replied, "O king, thy first vezír is a butcher's son; therefore did he draw to his origin. Thy second vezír is a cook's son, and he likewise proposed a punishment as became

---

versions of the Robbery of the King's Treasury, which are brought together in my work on the Migrations of Popular Tales and Fictions (Blackwood), vol. ii., pp. 113–165.

[1] A mythical saint, or prophet, who, according to the Muslim legend, was despatched by one of the ancient kings of Persia to procure him some of the Water of Life. After a tedious journey, Khizr reached the Fountain of Immortality, but having drank of its waters, it suddenly vanished. Muslims believe that Khizr still lives, and sometimes appears to favoured individuals, always clothed in green, and acts as their guide in difficult enterprises.

[2] "Spake these words to the king" — certainly not those immediately preceding! but that, if the king would provide for him during three years, at the end of that period he would show Khizr to the king.

his origin. Thy third vezír is a baker's son; he likewise proposed a punishment as became his origin. But thy fourth vezír is of gentle birth; compassion therefore becomes his origin, so he had compassion on that hapless one, and sought to do good and counselled liberation. O king, all things return to their origin." [1] And he gave the king much counsel, and at last said, "Lo, I am Khizr," and vanished.[2]

The discovery of the king's illegitimate birth, which occurs in so many versions, has its parallels in the story of the Nephew of Hippocrates in the "Seven Wise Masters," and the Lady's 2nd Story in Mr. Gibb's translation of the "Forty Vezírs." The extraordinary sensitiveness of the third young Bráhman, in the Vetála story, whose side was scratched by a hair that was under the seventh of the mattresses on which he lay, Rohde (says Tawney), in his "Greichische Novellistik," p. 62, compares with a story told by Aelian of the Sybarite Smindyrides, who slept on a bed of rose-leaves and got up in the morning covered with blisters. He also quotes from the Chronicle of Tabari a story of a princess who was made to bleed by a rose-leaf lying in her bed.[3]

The eleventh recital of the Vetála is about a king's three sensitive wives: As one of the queens was playfully pulling the hair of the king, a blue lotus leaped from her ear and fell on her lap; immediately a wound was produced on the front of her thigh by the blow, and the delicate princess exclaimed "Oh! oh!" and fainted. At night, the second retired with the king to an apartment on the roof of the palace exposed to the rays of the moon, which fell on the body of the queen, who was sleeping by the king's side, where it was exposed by her garment blowing aside; immediately she woke up, exclaiming, "Alas! I am burnt," and rose up from the bed rubbing her limbs. The king woke up in a state of alarm, crying out, "What is the meaning of this?" Then he got up and saw that blisters had been produced on the queen's body. In the meanwhile the king's third wife heard of it and left her palace to come to him. And when she got into the open air, she heard distinctly, as the night was still, the sound of a pestle pounding in a distant house. The moment the gazelle-eyed one heard it, she said "Alas! I am killed," and she sat down on the path, shaking her hands in an agony of pain. Then the girl turned back, and was conducted by her attendants to her own chamber, where she fell on her bed and groaned. And when her weeping attendants examined her, they saw that her hands were covered with bruises, and looked like lotuses upon which black beetles had settled.

To this piteous tale of the three very sensitive queens Tawney appends the following note: Rohde, in his "Greichische Novellistik," p. 62, compares with this a story told by Timæus, of a Sybarite who saw a husbandman hoeing a field, and contracted rupture from it. Another Sybarite, to whom he told the tale of his sad mishap, got ear-ache from hearing it. Oesterley, in his German translation of the Baitál Pachísí, points out that Grimm, in his "Kindermärchen," iii. p. 238, quotes a similar incident from the travels of the Three Sons of Giaffar: out of four princesses, one faints because a rose-twig is thrown into her face among

---

[1] Mr. Gibb compares with this the following passage from Boethius, "De Consolatione Philosophiæ," as translated by Chaucer: "All thynges seken ayen to hir propre course, and all thynges rejoysen on hir retourninge agayne to hir nature."

[2] In this tale, we see, Khizr appears to the distressed man in *white* raiment.

[3] In an old English metrical version of the "Seven Sages," the tutors of the prince, in order to test his progress in general science, secretly place an ivy leaf under each of the four posts of his bed, and when he awakes in the morning —

> "Par fay!" he said, "a ferli cas!
> Other ich am of wine y-drunk,
> Other the firmament is sunk,
> Other wexen is the ground,
> The thickness of four leavès round!
> So much to-night higher I lay,
> Certes, than yesterday."

some roses; a second shuts her eyes in order not to see the statue of a man; a third says, "Go away; the hairs in your fur cloak run into me;" and the fourth covers her face, fearing that some of the fish in a tank may belong to the male sex. He also quotes a striking parallel from the "Elites des contes du Sieur d'Onville:" Four ladies dispute as to which of them is the most delicate. One has been lame for three months owing to a rose-leaf having fallen on her foot; another has had three ribs broken by a sheet in her bed having been crumpled; a third has held her head on one side for six weeks owing to one half of her head having three more hairs on it than the other; a fourth has broken a blood-vessel by a slight movement, and the rupture cannot be healed without breaking the whole limb. [Poor things!]

THE PRINCE WHO FELL IN LOVE WITH THE PICTURE. *Vol. XI. p.* 153.

IN the Persian tales of "The Thousand and One Days," a young prince entered his father's treasury one day, and saw there a little cedar chest "set with pearls, diamonds, emeralds, and topazes;" on opening it (for the key was in the lock) he beheld the picture of an exceedingly beautiful woman, with whom he immediately fell in love. Ascertaining the name of the lady from an inscription on the back of the portrait, he sets off with a companion to discover her, and having been told by an old man at Baghdád that her father at one time reigned in Ceylon, he continued his journey thither, encountering many unheard-of adventures by the way. Ultimately he is informed that the lady with whose portrait he had become enamoured was one of the favourites of King Solomon. One should suppose that this would have effectually cured the love-sick prince; but no: he "could never banish her sweet image from his heart." [1]

Two instances of falling in love with the picture of a pretty woman occur in the "Kathá Sarít Ságara." In Book ix., chap. 51, a painter shows King Prithvirúpa the "counterfeit presentment" of the beauteous Princess Rapalatá, and "as the king gazed on it his eye was drowned in that sea of beauty her person, so that he could not draw it out again. For the king, whose longing was excessive, could not be satisfied with devouring her form, which poured forth a stream of the nectar of beauty, as the partridge cannot be satisfied with devouring the moonlight." In Book xii., chap. 100, a female ascetic shows a wandering prince the portrait of the Princess Mandáravatí, "and Sundarasena when he beheld that maiden, who, though she was present there only in a picture, seemed to be of romantic beauty and like a flowing forth of joy, immediately felt as if he had been pierced with the arrows of the god of the flowery bow [*i.e.* Káma]." In chapter 35 of Scott's translation of the "Bahár-i-Dánish," Prince Ferokh-Faul opens a volume, "which he had scarcely done when the fatal portrait of the fair princess who, the astrologers had foretold, was to occasion him so many perils, presented itself to his view. He instantly fainted, when the slave, alarmed, conveyed intelligence of his condition to the sultan, and related the unhappy cause of the disorder." In Gomberville's romance of Polexandre, the African prince, Abd-el-Malik, falls in love with the portrait of Alcidiana, and similar incidents occur in the romance of Agesilaus of Colchos and in the Story of the Seven Wazírs (vol. vi.); but why multiply instances? Nothing is more common in Asiatic fictions.

THE FULLER, HIS WIFE, AND THE TROOPER. *Vol. XI. p.* 157.

IN addition to the versions of this amusing story referred to on p. 157—all of which will be found in the second volume of my work on "Popular Tales and Fictions," pp. 212-228—

---

[1] See also the same story in The Nights, vols. vii. and viii., which Mr. Kirby considers as probably a later version. (App. vol. x. of The Nights, p. 442).

there is yet another in a Persian story-book, of unknown date, entitled, 'Shamsa ú Kuhkuha," written by Mirza Berkhorder Turkman, of which an account, together with specimens, is given in a recently-published little book (Quaritch), "Persian Portraits, a sketch of Persian History, Literature, and Politics, " by Mr. F. F. Arbuthnot, author of "Early Ideas: a Group of Hindoo Stories."

This version occurs in a tale of three artful wives—or, to employ the story-teller's own graphic terms, "three whales of the sea of fraud and deceit: three dragons of the nature of thunder and the quickness of lightning; three defamers of honour and reputation; namely, three men - deceiving, lascivious women, each of whom had from the chicanery of her cunning issued the diploma of turmoil to a hundred cities and countries, and in the arts of fraud they accounted Satan as an admiring spectator in the theatre of their stratagems.[1] One of them was sitting in the court of justice of the kazi's embrace; the second was the precious gem of the bazaar-master's diadem of compliance; and the third was the beazle and ornament of the signet-ring of the life and soul of the superintendent of police. They were constantly entrapping the fawns of the prairie of deceit within the grasp of cunning, and plundered the wares of the caravan of tranquillity of hearts of strangers and acquaintances, by means of the edge of the scimitar of fraud. One day this trefoil of roguery met at the public bath, and, according to their homogeneous nature they intermingled as intimately as the comb with the hair; they tucked up their garment of amity to the waist of union, entered the tank of agreement, seated themselves in the hot-house of love, and poured from the dish of folly, by means of the key of hypocrisy, the water of profusion upon the head of intercourse; they rubbed with the brush of familiarity and the soap of affection the stains of jealousies from each other's limbs. After a while, when they had brought the pot of concord to boil by the fire of mutual laudation, they warmed the bath of association with the breeze of kindness, and came out. In the dressing-room all three of them happened simultaneously to find a ring, the gem of which surpassed the imagination of the jeweller of destiny, and the like of which he had never beheld in the storehouse of possibility. In short, these worthy ladies contended with each other for possession of the ring, until at length the mother of the bathman came forward and proposed that they should entrust the ring to her in the meanwhile, and it should be the prize of the one who most cleverly deceived and befooled her husband, to which they all agreed, and then departed for their respective domiciles."[2]

Mr. Arbuthnot's limits permitted only of abstracts of the tricks played upon their husbands by the three ladies—which the story-teller gives at great length—and that of the kazi's wife is as follows:

The kazi's wife knows that a certain carpenter, who lived close to her, was very much in love with her. She sends her maid to him with a message to say that the flame of his love had taken effect upon her heart, and that he must make an underground passage between his house and her dwelling, so that they might communicate with each other freely by

---

[1] So, too, in the "Bahár-i-Dánish" a woman is described as being so able a professor in the school of deceit, that she could have instructed the devil in the science of stratagem; of another it is said that by her wiles she could have drawn the devil's claws; and of a third the author declares, that the devil himself would own there was no escaping from her cunning!

[2] There is a similar tale by the Spanish novelist Isidro de Robles (circa 1660), in which three ladies find a diamond ring in a fountain; each claims it; at length they agree to refer the dispute to a count of their acquaintance who happened to be close by. He takes charge of the ring and says to the ladies, "Whoever in the space of six weeks shall succeed in playing off on her husband the most clever and ingenious trick (always having due regard to his honour) shall possess the ring; in the meantime it shall remain in my hands." (See Roscoe's "Specimens of the Spanish Novelists," Chandos edition, p. 438 ff.). This story was probably brought by the Moors to Spain, whence it may have passed into France, since it is the subject of a *fabliau*, by Haisiau the trouvrè, entitled "Des Trois Dames qui trouverent un Anel," which is found in Méon's edition of Barbazan, 1808, tome iii. pp. 220–229, and in Le Grand, ed. 1781, tome iv. pp. 163–165.

means of the mine. The carpenter digs the passage, and the lady pays him a visit, and says to him, "To-morrow I shall come here, and you must bring the kazi to marry me to you." The next day the kazi goes to his office; the lady goes to the carpenter's house, and sends him to bring her husband, the kazi, to marry them. The carpenter fetches him, and, as the kazi hopes for a good present, he comes willingly enough, but is much surprised at the extreme likeness between the bride and his own wife. The more he looks at her, the more he is in doubt; and at last, offering an excuse to fetch something, he rushes off to his own house, but is forestalled by his spouse, who had gone thither by the passage, and on his arrival is lying on her bed. The kazi makes some excuses for his sudden entry into her room, and, after some words, goes back to the carpenter's house; but his wife had preceded him, and is sitting in her place. Again he begins the ceremony, but is attracted by a black mole on the corner of the bride's lip, which he could have sworn was the same as that possessed by his wife. Making more excuses, and in spite of the remonstrances of the carpenter, he hurries back to his house once more; but his wife had again got there before him, and he finds her reading a book, and much astonished at his second visit. She suggests that he is mad, and he admits that his conduct is curious, and returns to the carpenter's house to complete the ceremony. This is again frequently interrupted, but finally he marries his own wife to the carpenter, and, having behaved in such an extraordinary manner throughout, is sent off to a lunatic asylum.

For the tricks of the two other ladies, and for many other equally diverting tales, I refer the reader to Mr. Arbuthnot's pleasing and instructive little book, which is indeed an admirable epitome of the history and literature of Persia, and one which was greatly wanted in these days, when most men, "like the dogs in Egypt for fear of the crocodiles, must drink of the waters of information as they run, in dread of the old enemy Time."

I have discussed the question of the genealogy of this tale elsewhere, but, after a somewhat more minute comparative analysis of the several versions, am disposed to modify the opinion which I then entertained. I think we must consider as the direct or indirect source of the versions and variants the "Miles Gloriosus" of Plautus, the plot of which, it is stated in the prologue to the second act, was taken from a Greek play. It is, however, not very clear whether Berni adapted his story from Plautus or the "Seven Wise Masters"; probably from the former, since in both the lady is represented, to the captain and the cuckold, as a twin sister, while in the S. W. M. the crafty knight pretends that she is his leman, come from Hungary with tidings that he may now with safety return home. On the other hand, in the S. W. M., as in Plautus, the lovers make their escape by sea, an incident which Berni has altered to a journey by land—no doubt, in order to introduce further adventures for the development of his main plot. But then we find a point of resemblance between Berni and the S. W. M., in the incident of the cuckold accompanying the lovers part of their way—in the latter to the sea-shore; while in Plautus the deceived captain remains at home to prosecute an amour and get a thrashing for his reward (in Plautus, instead of a wife, it is the captain's slave-girl). It is curious that amidst all the masquerade of the Arabian story the cuckold's wife also personates her supposititious twin-sister, as in Plautus and Berni. In Plautus the houses of the lover and the captain adjoin, as is also the case in the modern Italian and Sicilian versions; while in Berni, the S. W. M., the Arabian, and the Persian story cited in this note they are at some distance. With these resemblances and variations it is not easy to say which version was derived from another. Evidently the Arabian story has been deliberately modified by the compiler, and he has, I think, considerably improved upon the original: the ludicrous perplexity of the poor fuller when he awakes, to find himself apparently transformed into a Turkish trooper, recalls the nursery rhyme of the little woman "who went to market her eggs for to sell," and falling asleep on the king's highway a pedlar cut off her petticoats up to the knees, and when she awoke and saw her condition she exclaimed, "Lawk-a-mercy me, this is none of I!" and so on. And not less diverting is the pelting the blockhead receives from his brother fullers—altogether, a capital story.

TALE OF THE SIMPLETON HUSBAND.—Vol. XI. p. 162.

THE "curious" reader will find European and Asiatic versions of this amusing story in "Originals and Analogues of some of Chaucer's Canterbury Tales." published for the Chaucer Society, pp. 177-188 and (in a paper contributed by me: "The Enchanted Tree") p. 341-364.

TALE OF THE THREE MEN AND OUR LORD ISA.—Vol. XI. p. 170.

UNDER the title of "The Robbers and the Treasure-Trove" I have brought together many European and Asiatic versions of this wide-spread tale in "Chaucer Analogues," pp. 415-436.

THE MELANCHOLIST AND THE SHARPER.—Vol. XI. p. 180.

A SIMILAR but much shorter story is found in Gladwin's "Persian Moonshee," and story-books in several of the Indian vernaculars which have been rendered into English:
    A miser said to a friend, "I have now a thousand rupees, which I will bury out of the city, and I will not tell the secret to any one besides yourself." They went out of the city together, and buried the money under a tree. Some days after the miser went alone to the tree and found no signs of his money. He said to himself, "Excepting that friend, no other has taken it away; but if I question him he will never confess." He therefore went to his (the friend's) house and said, "A great deal of money is come into my hands, which I want to put in the same place; if you will come to-morrow, we will go together." The friend, by coveting this large sum, replaced the former money, and the miser next day went there alone and found it. He was delighted with his own contrivance, and never again placed any confidence in friends.
    One should suppose a miser the last person to confide the secret of his wealth to any one; but the Italian versions bear a closer resemblance to the Arabian story. From No. 74 of the "Cento Novelle Antiche" Sacchetti, who was born in 1335 and is ranked by Crescimbini as next to Boccaccio, adapted his 198th novella, which is a most pleasing version of the Asiatic story:

ITALIAN VERSION.

A BLIND man of Orvieto, of the name of Cola, hit upon a device to recover a hundred florins he had been cheated of, which showed he was possessed of all the eyes of Argus, though he had unluckily lost his own. And this he did without wasting a farthing either upon law or arbitration, by sheer dexterity; for he had formerly been a barber, and accustomed to shave very close, having then all his eyes about him, which had been now closed for about thirty years. Alms seemed then the only resource to which he could betake himself, and such was the surprising progress he in a short time made in his new trade that he counted a hundred florins in his purse, which he secretly carried about him until he could find a safer place. His gains far surpassed anything he had realised with his razor and scissors; indeed, they increased so fast that he no longer knew where to bestow them; until one morning happening to remain the last, as he believed, in the church, he thought of depositing his purse of a hundred florins under a loose tile in the floor behind the door, knowing the situation of the place perfectly well. After listening some time without hearing a foot stirring, he very cautiously laid it in the spot; but unluckily there remained a certain Juccio Pezzichernolo, offering his adoration before an image of San Giovanni Boccadoro, who happened to see Cola busily engaged behind the door. He continued his adorations until he saw the blind man depart, when, not in the least suspecting the truth, he approached and searched the place. He soon found the identical tile, and on removing it with the help of his knife, he found the purse, which he very quietly put into his pocket, replacing the tiles just as they were, and, resolving to say nothing about it, he went home.

At the end of three days the blind mendicant, desirous of inspecting his treasure, took a quiet time for visiting the place, and removing the tile searched a long while in great perturbation, but all in vain, to find his beloved purse. At last, replacing things just as they were, he was compelled to return in no very enviable state of mind to his dwelling; and there meditating on his loss, the harvest of the toil of so many days, by dint of intense thinking a bright thought struck him (as frequently happens by cogitating in the dark), how he had yet a kind of chance of redeeming his lost spoils. Accordingly in the morning he called his young guide, a lad about nine years old, saying, "My son, lead me to church," and before setting out he tutored him how he was to behave, seating himself at his side before the entrance, and particularly remarking every person who should enter into the church. "Now, if you happen to see any one who takes particular notice of me, and who either laughs or makes any sign, be sure you observe it and tell me." The boy promised he would; and they proceeded accordingly and took their station before the church.

When the dinner-hour arrived, the father and son prepared to leave the place, the former inquiring by the way whether his son had observed any one looking hard at him as he passed along. "That I did," answered the lad, "but only one, and he laughed as he went past us. I do not know his name, but he is strongly marked with the small-pox and lives somewhere near the Frati Minori." "Do you think, my dear lad," said his father, "that you could take me to his shop, and tell me when you see him there?" "To be sure I could," said the lad. "Then come, let us lose no time," replied the father; "and when we are there tell me, and while I speak to him you can step on one side and wait for me." So the sharp little fellow led him along the way until he reached a cheesemonger's stall, when he acquainted his father, and brought him close to it. No sooner did the blind man hear him speaking with his customers than he recognised him for the same Juccio with whom he had formerly been acquainted during his days of light. When the coast was a little clear, our blind hero entreated some moments' conversation, and Juccio, half suspecting the occasion, took him on one side into a little room, saying, "Cola, friend, what good news?" "Why," said Cola, "I am come to consult you, in great hopes you will be of use to me. You know it is a long time since I lost my sight, and being in a destitute condition, I was compelled to earn my subsistence by begging alms. Now, by the grace of God, and with the help of you and of other good people of Orvieto, I have saved a sum of two hundred florins, one hundred of which I have deposited in a safe place, and the other is in the hands of my relations, which I expect to receive with interest in the course of a week. Now if you would consent to receive, and to employ for me to the best advantage, the whole sum of two hundred florins it would be doing me a great kindness, for there is no one besides in all Orvieto in whom I dare to confide; nor do I like to be at the expense of paying a notary for doing business which we can as well transact ourselves. Only I wish you would say nothing about it, but receive the two hundred florins from me to employ as you think best. Say not a word about it, for there would be an end of my calling were it known I had received so large a sum in alms." Here the blind mendicant stopped; and the sly Juccio, imagining he might thus become master of the entire sum, said he should be very happy to serve him in every way he could, and would return an answer the next morning as to the best way of laying out the money. Cola then took his leave, while Juccio, going directly for the purse, deposited it in its old place being in full expectation of soon receiving it again with the addition of the other hundred, as it was clear that Cola had not yet missed the money. The cunning old mendicant on his part expected that he would do no less, and trusting that his plot might have succeeded, he set out the very same day to the church, and had the delight, on removing the tile, to find his purse really there. Seizing upon it with the utmost eagerness, he concealed it under his clothes, and placing the tiles exactly in the same position, he hastened home whistling, troubling himself very little about his appointment of the next day.

The sly thief Juccio set out accordingly the next morning to see his friend Cola, and actually met him on the road. "Whither are you going?" inquired Juccio. "I was going," said Cola, "to your house." The former, then taking the blind man aside, said, "I am resolved to do what you ask; and since you are pleased to confide in me, I will tell you of a plan that I have in hand for laying out your money to advantage. If you will put the two hundred florins into my possession, I will make a purchase in cheese and salt meat, a speculation which cannot fail to turn to good account." "Thank you," quoth Cola, "I am going to-day for the other hundred, which I mean to bring, and when you have got them both, you can do with them what you think proper." Juccio said, "Then let me have them soon, for I think I can secure this bargain; and as the soldiers are come into the town, who are fond of these articles, I think it cannot fail to answer; so go, and Heaven speed you." And Cola went; but with very different intentions from those imagined by his friend—Cola being now clearsighted, and Juccio truly blind. The next day Cola called on his friend with very downcast and melancholy looks, and when Juccio bade him good day, he said, "I wish from my soul it were a good, or even a middling, day for me." "Why, what is the matter?" "The matter?" echoed Cola; "why, it is all over with me: some rascal has stolen a hundred florins from the place where they were hidden, and I cannot recover a penny from my relations, so that I may eat my fingers off for anything I have to expect." Juccio replied, "This is like all the rest of my speculations. I have invariably lost where I expected to make a good hit. What I shall do I know not; for if the person should choose to keep me to the agreement I made for you, I shall be in a pretty dilemma indeed." "Yet," said Cola, "I think my condition is still worse than yours. I shall be sadly distressed and shall have to amass afresh capital, which will take me ever so long. And when I have got it, I will take care not to conceal it in a hole in the floor, or trust it, Juccio, into any friend's hands." "But," said Juccio, "if we could contrive to recover what is owing by your relations, we might still make some pretty profit of it, I doubt not." For he thought, if he could only get hold of the hundred he had returned it would still be something in his way. "Why," said Cola, "to tell the truth, if I were to proceed against my relations I believe I might get it; but such a thing would ruin my business, my dear Juccio, for ever: the world would know I was worth money, and I should get no more money from the world; so I fear I shall hardly be able to profit by your kindness, though I shall always consider myself as much obliged as if I had actually cleared a large sum. Moreover, I am going to teach another blind man my profession, and if we have luck you shall see me again, and we can venture a speculation together." So far the wily mendicant, to whom Juccio said,"Well, go and try to get money soon, and bring it; you know where to find me, but look sharp about you and the Lord speed you; farewell." "Farewell," said Cola; "and I am well rid of thee," he whispered to himself; and going upon his way, in a short time he doubled his capital; but he no longer went near his friend Juccio to know how he should invest it. He had great diversion in telling the story to his companions during their feasts, always concluding, "By St. Lucia! Juccio is the blinder man of the two: he thought it was a bold stroke to risk his hundred to double the amount."

For my own part, I think the blind must possess a more acute intellect than other people, inasmuch as the light, exhibiting such a variety of objects to view, is apt to distract the attention, of which many examples might be adduced. For instance, two gentlemen may be conversing together on some matter of business, and in the middle of a sentence a fine woman happens to pass by, and they will suddenly stop, gazing after her; or a fine equipage, or any other object is enough to turn the current of their thoughts. And then we are obliged to recollect ourselves, saying, "Where was I?" "What was it that I was observing?" — a thing which never occurs to a blind man. The philosopher Democritus very properly on this account knocked his eyes out in order to catch objects in a juster light with his mind's eye.

It is impossible to describe Juccio's vexation on going to church and finding the florins were gone. His regret was far greater than if he had actually lost a hundred of his own; as is known to be the case with all inveterate rogues, half of whose pleasure consists in depriving others of their lawful property.

There are many analogous stories, one of which is the well-known tale of the merchant, who, before going on a journey, deposited with a dervish 1,000 sequins, which he thought it prudent to reserve in case of accidents. When he returned and requested his deposit, the dervish flatly denied that he ever had any of his money. Upon this the merchant went and laid his case before the kazi, who advised him to return to the dervish and speak pleasantly to him, which he does, but receives nothing but abuse. He informed the kazi of this, and was told not to go near the dervish for the present, but to be at ease for he should have his money next day. The kazi then sent for the dervish, and after entertaining him sumptuously, told him that, for certain reasons, he was desirous of removing a considerable sum of money from his house; that he knew of no person in whom he could confide so much as himself; and that if he would come the following evening at a late hour, he should have the precious deposit. On hearing this, the dervish expressed his gratification that so much confidence should be placed in his integrity, and agreed to take charge of the treasure. Next day the merchant returned to the kazi, who bade him go back to the dervish and demand his money once more, and should he refuse, threaten to complain to the kazi. The result may be readily guessed: no sooner did the merchant mention the kazi than the rascally dervish said, "My good friend, what need is there to complain to the kazi? Here is your money; it was only a little joke on my part." But in the evening, when he went to receive the kazi's pretended deposit, he experienced the truth of the saw, that "covetousness sews up the eyes of cunning."

A variant of this found in the continental "Gesta Romanorum" (ch. cxviii. of Swan's translation), in which a knight deposits ten talents with a respectable old man, who when called upon to refund the money denies all knowledge of it. By the advice of an old woman, the knight has ten chests made, and employs a person to take them to the old man and represent them as containing treasure; and while one of them is being carried into his house the knight enters and in the stranger's presence demands his money, which is at once delivered to him.

In Mr. Edward Rehatsek's translated selections from the Persian story-book "Shamsa ú Kuhkuha" (see *ante*, p. 237), printed at Bombay in 1871, under the title of "Amusing Stories," there is a tale (No. xviii.) which also bears some resemblance to that of the Melancholist and the Sharper; and as Mr. Rehatsek's little work is exceedingly scarce, I give it in extenso as follows:

There was in Damascus a man of the name of Zayn el-Arab, with the honey of whose life the poison of hardships was always mixed. Day and night he hastened like the breeze from north to south in the world of exertion, and he was burning brightly like straw, from his endeavours in the oven of acquisition in order to gain a loaf of bread and feed his family. In course of time, however, he succeeded in accumulating a considerable sum of money, but as he had tasted the bitter poison of destitution, and had for a very long time carried the heavy load of poverty upon his back, and fearing to lose his property by the chameleon-like changes of fortune, he took up his money on a certain night, carried it out of the city, and buried it under a tree. After some time had passed he began sorely to miss the presence of his treasure, and betook himself to the tree to refresh his eyes with the sight of it. But when he dug up the ground at the foot of the tree he discovered that his soul-exhilarating deposit was refreshing the palate of some one else. The morning of his prosperity was suddenly changed into the evening of bitterness and disappointment. He was perplexed to what friend to confide his secret, and to what remedy to fly for the recovery of his treasure. The lancet of grief had pierced the liver of his peace, and the huntsman of distress had tied up the wings and feet of the bird of his serenity. One day he went on some business to a learned and wise man of the city with whom he was on a footing of intimacy. This man said to him, "It is some time since I perceived the glade of your circumstances to have been destroyed by the burning coals of restlessness, and a sad change to have taken place in your health. I do not know the reason, nor what thorn of misfortune has pierced the foot of your heart, nor what hardship has dawned from the east of your mind." Zayn el-Arab wept tears of sadness and said, "O thou standard coin from the mint of love! the treachery of misfortune has brought a strange accident upon me, and the bow of destiny has let fly an unpropitious arrow upon my feeble target. I have a heavy heart and great sorrow, and were I to reveal it to you perhaps it would be of no use and would plunge you also into grief." The learned man said, "Since the hearts of intimate friends are like looking-glasses and are receiving the figures of mutual secrets, it is at all times necessary that they should communicate to each other any difficulties which they have fallen into, that they may remove them by taking in common those steps which prudence and foresight should recommend." Zayn el-Arab replied, "Dear friend, I had some gold, and fearing lest it should be stolen, I carried it to such and such a place and buried it under a tree, and when I again visited the place, I perceived the garment of my beloved Joseph to be sprinkled with the blood of the wolf of deception." The learned man said, "This is a grave accident, and it will be difficult to get on the track of your gold. Perhaps some one saw you bury it: he who has taken it will have to give an account of it in the next world, for God is omniscient. Give me ten days' delay, that I may study the book of expedients and stratagems, when mayhap somewhat will occur to me."

That knowing man sat down for ten days in the school of meditation, and how much so ever he turned over the leaves of the volume of his mind from the preface to the epilogue, he could hit upon no plan. On the tenth day they again met in the street, and he said to Zayn el-Arab, "Although the diver of my mind has plunged deeply and searched diligently in this deep sea, he has been unable to seize the precious pearl of a wise plan of operation: may God recompense you from the stores of His hidden treasury!" They were conversing in this way when a lunatic met them and said, "Well, my boys, what secret-mongering have you got between you?" The learned man said to Zayn el-Arab, "Come, let us relate our case to this crazy fellow, to see the flower of the plant that may bloom from his mind." Zayn el-Arab replied, "Dear friend, you, with all your knowledge, cannot devise anything during ten days: what information are we likely to gain from a poor lunatic who does not know whether it is now day or night?" The learned man said, "There is no telling what he may say to us. But you know that the most foolish as well as the most wise have ideas, and a sentence uttered at random has sometimes furnished a clue by which the desired object may be attained." Meanwhile a little boy also came up, and perceiving the lunatic stopped to see his tricks. The two friends explained their case to the lunatic, who then seemed immersed in thought for some time, after which he said, "He who took the root of that tree for a medicine also took the gold," and having thus spoken, he turned his back upon them and went his way. They consulted with each other what indication this remark might furnish, when the little boy who had overheard the conversation, asked what kind of tree it was. Zayn el-Arab replied that it was a jujube tree. The boy said, "This is an easy matter: you ought to inquire of all the doctors of this town for whom a medicine has been prescribed of the roots of this tree." They greatly admired the boy's acuteness and also of the lunatic's lucky thought.[1] The learned man was well acquainted with all the physicians of the city and made his enquiries, till he met with one who informed him that about twenty days ago he had prescribed for a merchant of the name of Khoja Semender, who suffered from asthma, and that one of the remedies was the root of that jujube tree. The learned man soon discovered the merchant's house, found him enjoying excellent health, and said to him, "Ah, Khoja, all the goods of this world ought to be surrendered to procure health. By the blessing of God, you have recovered your health, and you ought to give up what you found at the root of that tree, because the owner of it is a worthy man and possesses nothing else." The honest merchant answered, "It is true, I have found it, and it is with me. If you will describe it I will deliver it into your hands." The exact sum being stated, the merchant at once delivered up the gold.

---

[1] Idiots and little boys often figure thus in popular tales: readers of Rabelais will remember his story of the Fool and the Cook; and there is a familiar example of a boy's precocity in the story of the Stolen Purse — "Craft and Malice of Women," or the Seven Wazírs, vol. vi. of The Nights.

In the "Kathá Sarit Ságara," Book vi. ch. 33, we have proably the original of this last story: A wealthy merchant provided a Bráhman with a lodging near his own house, and every day gave him a large quantity of unhusked rice and other presents, and in course of time he received like gifts from other great merchants. In this way the miserly fellow gradually accumulated a thousand dínárs, and going into the forest he dug a hole and buried it in the ground, and he went daily to carefully examine the spot. One day, however, he discovered that his hoard had been stolen, and he went to his friend the merchant near whose house he lived, and, weeping bitterly, told him of his loss, and that he had resolved to go to a holy bathing-place and there starve himself to death. The merchant tried to console him and dissuade him from his resolution, saying, "Bráhman, why do you long to die for the loss of your wealth? Wealth, like an unseasonable cloud, suddenly comes and goes." But the Bráhman would not abandon his fixed determination to commit suicide, for wealth is dearer to the miser than life itself. When he was about to depart for the holy place, the king, having heard of it, came and asked him, "Bráhman, do you know of any mark by which you can distinguish the place where you buried your dínárs?" He replied, "There is a small tree in the wood, at the foot of which I buried that money." Then said the king, "I will find the money and give it back to you, or I will give it you from my own treasury; — do not commit suicide, Bráhman."

When the king returned to his palace, he pretended to have a headache, and summoned all the physicians in the city by proclamation with beat of drum. And he took aside every one of them singly and questioned them privately, saying, "What patients have you, and what medicines have you prescribed for each?" And they thereupon, one by one, answered the king's questions. At length a physician said, "The merchant Mátridatta has been out of sorts, O king, and this is the second day I have prescribed for him *nágabalá* (the plant *Uraria Lagopodioides*)." Then the king sent for the merchant, and said to him, "Tell me, who fetched you the *nagabala?*" The merchant replied, "My servant, your highness." On hearing this, the king at once summoned the servant and said to him, "Give up that treasure belonging to a Bráhman, consisting of a store of dínárs, which you found when you were digging at the foot of the tree for *nagabala*." When the king said this to him the servant was frightened, and confessed immediately; and bringing the money left it there. Then the king summoned the Bráhman and gave him, who had been fasting meanwhile, the dínárs, lost and found again, like a second soul external to his body. Thus did the king by his wisdom recover to the Bráhman his wealth which had been taken away from the root of the tree, knowing that that simple grew in such spots.

TALE OF THE DEVOUT WOMAN ACCUSED OF LEWDNESS. — Vol. XI. p. 184.

This is one of three Arabian variants of Chaucer's Man of Law's Tale (the Story of Constance), of which there are numerous versions — see my paper entitled "The Innocent Persecuted Wife," pp. 365–414 of "Originals and Analogues of some of Chaucer's Canterbury Tales."

THE WEAVER WHO BECAME A LEACH BY ORDER OF HIS WIFE.
Vol. XI. p. 194

Somewhat resembling his, but much more elaborate, is the amusing story of Ahmed the Cobbler, in Sir John Malcolm's "Sketches of Persia," ch. xx., the original of which is probably found in the tale of Harisarman, book vi. ch. 30, of the "Kathá Sarit Ságara," and it has many European variants, such as the German story of Doctor Allwissend, in Grimm's collection, and that of the Charcoal Burner in Sir George Dasent's "Tales from the Fjeld. — According to the Persian story, Ahmed the Cobbler had a young and pretty wife, of whom he was very fond. She was ever forming grand schemes of riches and splendour, and was firmly persuaded that she was destined to great fortune. It happened one evening, while in this frame of mind, that she went to the public baths, where she saw a lady retiring dressed in a magnificent robe, covered with jewels, and surrounded by slaves. This was the very condition she had always longed for, and she eagerly inquired the name of the happy person who had so many attendants and such fine jewels. She learned it was the wife of the chief astrologer to the king. With this information she returned home. Ahmed met her at the door, but was received with a frown, nor could all his caresses obtain a smile or a word; for several hours she continued silent, and in apparent misery; at length she said, "Cease your caresses, unless you are ready to give me a proof that you do really and sincerely love me." "What proof of love," exclaimed poor Ahmed, "can you desire that I will not give?" "Give over cobbling; it is a vile, low trade, and never yields more than ten or twelve dínars a day. Turn astrologer; your fortune will be made, and I shall have all I wish and be happy." "Astrologer!" cried Ahmed — "astrologer! Have you forgotten who I am — a cobbler, without any learning — that you want me to engage in a profession which requires so much skill and knowledge?" "I neither think nor care about your qualifications," said the enraged wife; "all I know is that if you do not turn astrologer immediately, I will be divorced from you to-morrow." The cobbler remonstrated, but in vain. The figure of the astrologer's wife, with her jewels and her slaves, took complete possession of her imagination. All night it haunted her: she dreamt of nothing else, and on awakening declared that she would leave the house if her husband did not comply with her wishes. What could poor Ahmed do? He was no astrologer; but he was dotingly fond of his wife, and he could not bear the idea of losing her. He promised to obey; and having sold his little stock, bought an astrolabe, an astronomical almanac, and a table of the twelve signs of the zodiac. Furnished with these, he went to the market-place, crying, "I am an astrologer! I know the sun, and the moon, and the stars, and the twelve signs of the zodiac; I can calculate nativities; I can foretell everything that is to happen." No man was better known than Ahmed the Cobbler. A crowd soon gathered round him. "What, friend Ahmed," said one, "have you worked till your head is turned?" "Are you tired of looking down at your last," cried another, "that you are now looking up at the stars?" These and a thousand other jokes assailed the ears of the poor cobbler, who notwithstanding continued to exclaim that he was an astrologer, having resolved on doing what he could to please his beautiful wife.

It so happened that the king's jeweller was passing by. He was in great distress, having lost the richest ruby belonging to the king. Every search had been made to recover this inestimable jewel, but to no purpose; and as the jeweller knew he could no longer conceal its loss from the king, he looked forward to death as inevitable. In this hopeless state, while wandering about the town, he reached the crowd around Ahmed, and asked what was the matter. "Don't you know Ahmed the Cobbler?" said one of the bystanders, laughing. "He has been inspired and is become an astrologer." A drowning man will catch at a broken reed: the jeweller no sooner heard the sound of the word astrologer than he went up to Ahmed, told him what had happened, and said, "If you understand your art, you must be able to discover the king's ruby. Do so, and I will give you two hundred pieces of gold. But if you do not succeed within six hours, I will use my influence at court to have you put to death as an impostor." Poor Ahmed was thunderstruck. He stood long without being able to speak, reflecting on his misfortunes, and grieving, above all, that his wife, whom he so loved, had, by her envy and selfishness, brought him to such a fearful alternative. Full of these sad thoughts, he exclaimed aloud, "O woman! woman! thou art more baneful to the happiness of man than the poisonous dragon of the desert!" Now the lost ruby had been secreted by the jeweller's wife, who, disquieted by those alarms which ever attend guilt, sent one of her female slaves to watch her husband. This slave, on seeing her master speak to the astrologer, drew near; and when she heard Ahmed, after some moments of abstraction, compare a woman to a poisonous dragon, she was satisfied that he must know everything. She ran to her mistress, and, breathless with fear, cried, "You are discovered by a vile astrologer! Before six hours are past the whole story will be known, and you will become infamous, if you are even so fortunate as to escape with life, unless you can find some way of prevailing on him to be merciful." She then related what she had seen and heard; and Ahmed's exclamation carried as complete conviction to the mind of the terrified lady as it had done to that of her slave. The jeweller's wife, hastily throwing on her veil, went in search of the dreaded astrologer. When she found him, she cried, "Spare my honour and my life, and I will confess everything." "What can you have to confess to me?" said Ahmed, in amazement. "O nothing — nothing with which you are not already acquainted. You know too well that I stole the king's ruby. I did so to punish my husband, who uses me most cruelly; and I thought by this means to obtain riches for myself and have him put to death. But you, most wonderful man, from whom nothing is hidden, have discovered and defeated my wicked plan. I beg only for mercy, and will do whatever you command me." An angel from heaven could not have brought more consolation to Ahmed than did the jeweller's wife. He assumed all the dignified solemnity that became his new character, and said, "Woman! I know all thou hast done, and it is fortunate for thee that thou hast come to confess thy sin and beg for mercy before it was too late. Return to thy house; put the ruby under the pillow of the couch on which thy husband sleeps; let it be laid on the side farthest from the door; and be satisfied thy guilt shall never be even suspected." The jeweller's wife went home and did as she was instructed. In an hour Ahmed followed her, and told the jeweller he had made his calculations, and found by the aspect of the sun and moon, and by the configuration of the stars, that the ruby was at that moment lying under the pillow of his couch on the side farthest from the door. The jeweller thought Ahmed must be crazy; but as a ray of hope is like a ray from heaven to the wretched, he ran to his couch, and there, to his joy and wonder, found the ruby in the very place described. He came back to Ahmed, embraced him, called him his dearest friend and the preserver of his life, gave him two hundred pieces of gold, declaring that he was the first astrologer of the age.

Ahmed returned home with his lucky gains, and would gladly have resumed his cobbling, but his wife insisting on his continuing to practice his new profession, there was no help but to go out again next day and proclaim his astrological accomplishments. By mere chance he is the means of a lady recovering a valuable necklace which she had lost at the bath, and forty chests of gold stolen from the king's treasury, and is finally rewarded with the hand of the king's daughter in marriage.

STORY OF THE KING WHO LOST KINGDOM, WIFE AND WEALTH.
Vol. XI. p. 221.

IN the "Indian Antiquary" for June 1886 the Rev. J. Hinton Knowles gives a translation of what he terms a Kashmírí Tale, under the title of "Pride Abased," which, he says, was told him by "a Brahman named Mukund Báyú, who resides at Suthú, Srínagar," and which is an interesting variant of the Wazír Er-Rahwan's second story of the King who lost his Realm and Wealth:

KASHMIRI VERSION.[1]

THERE was once a king who was noted throughout his dominions for daily boasting of his power and riches. His ministers at length became weary of this self-glorification, and one day when he demanded of them, as usual, whether there existed in the whole world another king as powerful as he, they plainly told him that there was such another potentate; upon which he assembled his troops and rode forth at their head, challenging the neighbouring

---

[1] I have considerably abridged Mr. Knowles' story in several places.

kings to fight with him. Ere long he met with more than his match, for another king came with a great army and utterly defeated him, and took possession of his kingdom. Disguising himself, the humbled king escaped with his wife and two boys, and arriving at the sea shore, found a ship about to sail. The master agreed to take him and his family and land them at the port for which he was bound. But when he beheld the beauty of the queen, he became enamoured of her, and determined to make her his own. The queen was the first to go on board the ship, and the king and his two sons were about to follow, when they were seized by a party of ruffians, hired by the shipmaster, and held back until the vessel had got fairly under way. The queen was distracted on seeing her husband and children left behind, and refused to listen to the master's suit, who, after having tried to win her love for several days without success, resolved to sell her as a slave. Among the passengers was a merchant, who, seeing that the lady would not accept the shipmaster for her husband, thought that if he bought her, he might in time gain her affection. Accordingly he purchased her of the master for a large sum of money, and then told her that he had done so with a view of making her his wife. The lady replied that, although the shipman had no right thus to dispose of her, yet she would consent to marry him at the end of two years, if she did not during that period meet with her husband and their two sons; and to this condition the merchant agreed. In the meanwhile the king, having sorrowfully watched the vessel till it was out of sight, turned back with his two boys, who wept and lamented as they ran beside him. After walking a great distance, he came to a shallow but rapid river, which he wished to cross, and, as there was no boat or bridge, he was obliged to wade through the water. Taking up one of his sons he contrived to reach the other side in safety, and was returning for the other when the force of the current overcame him and he was drowned.

When the two boys noticed that their father had perished, they wept bitterly. Their separation, too, was a further cause for grief. There they stood, one on either side of the river, with no means of reaching each other. They shouted, and ran about hither and thither in their grief, till they had almost wearied themselves into sleep, when a fisherman came past, who, seeing the great distress of the boys, took them into his boat, and asked them who they were, and who were their parents; and they told him all that had happened. When he had heard their story, he said, "You have not a father or mother, and I have not a child. Evidently God has sent you to me. Will you be my own children and learn to fish, and live in my house?" Of course, the poor boys were only too glad to find a friend and shelter. "Come," said the fisherman kindly, leading them out of the boat to a house close by, "I will look after you." The boys followed most happily, and went into the fisherman's house; and when they saw his wife they were still better pleased, for she was very kind to them, and treated them as if they had been her own children. The two boys went to school, and when they had learned all that the master could teach them, they began to help their adoptive father, and in a little while became most expert and diligent young fishermen.

Thus time was passing with them, when it happened that a great fish threw itself on to the bank of the river and could not get back again into the water. Everybody in the village went to see the monstrous fish, and cut a slice of its flesh and took it home. A few people also went from the neighbouring villages, and amongst them was a maker of earthernware. His wife had heard of the great fish and urged him to go and get some of the flesh. So he went, although the hour was late. On his arrival he found that all the people had returned to their homes. The potter had taken an axe with him, thinking that the bones would be so great and strong as to require its use in breaking them. When he struck the first blow a voice came out of the fish, like that of some one in pain, at which the potter was greatly surprised. "Perhaps," thought he, "the fish is possessed by a bhút.[1] I'll try again;" whereupon he struck another blow with his axe. Again the voice came forth from the fish, saying, "Woe is me! woe is me!" On hearing this, the potter thought, "Well,

---

[1] A species of demon.

this is evidently not a bhút, but the voice of an ordinary man. I'll cut the flesh carefully. May be that I shall find some poor distressed person." So he began to cut away the flesh carefully, and presently he perceived a man's foot, then the legs appeared, and then the entire body. "Praise be to God," he cried, "the soul is yet in him." He carried the man to his house as fast as he could, and on arriving there did everything in his power to recover him. A large fire was soon got ready, and tea and soup given the man, and great was the joy of the potter and his wife when they saw him reviving.[1] For some months the stranger lived with those good people, and learnt how to make pots and pans and other articles, and thereby helped them considerably. Now it happened that the king of that country died, and it was the custom of the people to take for their sovereign whomsoever the late king's elephant and hawk should select. And so on the death of the king the royal elephant was driven all over the country, and the hawk was made to fly about, in search of a successor, and it came to pass that the person before whom the elephant saluted and on whom the hawk alighted was considered as the divinely-chosen one. Accordingly the elephant and the hawk went about the country, and in the course of their wanderings came by the house of the potter who had so kindly succoured the poor man whom he found in the belly of the monstrous fish; and it chanced that as they passed the place the stranger was standing by the door, and behold, no sooner did the elephant and hawk see him than the one bowed down before him and the other perched on his hand. "Let him be king! let him be king!" shouted the people who were in attendance on the elephant, and they prostrated themselves before the stranger and begged him to accompany them to the palace.[2]

The ministers were glad when they heard the news, and most respectfully welcomed their new king. As soon as the rites and ceremonies necessary for the installation of a king had been observed, his majesty entered on his duties. The first thing he did was to send for the potter and his wife and grant them some land and money. In this and other ways, such as just judgments, proper laws, and kindly notices of all who were clever and good, he won for himself the good opinion and affection of his subjects and prospered in consequence thereof. After a few months, however, his health was impaired, and his physicians advised

---

[1] This is one of the innumerable parallels to the story of Jonah in the "whale's" belly which occur in Asiatic fictions. See, for some instances, Tawney's translation of the "Kathá Sarit Ságara," ch. xxxv. and lxxiv.; "Indian Antiquary," Sept. 1885, Legend of Ahlá; Miss Stokes' "Indian Fairy Tales," pp. 75, 76; and Steel and Temple's "Wide-Awake Stories from the Panjáb and Kashmír," p. 411. In Lucian's "Vera Historia," a monster fish swallows a ship and her crew, who live a long time in the extensive regions comprised in its internal economy. See also Herrtage's "Gesta Romanorum" (Early English Text Society), p. 297.

[2] In the Arabian version the people resolve to leave the choice of a new king to the royal elephant because they could not agree among themselves (vol. i., p. 224); but in Indian fictions such an incident frequently occurs as a regular custom. In the "Sivandhi Sthala Purana," a legendary account of the famous temple at Trichinopoli, as supposed to be told by Gautama to Matanga and other sages, it is related that a certain king having mortally offended a holy devotee, his capital and all its inhabitants were, in consequence of a curse pronounced by the enraged saint, buried beneath a shower of dust. "Only the queen escaped, and in her flight she was delivered of a male-child. After some time, the chiefs of the Chola kingdom, proceeding to elect a king, determined, by the advice of the saint, to crown whomsoever the late monarch's elephant should pitch upon. Being turned loose for this purpose, the elephant discovered and brought to Trisira-málí the child of his former master, who accordingly became the Chola king." (Wilson's Desc. Catal. of Mackenzie MSS., i. 17.) In a Manipurí story of two brothers, Turi and Basanta — "Indian Antiquary," vol. iii. — the elder is chosen king in like manner by an elephant who meets him in the forest, and takes him on his back to the palace, where he is immediately placed on the throne. See also "Wide-Awake Stories from the Panjáb and Kashmír," by Mrs. Steel and Captain Temple, p. 141; and Rev. Lal Behari Day's "Folk-Tales of Bengal," p. 100, for similar instances. The hawk taking part, in this story, with the elephant in the selection of a king does not occur in any other tale known to me.

him to take out-door exercise. Accordingly, he alternately rode, hunted and fished. He was especially fond of fishing, and whenever he indulged in this amusement, he was attended by two sons of a fisherman, who were clever and handsome youths.

About this time the merchant who bought the wife of the poor king that was carried away by the rapid river visited that country for purposes of trade. He obtained an interview with the king, and displayed before him all his precious stones and stuffs. The king was much pleased to see such treasures, and asked many questions about them and the countries whence they had been brought. The merchant satisfied the king's curiosity, and then begged permission to trade in that country, under his majesty's protection, which the king readily granted, and ordered that some soldiers should be placed on guard in the merchant's courtyard, and sent the fisherman's two sons to sleep in the premises.

One night those two youths not being able to sleep, the younger asked his brother to tell him a story to pass the time, so he replied, "I will tell you one out of our own experience: Once upon a time there lived a great and wealthy king, who was very proud, and his pride led him to utter ruin and caused him the sorest afflictions. One day when going about with his army, challenging other kings to fight with him, a great and powerful king appeared and conquered him. He escaped with his wife and two sons to the sea, hoping to find a vessel, by which he and his family might reach a foreign land. After walking several miles they reached the sea-shore and found a ship ready to sail. The master of the vessel took the queen, but the king and his two sons were held back by some men, who had been hired by the master for this purpose, until the ship was under way. The poor king after this walked long and far till he came to a rapid river. As there was no bridge or boat near, he was obliged to wade across. He took one of his boys and got over safely, and was returning for the other when he stumbled over a stone, lost his footing, and was carried down the stream; and he has not been heard of since. A fisherman came along, and, seeing the two boys crying, took them into his boat, and afterwards to his house, and became very fond of them, as did also his wife, and they were like father and mother to them. All this happened a few years ago, and the two boys are generally believed to be the fisherman's own sons. O brother, we are these two boys! And there you have my story."

The tale was so interesting and its conclusion so wonderful that the younger brother was more awake than before. It had also attracted the attention of another. The merchant's promised wife, who happened to be lying awake at the time, and whose room was separated from the warehouse by a very thin partition, overheard all that had been said, and she thought within herself, "Surely these two boys must be my own sons." Presently she was sitting beside them and asking them many questions. Two years or more had made great difference in the persons of both the boys, but there were certain signs which a hundred years could not efface from a mother's memory. These, together with the answers which she elicited from them, assured her that she had found her own sons again. Tears streamed down her face as she embraced them, and revealed to them that she was the queen, their mother, about whom they had just been speaking. She then told them all that had happened to her since she had been parted from them and their poor father, the king; after which she explained that although the merchant was a good man and very wealthy yet she did not like him well enough to become his wife, and proposed a plan for her getting rid of him. "My device," said she, "is to pretend to the merchant that you attempted my honour. I shall affect to be very angry and not give him any peace until he goes to the king and complains against you. Then will the king send for you in great wrath and inquire into this matter. In reply you may say it is all a mistake, for you regard me as your own mother, and in proof of this you will beg the king to summon me into his presence, that I may corroborate what you say. Then I will declare that you are really my own sons, and beseech the king to free me from the merchant and allow me to live with you in any place I may choose for the rest of my days."

The sons agreed to this proposal, and next night, when the merchant was also sleeping in the house, the woman raised a great cry, so that everybody was awakened by the noise. The merchant came and asked the cause of the outcry, and she answered, "The two youths who look after your warehouse have attempted to violate me, so I screamed in order to make them desist." On hearing this the merchant was enraged. He immediately bound the two youths, and, as soon as there was any chance of seeing the king, took them before him and preferred his complaint. "What have you to say in your defence?" said the king, addressing the youths; "because, if what this merchant charges against you be true, I will have you at once put to death. Is this the gratitude you manifest for all my kindness and condescension towards you? Say quickly what you have to say." "O king, our bene-factor," replied the elder brother, "we are not affrighted by your words and looks, for we are true servants. We have not betrayed your trust in us, but have always tried to fulfil your wishes to the utmost of our power. The charges brought against us by this merchant are unfounded. We have not attempted to dishonour his wife; we have rather always re-garded her as our own mother. May it please your majesty to send for the woman and inquire further into this matter."

The king consented, and the woman was brought before him. "Is it true," he asked her, "what the merchant, your affianced husband, witnesses against these two youths?" "O king," she replied, "the youths whom you gave to help the merchant have most carefully tried to carry out your wishes. But the night before last I heard their conversation. The elder was telling the younger a tale, from his own experience, he said. It was a story of a conceited king who had been defeated by another more powerful than he, and obliged to fly with his wife and two children to the sea. There, through the vile trickery of the master of a vessel, the wife was stolen and taken away to far distant lands, where she became engaged to a wealthy trader; while the exiled king and his two sons wandered in another direction, till they came to a river, in which the king was drowned. The two boys were found by a fisherman and brought up as his own sons. These two boys, O king, are before you, and I am their mother, who was taken away and sold to the trader, and who after two days must be married to him. For I promised that if within a certain period I should not meet with my husband and two sons I would be his wife. But I entreat your majesty to free me from this man. I do not wish to marry again, now that I have found my two sons. In order to obtain an audience of your majesty, this trick was arranged with the two youths."

By the time the woman had finished her story the king's face was suffused with tears, and he was trembling visibly. When he had somewhat recovered he rose from the throne, and going up to the woman and the two youths embraced them long and fervently. "You are my own dear wife and children," he cried. "God has sent you back to me. I, the king, your husband, your father, was not drowned as you supposed; but was swallowed by a great fish and nourished by it for some time, and then the monster threw itself upon the river's bank and I was extricated. A potter and his wife had pity on me and taught me their trade, and I was just beginning to earn my living by making earthen vessels when the late king of this country died, and I was chosen king by the royal elephant and hawk — I who am now standing here." Then his majesty ordered the queen and her two sons to be taken into the inner apartments of the palace, and explained his conduct to the people assembled. The merchant was politely dismissed from the country. And as soon as the two princes were old enough to govern the kingdom, the king committed to them the charge of all affairs, while he retired with his wife to a sequestered spot and passed the rest of his days in peace.

The tale of Sarwar and Nír, "as told by a celebrated Bard from Baraut, in the Merath district," in vol. iii. of Captain R. C. Temple's "Legends of the Panjáb" (pp. 97–125), though differing in form somewhat from the Kashmírí version, yet possesses the leading incidents in common with it, as will be seen from the following abstract:

PANJABI VERSION.

AMBA the rájá of Púná had a beautiful wife named Amlí and two young sons, Sarwar and Nír. There came to his court one day a fakír. The rájá promised to give him whatsoever he should desire. The fakír required Ambá to give up to him all he possessed, or lose his virtue, and the rájá gave him all, save his wife and two children, receiving in return the blessings of the fakír, Then the rájá and the rání went away; he carrying Sarwar in his bosom, and she with Nír in her lap.   For a time they lived on the fruits and roots of the forest.   At length the rání gave her husband her (jewelled) bodice to sell in the bázár, in order to procure food.   He offered it to Kundan the merchant, who made him sit down and asked him where he had left the rání, and why he did not bring her with him.   Ambá told him that he had left her with their two boys under the banyan-tree.   Then Kundan, leaving Ambá in the shop, went and got a litter, and proceeding to the banyan-tree showed the rání the bodice, and said, "Thy husband wishes thee to come to him."   Nothing doubt-ing, the rání entered the litter, and the merchant sent it off to his own house.   Leaving the boys in the forest, he returned to Ambá, and said to him that he had not enough money to pay the price of the bodice, so the rájá must take it back.   Ambá took the bodice, and coming to the boys, learned from Sarwar how their mother had been carried away in a litter, and he was sorely grieved in his heart, but consoled the children, saying that their mother had gone to her brother's house, and that he would take them to her at once.   Placing the two boys on his shoulders he walked along till he came to a river.   He set down Nír, and carried Sarwar safely across, but as he was going back for the other, behold, an alligator seized him.   It was the will of God: what remedy is there against the writing of Fate?   The two boys, separated by the river, sat down and wept in their sorrow.   In the early morning a washerman was up and spreading his clothes.   He heard the two boys weeping and came to see.   He had pity on them and brought them together.   Then he took them to his house, and washed their faces and gave them food.   He put them into a separate house and a Bráhman cooked for them and gave them water.[1]   He caused the brothers to be taught all kinds of learning, and at the end of twelve years they both set out together to seek their living.   They went to the city of Ujjain, and told the rájá their history — how they had left their home and kingdom.   The rájá gave them arms and suitable clothing, and ap-pointed them guards over the female apartments.[2]   One day a fisherman caught an alligator in his net.   When he cut open its body, he found in it Rájá Ambá, alive.[3]   So he took him to the rájá of Ujjain, and told how he had found him in the stomach of an alligator.   Ambá related his whole history to the rájá; how he gave up all his wealth and his kingdom to a fakír; how his wife had been stolen from him; and how after safely carrying one of his young sons over the river in returning for the other he had been swallowed by an alligator.   On hearing of all these misfortunes the rájá of Ujjain pitied him and loved him in his heart: he adopted Ambá as his son; and they lived together twenty years, when the rájá died and Ambá obtained the throne.

Meanwhile the beautiful Rání Amlí, the wife of Ambá, had continued to refuse the mer-chant Kundan's reiterated proffers of love.   At length he said to her, "Many days have passed over thee, live now in my house as my wife."   And she replied, "Let me bathe in the Ganges, and then I will dwell in thy house."   So he took elephants and horses and lákhs of coin, and set the rání in a litter and started on the journey.   When he reached the city of Ujjain, he made a halt and pitched his tents.   Then he went before Rájá Ambá and said, "Give me a guard, for the nights are dark.   Hitherto I have had much trouble and no ease at nights.   I am going to bathe in the Ganges, to give alms and much food to Bráhmans. I am come, rájá, to salute thee, bringing many things from my house."

The rájá sent Sarwar and Nír as guards.   They watched the tents, and while the rain was falling the two brothers began talking over their sorrows, saying "What can our mother be doing?   Whither hath our father gone?"   Their mother overheard them talking, and by the will of God she recognised the princes; then she tore open the tent, and cried aloud, "All

---

[1] So that their caste might not be injured.   A dhobí, or washerman, is of much lower caste than a Bráhman or a Khshatriya.

[2] A responsible position in a rájá's palace.

[3] "And Jonah was in the belly of the fish three days and three nights."   Rájá Ambá must have been fully twelve years in the stomach of the alligator.

my property is gone! Who brought this thief to my tent?" The ráni had both Sarwar and Nír seized, and brought before Rájá Ambá on the charge of having stolen her property. The rájá held a court, and began to ask questions, saying, "Tell me what hath passed during the night. How much of thy property hath gone, my friend? I will do thee justice, according to thy desire: my heart is grieved that thy goods are gone." Then said the ráni, "Be careful of the young elephant! The lightning flashes and the heavy rain is falling. Said Nír, 'Hear, brother Sarwar, who knows whither our mother hath gone?' And I recognised my son; so I made all this disturbance, rájá [in order to get access to thee]". [1] Hearing this, Rájá Ambá rose up and took her to his breast—Amlí and Ambá met again through the mercy of God. The rájá gave orders to have Kundan hanged, saying, "Do it at once; he is a scoundrel; undo him that he may not live." They quickly fetched the executioners and put on the noose; and then was Kundan strangled. The ráni dwelt in the palace and all her troubles passed far away. She fulfilled all her obligations, and obtained great happiness through her virtue.

TIBETAN VERSION.

UNDER the title of "Krisa Gautami" in the collection of "Tibetan Tales from Indian Sources," translated by Mr. Ralston from the German of Von Schiefner, we have what appears to be a very much garbled form of an old Buddhist version of our story. The heroine is married to a young merchant, whose father gives him some arable land in a hill district, where he resides with Krisa Guatami his wife.

When the time came for her to expect her confinement, she obtained leave of her husband to go to her parents' house in order that she might have the attendance of her mother. After her confinement and the naming of the boy, she returned home. When the time of her second confinement drew near, she again expressed to her husabnd a desire to go to her parents. Her husband set out with her and the boy in a waggon; but by the time they had gone half way she gave birth to a boy. When the husband saw that this was to take place, he got out of the waggon, sat under a tree, and fell asleep. While he was completely overcome by slumber a snake bit him and he died. When his wife in her turn alighted from the waggon, and went up to the tree in order to bring him the joyful tidings that a son was born unto him, he, as he had given up the ghost, made no reply. She seized him by the hand and found that he was dead. Then she began to weep. Meantime a thief carried off the oxen. After weeping for a long time, and becoming very mournful, she looked around on every side, pressed the new-born babe to her bosom, took the elder child by the hand, and set out on her way. As a heavy rain had unexpectedly fallen, all the lakes, ponds, and springs were full of water, and the road was flooded by the river. She reflected that if she were to cross the water with both the children at once, she and they might meet with a disaster, and therefore the children had better be taken over separately. So she seated the elder boy on the bank of the river, and took the younger one in her arms, walked across to the other side, and laid him down upon the bank. Then she went back for the elder boy. But while she was in the middle of the river, the younger boy was carried off by a jackal. The elder boy thought that his mother was calling him, and sprang into the water. The bank was very steep, so he fell down and was killed. The mother hastened after the jackal, who let the child drop and ran off. When she looked at it, she found that it was dead. So after she had wept over it, she threw it into the water. When she saw that the elder was being carried along by the stream, she became still more distressed. She hastened after him, and found that he was dead. Bereft of both husband and children, she gave way to despair, and sat down alone on the bank, with only the lower part of her body covered. There she listened to the howling of the wind, the roaring of the forest and of the waves, as well as the singing of various kinds of birds. Then wandering to and fro, with sobs and tears of woe, she lamented the loss of her husband and her two children.

---

[1] This device of the mother to obtain speech of the king is much more natural than that adopted in the Kashmíri version.

She meets with one of her father's domestics, who informs her that her parents and their servants had all been destroyed by a hurricane, and that "he only had escaped" to tell her the sad tidings. After this she is married to a weaver, who ill-uses her, and she escapes from him one night. She attaches herself to some travellers returning from a trading expedition in the north, and the leader of the caravan takes her for his wife. The party are attacked by robbers and the leader is killed. She then becomes the wife of the chief of the robbers, who in his turn finds death at the hands of the king of that country, and she is placed in his zenana.

The king died, and she was buried alive in his tomb, after having had great honour shown to her by the women, the princes, the ministers, and a vast concourse of people. Some men from the north who were wont to rob graves broke into this one also. The dust they raised entered into Krisa Gautami's nostrils, and made her sneeze. The grave-robbers were terrified, thinking that she was a demon (*vetála*), and they fled; but Krisa Gautami escaped from the grave through the opening which they had made. Conscious of all her troubles, and affected by the want of food, just as a violent storm arose, she went out of her mind. Covered with merely her underclothing, her hands and feet foul and rough, with long locks and pallid complexion, she wandered about until she reached Sravastí. There, at the sight of Bhagavant, she recovered her intellect. Bhagavant ordered Ananda to give her an overrobe, and he taught her the doctrine, and admitted her into the ecclesiastical body, and he appointed her the chief of the Bhikshunís who had embraced discipline.[1]

This remarkable story is one of those which reached Europe long anterior to the Crusades. It is found in the Greek martyr acts, which were probably composed in the eighth century, where it is told of Saint Eustache, who was before his baptism a captain of Trajan, named Placidus, and the same legend reappears, with modifications of the details, in many mediæval collections and forms the subject of several romances. In most versions the *motif* is similar to that of the story of Job. The following is the outline of the original legend, according to the Greek martyr acts:

LEGEND OF ST. EUSTACHE.

As Placidus one day hunted in the forest, the Saviour appeared to him between the antlers of a hart, and converted him. Placidus changed his name into Eustache, when he was baptised with his wife and sons. God announced to him by an angel his future martyrdom. Eustache was afflicted by dreadful calamities, lost all his estate, and was compelled to go abroad as a beggar with his wife and his children. As he went on board a ship bound for Egypt, his wife was seized by the shipmaster and carried off. Soon after, when Eustache was travelling along the shore, his two children were borne off by a lion and a leopard. Eustache then worked for a long time as journeyman, till he was discovered by the emperor Trajan, who had sent out messengers for him, and called him to court. Reappointed captain, Eustache undertook an expedition against the Dacians. During this war he found his wife in a cottage as a gardener—the shipmaster had fallen dead to the ground as he ventured to touch her—and in the same cottage he found again his two sons as soldiers: herdsmen had rescued them from the wild beasts and brought them up. Glad was their meeting again! But as they returned to Rome they were all burnt in a glowing bull of brass by the emperor's order, because they refused to sacrifice to the heathen gods.[2]

---

[1] The story of Abú Sábir (see vol. i. p. 58 ff.) may also be regarded as an analogue. He is unjustly deprived of all his possessions, and, with his wife and two young boys, driven forth of his village. The children are borne off by thieves, and their mother forcibly carried away by a horseman. Abú Sabir, after many sufferings, is raised from a dungeon to a throne. He regains his two children and his wife, who had steadfastly refused to cohabit with her captor.

[2] Introduction to the romance of "Torrent of Portingale," re-edited (for the Early English Text Society, 1886) by E. Adam, Ph.D., pp. xxi. xxii.

The story of Placidus, which forms chapter 110 of the continental "Gesta Romanorum," presents few and unimportant variations from the foregoing: Eustatius came to a river the water of which ran so high that it seemed hazardous to attempt to cross it with both the children at the same time; one therefore he placed upon the bank, and then passed over with the other in his arms, and having laid it on the ground, he returned for the other child. But in the midst of the river, looking back, he beheld a wolf snatch up the child he had just carried over and run with it into the adjoining wood. He turned to rescue it, but at that instant a huge lion approached the other child and disappeared with it. After the loss of his two boys Eustatius journeyed on till he came to a village, where he remained for fifteen years, tending sheep as a hired servant, when he was discovered by Trajan's messengers, and so on.

The story is so differently told in one of the Early English translations of the "Gesta Romanorum" in the Harleian MSS. 7333 (re-edited by Herrtage for the E.E.T. Soc., pp. 87-91) that it is worth while, for purposes of comparison, reproducing it here in full:

OLD ENGLISH "GESTA" VERSION.

AVERIOS was a wise emperour regnyng in the cite of Rome; and he let crye a grete feste, and who so ever wold come to that feste, and gete victory in the tournement, he shuld have his doughter to wyf, after his decesse. So there was a doughti knyght, and hardy in armys, and specially in tournement, the which hadde wyf, and two yong children of age of thre yere; and when this knyght had herd this crye, in a clere morowenyng[1] he entred in to a forest, and there he herd a nyghtingale syng upon a tre so swetly, that he herd never so swete a melody afore that tyme. The knyght sette him doun undre the tre, and seid to him self, "Now, Lord, if I myght knowe what this brid[2] shold bemene!" [3] There come an old man, and seid to him, "That thou shalt go within thes thre daies to the emperours feste, and thou shalt suffre grete persecution or thou come there; and if thou be constant, and pacient in all thi tribulacion, thy sorowe shal turne the[4] to grete joy; and, ser, this is the interpretacion of his song." When this was seid, the old man vanysshed, and the brid fly away. Tho[5] the knyght had grete merviell; he yede[6] to his wif, and told her the cas.[7] "Ser," quod she, "the will of God be fulfilled, but I counsell that we go to the feste of the emperour, and that ye thynk on the victory in the tournement, by the which we may be avaunced[8] and holpen."[9] When the knyght had made all thing redy, there come a grete fire in the nyght; and brent[10] up all his hous, and all his goodis, for which he had grete sorowe in hert; nevertheles, notwithstondyng all this, he yede forthe toward the see, with his wife, and with his two childryn; and there he hired a ship, to passe over. When thei come to londe, the maister of the shippe asked of the knyght his hire for his passage, for him, and for his wif, and for his two childryn. "Dere frend," said the knyght to him, "dere frend, suffre me, and thou shalt have all thyn, for I go now to the feste of the emperour, where I trust to have the victory in turnement, and then thou shalt be wele ypaied." "Nay, by the feith that I owe to the emperour," quod that other, "hit shal not be so, for but if[11] you pay now, I shal holde thi wif to wed,[12] tyll tyme that I be paied fully my salary." And he seid that, for he desired the love of the lady. Tho the knyght profren his two childryn to wed, so that he myght have his wif; and the shipman seid, "Nay, such wordis beth[13] vayn, for," quod he, "or[14] I wol have my mede, or els I wolle holde thi wif." So the knyght lefte his wif with him, and kyst her with bitter teris; and toke the two childryn, scil. oon on his arme,

---

[1] Morning.	[8] *Avaunced:* advanced; promoted.
[2] Bird.	[9] *Holpen:* helped.
[3] Mean; betoken.	[10] *Brent:* burnt.
[4] Thee.	[11] *But if:* unless.
[5] *Tho:* then.	[12] *To wed:* in pledge, in security.
[6] *Yede:* went.	[13] *Beth:* are.
[7] Case.	[14] *Or:* either.

and that othir in his nek, and so he yede forth to the turnement. Aftir, the maister of the shippe wolde have layn by the lady, but she denyed hit, and seid, that she had lever dey[1] than consente therto. So within short tyme, the maister drew to a fer[2] lond, and there he deied; and the lady beggid her brede fro dore to dore, and knew not in what lond her husbond was duellinge. The knyght was gon toward the paleis, and at the last he come by a depe water, that was impossible to be passid, but[3] hit were in certein tyme, when hit was at the lowist. The knyght sette doun oo[4] child, and bare the othir over the water; and aftir that he come ayen[5] to fecche over the othir, but or[6] he myght come to him, there come a lion, and bare him awey to the forest. The knyght pursued aftir, but he myght not come to the lion; and then he wept bitterly, and yede ayen over the water to the othir child; and or he were ycome, a bere had take the child, and ran therwith to the forest. When the knyght saw that, sore he wepte, and seid, "Allas! that ever I was bore, for now have I lost wif and childryn. O thou brid! thi song that was so swete is yturned in to grete sorowe, and hath ytake away myrth fro my hert." Aftir this he turned toward the feste, and made him redy toward the turnement; and there he bare him so manly, and so doutely in the turnement, and that twies or thries, that he wan the victory, and worship, and wynnyng of that day. For the emperour hily avauncid him, and made him maister of his oste,[7] and commaundid that all shuld obey to him; and he encresid, and aros from day to day in honure and richesse. And he went aftirward in a certain day in the cite, [and] he found a precious stone, colourid with thre maner of colours, as in oo partie[8] white, in an othir partie red, and in the thrid partie blak. Anon he went to a lapidary, that was expert in the vertue of stonys; and he seid, that the vertue of thilke[9] stone was this, who so ever berith the stone upon him, his hevynesse[10] shall turne in to joy; and if he be povere,[11] he shal be made riche; and if he hath lost anything, he shall fynde hit ayen with grete joy. And when the knyght herd this, he was glad and blith, and thought in him self, "I am in grete hevynesse and poverte, for I have lost all that I had, and by this stone I shal recovere all ayen, whether hit be so or no, God wote!" Aftir, when he must go to bataile of the emperour he gadrid to-gidre[12] all the oste, and among them he found two yong knyghtis, semely in harneis,[13] and wele i-shape, the which he hired for to go with him yn bataill of the emperour. And when thei were in the bataill, there was not oon in all the batail that did so doutely,[14] as did tho[15] two knyghtis that he hired; and therof this knyght, maister of the ost, was hily gladid. When the bataill was y-do,[16] thes two yong knyghtes yede to her oste[17] in the cite; and as they sat to-gidir, the elder seid to the yonger, "Dere frend, hit is long sithen[18] that we were felawys,[19] and we have grete grace of God, for in every batail we have the victory; and therfore I pray you, telle me of what contre ye were ybore, and in what nacion? For I askid never this of the or now; and if thou wilt telle me soth,[20] I shall telle my kynrede and where I was borne." And when oo felawe spak thus to the othir, a faire lady was loggid[21] in the same ostry;[22] and when she herd the elder knyght speke, she herkened to him; but she knew neither of hem,[23] and yit she was modir of both, and wyf of the maister of the oste,[24] the which also the maister of the shippe withheld for ship-hire, but ever God kept her fro synne. Then spake the yonger knyght, "Forsoth, good man, I note[25] who was my fader

---

1 *Lever dey:* rather die.
2 Far; distant.
3 Unless.
4 *Oo:* one.
5 *Ayen:* again.
6 *Or:* ere; before.
7 Army; host.
8 Part.
9 That.
10 Grief; sorrow.
11 Poor.
12 Gathered, or collected, together.
13 Arms; accoutrements; dress.

14 Bravely.
15 Those.
16 Done; ended.
17 Their lodgings; inn.
18 Since.
19 Comrades.
20 Truly.
21 Lodged.
22 Inn.
23 *Hem:* them.
24 Chief of the army.
25 *I note :* I know not.

or who was my modir, ne[1] in what stede[2] I was borne; but I have this wele in mynde,
that my fader was a knyght, and that he bare me over the water, and left my eldir brothir
in the lond; and as he passid over ayen to fecche him, there come a lion, and toke me up,
but a man of the cite come with houndis, and when he saw him, he made him to leve me
with his houndis."[3]   "Now sothly," quod that othir, "and in the same maner hit happid
with me. For I was the sone of a knyght, and had only a brothir; and my fader brought me
and my brothir, and my modir, over the see toward the emperour; and for my fader had
not to pay to the maister of the ship for the fraught, he left my modir to wed; and then my
fader toke me with my yong brothir, and brought us on his bak, and in his armys, tyll
that we come unto a water, and there left me in a side of the water, and bare over my yong
brothir; and or my fader myght come to me ayene, to bare me over, ther come a bere, and
bore me to wode;[4] and the people that saw him, make grete cry, and for fere the bere let me
falle, and so with thelke[5] poeple I duellid x. yere, and ther I was y-norisshed." When the
modir herd thes wordis, she seid, "Withoute doute thes ben my sonys;" and ran to hem
anon, and fil upon her[6] nekkes, and wepte sore for joy, and seid, "A! dere sonys, I am
your modir, that your fader left with the maister of the shippe; and I know wele by your
wordis and signes that ye beth true brethern. But how it is with your fader, that I know
not, but God, that all seth,[7] yeve[8] me grace to fynd my husbond." And alle that nyght
thes thre were in gladnes. On the morow the modir rose up, and the childryn, scil. the
knyghtis, folowid; and as thei yede, the maister of the oste mette with hem in the strete,
and though he were her fader, he knew hem not, but[9] as thei had manli fought the day afore;
and therfor he salued hem honurably, and askid of hem what feir lady that was, that come
with hem? Anon as his lady herd his voys, and perceyved a certeyn signe in his frount,[10]
she knew fully therby that it was her husbond; and therfore she ran to him, and clypt him,
and kyst him, and for joy fille doun to the erth, as she had be ded. So aftir this passion, she
was reised up; and then the maister seid to her, "Telle me, feir woman, whi thou clippest
me, and kyssist me so?" She seid, "I am thi wif, that thou leftist with the maister of the
ship; and thes two knyghtis bene your sonys. Loke wele on my front, and see." Then the
knyght byheld her wele, with a good avisement,[11] and knew wele by diverse tokyns that she
was his wif; and anon kyst her, and the sonys eke; and blessid hiely God, that so had
visited hem. Tho went he ayen to his lond, with his wif, and with his children, and endid
faire his lif.

From the legend of St. Eustache the romances of Sir Isumbras, Octavian, Sir Eglamour
of Artois, and Sir Torrent of Portugal are derived. In the last, while the hero is absent,
aiding the king of Norway with his sword, his wife Desonelle is delivered of twins, and her
father, King Calamond, out of his hatred of her, causes her and the babes to be put to sea
in a boat; but a favourable wind saves them from destruction, and drives the boat upon the
coast of Palestine. As she is wandering aimlessly along the shore, a huge griffin appears,
and seizes one of her children, and immediately after a leopard drags away the other. With
submission she suffers her miserable fate, relying on the help of the Holy Virgin. The
king of Jerusalem, just returning from a voyage, happened to find the leopard with the
child, which he ordered to be saved and delivered to him. Seeing from the foundling's
golden ring that the child was of noble descent, and pitying its helpless state, he took it into
his palace, and brought him up as if he were his own son, at his court. The dragon with
the other child was seen by a pious hermit, St. Antony, who, though son of the king of
Greece, had in his youth forsaken the world. Through his prayer St. Mary made the dragon
put down the infant. Antony carried him to his father, who adopted him and ordered him

---

1 Nor.
2 Place.
3 That is, by means of his hounds.
4 A wood.
5 Those.
6 *Her:* their.

7 Looks towards; attends to.
8 Give.
9 Excepting; unless.
10 Face; countenance.
11 Care; close examination.

to be baptised. Desonelle wandered up and down, after the loss of her children, till she happened to meet the king of Nazareth hunting. He, recognising her as the king of Portugal's daughter, gave her a kind welcome and assistance, and at his court she lived several years in happy retirement. Ultimately she is re-united to her husband and her two sons, when they have become famous knights.

The following is an epitome of "Sir Isumbras," from Ellis's "Specimens of Early English Metrical Romances" (Bohn's ed. p. 479 ff.):

ROMANCE OF SIR ISUMBRAS.

THERE was once a knight, who, from his earliest infancy, appeared to be the peculiar favourite of Fortune. His birth was noble; his person equally remarkable for strength and beauty; his possessions so extensive as to furnish the amusements of hawking and hunting in the highest perfection. Though he had found no opportunity of signalising his courage in war, he had borne away the prize at numberless tournaments; his courtesy was the theme of general praise; his hall was the seat of unceasing plenty; it was crowded with minstrels, whom he entertained with princely liberality, and the possession of a beautiful wife and three lovely children completed the sum of earthly happiness.

Sir Isumbras had many virtues, but he had one vice. In the pride of his heart he forgot the Giver of all good things, and considered the blessings so abundantly showered upon him as the proper and just reward of his distinguished merit. Instances of this overweening presumption might perhaps be found in all ages among the possessors of wealth and power; but few sinners have the good fortune to be recalled, like Sir Isumbras, by a severe but salutary punishment, to the pious sentiments of Christian humility.

It was usual with knights to amuse themselves with hawking or hunting whenever they were not occupied by some more serious business; and, as business seldom intervened, they thus amused themselves every day in the year. One morning, being mounted on his favourite steed, surrounded by his dogs, and with a hawk on his wrist, Sir Isumbras cast his eyes on the sky, and discovered an angel, who, hovering over him, reproached him with his pride, and announced the punishment of instant and complete degradation. The terrified knight immediately fell on his knees; acknowledged the justice of his sentence; returned thanks to Heaven for deigning to visit him with adversity while the possession of youth and health enabled him to endure it; and, filled with contrition, prepared to return from the forest. But scarcely had the angel disappeared when his good steed suddenly fell dead under him; the hawk dropped from his wrist; his hounds wasted and expired; and, being thus left alone, he hastened on foot towards his palace, filled with melancholy forebodings, but impatient to learn the whole extent of his misfortune.

He was presently met by a part of his household, who, with many tears, informed him that his horses and oxen had been suddenly struck dead with lightning, and that his capons were all stung to death with adders. He received the tidings with humble resignation, commanded his servants to abstain from murmurs against Providence, and passed on. He was next met by a page, who related that his castle was burned to the ground, that many of his servants had lost their lives, and that his wife and children had with great difficulty escaped from the flames. Sir Isumbras, rejoiced that Heaven had yet spared those who were most dear to him, bestowed upon the astonished page his purse of gold as a reward for the intelligence.

A doleful sight then gan he see;
His wife and children three
Out of the fire were fled:
There they sat, under a thorn,
Bare and naked as they were born,
Brought out of their bed.

A woful man then was he,
When he saw them all naked be,
    The lady said, all so blive,
"For nothing, sir, be ye adrad."
He did off his surcoat of pallade,[1]
    And with it clad his wife.
His scarlet mantle then shore[2] he;
Therein he closed his children three
    That naked before him stood.

He then proposed to his wife that, as an expiation of their sins, they should at once undertake a pilgrimage to Jerusalem; so, cutting with his knife a sign of the cross on his bare
shoulder, he set off with the four companions of his misery, resolving to beg his bread till
they should arrive at the Holy Sepulchre. After passing through "seven lands," supported
by the scanty alms of the charitable, they arrived at length at a forest, where they wandered
during three days without meeting a single habitation. Their food was reduced to the few
berries which they were able to collect; and the children, unaccustomed to such hard fare,
began to sink under the accumulated difficulties of their journey. In this situation they
were stopped by a wide and rapid though shallow river. Sir Isumbras, taking his eldest
son in his arms, carried him over to the opposite bank, and placing him under a bush of
broom, directed him to dry his tears, and amuse himself by playing with the blossoms till
his return with his brothers. But scarcely had he left the place when a lion, starting from a
neighbouring thicket, seized the child and bore him away into the recesses of the forest.
The second son became, in like manner,· the prey of an enormous leopard; and the disconsolate mother, when carried over with her infant to the fatal spot, was with difficulty persuaded to survive the loss of her two elder children. Sir Isumbras, though he could not
repress the tears extorted by this cruel calamity, exerted himself to console his wife, and,
humbly confessing his sins, contented himself with praying that his present misery might
be accepted by Heaven as a partial expiation.

Through forest they went days three,
Till they came to the Greekish sea;
    They grette,[3] and were full wo!
As they stood upon the land,
They saw a fleet sailand,[4]
    Three hundred ships and mo.[5]
With top-castels set on-loft,
Richly then were they wrought,
    With joy and mickle[6] pride:
A heathen king was therein,
That Christendom came to win;
    His power was full wide.

It was now seven days since the pilgrims had tasted bread or meat; the soudan's[7] galley,
therefore, was no sooner moored to the beach than they hastened on board to beg for food.
The soudan, under the apprehension that they were spies, ordered them to be driven back
on shore; but his attendants observed to him that these could not be common beggars;
that the robust limbs and tall stature of the husband proved him to be a knight in disguise;

---

[1] *Palata*, Lat. (*Paletot*, O. Fr.), sometimes signifying a particular stuff, and sometimes a
particular dress. See Du Cange.
[2] Cut; divided.
[3] Wept.
[4] Sailing.   [5] More.   [6] Much.   [7] Sultan.

and that the delicate complexion of the wife, who was "bright as blossom on tree," formed a striking contrast to the ragged apparel with which she was very imperfectly covered. They were now brought into the royal presence; and the soudan, addressing Sir Isumbras, immediately offered him as much treasure as he should require, on condition that he should renounce Christianity and consent to fight under the Saracen banners. The answer was a respectful but peremptory refusal, concluded by an earnest petition for a little food; but the soudan, having by this time turned his eyes from Sir Isumbras to the beautiful companion of his pilgrimage, paid no attention to his request.

> The soudan beheld that lady there,
> Him thought an angel that she were,
>   Comen a-down from heaven;
> "Man! I will give thee gold and fee,
> An thou that woman will sellen me,
>   More than thou can neven.[1]
> I will give thee an hundred pound
> Of pennies that been whole and round,
>   And rich robes seven:
> She shall be queen of my land,
> And all men bow unto her hand,
>   And none withstand her steven." [2]
> Sir Isumbras said, "Nay!
> My wife I will nought sell away,
>   Though ye me for her sloo! [3]
> I weddid her in Goddislay,
> To hold her to mine ending day,
>   Both for weal and wo."

It evidently would require no small share of casuistry to construe this declaration into an acceptance of the bargain; but the Saracens, having heard the offer of their sovereign, deliberately counted out the stipulated sum on the mantle of Sir Isumbras; took possession of the lady; carried the knight with his infant son on shore; beat him till he was scarcely able to move; and then returned for further orders. During this operation, the soudan, with his own hand, placed the regal crown on the head of his intended bride; but recollecting that the original project of the voyage to Europe was to conquer it, which might possibly occasion a loss of some time, he delayed his intended nuptial, and ordered a fast-sailing vessel to convey her to his dominions, providing her at the same time with a charter addressed to his subjects, in which he enjoined them to obey her, from the moment of her landing, as their legitimate sovereign.

The lady, emboldened by these tokens of deference on the part of her new lord, now fell on her knees and entreated his permission to pass a few moments in private with her former husband, and the request was instantly granted by the complaisant Saracen. Sir Isumbras still smarting from his bruises, was conducted with great respect and ceremony to his wife, who, embracing him with tears, earnestly conjured him to seek her out as soon as possible in her new dominions, to slay his infidel rival, and to take possession of a throne which was probably reserved to him by Heaven as an indemnification for his past losses. She then supplied him with provisions for a fortnight; kissed him and her infant son; swooned three times; and then set sail for Africa.

Sir Isumbras, who had been set on shore quite confounded by this quick succession of strange adventures, followed the vessel with his eyes till it vanished from his sight, and then taking his son by the hand led him up to some rocky woodlands in the neighbourhood. Here they sat down under a tree, and after a short repast, which was moistened with their

---

[1] Name.   [2] Voice, *i.e.*, command.   [3] Slew.

tears, resumed their journey. But they were again bewildered in the forest, and, after gaining the summit of the mountain without being able to descry a single habitation, lay down on the bare ground and resigned themselves to sleep. The next morning Sir Isumbras found that his misfortunes were not yet terminated. He had carried his stock of provisions, together with his gold, the fatal present of the soudan, enveloped in a scarlet mantle; and scarcely had the sun darted its first rays on the earth when an eagle, attracted by the red cloth; swooped down upon the treasure and bore it off in his talons. Sir Isumbras, waking at the moment, perceived the theft, and for some time hastily pursued the flight of the bird, who, he expected, would speedily drop the heavy and useless burthen; but he was disappointed; for the eagle, constantly towering as he approached the sea, at length directed his flight towards the opposite shore of Africa. Sir Isumbras slowly returned to his child, whom he had no longer the means of feeding; but the wretched father only arrived in time to behold the boy snatched from him by a unicorn. The knight was now quite disheartened. But his last calamity was so evidently miraculous that even the grief of the father was nearly absorbed by the contrition of the sinner. He fell on his knees and uttered a most fervent prayer to Jesus and the Virgin, and then proceeded on his journey.

His attention was soon attracted by the sound of a smith's bellows: he quickly repaired to the forge and requested the charitable donation of a little food; but was told by the labourers that he seemed as well able to work as they did, and they had nothing to throw away in charity.

> Then answered the knight again,
> "For meat would I swink[1] fain."
>   Fast he bare and drow;[2]
> They given him meat and drink anon.
> And taughten him to bear stone:
>   Then had he shame now.

This servitude lasted a twelvemonth, and seven years expired before he had fully attained all the mysteries of his new profession. He employed his few leisure hours in fabricating a complete suit of armour: every year had brought him an account of the progress of the Saracens; and he could not help entertaining a hope that his arm, though so ignobly employed, was destined at some future day to revenge the wrongs of the Christians, as well as the injury which he had personally received from the unbelievers.

At length he heard that the Christian army had again taken the field; that the day was fixed for a great and final effort; and that a plain at an inconsiderable distance from his shop was appointed for the scene of action. Sir Isumbras rose before day, buckled on his armour, and mounting a horse which had hitherto been employed in carrying coals, proceeded to the field and took a careful view of the dispositoin of both armies. When the trumpets gave the signal to charge, he dismounted, fell on his knees, and after a short but fervent prayer to Heaven, again sprang into his saddle and rode into the thickest ranks of the enemy. His uncouth war-horse and awkward armour had scarcely less effect than his wonderful address and courage in attracting the attention of both parties; and when after three desperate charges, his sorry steed was slain under him, one of the Christian chiefs make a powerful effort for his rescue, bore him to a neighbouring eminence, and presented to him a more suitable coat of armour, and a horse more worthy of the heroic rider.

> When he was armed on that stead,
> It is seen where his horse yede,[3]
>   And shall be evermore.
> As sparkle glides off the glede,[4]

---

[1] Labour.
[2] Drew.

[3] Went.
[4] Burning coal.

In that stour he made many bleed,
  And wrought hem wonder sore.
He rode up into the mountain,
  The soudan soon hath he slain,
  And many that with him were.
All that day lasted the fight;
Sir Isumbras, that noble knight,
  Wan the battle there.
Knights and squires have him sought,
And before the king him brought;
  Full sore wounded was he.
They asked what was his name;
He said, "Sire, a smith's man;
  What will ye do with me?"
The Christian king said, than,
  "I trow never smith's man
  In war was half so wight."
"I bid[1] you, give me meat and drink
And what that I will after think,
  Till I have kevered[2] my might."
The king a great oath sware,
As soon as he whole were,
  That he would dub him knight.
In a nunnery they him leaved,
To heal the wound in his heved,[3]
  That he took in that fight.
The nuns of him were full fain,
For he had the soudan slain,
  And many heathen hounds;
For his sorrow they gan sore rue;
Every day they salved him new,
  And stopped well his wounds.

We may fairly presume, without derogating from the merit of the holy sisters or from the virtue of their salves and bandages, that the knight's recovery was no less accelerated by the pleasure of having chastised the insolent possessor of his wife and the author of his contumelious beating. In a few days his health was restored; and having provided himself with a "scrip and pike" and the other accoutrements of a palmer, he took his leave of the nuns, directed his steps once more to the "Greekish Sea," and, embarking on board of a vessel which he found ready to sail, speedily arrived at the port of Acre.

During seven years, which were employed in visiting every part of the Holy Land, the penitent Sir Isumbras led a life of continued labour and mortification: fed during the day by the precarious contributions of the charitable, and sleeping at night in the open air, without any addition to the scanty covering which his pilgrim's weeds, after seven years service, were able to afford. At length his patience and contrition were rewarded. After a day spent in fruitless applications for a little food,

Beside the burgh of Jerusalem
He set him down by a well-stream,
  Sore wepand[4] for his sin.
And as he sat, about midnight,
There came an angel fair and bright,

---

[1] Pray; beg.   [3] Head.
[2] Recovered.   [4] Weeping.

> And brought him bread and wine;
> He said, "Palmer, well thou be!
> The King of Heaven greeteth well thee;
> Forgiven is sin thine."

Sir Isumbras accepted with pious gratitude the donation of food, by which his strength was instantly restored, and again set out on his travels; but he was still a widower, still deprived of his children, and as poor as ever; nor had his heavenly monitor afforded him any hint for his future guidance. He wandered therefore through the country, without any settled purpose, till he arrived at a "rich burgh," built round a "fair castle," the possessor of which, he was told, was a charitable queen, who daily distributed a florin of gold to every poor man who approached her gates, and even condescended to provide food and lodging within her palace for such as were distinguished by superior misery. Sir Isumbras presented himself with the rest; and his emaciated form and squalid garments procured him instant admittance.

> The rich queen in hall was set;
> Knights her served, at hand and feet,
> In rich robes of pall:
> In the floor a cloth was laid;
> "The poor palmer," the steward said,
> "Shall sit above you all."
> Meat and drink forth they brought;
> He sat still, and ate right nought,
> But looked about the hall.
> So mickle he saw of game and glee
> (Swiche mirthis he was wont to see),
> The tears he let down fall.

Conduct so unusual attracted the attention of the whole company, and even of the queen, who, ordering "a chair with a cushion" to be placed near the palmer, took her seat in it, entered into conversation with him on the subject of his long and painful pilgrimage, and was much edified by the moral lessons which he interspersed in his narrative. But no importunity could induce him to taste food: he was sick at heart, and required the aid of solitary meditation to overcome the painful recollections which continually assailed him. The queen was more and more astonished, but at length left him to his reflections, after declaring that, "for her lord's soul, or for his love, if he were still alive," she was determined to retain the holy palmer in her palace, and to assign him a convenient apartment, together with a servant to attend him.

An interval of fifteen years, passed in the laborious occupations of blacksmith and pilgrim, may be supposed to have produced a very considerable alteration in the appearance of Sir Isumbras; and even his voice, subdued by disease and penance, may have failed to discover the gallant knight under the disguise which he had so long assumed. But that his wife (for such she was) should have been equally altered by the sole operation of time; that the air and gestures and action of a person once so dear and so familiar to him should have awakened no trace of recollection in the mind of a husband, though in the midst of scenes which painfully recalled the memory of his former splendour, is more extraordinary. Be this as it may, the knight and the queen, though lodged under the same roof and passing much of their time together, continued to bewail the miseries of their protracted widowhood.

Sir Isumbras, however, speedily recovered, in the plentiful court of the rich queen, his health and strength, and with these the desire of returning to his former exercises. A tournament was proclaimed; and the lists, which were formed immediately under the windows of the castle, were quickly occupied by a number of Saracen knights, all of whom Sir Isumbras successively overthrew. So dreadful was the stroke of his spear, that many were killed at the first encounter; some escaped with a few broken bones; others were thrown headlong into the castle ditch; but the greater number consulted their safety by a timely flight; while the queen contemplated with pleasure and astonishment the unparalleled exploits of her favourite palmer.

> Then fell it, upon a day,
> The Knight went him for to play,
>   As it was ere his kind;
> A fowl's nest he found on high;
> A red cloth therein he seygh[1]
>   Wavand[2] in the wind.
> To the nest he gan win;[3]
> His own mantle he found therein;
>   The gold there gan he find.

The painful recollection awakened by this discovery weighed heavily on the soul of Sir Isumbras. He bore the fatal treasure to his chamber, concealed it under his bed, and spent the remainder of the day in tears and lamentations. The images of his lost wife and children now began to haunt him continually; and his altered demeanour attracted the attention and excited the curiosity of the whole court, and even of the queen, who could only learn from the palmer's attendant that his melancholy seemed to originate in the discovery of something in a bird's nest. With this strange report she was compelled to be satisfied, till Sir Isumbras, with the hope of dissipating his grief, began to resume his usual exercises in the field; but no sooner had he quitted his chamber than the "squires" by her command broke open the door, discovered the treasure, and hastened with it to the royal apartment. The sight of the gold and the scarlet mantle immediately explained to the queen the whole mystery of the palmer's behaviour. She burst into tears; kissed with fervent devotion the memorial of her lost husband; fell into a swoon; and on her recovery told the story to her attendants, and enjoined them to go in quest of the palmer, and to bring him at once before her. A short explanation removed her few remaining doubts; she threw herself into the arms of her husband, and the reunion of this long separated couple was immediately followed by the coronation of Sir Isumbras and by a protracted series of festivities.

The Saracen subjects of the Christian sovereign continued, with unshaken loyalty, to partake of the plentiful entertainments provided for all ranks of people on this solemn occasion; but no sooner had the pious Sir Isumbras signified to them the necessity of their immediate conversion, than his whole "parliament" adopted the resolution of deposing and committing to the flames their newly-acquired sovereign, as soon as they should have obtained the concurrence of the neighbouring princes. Two of these readily joined their forces for the accomplishment of this salutary purpose, and invading the territories of Sir Isumbras with an army of thirty thousand men, sent him, according to usual custom, a solemn defiance. Sir Isumbras boldly answered the defiance, issued the necessary orders, called for his arms, sprang upon his horse, and prepared to march out against the enemy; when he discovered that his subjects had, to a man, abandoned him, and that he must encounter singly the whole host of the invaders.

> Sir Isumbras was bold and keen,
> And took his leave at the queen,
>   And sighed wonder sore:
> He said, "Madam, have good day!
> Sickerly, as you I say,
>   For now and evermore!"
> "Help me, sir, that I were dight
> In arms, as it were a knight;

---

[1] Saw.   [2] Waving.   [3] Began to climb.

> I will with you fare:
> Gif God would us grace send,
> That we may together end,
>   Then done were all my care."
> Soon was the lady dight
> In arms, as it were a knight;
>   He gave her spear and shield:
> Again[1] thirty thousand Saracens and mo.[2]
> There came no more but they two,
>   When they met in field.

Never, probably, did a contest take place between such disproportioned forces. Sir Isumbras was rather encumbered than assisted by the presence of his beautiful but feeble helpmate; and the faithful couple were upon the point of being crushed by the charge of the enemy, when three unknown knights suddenly made their appearance, and as suddenly turned the fortune of the day. The first of these was mounted on a lion, the second on a leopard, and the third on a unicorn. The Saracen cavalry, at the first sight of these unexpected antagonists, dispersed in all directions. But flight and resistance were equally hopeless: three and twenty thousand unbelievers were soon laid lifeless on the plain by the talons of the lion and leopard and by the resistless horn of the unicorn, or by the swords of their young and intrepid riders; and the small remnant of the Saracen army who escaped from the general carnage quickly spread, through every corner of the Mohammedan world, the news of this signal and truly miraculous victory.

Sir Isumbras, who does not seem to have possessed the talent for unravelling mysteries, had never suspected that his three wonderful auxiliaries were his own children whom Providence had sent to his assistance at the moment of his greatest distress; but he was not the less thankful when informed of the happy termination of all his calamities. The royal family were received in the city with every demonstration of joy by his penitent subjects, whose loyalty had been completely revived by the recent miracle. Magnificent entertainments were provided; after which Sir Isumbras, having easily overrun the territories of his two pagan neighbours, who had been slain in the last battle, proceeded to conquer a third kingdom for his youngest son; and the four monarchs, uniting their efforts for the propagation of the true faith, enjoyed the happiness of witnessing the baptism of all the inhabitants of their respective dominions.

> They lived and died in good intent;
> Unto heaven their souls went,
>   When that they dead were.
> Jesu Christ, heaven's king,
> Give us, aye, his blessing,
>   And shield us from care!

On comparing these several versions it will be seen that, while they differ one from another in some of the details, yet the fundamental outline is identical, with the single exception of the Tibetan story, which, in common with Tibetan tales generally, has departed very considerably from the original. A king, or knight, is suddenly deprived of all his possessions, and with his wife and two children becomes a wanderer on the face of the earth; his wife is forcibly taken from him; he afterwards loses his two sons; he is once more raised to affluence; his sons, having been adopted and educated by a charitable person, enter

---

[1] Against.   [2] More.

his service; their mother recognises them through overhearing their conversation; finally husband and wife and children are happily re-united. Such is the general outline of the story, though modifications have been made in the details of the different versions—probably through its being transmitted orally in some instances. Thus in the Arabian story, the king is ruined apparently in consequence of no fault of his own; in the Panjábí version, he relinquishes his wealth to a fakír as a pious action; in the Kashmírí and in the romance of Sir Isumbras, the hero loses his wealth as a punishment for his overweening pride; in the legend of St. Eustache, as in the story of Job, the calamities which overtake the Christian convert are designed by Heaven as a trial of his patience and fortitude; while even in the corrupted Tibetan story the ruin of the monarch is reflected in the destruction of the parents of the heroine by a hurricane. In both the Kashmírí and the Panjábí versions, the father is swallowed by a fish (or an alligator) in re-crossing the river to fetch his second child; in the Tibetan story the wife loses her husband, who is killed by a snake, and having taken one of her children over the river, she is returning for the other when, looking back, she discovers her babe in the jaws of a wolf: both her children perish: in the European versions they are carried off by wild beasts and rescued by strangers—the romance of Sir Isumbras is singular in representing the number of children to be three. Only in the Arabian story do we find the father carrying his wife and children in safety across the stream, and the latter afterwards lost in the forest. The Kashmírí and "Gesta" versions correspond exactly in representing the shipman as seizing the lady because her husband could not pay the passage-money: in the Arabian she is entrapped in the ship, owned by a Magian, on the pretext that there is on board a woman in labour; in Sir Isumbras she is forcibly "bought" by the Soudan. She is locked up in a chest by the Magian; sent to rule his country by the Soudan; respectfully treated by the merchant in the Kashmírí story, and, apparently, also by Kandan in the Panjábí legend; in the story of St. Eustache her persecutor dies and she is living in humble circumstances when discovered by her husband.—I think there is internal evidence, apart from the existence of the Tibetan version, to lead to the conclusion that the story is of Buddhist extraction, and if such be the fact, it furnishes a further example of the indebtedness of Christian hagiology to Buddhist tales and legends.

AL-MALIK AL-ZAHIR AND THE SIXTEEN CAPTAINS OF POLICE.

Vol. XII. p. 1.

WE must, I think, regard this group of tales as being genuine narratives of the exploits of Egyptian sharpers. From the days of Herodotus to the present time, Egypt has bred the most expert thieves in the world. The policemen don't generally exhibit much ability for coping with the sharpers whose tricks they so well recount; but indeed our home-grown "bobbies" are not particularly quick-witted.

THE THIEF'S TALE.—Vol. XII. p. 28.

A PARALLEL to the woman's trick of shaving off the beards and blackening the faces of the robbers is found in the well-known legend, as told by Herodotus (Euterpe, 121), of the robbery of the treasure-house of Rhampsinitus king of Egypt, where the clever thief, having made the soldiers dead drunk, shaves off the right side of their beards and then decamps with his brother's headless body.

THE NINTH CONSTABLE'S STORY.—Vol. XII. p. 29.

THE narrow escape of the singing-girl hidden under a pile of *halfah* grass may be compared with an adventure of a fugitive Mexican prince whose history, as related by Prescott, is as full of romantic daring and hair's-breadth 'scapes as that of Scanderbeg or the "Young Chevalier." This prince had just time to turn the crest of a hill as his enemies were climbing it on the other side, when he fell in with a girl who was reaping *chian*, a Mexican plant, the seed of which is much used in the drinks of the country. He persuaded her to cover him with the stalks she had been cutting. When his pursuers came up and inquired if she had seen the fugitive, the girl coolly answered that she had, and pointed out a path as the one he had taken.

THE FIFTEENTH CONSTABLE'S STORY.—Vol. XII. p. 40.

THE concluding part of this story differs very materially from that of the Greek legend of Ibycus (fl. B.C. 540), which is thus related in a small MS. collection of Arabian and Persian anecdotes in my possession, done into English from the French:

It is written in the history of the first kings that in the reign of a Grecian king there lived a philosopher named Ibycus, who surpassed in sagacity all other sages of Greece. Ibycus was once sent by the king to a neighbouring court. On the way he was attacked by robbers who, suspecting him to have much money, formed the design of killing him. "Your object in taking my life," said Ibycus, "is to obtain my money; I give it up to you, but allow me to live." The robbers paid no attention to his words, and persisted in their purpose. The wretched Ibycus, in his despair, looked about him to see if any one was coming to his assistance, but no person was in sight. At that very moment a flock of cranes flew overhead. "O cranes!" cried Ibycus, "know that I have been seized in this desert by these wicked men, and I die from their blows. Avenge me, and demand from them my blood." At these words the robbers burst into laughter: "To take away life from those who have lost their reason," they observed, "is to add nothing to their hurt." So saying, they killed Ibycus and divided his money. On receipt of the news that Ibycus had been murdered, the inhabitants of the town were exasperated and felt great sorrow. They caused strict inquiries to be made for the murderers, but they could not be found. After some time the Greeks were celebrating a feast. The inhabitants of the adjoining districts came in crowds to the temples. The murderers of Ibycus also came, and everywhere showed themselves. Meanwhile a flock of cranes appeared in the air and hovered above the people, uttering cries so loud and prolonged that the prayers and ceremonies were interrupted. One of the robbers looked with a smile at his comrades, saying, by way of joke, "These cranes come without doubt to avenge the blood of Ibycus." Some one of the town, who was near them, heard these words, repeated them to his neighbour, and they together reported them to the king. The robbers were taken, strictly cross-examined, confessed their crime, and suffered for it a just punishment. In this way the cranes inflicted vengeance on the murderers of Ibycus. But we ought to see in this incident a matter which is concealed in it: This philosopher, although apparently addressing his words to the cranes, was really imploring help from their Creator; he hoped, in asking their aid, that He would not suffer his blood to flow unavenged. So God accomplished his hopes, and willed that cranes should be the cause that his death was avenged in order that the sages of the world should learn from it the power and wisdom of the Creator.

This ancient legend was probably introduced into Arabian literature in the 9th century, when translations of so many of the best Greek works were made; and, no doubt, it was adapted in the following Indian (Muslim) story:[1]

---

[1] From an early volume of the "Asiatic Journal," the number of which I did not "make a note of"—thus, for once at least, disregarding the advice of the immortal Captain Cuttle.

There was a certain *pir*, or saint, of great wisdom, learning, and sanctity, who sat by the wayside expounding the Kurán to all who would listen to him. He dwelt in the out-buildings of a ruined mosque close by, his only companion being a maina, or hill-starling, which he had taught to proclaim the excellence of the formula of his religion, saying, "The Prophet is just!" It chanced that two travellers passing that way beheld the holy man at his devotions, and though far from being religious persons yet tarried a while to hear the words of truth. Evening now drawing on, the saint invited his apparently pious auditors to his dwelling, and set before them such coarse food as he had to offer. Having eaten and refreshed themselves, they were astonished at the wisdom displayed by the bird, who continued to repeat holy texts from the Kurán. The meal ended, they all lay down to sleep, and while the good man reposed, his treacherous guests, who envied him the posses-sion of a bird that in their hands might be the means of enriching them, determined to steal the treasure and murder its master. So they stabbed the sleeping devotee to the heart and then seized hold of the bird's cage. But, unperceived by them, the door of it had been left open and the bird was not to be found. After searching for the bird in vain, they con-sidered it necessary to dispose of the body, since, if discovered, suspicion would assuredly fall upon them; and carrying it away to what they deemed a safe distance they buried it. Vexed to be obliged to leave the place without obtaining the reward of their evil deeds, they again looked carefully for the bird, but without success; it was nowhere to be seen, and so they were compelled to go forward without the object of their search. The maina had witnessed the atrocious deed, and unseen had followed the murderers to the place were they had buried the body; it then perched upon the tree beneath which the saint had been wont to enlighten the minds of his followers, and when they assembled flew into their midst, exclaiming, "The Prophet is just!" making short flights and then returning. These unusual motions, together with the absence of their preceptor, induced the people to follow it, and directing its flight to the grave of its master, it uttered a mournful cry over the newly-covered grave. The villagers, astonished, began to remove the earth, and soon discovered the bloody corse. Surprised and horror-stricken, they looked about for some traces of the murderers, and perceiving that the bird had resumed the movements which had first induced them to follow it, they suffered it to lead them forward. Before evening fell, the avengers came up with two men, who no sooner heard the maina exclaim, "The Prophet is just!" and saw the crowd that accompanied it, than they fell upon their knees, confessing that the Prophet had indeed brought their evil deeds to light; so, their crime being thus made manifest, summary justice was inflicted upon them.

TALE OF THE DAMSEL TOHFAT AL-KULUB.—Vol. XII. p. 47.

AN entertaining story, but very inconsistent in the character of Iblis, who is constantly termed, in good Muslim fashion, "the accursed," yet seems to be somewhat of a follower of the Prophet, and on the whole a good-natured sort of fellow. His mode of expressing his approval of the damsel's musical "talent" is, to say the least, original.

WOMEN'S WILES.—Vol. XII. p. 99.

A VARIANT—perhaps an older form—of this story occurs in the tale of Prince Fadlallah, which is interwoven with the History of Prince Calaf and the Princess of China, in the Persian tales of "The Thousand and One Days":

The prince, on his way to Baghdád, is attacked by robbers, his followers are all slain, and himself made prisoner, but he is set at liberty by the compassionate wife of the robber-chief during his absence on a plundering expedition. When he reaches Baghdád he has no re-source but to beg his bread, and having stationed himself in front of a large mansion, an old female slave presently comes out and gives him a loaf. At this moment a gust of wind blew aside the curtain of a window and discovered to his admiring eyes a most beautiful damsel, of whom he became immediately enamoured. He inquired of a passerby the name of the owner of the mansion, and was informed that it belonged to a man called Mouaffac, who had been lately governor of the city, but having quarrelled with the kází, who was of a revengeful disposition, the latter had found means to disgrace him with the khalíf and to have him deprived of his office. After lingering near the house in vain till night-fall, in hopes of once more obtaining a glimpse of this beauty, he retired for the night to a burying-ground, where he was soon joined by two thieves, who pressed upon him a share of the good cheer with which they had provided themselves; but while the thieves were feasting and talking over a robbery which they had just accomplished, the police suddenly pounced upon them, and took all three and cast them into prison.

In the morning they were examined by the kází, and the thieves, seeing it was useless to deny it, confessed their crime. The prince then told the kází how he chanced to fall into company of the thieves, who confirmed all he said, and he was set at liberty. Then the kází began to question him as to how he had employed his time since he came to Baghdád, to which he answered very frankly but concealed his rank. On his mentioning the brief glance he had of the beautiful lady at the window of the ex-governor's house, the kází's eyes sparkled with apparent satifaction, and he assured the prince that he should have the lady for his bride; for, believing the prince to be a mere beggarly adventurer, he resolved to foist him on Mouaffac as the son of a great monarch. So, having sent the prince to the bath and provided him with rich garments, the kází dispatched a messenger to request Mou-affac to come to him on important business. When the ex-governor arrived, the kází told him blandly that there was now an excellent opportunity for doing away the ill will that had so long existed between them. "It is this," continued he: "the prince of Basra, having fallen in love with your daughter from report of her great beauty, has just come to Bagh-dád, unknown to his father, and intends to demand her of you in marriage. He is lodged in my house, and is most anxious that this affair should be arranged by my interposition, which is the more agreeable to me, since it will, I trust, be the means of reconciling our differences." Mouaffac expressed his surprise that the prince of Basra should think of marrying his daughter, and especially that the proposal should come through the kází, of all men. The kází begged him to forget their former animosity and consent to the imme-diate celebration of the nuptials. While they were thus talking, the prince entered, in a magnificent dress, and was not a little astonished to be presented to Mouaffac by the treacherous kází as the prince of Basra, who had come as a suitor for his daughter in mar-riage. The ex-governor saluted him with every token of profound respect, and expressed his sense of the honour of such an alliance: his daughter was unworthy to wait upon the meanest of the prince's slaves. In brief, the marriage is at once celebrated, and the prince duly retires to the bridal chamber with the beauteous daughter of Mouaffac. But in the morning, at an early hour, a servant of the kází knocks at his door, and, on the prince opening it, says that he brings him his rags of clothes and is required to take back the dress which the kází had lent him yesterday to personate the prince of Basra. The prince, having donned his tattered garments, said to his wife, "The kází thinks he has married you to a wretched beggar, but I am no whit inferior in rank to the prince of Basra — I am also a prince, being the only son of the king of Mosel," and then proceeded to recount all his ad-ventures. When he had concluded his recital, the lady despatched a servant to procure a suitable dress for the prince, which when he had put on, she said, "I see it all: the kází, no doubt, believes that by this time we are all overwhelmed with shame and grief. But what must be his feelings when he learns that he has been a benefactor to his enemies! Before you disclose to him your real rank, however, we must contrive to punish him for his malicious intentions. There is a dyer in this town who has a frightfully ugly daughter — but leave this affair in my hands."

The lady then dressed herself in plain but becoming apparel, and went out of the house alone. She proceeded to the court of the kází, who no sooner cast his eyes upon her than he was struck with her elegant form. He sent an officer to inquire of her who she was and what she had come about. She made answer that she was the daughter of an artisan in the city, and that she desired to have some private conversation with the kází. When the officer reported the lady's reply, the kází directed her to be conducted into a private chamber, where he presently joined her, and gallantly placed his services at her disposal. The lady now removed her veil, and asked him whether he saw anything ugly or repulsive in her features. The kází on seeing her beautiful face was suddenly plunged in the sea of love, and declared that her forehead was of polished silver, her eyes were sparkling diamonds, her mouth a ruby casket containing a bracelet of pearls. Then she displayed her arms, so white and plump, the sight of which threw the kází into ecstasies and almost caused him to faint. Quoth the lady, "I must tell you, my lord, that with all the beauty I possess, my father, a dyer in the city, keeps me secluded, and declares to all who come to ask me in marriage that I am an ugly, deformed monster, a mere skeleton, lame, and full of diseases." On this the kází burst into a tirade against the brutal father who could thus traduce so much beauty, and vowed that he would make her his wife that same day. The lady, after expressing her fears that he would not find it easy to gain her father's consent, took her leave and returned home.

The kází lost no time in sending for the dyer, and, after complimenting him upon his reputation for piety, said to him, "I am informed that behind the curtain of chastity you have a daughter ripe for marriage. Is not this true?" Replied the dyer, "My lord, you have been rightly informed. I have a daughter who is indeed fully ripe for marriage, for she is more than thirty years of age; but the poor creature is not fit to be a wife to any man. She is very ugly, lame, leprous, and foolish. In short, she is such a monster that I am obliged to keep her out of all people's sight." "Ha!" exclaimed the kází, "you can't impose on me with such a tale. I was prepared for it. But let me tell you that I myself am ready and willing to marry that same ugly and leprous daughter of yours, with all her defects." When the dyer heard this, he looked the kází full in the face and said, "My lord, you are welcome to divert yourself by making a jest of my daughter." "No," replied the kází, "I am quite in earnest. I demand your daughter in marriage." The dyer broke into laughter, saying, "By Allah, some one has meant to play you a trick, my lord. I forewarn you that she is ugly, lame, and leprous." "True," responded the kází, with a knowing smile; "I know her by these tokens. I shall take her notwithstanding." The dyer, seeing him determined to marry his daughter, and being now convinced that he had been imposed upon by some ill-wisher, thought to himself, "I must demand of him a round sum of money which may cause him to cease troubling me any further about my poor daughter." So he said to the kází, "My lord, I am ready to obey your command; but I will not part with my daughter unless you pay me beforehand a dowry of a thousand sequins." Replied the kází, "Although, methinks, your demand is somewhat exorbitant, yet I will pay you the money at once," which having done, he ordered the contract to be drawn up. But when it came to be signed the dyer declared that he would not sign save in the presence of a hundred men of the law. "Thou art very distrustful," said the kází, "but I will comply in everything, for I am resolved to make sure of thy daughter." So he sent for all the men of law in the city, and when they were assembled at the house of the kází, the dyer said that he was now willing to sign the contract; "But I declare," he added, "in the presence of these honourable witnesses, that I do so on the condition that if my daughter should not prove to your liking when you have seen her, and you should determine to divorce her, you shall oblige yourself to give her a thousand sequins of gold in addition to the same amount which I have already received from you." "Agreed," said the kází, "I oblige myself to it, and call this whole assembly to be witnesses. Art thou now satisfied?" "I am," replied the dyer, who then went his way, saying that he would at once send him his bride.

As soon as the dyer was gone, the assembly broke up, and the kází was left alone in his house. He had been two years married to the daughter of a merchant of Baghdád, with whom he had hitherto lived on very amicable terms. When she heard that he was arranging for a second marriage, she came to him in a great rage. "How now," said she, "two hands in one glove! two swords in one scabbard! two wives in one house! Go, fickle man! Since the caresses of a young and faithful wife cannot secure your constancy, I am ready to yield my place to my rival and retire to my own family. Repudiate me—return my dowry —and you shall never see me more." "I am glad you have thus anticipated me," answered the kází, "for I was somewhat perplexed how to acquaint you of my new marriage." So saying, he opened a coffer and took out a purse of five hundred sequins of gold, and putting it into her hands, "There, woman," said he, "thy dowry is in that purse: begone, and take with you what belongs to you. I divorce thee once; I divorce thee twice; three times I divorce thee. And that thy parents may be satisfied thou art divorced from me, I shall give thee a certificate signed by myself and my nayb." This he did accordingly, and his wife went to her father's house, with her bill of divorce and her dowry.

The kází then gave orders to furnish an apartment sumptuously for the reception of his bride. The floor was spread with velvet carpets, the walls were hung with rich tapestry, and couches of gold and silver brocade were placed around the room. The bridal chamber was decked with caskets filled with the most exquisite perfumes. When everything was in readiness, the kází impatiently expected the arrival of his bride, and at last was about to despatch a messenger to the dyer's when a porter entered, carrying a wooden chest covered with a piece of green taffeta. "What hast thou brought me there, friend?" asked the kází. "My lord," replied the porter, setting the chest on the floor, "I bring your bride." The kází opened the chest, and discovered a woman of three feet and a half, defective in every limb and feature. He was horrified at the sight of this object, and throwing the covering hastily over it, demanded of the porter, "What wouldst thou have me do with this frightful creature?" "My lord," said the porter, "this is the daughter of Omar the dyer, who told me that you had espoused her out of pure inclination." "O Allah!" exclaimed the kází, "is it possible to marry such a monster as this?" Just then, the dyer, well knowing that the kází must be surprised, came in. "Thou wretch," cried the kází, "how dost thou dare to trifle with me? In place of this hideous object, send hither your other daughter, whose beauty is beyond comparison; otherwise thou shalt soon know what it is to insult me." Quoth the dyer, "My lord, I swear, by Him who out of darkness produced light, that I have no other daughter but this. I told you repeatedly that she was not for your purpose, but you would not believe my words. Who, then, is to blame?" Upon this the kází began to cool, and said so the dyer, "I must tell you, friend Omar, that this morning there came to me a most beautiful damsel, who pretended that you were her father, and that you represented her to everybody as a monster, on purpose to deter all suitors that came to ask her in marriage." "My lord," answered the dyer, "this beautiful damsel must be an impostor; some one, undoubtedly, owes you a grudge." Then the kází, having reflected for a few minutes, said to the dyer, "Bid the porter carry thy daughter home again. Keep the thousand sequins of gold which I gave thee, but ask no more of me, if thou desirest that we should continue friends." The dyer, knowing the implacable disposition of the kází, thought it advisable to content himself with what he had already gained, and the kází, having formally divorced his hideous bride, sent her away with her father. The affair soon got wind in the city and everybody was highly diverted with the trick practised on the kází.

It will be observed that in the Arabian story there are two clever devices: that of the lady who tricks the boastful merchant, whose motto was that men's craft is superior to women's craft, into marrying the ugly daughter of the kází; and that of the merchant to get rid of his bad bargain by disgusting the kází with the alliance. The scene at the house of the worthy judge—the crowd of low rascals piping, drumming, and capering, and felicitating themselves on their pretended kinsman the merchant's marriage—is highly humorous. This does not occur in the Persian story, because it is the kází who has been duped into marrying the dyer's deformed daughter, and she is therefore simply packed off again to her father's house.

That the tales of the "Thousand and One Days" are not (as is supposed by the writer of an article on the several English versions of The Nights in the "Edinburgh Review" for

July 1886, p. 167) mere imitations of Galland[1] is most certain, apart from the statement in the preface to Petis' French translation, which there is no reason to doubt—see vol. x. of The Nights, p. 166, note 1. Sir William Ouseley, in his *Travels*, vol. ii., p. 21, note, states that he brought from Persia a manuscript which comprised, *inter alia*, a portion of the "Hazár ú Yek Rúz," or the Thousand and One Days, which agreed with Petis' translation of the same stories. In the Persian collection entitled "Shamsa ú Kuhkuha" occur several of the tales and incidents, for example, the Story of Nasiraddoli King of Mousel, the Merchant of Baghdád, and the Fair Zeinib, while the Story of the King of Thibet and the Princess of the Naimans has its parallel in the Turkish "Kirk Vazír," or Forty Vazírs. Again, the Story of Couloufe and the Beautiful Dilara reminds us of that of Haji the Cross-grained in Malcolm's "Sketches of Persia." But of the French translation not a single good word can be said—the Oriental "costume" and phraseology have almost entirely disappeared, and between Petis de la Croix and the author of "Gil Blas"—who is said to have had a hand in the work—the tales have become ludicrously Frenchified. The English translation made from the French is, if possible, still worse. We there meet with "persons of quality," "persons of fashion," with "seigneurs," and a thousand and one other inconsistencies and absurdities. A new translation is much to be desired. The copy of the Persian text made by Petis is probably in the Paris Library and Ouseley's fragment is doubtless among his other Oriental MSS. in the Bodleian. But one should suppose that copies of the "Hazár ú Yek Rúz" may be readily procured at Ispahán or Tehrán, and at a very moderate cost, since the Persians now-a-days are so poor in general that they are eager to exchange any books they possess for the "circulating medium."

NUR AL-DIN AND THE DAMSEL SITT AL-MILAH.—Vol. XII. p. 107.

This is an excellent tale; the incidents occur naturally and the reader's interest in the fortunes of the hero and heroine never flags. The damsel's sojourn with the old Muezzin—her dispatching him daily to the shroff—bears some analogy to part of the tale of Ghanim the Slave of Love (vol. ii. of The Nights), which, by the way, finds close parallels in the Turkish "Forty Vazírs" (the Lady's 18th story in Mr. Gibb's translation), the Persian "Thousand and One Days" (story of Aboulcasem of Basra), and the "Bagh o Bahár" (story of the First Dervish). This tale is, in fact, a compound of incidents occurring in a number of different Arabian fictions.

TALE OF KING INS BIN KAYS AND HIS DAUGHTER.—Vol. XII. p. 138.

Here we have another instance of a youth falling in love with the portrait of a pretty girl (see *ante*, p. 236). The doughty deeds performed by the young prince against thousands of his foes throw into the shade the exploits of the Bedouin hero Antar, and those of our own famous champions Sir Guy of Warwick and Sir Bevis of Hampton.

ADDITIONAL NOTES.

FIRUZ AND HIS WIFE, p. 216.

I find yet another variant of this story in my small MS. collection of Arabian and Persian anecdotes, translated from the French (I have not ascertained its source):

---

[1] "It was no wonder," says this writer, "that his (*i.e.* Galland's) version of the 'Arabian Nights' achieved a universal popularity, and was translated into many languages, and that it provoked a crowd of imitations, from 'Les Mille et Un Jours' to the 'Tales of the Genii.'"

They relate that a lord of Basra, while walking one day in his garden, saw the wife of his gardener, who was very beautiful and virtuous. He gave a commission to his gardener which required him to leave his home. He then said to his wife, "Go and shut all the doors." She went out and soon returned, saying, "I have shut all the doors except one, which I am unable to shut." The lord asked, "And where is that door?" She replied, "That which is between you and the respect due to your Maker: there is no way of closing it." When the lord heard these words, he asked the woman's pardon, and became a better and a wiser man.

We have here a unique form of the wide-spread tale of "The Lion's Track," which, while it omits the husband's part, yet reflects the virtuous wife's rebuke of the enamoured sultan.

THE SINGER AND THE DRUGGIST, *p.* 219.

IF Straparola's version is to be considered as an adaptation of Ser Giovanni's novella — which I do not think very probable — it must be allowed to be an improvement on his model. In the Arabian story the singer is first concealed in a mat, next in the oven, and again in the mat, after which he escapes by clambering over the parapet of the druggist's roof to that of an adjoining house, and his subsequent adventures seem to be added from a different story. In Ser Giovanni's version the lover is first hid beneath a heap of half-dried clothes, and next behind the street door, from which he escapes the instant the husband enters, and the latter is treated as a madman by the wife's relatives and the neighbours —an incident which has parallels in other tales of women's craft and its prototype, perhaps, in the story of the man who compiled a book of the Wiles of Woman, as told in "Syntipas," the Greek version of the Book of Sindibad. In Straparola the lover — as in the Arabian story — is concealed three times, first in a basket, then between two boardings, and lastly in a chest containing law papers; and the husband induces him to recount his adventures in presence of the lady's friends, which having concluded, the lover declares the story to be wholly fictitious: this is a much more agreeable ending than that of Giovanni's story, and, moreover, it bears a close analogy to the latter part of the Persian tale, where the lover exclaims he is right glad to find it all a dream. Straparola's version has another point of resemblance in the Persian story — so far as can be judged from Scott's abstract — and also in the Arabian story: the lover discovers the lady by chance, and is not advised to seek out some object of love, as in Giovanni; in the Arabian the singer is counselled by the druggist to go about and entertain wine parties. Story-comparers have too much cause to be dissatisfied with Jonathan Scott's translation of the "Bahár-i-Dánish" — a work avowedly derived from Indian sources — although it is far superior to Dow's garbled version. The abstracts of a number of the tales which Scott gives in an appendix, while of some use, are generally tantalising: some stories he has altogether omitted "because they are similar to tales already well known" (unfortunately the comparative study of popular fictions was hardly begun in his time); while of others bare outlines are furnished, because he considered them "unfit for general perusal." But his work, even as it is, has probably never been "generally" read, and he seems to have had somewhat vague notions of "propriety," to judge by his translations from the Arabic and Persian. A complete English rendering of the "Bahár-i-Dánish" would be welcomed by all interested in the history of fiction.

THE FULLER, HIS WIFE AND THE TROOPER, *p.* 236.

THE trick played on the silly fuller of dressing him up as a Turkish soldier resembles that of the Three Deceitful Women who found a gold ring in the public bath, as related in the Persian story-book, "Shamsa ú Kuhkuha:"

When the wife of the superintendent of police was apprised that her turn had come, she revolved and meditated for some time what trick she was to play off on her lord, and after having come to a conclusion she said one evening to him, "To-morrow I wish that we should both enjoy ourselves at home without interruptions, and I mean to prepare some cakes." He replied, "Very well, my dear; I have also longed for such an occasion." The lady had a servant who was very obedient and always covered with the mantle of attachment to her. The next morning she called this youth and said to him, "I have long contemplated the hyacinth grove of thy symmetrical stature; and I know that thou travellest constantly and faithfully on the road of compliance with all my wishes, and that thou seekest to serve me. I have a little business which I wish thee to do for me." The servant answered, "I shall be happy to comply." Then the lady gave him a thousand dinars and said, "Go to the convent which is in our vicinity; give this money to one of the kalandars there and say to him, 'A prisoner whom the Amír had surrendered to the police has escaped last night. He closely resembles thee, and as the superintendent of the police is unable to account to the Amír, he has sent a man to take thee instead of the escaped criminal. I have compassion for thee and mean to rescue thee. Take this sum of money; give me thy dress; and flee from the town; for if thou remainest in it till the morning thou wilt be subjected to torture and wilt lose thy life.' " The servant acted as he was bid, and brought the garments to his mistress. When it was morning she said to her husband, "I know you have long wished to eat sweetmeats, and I shall make some to-day." He answered, "Very well." His wife made all her preparations and commenced to bake the sweetmeats. He said to her, "Last night a theft was committed in a certain place, and I sat up late to extort confessions; and as I have spent a sleepless night, I feel tired and wish to repose a little." The lady replied, "Very well."

Accordingly the superintendent of the police reclined on the pillow of rest; and when the sweetmeat was ready his wife took a little and putting an opiate into it she handed it to him, saying, "How long will you sleep? To-day is a day of feasting and pleasure, not of sleep and laziness. Lift up your head and see whether I have made the sweets according to your taste." He raised his head, swallowed a piece of the hot cake and lay down again. The morsel was still in his throat when consciousness left and a deep sleep overwhelmed him. His wife immediately undressed him and put on him the garments of the kalandar. The servant shaved his head and made some tattoo marks on his body. When the night set in the lady called her servant and said, "Hyacinth, be kind enough to take the superintendent on thy back, and carry him to the convent instead of that kalandar, and if he wishes to return to the house in the morning, do not let him." The servant obeyed. Towards dawn the superintendent recovered his senses a little; but as the opiate had made his palate very bitter, he became extremely thirsty. He fancied that he was in his own house, and so he exclaimed, "Narcissus, bring water." The kalandars awoke from sleep, and after hearing several shouts of this kind, they concluded that he was under the influence of bang, and said, "Poor fellow! the narcissus is in the garden; this is the convent of sufferers, and there are green garments enough here. Arise and sober thyself, for the morning and harbinger of benefits as well as of the acquisition of the victuals for subsistence is approaching." When the superintendent heard these words he thought they were a dream, for he had not yet fully recovered his senses. He sat quietly, but was amazed on beholding the walls and ceiling of the convent: he got up, looked at the clothes in which he was dressed and at the marks tattooed on his body, and began to doubt whether he was awake or asleep. He washed his face, and perceived that the caravan of his mustachios had likewise departed from the plain of his countenance.

In this state of perplexity he went out of the convent and proceeded to his house. There his wife, with her male and female servants, was expecting his arrival. He approached the house and placed his hand on the knocker of the door, but was received by Hyacinth, who said, "Kalandar, whom seekest thou?" The superintendent rejoined, "I want to enter the house." Hyacinth continued, "Thou hast to-day evidently taken thy morning draught of bang earlier and more copiously than usual, since thou hast foolishly mistaken the road to thy convent. Depart! This is not a place in which vagabond kalandars are harboured. This is the palace of the superintendent of the police; and if the symurgh looks with incivility from the fastness of the west of Mount Káf at this place, the wings of its impertinence will at once become singed." The superintendent said, "What nonsense art thou speaking? Go out of my way, for I do not relish thy imbecile prattle." But when he wanted to enter, Hyacinth struck him with a bludgeon on the shoulder, which the superintendent returned with a box on the ear, and both began to wrestle together. At that moment the lady and her maid-servants rushed forth from the rear and assailed him with sticks and stones, shouting, "This kalandar wishes in plain daylight to force his way into the house of the superintendent. What a pity that the superintendent is sick, or else this crime would have to be expiated on the gallows!" In the meantime all the neighbours assembled, and on seeing the shameless kalandar's proceedings they cried, "Look at that impudent kalandar who wants forcibly to enter the house of the superintendent." Ultimately the crowd amounted to more than five hundred persons, and the gentleman was put to flight and pursued by all the little boys, who pelted him with stones till they expelled him from the town.

At the distance of three farsangs from the town there was a village where the superintendent concealed himself in the corner of a mosque. During the evenings he went from house to house and begged for food to sustain life, until his mustachios again grew and the tattooed scars gradually began to disappear. Whenever anyone inquired for the superintendent at his house, he was informed by the servants that the gentleman was sick. After one month had expired, the grief of separation and the misery of his condition had again driven him back to the city. He went to the convent because fear hindered him from going to the house. His wife happened one day to catch a glimpse of him from her window, and perceived him sitting in the same dress with a company of kalandars. She felt compassion for him, called the servant and said, "The superintendent has had enough of this!" She made a loaf of bread and put some opiate into it, and said, "When the kalandars are asleep, you must go and place this loaf under the pillow of the superintendent." The servant obeyed, and when the gentleman awoke in the middle of the night he was surprised to find the loaf. He fancied that when his companions had during the night returned from begging, they had placed it there, and so he ate some of it. During the same night the servant went there by the command of the lady, took his master on his back and carried him home. When it was morning, the lady took off the kalandar's clothes from her husband and dressed him in his own garments, and began to make sweetmeats as on the former occasion. After some time he began to move, and his wife exclaimed, "O superintendent, do not sleep so much. I have told you that we shall spend this day in joy and pleasure, and it was not fair of you to pass the time in this lazy way. Lift up your head and see what beautiful sweetmeats I have baked for you." When he opened his eyes, and saw himself dressed in his own clothes and at home, the rosebush of his amazement again brought forth the flowers of astonishment, and he said, "God be praised! What has happened to me?" He sat up, and exclaimed, "Wife, things have happened to me which I can scarcely describe." She replied, "From the uneasy motions which you have made in your sleep, it appears you must have had extraordinary dreams." "Dreams, forsooth," said he; "since the moment I lay down I have experienced the most strange adventures." "Certainly," rejoined the lady, "last night you have been eating food disagreeing with your constitution, and to-day the vapours of it have ascended into your brains, and have caused you all this distress." The superintendent said, "Yes, last night we went to a party in the house of Serjeant Bahman, and there was roasted pillau, of which I ate somewhat more than usual, and the vapour of it has occasioned me all this trouble." [1]

---

[1] This is a version of The Sleeper and the Waker — with a vengeance! Abú Hasan the Wag, the Tinker, and the Rustic, and others thus practised upon by frolic-loving princes and dukes, had each, at least, a most delightful "dream." But when a man is similarly handled by the "wife of his bosom" — in stories, only, of course — the case is very different, as the poor chief of police experienced. Such a "dream" as his wife induced upon him we may be sure he would remember "until that day that he did creep into his sepulchre!"

Strikingly similar to this story is the trick of the first lady on her husband in the "Fabliau des Trois Dames qui trouverent un Anel." Having made him drunk, she causes his head to be shaved, dresses him in the habit of a monk, and carries him, assisted by her lover, to the entrance of a convent. When he awakes and sees himself thus transformed he imagines that God by a miraculous exercise of His grace had called him to the monastic life. He presents himself before the abbot and requests to be received among the brethren. The lady hastens to the convent in well-feigned despair, and is exhorted to be resigned and to congratulate her husband on the saintly vow he has taken. "Many a good man," says the poet, "has been betrayed by woman and by her harlotry. This one became a monk in the abbey, where he abode a very long time. Wherefore, I counsel all people who hear this story told, that they ought not to trust in their wives, nor in their households, if they have not first proved that they are full of virtues. Many a man has been deceived by women and by their treachery. This one became monk against right, who would never have been such in his life, if his wife had not deceived him." [1]

The second lady's trick in the *fabliau* is a very close parallel to the story in The Nights, vol. v. p. 96.[2] She had for dinner on a Friday some salted and smoked eels, which her husband bade her cook, but there was no fire in the house. Under the pretext of going to have them cooked at a neighbour's fire she goes out and finds her lover, at whose house she remains a whole week. On the following Friday, at the hour of dinner, she enters a neighbour's house and asks leave to cook the eels, saying that her husband is angry with her for having no fire, and that she did not dare to go back, lest he should take off her head. As soon as the eels are cooked she carries them piping hot to her own house. The husband asks her where she has been for eight days, and commences to beat her. She cries for help and the neighbours come in, and amongst them the one at whose fire the eels had been cooked, who swears that the wife had only just left her house, and ridicules the husband for his assertion that she had been away a whole week. The husband gets into a great rage and is locked up for a madman.

The device of the third lady seems a reflection of the "Elopement," but without the underground tunnel between the houses of the wife and the lover. The lady proposes to her lover to marry him, and he believes that she is only jesting, seeing that she is already married, but she assures him that she is quite in earnest, and even undertakes that her husband will consent. The lover is to come for her husband and take him to the house of Dan Eustace, where he has a fair niece, whom the lover is to pretend he wishes to espouse, if he will give her to him. The wife will go thither, and she will have done her business with Eustace before they arrive. Her husband cannot but believe that he has left her at home, and she will be so apparelled that he cannot recognise her. This plan is accordingly carried out. The lover asks the husband for the hand of his niece in marriage, to which he joyously consents, and without knowing it makes a present of his own wife. "All his life long the lover possessed her, because the husband gave and did not lend her; nor could he ever get her back."

Le Grand mentions that this *fabliau* is told at great length in the tales of the Sieur d'Ouville, tome iv. p. 255. In the "Facetiæ Bebelianæ," p. 86, three women wager which of them will play the best trick on her husband. One causes him to believe he is a monk,

---

[1] I call this "strikingly similar" to the preceding Persian story, although it has fewer incidents and the lady's husband remains a monk; she could not have got him back even had she wished; for, having taken the vows, he was debarred from returning to "the world," which a kalandar or dervish may do as often as he pleases.
[2] "The Woman's trick against her Husband."

and he goes and sings mass; the second husband believed himself to be dead, and allows himself to be carried to that mass on a bier; and the third sings in it quite naked. (There is a very similar story in Campbell's "Popular Tales of the West Highlands.") It is also found, says Le Grand, in the "Convivales Sermones," tome i. p. 200; in the "Delices de Verboquet," p. 166; and in the Facetiæ of Lod. Doménichi, p. 172. In the "Contes pour Rire," p. 197, three women find a diamond, and the arbiter whom they select promises it, as in the *fabliau*, to her who concocts the best device for deceiving her husband, but their *ruses* are different.

INDEX.

———◇———

Perjury easily expiated amongst Moslems, 26.
Pilgrimage quoted —

"Plied him with wine," a favourite habit with mediæval Arabs, 35.

Poetry (Persian) often alludes to the rose, etc., 71.

Police (Eastern), 3.

Professional singers, becoming freed women and turning "respectable," 191.

Pummel of the saddle, 59.

QUARTERS containing rooms in which girls are sold, 48.

Queen Shu'á'ah = Queen Sunbeam, 78.

"Quench that fire for him" (i.e. hush up the matter), 10.

RAAS GHANAM = a head of sheep (form of expressing singularity common to Arabic), 151.

Raba' = lit. spring quarters (tr. "a lodging house"), 13.

Rasílah = a (she) partner (tr. "accompanyist"), 30.

Rayhánah, i.e. the "Basil," mostly a servile name, 14.

Red Camel (Ahmar), 185.

Rikkí al-Saut = soften the sound (or "lower thy voice"), 63.

Rúhí = lit. my breath (tr. "my sprite"), 88.

Rustaki, from Rustak, a quarter of Baghdad, 153.

SAFF KAMARÍYÁT MIN AL-ZUJÁJ = glazed and coloured lunettes, 27.

Sahbá = red wine, 70.

Sáhils, or shorelands, 1.

Sákiyah = waterwheel, 32.

Sammár = reciters, 2.

Santír = psalteries, 184.

Sat down (in sign of agitation), 154.

Sawákí = channels, 66.

Severance-spies = stars and planets, 175.

Shaking his clothes (in sign of quitting possession), 150.

Sharárah = a spark, 61.

Sharí'at, forbidding divorce by compulsion, 106.

Sharífí = a sequin, 104.

Sharkíyah (province in Egypt), 11.

Sharr fí al-Haramayn = wickedness in the two Holy Places, 162.

Shawáhid (meaning that heart testifies to heart) tr. "hearts have their witnesses," 60.

Shaybání (Al-) = "Of the Shaybán tribe," 138, 144.

Shaykh al-Hujjáj = Shaykh of the Pilgrims, 43.

"Shaykh al-Tawaif" may mean "Shaykh of the Tribes" (of Jinns), 85.

Shayyan li 'lláh = lit. (Give me some) Thing for (the love of) Allah (tr. "An alms, for the love of Allah"), 30.

Sházz = Voice (doubtful if girl's, nightingale's, or dove's), 181.

"She heard a blowing behind her" (a phenomena well known to spiritualists), 72.

"She will double thy store of presents," 80.

Shuhbá (Al-) = Ash-coloured, verging upon white, 80.

Sídí = "my lord" (here becomes part of a name), 107.

Sijn al-Dam = the Prison of Blood, 116.

Sim'án-son = son of Simeon, i.e. a Christian, 127.

Singing and music blameable (Makrúh), though not actually damnable, 32.

Sir fí hálik (pron. Sirfhák) = Go about thy business, 30.

Sirr (a secret), afterwards Kitmán (concealment) = keeping a lover downhearted, 160.

Sitt al-Miláh = Lady or princess of the Fair (ones), 111.

Slaves fond of talking over their sale, 67.

Sons of Adam = his Moslem neighbours, 20.

Yá Mu'arras = O fool and disreputable (*tr.* "O pimp"), 15.

Ya'tamidúna hudà-hum = purpose the right direction (*tr.* "those who seek their salvation"), 21.

Yá Zínat al-Nisá = O adornment of womankind, 151.

"Ye are quit of," etc. = You are welcome to it and so it becomes lawful (*halal*) to you, 115.

Yúnus = Ibn Habíb, a friend of Isaac of Musul, 47.

Zaʻamú = they opine, they declare (*tr.* "They set forth"), 38.

Zabídún (here probably a clerical error for Zabíd, Capital of Tahámah), 139.

Zafáir al-Jinn = Adiantum capillus Veneris, 67.

Zalamah (Al-) = the policeman (*tr.* "men of violence"), 36.

Zirtah = fart, 38.

Zur ghibban, tazid hibban = visits rare keep friendship fair, 152.

Zuwaylah Gate, 4.